The H[...]

"There are few trips [...] n the imagination of a bri[...] available in *The House* [...]. Although remote from our country and our time, the characters, their joys and their anguish, could not be more contemporary or immediate."

—Carol E. Rinzler, *Cosmopolitan*

"Spectacular ... An absorbing and distinguished work ... A novel of peace and reconciliation ... *The House of the Spirits*, with its all-informing, generous, and humane sensibility, is a unique achievement, both personal witness and possible allegory of the past, present, and future of Latin America. It is also a moving and compelling first novel, translated with grace and accuracy by Magda Bogin."

—Alexander Coleman, *The New York Times Book Review*

"A runaway bestseller in Europe, this accomplished first novel is a richly symbolic family saga by the niece of Chile's assassinated President Salvador Allende. It is both an engrossing narrative and an impassioned testimony to the people of Chile.... Because of its supple integration of the supernatural with the real, the book will be compared with Gabriel García Márquez's *One Hundred Years of Solitude*. Allende has her own distinctive voice, however; ... it has a whimsical charm, besides being clearer, more accessible, and more explicit about the contemporary situation in South America.... Richly and meticulously detailed."

—*Publishers Weekly*

"A strong, absorbing Chilean family chronicle, plushly upholstered—with mystical undercurrents ... There's a comfortable, appealing professionalism to Allende's narration, slowly turning the years through the Truebas' passions and secrets and fidelities.... The characters are clear and sharp ... A fine array of exotic, historical settings ... Uncommonly satisfying."

—*Kirkus Reviews*

"Allende's writing is so inventive, funny, and persuasive that in the process of creating a stimulating political novel she has also created a vivid, absorbing work of art. Her characters are fascinatingly detailed and human."

—Ralph Novak, *People*

"An alluring, sometimes magical tale ... In its tumultuous story of rebellion and love among three generations, it is an allegory in which any family should be able to recognize a bit of itself."

—Claudia Rosett, *The Wall Street Journal*

"Nothing short of astonishing ... In *The House of the Spirits*, Isabel Allende has indeed shown us the relationships between past and present, family and nation, city and country, spiritual and political values. She has done so with enormous imagination, sensitivity, and compassion."

—Jane Futcher, *San Francisco Chronicle*

"Magnificent ... Imaginative and compelling ... A truly enchanting world where hope is never lost."

—Charles Larson, *Detroit News*

"Haunting ... Rich and complex ... Gripping."

—Miriam Berkley, *Chicago Sun-Times*

"Compelling ... A splendid and fantastic meditation on a people and a nation."

—*Booklist*

"Her novel is possessed by an immense energy, a fecund imagination, and ... an elegant way with the language."

—Peter S. Prescott, *Newsweek*

"She can create diverse characters of depth, nudge the plot with ease, and shift ably from the domestic sphere to the political. She is, above all, another remarkable storyteller from a continent blessed with many such enchanters.... Allende has an affection for her characters quite beyond politics, and an estimable ability to bring them to life."

—Dan Cryer, *Newsday*

"Moving and powerful ... Her novel captivates and holds the reader throughout.... *The House of the Spirits* is full of marvelous and unforgettable women who add a special dimension to the book.... Magda Bogin's excellent translation captures the luminous prose of Isabel Allende and makes the reading of this novel an unforgettable experience."

—Marjorie Agosin, *The Christian Science Monitor*

"The only cause *The House of the Spirits* embraces is that of humanity, and it does so with such passion, humor, and wisdom that in the end it transcends politics.... The result is a novel of force and charm, spaciousness and vigor."

—Jonathan Yardley, *The Washington Post*

"Allende is a talented writer who deftly uses the techniques of magical realism but also shows great sensitivity in the delineation of character."

—*Library Journal*

"Isabel Allende's extraordinary first novel, *The House of the Spirits,* mixes fiction, journalism, and a sense of magic in an epic that qualifies her as one of Latin America's most inspired writers.... The richness and texture alone of Allende's book put it with the best of the sweeping family chronicles."

—Maggie Locke, *San Diego Tribune*

Isabel Allende

THE HOUSE OF
THE SPIRITS

*Translated from the Spanish
by Magda Bogin*

BANTAM BOOKS
TORONTO · NEW YORK · LONDON · SYDNEY · AUCKLAND

THE HOUSE OF THE SPIRITS

*A Bantam Book / published by arrangement with
Alfred A. Knopf, Inc.*

PRINTING HISTORY

Originally published in Spain as La Casa de los Espíritus by Plaza & Janes, S.A. Editores.

Knopf edition published May 1985
Three printings through June 1985
Bantam edition / August 1986

Grateful acknowledgment is made to Delacorte Press for permission to reprint an excerpt from the book Selected Poems by Pablo Neruda. Translated by Alastair Reid, edited by Nathaniel Tarn. Copyright © 1970 by Anthony Kerrigan, W.S. Merwin, Alastair Reid, and Nathaniel Tarn. Copyright © 1972 by Dell Publishing Company, Inc. Reprinted by permission of Delacorte Press/Seymour Lawrence.

Bantam Books are published by Bantam Books, Inc. Its trademark, consisting of the words "Bantam Books" and the portrayal of a rooster, is Registered in U.S. Patent and Trademark Office and in other countries. Marca Registrada. Bantam Books, Inc., 666 Fifth Avenue, New York, New York 10103.

To my mother, my grandmother,
and all the other extraordinary women
of this story

How much does a man live, after all?

Does he live a thousand days, or one only?

For a week, or for several centuries?

How long does a man spend dying?

What does it mean to say "for ever"?

PABLO NERUDA

THE HOUSE OF THE SPIRITS

ONE

Rosa the Beautiful

Barrabás came to us by sea, the child Clara wrote in her delicate calligraphy. She was already in the habit of writing down important matters, and afterward, when she was mute, she also recorded trivialities, never suspecting that fifty years later I would use her notebooks to reclaim the past and overcome terrors of my own. Barrabás arrived on a Holy Thursday. He was in a despicable cage, caked with his own excrement and urine, and had the lost look of a hapless, utterly defenseless prisoner; but the regal carriage of his head and the size of his frame bespoke the legendary giant he would become. It was a bland, autumnal day that gave no hint of the events that the child would record, which took place during the noon mass in the parish of San Sebastián, with her whole family in attendance. As a sign of mourning, the statues of the saints were shrouded in purple robes that the pious ladies of the congregation unpacked and dusted off once a year from a cupboard in the sacristy. Beneath these funereal sheets the celestial retinue resembled nothing so much as a roomful of furniture awaiting movers, an impression that the candles, the incense, and the soft moans of the organ were powerless to counteract. Terrifying dark bundles loomed where the life-size saints had stood, each with its influenza-pale expression, its elaborate wig woven from the hair of someone long dead, its rubies, pearls and emeralds of painted glass, and the rich gown of a Florentine aristocrat. The only one whose appearance was enhanced by mourning was the church's patron saint, Sebastián, for during Holy Week the faithful were spared the sight of that body twisted in the most indecent posture, pierced by arrows, and dripping with blood and tears like a suffering homosexual, whose wounds, kept miraculously fresh by Father Restrepo's brush, made Clara tremble with disgust.

It was a long week of penitence and fasting, during which there were no card games and no music that might lead to lust or abandon; and within the limits of possibility, the strictest sadness and chastity were observed, even though it was precisely at this time that the forked tail of the devil pricked most insistently at Catholic flesh. The fast consisted of soft puff pastries, delicious vegetarian dishes, spongy tortillas, and enormous cheeses from the countryside, with which each family commemorated the Passion of the Lord, taking every precaution not to touch the least morsel of meat or fish on pain of excommunication, as Father Restrepo had repeatedly made clear. No one had ever dared to disobey him. The priest was blessed with a long, incriminating finger, which he used to point out sinners in public, and a tongue well schooled in arousing emotions.

"There's the thief who steals from the collection box!" he shouted from the pulpit as he pointed to a gentleman who was busying himself with the lint on his lapel so as not to show his face. "And there's the shameless hussy who prostitutes herself down by the docks!" he accused Doña Ester Trueba, disabled by arthritis and a devotee of the Virgin del Carmen, who opened her eyes wide, not knowing the meaning of the word or where the docks were. "Repent, sinners, foul carrion, unworthy of our Lord's great sacrifice! Fast! Do penance!"

Carried away by vocational zeal, the priest had all he could do to avoid openly disobeying the instructions of his ecclesiastic superiors, who, shaken by the winds of modernism, were opposed to hair shirts and flagellation. He himself was a firm believer in the value of a good thrashing to vanquish the weaknesses of the soul and was famous for his unrestrained oratory. The faithful followed him from parish to parish, sweating as he described the torments of the damned in hell, the bodies ripped apart by various ingenious torture apparatuses, the eternal flames, the hooks that pierced the male member, the disgusting reptiles that crept up female orifices, and the myriad other sufferings that he wove into his sermons to strike the fear of God into the hearts of his parishioners. Even Satan was described in his most intimate perversions in the Galician accents of this priest whose mission in this world was to rouse the conscience of his indolent Creole flock.

Severo del Valle was an atheist and a Mason, but he had political ambitions and could not allow himself the luxury of missing the most heavily attended mass on Sundays and feast days, when everyone would have a chance to see him. His wife, Nívea, preferred to deal with God without benefit of intermediaries. She had a deep distrust of cassocks and was bored by descriptions of heaven, purgatory and hell, but she shared her husband's parliamentary ambitions, hoping that if he won a seat in Congress she would finally secure the vote for women, for which she had fought for the past ten years, permitting none of her numerous pregnancies to get in her way. On this Holy Thursday, Father Restrepo had led his audience to the limits of their endurance with his apocalyptic visions, and Nívea was beginning to feel dizzy. She wondered if she was pregnant again. Despite cleansings with vinegar and spongings with gall, she had given birth to fifteen children, of whom eleven were still alive, but she had good reason to suppose that she was settling into maturity, because her daughter Clara, the youngest of her children, was now ten. It seemed that the force of her astonishing fertility had finally begun to ebb. She was able to attribute her present discomfort to Father Restrepo when he pointed at her to illustrate a point about the Pharisees, who had tried to legalize bastards and civil marriage, thereby dismembering the family, the fatherland, private property, and the Church, and putting women on an equal footing with men—this in open defiance of the law of God, which was most explicit on the issue. Along with their children, Nívea and Severo took up the entire third row of benches. Clara was seated beside her mother, who squeezed her hand impatiently whenever the priest lingered too long on the sins of the flesh, for she knew that this would only lead the child to visualize with even greater accuracy aberrations that transcended reality. Clara was extremely precocious and had inherited the runaway imagination of all the women in her family on her mother's side. This was evident from the questions she asked, to which no one knew the answers.

The temperature inside the church had risen, and the penetrating odor of the candles, the incense, and the tightly packed crowd all contributed to Nívea's fatigue. She wished the ceremony would end at once so she could return to her cool house, sit down among the ferns, and taste the pitcher of barley water flavored with almonds that Nana always made on holidays. She looked around at her children. The younger ones were tired and rigid in their Sunday best, and the older ones were beginning to squirm. Her gaze rested on Rosa, the oldest of her living daughters, and, as always, she was surprised. The girl's strange beauty had a disturbing quality that even she could not help noticing, for this child of hers seemed to have been made of a different material from the rest of the human race. Even before she was born, Nívea had known she was not of this world, because she had already seen her in dreams. This was why she had not been surprised when the midwife screamed as the child emerged. At birth Rosa was white and smooth, without a wrinkle, like a porcelain doll, with green hair and yellow eyes—the most beautiful creature to be born on earth since the days of original sin, as the midwife put it, making the sign of the cross. From her very first bath, Nana had washed her hair with camomile, which softened its color, giving it the hue of old bronze, and put her out in the sun with nothing on, to strengthen her skin, which was translucent in the most delicate parts of her chest and armpits, where the veins and secret texture of the muscles could be seen. Nana's gypsy tricks did not suffice, however, and rumors quickly spread that Nívea had borne an angel. Nívea hoped that the successive and unpleasant stages of growth would bring her daughter a few imperfections, but nothing of the sort occurred. On the contrary, at eighteen Rosa was still slender and remained unblemished; her maritime grace had, if anything, increased. The tone of her skin, with its soft bluish lights, and of her hair, as well as her slow movements and silent character, all made one think of some inhabitant of the sea. There was something of the fish to her (if she had had a scaly tail, she would have been a mermaid), but her two legs placed her

squarely on the tenuous line between a human being and a
creature of myth. Despite everything, the young woman had
led a nearly normal life. She had a fiancé and would one day
marry, on which occasion the responsibility of her beauty
would become her husband's. Rosa bowed her head and a
ray of sunlight pierced the Gothic stained-glass windows of
the church, outlining her face in a halo of light. A few
people turned to look at her and whispered among themselves, as often happened as she passed, but Rosa seemed
oblivious. She was immune to vanity and that day she was
more absent than usual, dreaming of new beasts to embroider on her tablecloth, creatures that were half bird and half
mammal, covered with iridescent feathers and endowed with
horns and hooves, and so fat and with such stubby wings
that they defied the laws of biology and aerodynamics. She
rarely thought about her fiancé, Esteban Trueba, not because
she did not love him but because of her forgetful nature and
because two years' absence is a long time. He was working
in the mines in the North. He wrote to her regularly and
Rosa sometimes replied, sending him lines of poetry and
drawings of flowers she had copied out on sheets of parchment paper. Through this correspondence, which Nívea vio-
lated with impunity at regular intervals, she learned about
the hazards of a miner's life, always dreading avalanches,
pursuing elusive veins, asking for credit against good luck
that was still to come, and trusting that someday he would
strike a marvelous seam of gold that would allow him to
become a rich man overnight and return to lead Rosa by the
arm to the altar, thus becoming the happiest man in the
universe, as he always wrote at the end of his letters. Rosa,
however, was in no rush to marry and had all but forgotten
the only kiss they had exchanged when they said goodbye;
nor could she recall the color of her tenacious suitor's eyes.
Because of the romantic novels that were her only reading
matter, she liked to picture him in thick-soled boots, his skin
tanned from the desert winds, clawing the earth in search of
pirates' treasure, Spanish doubloons, and Incan jewels. It
was useless for Nívea to attempt to convince her that the
wealth of mines lay in rocks, because to Rosa it was incon-
ceivable that Esteban Trueba would spend years piling up
boulders in the hope that by subjecting them to God only

knew what wicked incinerating processes, they would eventually spit out a gram of gold. Meanwhile she awaited him without boredom, unperturbed by the enormous task she had taken upon herself: to embroider the largest tablecloth in the world. She had begun with dogs, cats, and butterflies, but soon her imagination had taken over, and her needle had given birth to a whole paradise filled with impossible creatures that took shape beneath her father's worried eyes. Severo felt that it was time for his daughter to shake off her lethargy, stand firmly in reality, and learn the domestic skills that would prepare her for marriage, but Nívea thought differently. She preferred not to torment her daughter with earthly demands, for she had a premonition that her daughter was a heavenly being, and that she was not destined to last very long in the vulgar traffic of this world. For this reason she left her alone with her embroidery threads and said nothing about Rosa's nightmarish zoology.

A bone in Nívea's corset snapped and the point jabbed her in the ribs. She felt she was choking in her blue velvet dress, with its high lace collar, its narrow sleeves, and a waist so tight that when she removed her belt her stomach jumped and twisted for half an hour while her organs fell back in place. She had often discussed this with her suffragette friends and they had all agreed that until women shortened their dresses and their hair and stopped wearing corsets, it made no difference if they studied medicine or had the right to vote, because they would not have the strength to do it, but she herself was not brave enough to be among the first to give up the fashion. She noticed that the voice from Galicia had ceased hammering at her brain. They were in one of those long breaks in the sermon that the priest, a connoisseur of unbearable silences, used with frequency and to great effect. His burning eyes glanced over the parishioners one by one. Nívea dropped Clara's hand and pulled a handkerchief from her sleeve to blot the drop of sweat that was rolling down her neck. The silence grew thick, and time seemed to stop within the church, but no one dared to cough or shift position, so as not to attract Father Restrepo's attention. His final sentences were still ringing between the columns.

Just at that moment, as Nívea would recall years later,

in the midst of all that anxiety and silence, the voice of little Clara was heard in all its purity.

"Psst! Father Restrepo! If that story about hell is a lie, we're all fucked, aren't we. . . ."

The Jesuit's index finger, which was already raised to illustrate additional tortures, remained suspended like a lightning rod above his head. People stopped breathing, and those whose heads had been nodding suddenly woke up. Señor and Señora del Valle were the first to react. They were swept by panic as they saw their children fidget nervously. Severo understood that he must act before collective laughter broke out around them or some divine cataclysm occurred. He grabbed his wife by the arm and Clara by the neck and walked out dragging them behind him with enormous strides, followed by his other children, who stampeded toward the door. They managed to escape before the priest could summon a ray of lightning to turn them all into pillars of salt, but from the threshold they could hear his dreadful voice of offended archangel.

"Possessed . . . She's possessed by the devil!"

These words of Father Restrepo were etched in the family memory with all the gravity of a diagnosis, and in the years to come they had more than one occasion to recall them. The only one who never thought of them again was Clara herself, who simply wrote them in her diary and forgot them. Her parents, however, could not forget, even though they both agreed that demonic possession was a sin too great for such a tiny child. They were afraid of other people's curses and Father Restrepo's fanaticism. Until that day they had never given a name to the eccentricities of their youngest daughter, nor had it ever crossed their minds to ascribe them to satanic influence. Clara's strangeness was simply an attribute of their youngest daughter, like Luis's limp or Rosa's beauty. The child's mental powers bothered no one and produced no great disorder; they almost always surfaced in matters of minor importance and within the strict confines of their home. It was true there had been times, just as they were about to sit down to dinner and everyone was in the large dining room, seated according to dignity and position, when the saltcellar would suddenly begin to shake and move among the plates and goblets without any visible source of energy or sign of illusionist's trick. Nívea would pull Clara's braids and that would be enough to wake her daughter from her mad distraction and return the saltcellar to immobility. The other children had organized a system so that in case of visitors, whoever was closest would reach out and stop whatever might be moving on the table before the guests noticed and were startled. The family continued eating without comment. They had also grown accustomed to the youngest daughter's prophecies. She would announce earthquakes in advance, which was quite useful in that country of catastrophes, for it gave them a chance to lock up the good dishes and place their slippers within reach in case they had to run out in the middle of the night. At the age of six, Clara had foreseen that the horse was going to throw Luis, but he refused to listen and had had a dislocated hip ever since. In time, his left leg had shortened and he had to wear a special shoe with an enormous platform that he made himself. After that Nívea had worried, but Nana reassured her by telling her that many children fly like birds, guess other people's dreams, and speak with ghosts, but that they all outgrow it when they lose their innocence.

"None of them reach adulthood like that," she explained. "Wait till she starts to 'demonstrate.' You'll see how fast she loses interest in making furniture move across the room and predicting disasters!"

Clara was Nana's pet. She had helped at her birth and was the only one who really understood the child's eccentricities. When Clara had emerged from her mother's womb, Nana had cradled and washed her, and from that time on she had felt a desperate love for this fragile creature whose lungs were always full of phlegm, who was always on the verge of losing her breath and turning purple, and whom she had had to revive so many times with the warmth of her huge breasts because she knew that this was the only cure for asthma, much more effective than Dr. Cuevas's fortified syrups.

On that particular Holy Thursday, Severo was pacing up and down the drawing room worrying about the scandal his daughter had provoked at mass. He reasoned that only a fanatic like Father Restrepo could believe in satanic possession in the heart of the twentieth century, this century of light, science, and technology, a time in which the devil had finally lost his reputation. Nívea interrupted him to say that was not the point. The seriousness of what had happened was that if word of their daughter's powers reached beyond the walls of the house and the priest began his own investigation, all their neighbors would find out.

"People are going to start lining up to look at her as if she were a monster," Nívea said.

"And the Liberal Party will go to hell," Severo added, anticipating the damage to his political career that could be caused by having a bewitched child in the family.

Just then Nana shuffled in with her sandals flapping, in her froufrou of starchy petticoats, to announce that a group of men were out in the courtyard unloading a dead man. And so they were. A four-horse carriage had drawn up outside occupying the whole first courtyard, trampling the camellias, and getting manure all over the shiny cobblestones, all this amidst a whirlwind of dust, a pawing of horses, and the curses of superstitious men who were gesticulating against the evil eye. They had come to deliver the body of Uncle Marcos and all his possessions. A honey-voiced man dressed in black, with a frock coat and a hat that was too big for him, was directing the tumult. He began a solemn speech explaining the circumstances of the case, but was brutally interrupted by Nívea, who threw herself on the dusty coffin that held the remains of her dearest brother. She was shouting for them to lift the cover so she could see him with her own two eyes. She had buried him once before, which explained why she had room for doubt whether this time his death was real. Her shouts brought the servants streaming from the house, as well as all her children, who came as fast as they could when they heard their uncle's name echoing amidst the cries of mourning.

It had been two years since Clara had last seen her Uncle Marcos, but she remembered him very well. His was the only perfectly clear image she retained from her whole childhood, and in order to describe him she did not need to consult the daguerreotype in the drawing room that showed him dressed as an explorer leaning on an old-fashioned double-barreled rifle with his right foot on the neck of a Malaysian tiger, the same triumphant position in which she had seen the Virgin standing between plaster clouds and pallid angels at the main altar, one foot on the vanquished devil. All Clara had to do to see her uncle was close her eyes and there he was, weather-beaten and thin, with a pirate's mustache through which his strange, sharklike smile peered out at her. It seemed impossible that he could be inside that long black box that was lying in the middle of the courtyard.

Each time Uncle Marcos had visited his sister Nívea's home, he had stayed for several months, to the immense joy of his nieces and nephews, particularly Clara, causing a storm in which the sharp lines of domestic order blurred. The house became a clutter of trunks, of animals in jars of formaldehyde, of Indian lances and sailor's bundles. In every part of the house people kept tripping over his equipment, and all sorts of unfamiliar animals appeared that had traveled from remote lands only to meet their death beneath Nana's irate broom in the farthest corners of the house. Uncle Marcos's manners were those of a cannibal, as Severo put it. He spent the whole night making incomprehensible movements in the drawing room; later they turned out to be exercises designed to perfect the mind's control over the body and to improve digestion. He performed alchemy experiments in the kitchen, filling the house with fetid smoke and ruining pots and pans with solid substances that stuck to their bottoms and were impossible to remove. While the rest of the household tried to sleep, he dragged his suitcases up and down the halls, practiced making strange, high-pitched sounds on savage instruments, and taught Spanish to a parrot whose native language was an Amazonic dialect. During the day, he slept in a hammock that he had strung between two columns in the hall, wearing only a loincloth that put Severo in a terrible mood but that Nívea forgave because Marcos had convinced her that it was the same costume in which Jesus of Nazareth had preached. Clara remembered perfectly, even though she had been only a tiny child, the first time her Uncle Marcos came to the house after one of his voyages. He settled in as if he planned to stay forever. After a short time, bored with having to appear at ladies' gatherings where the mistress of the house played the piano, with playing cards, and with dodging all his relatives' pressures to pull himself together and take a job as a clerk in Severo del Valle's law practice, he bought a barrel organ and took to the streets with the hope of seducing his Cousin Antonieta and entertaining the public in the bargain. The machine was just a rusty box with wheels, but he painted it with seafaring designs and gave it a fake ship's smokestack. It ended up looking like a coal stove. The organ played either a military march or a waltz, and in between turns of the handle the parrot, who had managed to learn Spanish although he had not lost his foreign accent, would draw a crowd with his piercing shrieks. He also plucked slips of paper from a box with his beak, by way of selling fortunes to the curious. The little pink, green, and blue papers were so clever that they always divulged the exact secret wishes of the customers. Besides fortunes there were little balls of sawdust to amuse the children and a special powder that was supposed to cure impotence, which Marcos sold under his breath to passersby afflicted with that malady. The idea of the organ was a last desperate attempt to win the hand of Cousin Antonieta after more conventional means of courting her had failed. Marcos thought no woman in her right mind could remain impassive before a barrel-organ serenade. He stood beneath her window one evening and played his military march and his waltz just as she was taking tea with a group of female friends. Antonieta did not realize the music was meant for her until the parrot called her by her full name, at which point she appeared in the window. Her reaction was not what her suitor had hoped for. Her friends offered to spread the news to every salon in the city, and the next day people thronged the downtown streets hoping to see Severo del Valle's brother-in-law playing the organ and selling little sawdust balls with a moth-eaten parrot, for the sheer pleasure of proving that even in the best of families there could be good reason for embarrassment. In the face of this stain to the family reputation, Marcos was forced to give up organ-grinding and resort to less conspicuous ways of winning over his Cousin Antonieta, but he did not renounce his goal. In any case, he did not succeed, because from one day to the next the young lady married a diplomat who was twenty years her senior; he took her to live in a tropical country whose name no one could recall, except that it suggested negritude, bananas, and palm trees, where she managed to recover from the memory of that suitor who had ruined her seventeenth year with his military march and his waltz. Marcos sank into a deep depression that lasted two or three days, at the end of which he announced that he would never marry and that he was embarking on a trip around the world. He sold his organ to a blind man and left the parrot to Clara, but Nana secretly poisoned it with an overdose of cod-liver oil, because no one could stand its lusty glance, its fleas, and its harsh, tuneless hawking of paper fortunes, sawdust balls, and powders for impotence.

That was Marcos's longest trip. He returned with a shipment of enormous boxes that were piled in the far courtyard, between the chicken coop and the woodshed, until the winter was over. At the first signs of spring he had them transferred to the parade grounds, a huge park where people would gather to watch the soldiers file by on Independence Day, with the goosestep they had learned from the Prussians. When the crates were opened, they were found to contain loose bits of wood, metal, and painted cloth. Marcos spent two weeks assembling the contents according to an instruction manual written in English, which he was able to decipher thanks to his invincible imagination and a small dictionary. When the job was finished, it turned out to be a bird of prehistoric dimensions, with the face of a furious eagle, wings that moved, and a propeller on its back. It caused an uproar. The families of the oligarchy forgot all about the barrel organ, and Marcos became the star attraction of the season. People took Sunday outings to see the bird; souvenir vendors and strolling photographers made a fortune. Nonetheless, the public's interest quickly waned. But then Marcos announced that as soon as the weather cleared he planned to take off in his bird and cross the mountain range. The news spread, making this the most talked-about event of the year. The contraption lay with its stomach on terra firma, heavy and sluggish and looking more like a wounded duck than like one of those newfangled airplanes they were starting to produce in the United States. There was nothing in its appearance to suggest that it could move, much less take flight across the snowy peaks. Journalists and the curious flocked to see it. Marcos smiled his immutable smile before the avalanche of questions and posed for photographers without offering the least technical or

scientific explanation of how he hoped to carry out his plan.
People came from the provinces to see the sight. Forty years
later his great-nephew Nicolás, whom Marcos did not live to
see, unearthed the desire to fly that had always existed in the
men of his lineage. Nicolás was interested in doing it for
commercial reasons, in a gigantic hot-air sausage on which
would be printed an advertisement for carbonated drinks.
But when Marcos announced his plane trip, no one believed
that his contraption could be put to any practical use. The
appointed day dawned full of clouds, but so many people
had turned out that Marcos did not want to disappoint them.
He showed up punctually at the appointed spot and did not
once look up at the sky, which was growing darker and
darker with thick gray clouds. The astonished crowd filled
all the nearby streets, perching on rooftops and the balconies
of the nearest houses and squeezing into the park. No political gathering managed to attract so many people until half a
century later, when the first Marxist candidate attempted,
through strictly democratic channels, to become President.
Clara would remember this holiday as long as she lived.
People dressed in their spring best, thereby getting a step
ahead of the official opening of the season, the men in white
linen suits and the ladies in the Italian straw hats that were
all the rage that year. Groups of elementary-school children
paraded with their teachers, clutching flowers for the hero.
Marcos accepted their bouquets and joked that they might as
well hold on to them and wait for him to crash, so they
could take them directly to his funeral. The bishop himself,
accompanied by two incense bearers, appeared to bless the
bird without having been asked, and the police band played
happy, unpretentious music that pleased everyone. The police, on horseback and carrying lances, had trouble keeping
the crowds far enough away from the center of the park,
where Marcos waited dressed in mechanic's overalls, with
huge racer's goggles and an explorer's helmet. He was also
equipped with a compass, a telescope, and several strange
maps that he had traced himself based on various theories of
Leonardo da Vinci and on the polar knowledge of the Incas.
Against all logic, on the second try the bird lifted off without
mishap and with a certain elegance, accompanied by the
creaking of its skeleton and the roar of its motor. It rose

flapping its wings and disappeared into the clouds, to a send-off of applause, whistlings, handkerchiefs, drumrolls, and the sprinkling of holy water. All that remained on earth were the comments of the amazed crowd below and a multitude of experts, who attempted to provide a reasonable explanation of the miracle. Clara continued to stare at the sky long after her uncle had become invisible. She thought she saw him ten minutes later, but it was only a migrating sparrow. After three days the initial euphoria that had accompanied the first airplane flight in the country died down and no one gave the episode another thought, except for Clara, who continued to peer at the horizon.

After a week with no word from the flying uncle, people began to speculate that he had gone so high that he had disappeared into outer space, and the ignorant suggested he would reach the moon. With a mixture of sadness and relief, Severo decided that his brother-in-law and his machine must have fallen into some hidden crevice of the *cordillera,* where they would never be found. Nívea wept disconsolately and lit candles to San Antonio, patron of lost objects. Severo opposed the idea of having masses said, because he did not believe in them as a way of getting into heaven, much less of returning to earth, and he maintained that masses and religious vows, like the selling of indulgences, images, and scapulars, were a dishonest business. Because of his attitude, Nívea and Nana had the children say the rosary behind their father's back for nine days. Meanwhile, groups of volunteer explorers and mountain climbers tirelessly searched peaks and passes, combing every accessible stretch of land until they finally returned in triumph to hand the family the mortal remains of the deceased in a sealed black coffin. The intrepid traveler was laid to rest in a grandiose funeral. His death made him a hero and his name was on the front page of all the papers for several days. The same multitude that had gathered to see him off the day he flew away in his bird paraded past his coffin. The entire family wept as befit the occasion, except for Clara, who continued to watch the sky with the patience of an astronomer. One week after he had been buried, Uncle Marcos, a bright smile playing behind his pirate's mustache, appeared in person in the doorway of Nívea and Severo del Valle's house. Thanks to the surreptitious prayers of the women and children, as he himself admitted, he was alive and well and in full possession of his faculties, including his sense of humor. Despite the noble lineage of his aerial maps, the flight had been a failure. He had lost his airplane and had to return on foot, but he had not broken any bones and his adventurous spirit was intact. This confirmed the family's eternal devotion to San Antonio, but was not taken as a warning by future generations, who also tried to fly, although by different means. Legally, however, Marcos was a corpse. Severo del Valle was obliged to use all his legal ingenuity to bring his brother-in-law back to life and the full rights of citizenship. When the coffin was pried open in the presence of the appropriate authorities, it was found to contain a bag of sand. This discovery ruined the reputation, up till then untarnished, of the volunteer explorers and mountain climbers, who from that day on were considered little better than a pack of bandits.

Marcos's heroic resurrection made everyone forget about his barrel-organ phase. Once again he was a sought-after guest in all the city's salons and, at least for a while, his name was cleared. Marcos stayed in his sister's house for several months. One night he left without saying goodbye, leaving behind his trunks, his books, his weapons, his boots, and all his belongings. Severo, and even Nívea herself, breathed a sigh of relief. His visit had gone on too long. But Clara was so upset that she spent a week walking in her sleep and sucking her thumb. The little girl, who was only seven at the time, had learned to read from her uncle's storybooks and been closer to him than any other member of the family because of her prophesying powers. Marcos maintained that his niece's gift could be a source of income and a good opportunity for him to cultivate his own clairvoyance. He believed that all human beings possessed this ability, particularly his own family, and that if it did not function well it was simply due to a lack of training. He bought a crystal ball in the Persian bazaar, insisting that it had magic powers and was from the East (although it was later found to be part of a buoy from a fishing boat), set it down on a background of black velvet, and announced that he could tell people's fortunes, cure the evil eye, and improve the quality of dreams, all for the modest sum of five centavos. His first customers were the maids from around the neighborhood. One of them had been accused of stealing, because her employer had misplaced a valuable ring. The crystal ball revealed the exact location of the object in question: it had rolled beneath a wardrobe. The next day there was a line outside the front door of the house. There were coachmen, storekeepers, and milkmen; later a few municipal employees and distinguished ladies made a discreet appearance, slinking along the side walls of the house to keep from being recognized. The customers were received by Nana, who ushered them into the waiting room and collected their fees. This task kept her busy throughout the day and demanded so much of her time that the family began to complain that all there ever was for dinner was old string beans and jellied quince. Marcos decorated the carriage house with some frayed curtains that had once belonged in the drawing room but that neglect and age had turned to dusty rags. There he and Clara received the customers. The two divines wore tunics "the color of the men of light," as Marcos called the color yellow. Nana had dyed them with saffron powder, boiling them in pots usually reserved for rice and pasta. In addition to his tunic, Marcos wore a turban around his head and an Egyptian amulet around his neck. He had grown a beard and let his hair grow long and he was thinner than ever before. Marcos and Clara were utterly convincing, especially because the child had no need to look into the crystal ball to guess what her clients wanted to hear. She would whisper in her Uncle Marcos's ear, and he in turn would transmit the message to the client, along with any improvisations of his own that he thought pertinent. Thus their fame spread, because all those who arrived sad and bedraggled at the consulting room left filled with hope. Unrequited lovers were told how to win over indifferent hearts, and the poor left with foolproof tips on how to place their money at the dog track. Business grew so prosperous that the waiting room was always packed with people, and Nana began to suffer dizzy spells from being on her feet so many hours a day. This time Severo had no need to intervene to put a stop to his brother-in-law's venture, for both Marcos and Clara, realizing that their unerring guesses could alter the fate of their clients, who always followed their advice to the letter, became frightened and decided that this was a job for swindlers. They abandoned their carriage-house oracle and split the profits, even though the only one who had cared about the material side of things had been Nana.

Of all the del Valle children, Clara was the one with the greatest interest in and stamina for her uncle's stories. She could repeat each and every one of them. She knew by heart words from several dialects of the Indians, was acquainted with their customs, and could describe the exact way in which they pierced their lips and earlobes with wooden shafts, their initiation rites, the names of the most poisonous snakes, and the appropriate antidotes for each. Her uncle was so eloquent that the child could feel in her own skin the burning sting of snakebites, see reptiles slide across the carpet between the legs of the jacaranda room-divider, and hear the shrieks of macaws behind the drawing-room drapes. She did not hesitate as she recalled Lope de Aguirre's search for El Dorado, or the unpronounceable names of the flora and fauna her extraordinary uncle had seen; she knew about the lamas who take salt tea with yak lard and she could give detailed descriptions of the opulent women of Tahiti, the rice fields of China, or the white prairies of the North, where the eternal ice kills animals and men who lose their way, turning them to stone in seconds. Marcos had various travel journals in which he recorded his excursions and impressions, as well as a collection of maps and books of stories and fairy tales that he kept in the trunks he stored in the junk room at the far end of the third courtyard. From there they were hauled out to inhabit the dreams of his descendants, until they were mistakenly burned half a century later on an infamous pyre.

Now Marcos had returned from his last journey in a coffin. He had died of a mysterious African plague that had turned him as yellow and wrinkled as a piece of parchment. When he realized he was ill, he set out for home with the hope that his sister's ministrations and Dr. Cuevas's knowl-edge would restore his health and youth, but he was unable to withstand the sixty days on ship and died at the latitude of Guayaquil, ravaged by fever and hallucinating about musky women and hidden treasure. The captain of the ship, an Englishman by the name of Longfellow, was about to throw

him overboard wrapped in a flag, but Marcos, despite his
savage appearance and his delirium, had made so many
friends on board and seduced so many women that the
passengers prevented him from doing so, and Longfellow
was obliged to store the body side by side with the vegetables of the Chinese cook, to preserve it from the heat and
mosquitoes of the tropics until the ship's carpenter had time
to improvise a coffin. At El Callao they obtained a more
appropriate container, and several days later the captain,
furious at all the troubles this passenger had caused the
shipping company and himself personally, unloaded him
without a backward glance, surprised that not a soul was
there to receive the body or cover the expenses he had
incurred. Later he learned that the post office in these lati-
tudes was not as reliable as that of far-off England, and that
all his telegrams had vaporized en route. Fortunately for
Longfellow, a customs lawyer who was a friend of the del
Valle family appeared and offered to take charge, placing
Marcos and all his paraphernalia in a freight car, which he
shipped to the capital to the only known address of the
deceased: his sister's house.

This would have been one of the most painful moments
in Clara's life if Barrabás had not arrived among her uncle's
things. Unaware of the commotion in the courtyard, she was
led by instinct directly to the corner where the cage had been
set down. In it was Barrabás. Or, rather, a pile of bones
covered with a skin of indefinite color that was full of
infected patches, with one eye sealed shut and the other
crusted over, rigid as a corpse in his own excrement. Despite
his appearance, the child had no trouble in identifying him.

"A puppy!" she cried.

The animal became her responsibility. She removed it
from the cage, rocked it in her arms, and with a missionary's
care managed to get water down his parched, swollen throat.
No one had bothered to feed him since Captain Longfellow—
who, like most Englishmen, was kinder to animals than to
people—had dropped him on the pier along with all the
other baggage. While the dog had been on board with his
dying master, the captain had fed him with his own hand and
taken him up on deck, lavishing on him every attention that
he had denied Marcos, but once on land he was treated as

part of the baggage. Without any competition for the job, Clara became the creature's mother, and she soon revived him. A few days later, after the storm of the corpse's arrival had died down and Uncle Marcos had been laid to rest, Severo noticed the hairy animal his daughter was holding in her arms.

"What's that?" he asked.

"Barrabás," Clara replied.

"Give him to the gardener so he can get rid of him. He might be contagious," Severo ordered.

But Clara had adopted him. "He's mine, Papa. If you take him away, I'll stop breathing and I promise you I'll die."

The dog remained in the house. Soon afterward he was running everywhere, devouring drape fringes, Oriental rugs, and all the table legs. He rapidly recovered from his terrible condition and began to grow. After he had had a bath, he was found to be black, with a square head, long legs, and short hair. Nana suggested cutting off his tail to make him more refined, but Clara had a tantrum that degenerated into an asthma attack and no one ever mentioned it again. Barrabás kept his tail, which in time grew to be as long as a golf club and developed a life all its own that led to lamps and china being swept from tabletops. He was of unknown pedigree. He had nothing in common with the stray dogs in the street, much less with the thoroughbred racers that assorted families of the aristocracy were raising. The veterinarian was unable to pinpoint his origin and Clara decided that he was from China, because most of her uncle's baggage was from that distant land. The dog had a seemingly unlimited capacity for growth. Within six months he was the size of a sheep, and at the end of a year he was as big as a colt. In desperation the family began to question whether he would ever stop growing and whether he really was a dog. They suggested that he might be some exotic animal their uncle had caught in some remote corner of the world and that perhaps in his natural habitat he was wild. Nívea looked at his crocodile claws and his sharp little teeth and her heart leapt at the thought that if in one bite he could snap the head off any grown-up, it would be even easier for him to gobble up one of her children. But Barrabás gave no indication of ferocity. On the contrary, he had all the captivating ways of a frolicsome kitten. He slept by Clara's side with his head on her feather pillow and a quilt up to his neck because he was very sensitive to cold, and later, when he was too big for the bed, he lay on the floor beside her, his horse's hoof resting on the child's hand. He never barked or growled. He was as black and silent as a panther, liked ham and every known type of marmalade, and whenever there was company and the family forgot to lock him up he would steal into the dining room and slink around the table, removing with the greatest delicacy all his favorite dishes, and of course none of the diners dared to interfere. Despite his docility, Barrabás inspired terror. Delivery men fled precipitously whenever he stuck his head out into the street, and once he caused a riot among the women who were lined up waiting to buy milk, startling the dray horse who took off like a shot, scattering milk pails every which way on the pavement. Severo had to pay for all the damage and ordered the dog tied up in the courtyard, but Clara had another fit and the decision was indefinitely postponed. Popular imagination and ignorance with respect to his past lent Barrabás the most mythological characteristics. It was said that he would not stop growing, and that if a butcher's cruelty had not put an end to his existence, he would have reached the size of a camel. Some people believed him to be a cross between a dog and a mare, and expected him to sprout wings and horns and acquire the sulfuric breath of a dragon, like the beasts Rosa was embroidering on her endless tablecloth. Tired of picking up broken china and hearing rumors of how he turned into a wolf when there was a full moon, Nana applied the same method she had used with the parrot, but the overdose of cod-liver oil did not kill the dog. It simply gave him a four-day case of diarrhea that covered the house from top to bottom and that she herself had to clean.

Those were difficult times. I was about twenty-five then, but I felt as if I had only a little life left ahead of me to build my future and attain the position that I wanted. I worked like a beast and the few times I sat down to rest, not by choice but forced by the tedium of Sunday afternoons, I felt as if I were losing precious moments of my life: each idle minute meant another century away from Rosa. I lived in the mine, in a wooden shack with a zinc roof that I built myself with the help of a few peons. It was just one square room, in which I had arranged all my belongings, with a crude window in each wall so that by day the stifling desert air would have a chance to circulate, and with shutters to keep out the glacial wind that blew at night. My furniture consisted of a chair, a cot, a rough table, a typewriter, and a heavy safe I had hauled across the desert on a mule, in which I kept the miners' logbooks, a few papers, and a canvas pouch containing the few sparkling pieces of gold that were the only fruit of all my effort. It wasn't very pleasant, but I was used to discomfort. I had never taken a hot bath, and my childhood memories were of cold, of loneliness, and of a perpetually empty stomach. There I ate, slept, and wrote for two long years, with no greater distraction than the handful of books I read and reread, a stack of old magazines, some English grammars, from which I pieced together the rudiments of that magnificent language, and a box with a key, in which I kept my correspondence with Rosa. I had got into the habit of typing all my letters to her, keeping a copy for myself that I filed along with the few letters I received from her. I ate the same food that was cooked for all the miners, and I had forbidden the drinking of alcoholic beverages within the mine. I kept none in my own house either, because I've always held that loneliness and boredom can lead a man to drink. It may have been the memory of my father—open-collared, his tie loosened and stained, his eyes clouded and his breath heavy, glass in hand—that made me a teetotaler. Besides, I don't hold my liquor well. I get drunk in nothing flat. I discovered this at the age of sixteen and I've never forgotten it. My granddaughter once asked me how I managed to live alone for so long far removed from civilization. The truth is I don't know. But it must have been easier for me than for most people, because I've never been particularly sociable; I have few friends and I don't enjoy parties or festivities. I'm much happier when I'm alone. At that time I had never lived with a woman, so I could hardly miss something I hadn't grown accustomed to. I wasn't the type who's always falling in love—I never have been. I'm the faithful type, though it's true that all it takes is the shadow of an arm, the curve of a waist, or the crease of a female knee to put ideas into my head even now when I'm so old that I don't recognize myself when I look in the mirror. I look like a twisted tree. I'm not trying to justify the sins of my youth by saying that I couldn't control my instincts: nothing of the sort. By that point I was used to having dead-end relationships with easy women, since there was no possibility of any other kind. In my generation we used to distinguish between decent women and all the rest, and we also divided up the decent ones into our own and others'. I had never thought of love until I met Rosa, and romance struck me as dangerous and pointless; if a young girl caught my eye, I didn't dare approach her, since I was afraid of being rejected and ridiculed. I've always been very proud, and because of my pride I've suffered more than most.

More than half a century has passed, but I can still remember the exact moment when Rosa the Beautiful entered my life like a distracted angel who stole my soul as she went by. She was with her Nana and another child, probably one of her younger sisters. I think she was wearing a violet dress, but I'm not sure, because I have no eye for women's clothes and because she was so beautiful that even if she had been wearing an ermine cape all I would have noticed was her face. I don't generally spend my time thinking about women, but only a fool could have failed to spot that apparition, who caused a stir wherever she went, and tied up traffic, with her incredible green hair, which framed her face like a fantastic hat, her fairy-tale manner, and her special way of moving as if she were flying. She crossed right in front of me without seeing me and floated into the pastry shop on the Plaza de Armas. Dumbstruck, I waited in the street while she bought licorice drops, which she selected one by one, with that tinkling laugh of hers, tossing some into her mouth and handing others to her sister. I wasn't the only one to stand there hypnotized, for within a few minutes a whole circle of men had formed, their noses pressed against the window. It was then that I reacted. It didn't cross my mind that since I had no fortune, was no one's idea of a proper young man, and faced a most uncertain future, I was far from being the ideal suitor for that heavenly girl. I didn't even know her! But I was bewitched, and I decided then and there that she was the only woman in the world who was worthy to be my wife, and that if I couldn't have her I would remain a bachelor. I followed her all the way home. I got on the same streetcar and took the seat behind her, unable to take my eyes off her perfect nape, her round neck, and her soft shoulders caressed by the green curls that had escaped from her coiffure. I didn't feel the motion of the car, because I was in a dream. Suddenly she swept down the aisle and as she passed me her astonishing gold eyes rested for a moment on my own. Part of me must have died. I couldn't breathe and my pulse stopped in its tracks. When I recovered my composure, I had to leap onto the sidewalk at the risk of breaking all my bones, and run toward the street down which she had already turned. Thanks to a cloud of violet disappearing behind a gate, I learned where she lived. From that day on I stood guard outside her house, pacing up and down the street like an orphaned dog, spying on her, slipping money to the gardener, engaging the maids in conversation, until I finally managed to speak to Nana, and she, God bless her, took pity on me and agreed to be our go-between, conveying my love letters, my flowers, and the innumerable boxes of licorice drops with which I tried to win Rosa's affection. I also sent her acrostics. I don't know how to write poetry, but there was a Spanish bookseller with a real genius for rhyme from whom I ordered poems and songs—anything whose raw material was paper and ink. My sister Férula helped me get closer to the del Valle family by uncovering distant links between our ancestors and theirs, and seeking out every opportunity to greet them as they came out of mass. That was how I was finally able to visit Rosa, but the day I entered her house and was within speaking range of her, I couldn't think of anything to say. I stood there mute, my hat in my hand and my mouth gaping, until her parents, who were well acquainted with such symptoms, came to my rescue. I can't imagine what Rosa could have seen in me—or why, with time, she came to accept me as her husband. I became her official suitor without having to perform any superhuman tasks because, despite her awesome beauty and her innumerable virtues, Rosa had no other wooers. Her mother explained it to me this way: she said that no one felt strong enough to spend his life protecting her from other men's desire. Many had circled around her, even fallen head over heels in love with her, but until I came along none had made up his mind. Her beauty struck fear into their hearts and they preferred to admire her from afar, not daring to approach her. That had never occurred to me, to tell you the truth. My problem was that I didn't have a cent, although I felt capable, through my love, of becoming a rich man. I looked around to find the quickest route within the limits of the honesty in which I had been raised, and I realized that success required godparents, advanced studies, or capital. It wasn't enough to have a respectable last name. I suppose that if I had had the money to start out with, I would have tried my luck at the gaming tables or the races, but since that was not the case I had to think of a line of work that, while it might entail certain risks, held out the promise of a fortune. Gold and silver mines were the dream of all adventurers: a mine could plunge you into abject poverty, kill you with tuberculosis, or make you a rich man overnight. It was a question of luck. Thanks to the prestige of my mother's name, I was able to obtain the concession for a mine in the North, for which the bank gave me a loan. I vowed to extract the last gram of precious metal even if it meant I had to crush the hills with my own hands and grind the rocks with my feet. For Rosa's sake, I was prepared to do that and much more.

At the end of autumn, when the family had calmed down about Father Restrepo, who was forced to mitigate his inquisitional behavior after the bishop had personally warned him to leave little Clara del Valle alone, and when they had all resigned themselves to the fact that Uncle Marcos was truly dead, Severo's political designs began to take shape. He had worked for years toward this end, so it was a personal triumph when he was invited to be the Liberal Party candidate in the upcoming Congressional elections, representing a southern province that he had never set foot in and that he had difficulty finding on the map. The party badly needed people and Severo was anxious for a seat in Congress, so they had no trouble convincing the downtrodden voters of the South to choose him as their candidate. Their invitation was supported by a monumental rose-colored roast pig, which the voters shipped directly to candidate del Valle's home. It arrived on an enormous wooden tray, scented and gleaming, with a sprig of parsley in its mouth and a carrot protruding from its rump, the whole reposing on a bed of tomatoes. Its stomach had been stitched closed, and it was stuffed with partridges that in turn were stuffed with plums. It was accompanied by a decanter containing half a gallon of the best brandy in the country. The idea of becoming a deputy or, better still, a senator, was a long-cherished dream of Severo's. Over the years he had been meticulously laying the groundwork, by means of contacts, friendships, secret meetings, discreet but effective public appearances, and gifts of money or favors made to the right people at the right moment. That southern province, however distant and unknown, was exactly what he had been waiting for.

The pig arrived on a Tuesday. On Friday, when the pig was no more than a heap of skin and bones that Barrabás was gnawing in the courtyard, Clara announced that there would soon be another death in the del Valle family.

"But it will be by mistake," she added.

On Saturday she slept badly and awoke screaming in the middle of the night. In the morning Nana made her a cup of linden tea but no one paid her much attention, because everyone was busy with the preparations for their father's southern trip, and because Rosa the Beautiful had developed a chill. Nívea gave orders for Rosa to remain in bed, and Dr. Cuevas said that it was nothing serious and that she should be given sugared lemonade with a splash of liquor to help bring down her fever. Severo went in to see his daughter and found her flushed and wide-eyed, sunk deep in the butter-colored lace sheets. He took her a dance card as a present and gave Nana permission to open the decanter of brandy and pour some in the lemonade. Rosa drank the lemonade, wrapped herself in her woolen shawl, and immediately fell asleep next to Clara, with whom she shared the room.

On the morning of that tragic Sunday, Nana woke up early as she always did. Before going to mass, she went into the kitchen to prepare breakfast for the family. The wood and coal stove had been readied the night before, and she lit the smoldering, still-warm embers. While the water heated and the milk boiled, she stacked the plates to be taken into the dining room. She put some oatmeal on the stove, strained the coffee, and toasted the bread. She arranged two trays, one for Nívea, who always breakfasted in bed, and one for Rosa, who by virtue of her illness was entitled to the same treatment as her mother. She covered Rosa's tray with a linen napkin that had been embroidered by the nuns, to keep the coffee warm and prevent flies from getting in the food, and stuck her head out in the courtyard to make sure Barrabás was not in sight. He had a penchant for leaping at her whenever she went by with the breakfast tray. She saw him in the corner playing with a hen and took advantage of his momentary distraction to begin her long trip across court-yards and through hallways, from the kitchen, which was in the middle of the house, all the way to the girls' room, which was on the other side. When she came to Rosa's door, she stopped, gripped by a premonition. She entered without knocking, as she always did, and immediately noticed the scent of roses, even though they were not in season. This was how Nana understood that an inescapable disaster had occurred. She set the tray down carefully beside the bed and walked slowly to the window. She opened the heavy drapes and let the pale morning sun into the room. Grief-stricken, she turned around and was not at all surprised to see Rosa lying dead upon the bed, more beautiful than ever, her hair strikingly green, her skin the tone of new ivory, and her honey-gold eyes wide open, staring at the ceiling. Little Clara was at the foot of the bed observing her sister. Nana fell to her knees beside the bed, took Rosa's hand in hers, and began to pray. She prayed for a long time, until the terrible moan of a lost freighter was heard throughout the house. It was the first and last time anyone heard Barrabás's voice. He mourned the dead girl all that day, fraying the nerves of the whole family and all the neighbors, who came running at the sound of his shipwrecked howls.

After taking one look at Rosa's body, Dr. Cuevas knew that she had died of no ordinary fever. He began to search the entire house, going over the kitchen inch by inch, sticking his fingers into pots, opening flour sacks and bags of sugar, prying the tops off boxes of dried fruit, and leaving a wake of destruction behind him. He rummaged through

Rosa's drawers, questioned the servants one by one, and harassed Nana until she was beside herself; finally his search led to the decanter of brandy, which he requisitioned instantly. He shared his doubts with no one, but he took the bottle to his laboratory. He returned three hours later, his rosy face transformed by horror into the pale mask he wore throughout that whole dreadful episode. He walked up to Severo, took him by the arm, and led him off to one side.

"There was enough poison in that brandy to fell an ox," he said between tight lips. "But in order to be sure that that's what killed the child, I'll have to do an autopsy."

"Does that mean you have to cut her open?" Severo moaned.

"Not completely. I won't have to touch her head, just her digestive tract," the doctor explained.

Severo was overcome.

By that point Nívea was worn out from weeping, but when she learned that they were thinking of taking her daughter to the morgue, she quickly regained her strength. She calmed down only when they swore that they would take Rosa directly from the house to the Catholic cemetery: only then did she accept the laudanum the doctor handed her. She slept for twenty hours.

When evening fell, Severo made his preparations. He sent his children up to bed and gave the servants permission to retire early. He allowed Clara, who was too upset by what had happened, to spend the night in the bedroom of another sister. When all the lights were out and the house was silent, Dr. Cuevas's assistant, a sickly, myopic young man with a stutter, arrived. They helped Severo carry his daughter's body into the kitchen and set it gently down on the slab of marble where Nana kneaded pastry and chopped vegetables. Despite his sturdy character, Severo was overcome when his daughter's nightgown was lifted to reveal the splendid body of a mermaid. He staggered out of the room, drunk with grief, and collapsed in an armchair, weeping like a child. Dr. Cuevas too, who had seen Rosa come into this world and knew her like the palm of his own hand, was taken aback at the sight of her nude body. The young assistant began to pant, so overwhelmed was he, and he panted for years to come, every time he recalled the extraordinary sight of Rosa naked and asleep on the kitchen table, her long hair sweeping to the floor in a cascade of green.

While they were at work on their terrible task, Nana, bored with weeping and prayer and sensing that something strange was going on in her domain, got up, wrapped her shawl around her shoulders, and set out through the house. She saw a light in the kitchen, but the door and wooden shutters were closed. She continued down the frozen, silent hallways, crossing the three wings of the house, until she came to the drawing room. Through the open door she could see her employer pacing up and down with a desolate air. The fire in the fireplace had long since gone out. She stepped into the room.

"Where is Rosa?" she asked.

"Dr. Cuevas is with her, Nana," he replied. "Come have a drink with me."

Nana remained standing, her crossed arms holding her shawl against her chest. Severo pointed to the sofa and she approached shyly. She sat down beside him. It was the first time she had been this close to her employer since she had lived in his house. Severo poured them each a glass of sherry and downed his in a single gulp. He buried his head in his hands, tearing his hair and murmuring a strange litany between his teeth. Nana, who was sitting stiffly on the edge of her seat, relaxed when she saw him cry. She stretched out her rough, chapped hand and, with a gesture that came automatically, smoothed his hair with the same caress she had used to console his children for the past twenty years. He glanced up and when he saw the ageless face, the Indian cheekbones, the black bun, the broad lap against which he had seen all his descendants burped and rocked to sleep, he felt that this woman, as warm and generous as the earth itself, would be able to console him. He leaned his forehead on her skirt, inhaled the sweet scent of her starched apron, and broke into the sobs of a small boy, spilling all the tears he had held in during his life as a man. Nana scratched his back, patted him gently, spoke to him in the half-language that she used to put the littlest ones to sleep, and sang him one of her peasant ballads until he had calmed down. They remained seated side by side, sipping sherry and weeping from time to time as they recalled the happy days when Rosa scampered in the garden startling the butterflies with her beauty that could only have come from the bottom of the sea.

In the kitchen, Dr. Cuevas and his assistant prepared their dread utensils and foul-smelling jars, donned rubber aprons, rolled up their sleeves, and proceeded to poke around in Rosa's most intimate parts until they had proven beyond a shadow of a doubt that the girl had swallowed an extraordinary quantity of rat poison.

"This was meant for Severo," the doctor concluded, washing his hands in the sink.

The assistant, overcome by the young girl's beauty, could not resign himself to leaving her sewn up like a jacket and suggested that they fix her up a bit. Both men plunged into the work of preserving her with unguents and filling her with mortician's paste. They worked until four o'clock in the morning, when Dr. Cuevas announced that he was too tired and too sad to continue. He went out of the room and Rosa was left in the hands of the assistant, who wiped the blood-stains from her skin with a sponge, put her embroidered nightgown back over her chest to cover up the seam that ran from her throat all the way to her sex, and arranged her hair. Then he cleaned up the mess that he and the doctor had made.

Dr. Cuevas walked into the living room and found Severo and Nana half drunk with tears and sherry.

"She's ready," he said. "We've fixed her up a little so her mother can go in and have a look at her."

He told Severo that his doubts had been well founded and that in his daughter's stomach he had found the same lethal substance as in the gift of brandy. It was then that Severo recalled Clara's prediction and lost whatever remained of his composure, for he was incapable of thinking that his daughter had died instead of him. He crumpled to the floor, moaning that he was the guilty one because of his ambition and bluster, that no one had told him to get involved in politics, that he had been much better off as an ordinary lawyer and family man, and that from then on he was renouncing his accursed candidacy, resigning from the Liberal Party and from all his public deeds and works, and that he hoped none of his descendants would ever get mixed up in politics, which was a trade for butchers and bandits—till finally Dr. Cuevas took pity on him and did him the favor of getting him drunk. The sherry was stronger than his suffering and guilt. Nana and the doctor carried him up to his bedroom, removed his clothes, and put him in his bed. Then they went into the kitchen, where the assistant was just putting the final touches on Rosa.

Nívea and Severo del Valle woke up late the following morning. Their relatives had hung the house in mourning. The curtains were drawn and bore black crepe ribbons, and the walls were piled with wreaths of flowers whose sickly sweet odor filled the halls. A funeral chapel had been set up in the dining room. There on the big table, covered with a black cloth with gold fringes, lay Rosa's white coffin with its silver rivets. Twelve yellow candles in bronze candelabras cast a dusky light over the girl. They had dressed her in the white gown and crown of wax orange blossoms that were being saved for her wedding day.

At twelve o'clock the parade of friends, relatives, and acquaintances began to file in to express their sympathy to the family. Even their most confirmed enemies appeared at the house, and Severo del Valle interrogated each pair of eyes in the hope of discovering the identity of the assassin; but in each, even those of the president of the Conservative Party, he saw the same innocence and grief.

During the wake, the men wandered through the sitting rooms and hallways of the house, speaking softly of business. They kept a respectful silence whenever any member of the family approached. When the time came to enter the dining room and pay their last respects to Rosa, everyone trembled, for if anything her beauty had grown more remarkable in death. The ladies moved into the living room, where they arranged the chairs in a circle. There they could weep at leisure, unburdening themselves of their own troubles as they wept for someone else's death. The weeping was copious, but it was dignified and muted. Some of the women murmured prayers under their breath. The maids moved back and forth through the sitting rooms and halls, distributing tea and cognac, homemade sweets, handkerchiefs for the women, and cold compresses soaked in ammonia for those ladies who felt faint from the lack of air, the scent of candles, and the weight of their emotion. All the del Valle sisters except Clara, who was still only a child, were dressed in black from head to toe and flanked their mother like a row of crows. Nívea, who had shed all her tears, sat rigid on her chair without a sigh, without a word, and without ammonia, to which she was allergic. As they arrived at the house, visitors stopped in to pay her their condolences. Some kissed her on both cheeks and others held her tight for a few seconds, but she seemed not to recognize even those she numbered among her closest friends. She had seen others of her children die in early childhood or at birth, but none had caused the sense of loss that she felt now.

All the brothers and sisters said goodbye to Rosa with a kiss on her cold forehead except for Clara, who refused to go anywhere near the dining room. They did not insist, because of both her extreme sensitivity and her tendency to sleepwalk whenever her imagination ran away with her. She stayed by herself in the garden curled up beside Barrabás, refusing to eat or have anything to do with the funeral. Only Nana kept an eye on her and tried to comfort her, but Clara pushed her away.

Despite the care Severo took to hush all speculation, Rosa's death became a public scandal. To anyone who listened, Dr. Cuevas offered the most logical explanation of her death, which was due, he said, to galloping pneumonia. But rumor had it that she had mistakenly been poisoned in her father's stead. In those days political assassinations were unknown in the country, and in any case poison was a method only whores and fishwives would resort to, a lowly technique that had not been seen since colonial times; even crimes of passion were nowadays resolved face to face. There was a great uproar over the attempt on his life, and before Severo could do anything to stop it, an announcement appeared in the opposition paper in which veiled accusations were made against the oligarchy and it was asserted that the conservatives were even capable of this act, because they could not forgive Severo del Valle for throwing his lot in with the liberals despite his social class. The police tried to pursue the clue of the brandy decanter, but all they were able to learn was that its source was not the same as that of the roast pig stuffed with partridges and plums and that the voters of the South had nothing to do with the whole matter. The mysterious decanter had been found outside the service door to the del Valle house on the same day and at the same time that the roast pig was delivered. The cook had simply assumed that it was part of the same gift. Neither the zeal of the police nor Severo's own investigation, which was carried out with the help of a private detective he engaged, shed any light on the identity of the assassin, and the shadow of suspended vengeance has continued to hang over succeeding generations. It was the first of many acts of violence that marked the fate of the del Valle family.

I remember perfectly. It had been a very happy day for me, because a new lode had appeared, the thick, magnificent seam that had eluded me throughout that time of sacrifice, absence, and hope, and that might represent the wealth I had been seeking for so long. I was sure that within six months I would have enough money to get married, and that by the time the year was out I would be able to call myself a wealthy man. I was very lucky, because in the mines there were more men who lost the little that they had than those who made a fortune, which is just what I was writing to Rosa that evening as I sat there so euphoric and so impatient that my fingers locked on the old typewriter and all the words came out jammed together. I was in the middle of the letter when I heard the pounding at the door that would cut off my inspiration forever. It was a peasant, with a team of mules, who had brought a telegram from town, sent by my sister Férula, telling me of Rosa's death.

I had to read the scrap of paper three times through before I understood the extent of my grief. The only thought that had never crossed my mind was that Rosa could be mortal. I suffered greatly whenever it occurred to me that, bored with waiting for me, she might marry someone else, or that the cursed vein that would spell my fortune might never turn up, or that the mine might cave in, squashing me like a cockroach. I had thought of all these possibilities and more, but never that of Rosa's death, despite my proverbial pessimism, which always leads me to expect the worst. I felt that without Rosa life no longer had any meaning. All the air went out of me as if I were a punctured balloon; all my enthusiasm vanished. God only knows how long I sat there in my chair, staring out the window at the desert, until my soul gradually returned to my body. My first reaction was one of rage. I turned against the walls, pounding the flimsy wooden planks until my knuckles bled. Then I tore all of Rosa's letters and drawings and the copies of my letters to her into a thousand pieces, stuffed my clothing, my papers, and my canvas pouch filled with gold into my suitcase, and went to find the foreman so I could leave him the logbooks and the keys to the warehouse. The mule driver offered to take me to the train. We had to travel almost the whole night on the animals' backs, with thin Spanish blankets as our only shield against the freezing mist, advancing at a snail's pace through that endless wasteland in which only the instinct of my guide guaranteed our safe arrival, for there were no points of reference. The night was clear and full of stars. I felt the cold pierce my bones, cut off the circulation in my hands, and seep into my soul. I was thinking of Rosa and wishing with an unreasoning violence that her death wasn't true, desperately begging the heavens for it all to turn out to be a terrible mistake, and praying that, revived by the force of my love, she would rise like Lazarus from her deathbed. I wept inwardly, sunk in my grief and in the icy night, cursing at the mule who was so slow, at Férula, the bearer of bad news, at Rosa herself for having died, and at God for having let her, until light appeared over the horizon and I saw the star fade away and the first shades of dawn appear, dyeing the landscape red and orange. With the light, I regained some of my strength. I began to resign myself to my misfortune and to ask no longer that she be resurrected but simply that I would arrive in time to see her one last time before they buried her. We doubled our pace and an hour later the driver took leave of me outside the tiny train station where I caught the narrow-gauge locomotive that linked the civilized world and the desert where I had spent two years.

I traveled more than thirty hours without stopping to eat, not even noticing my thirst, and I managed to reach the del Valle home before the funeral. They say that I arrived covered with dust, without a hat, filthy and bearded, thirsty and furious, shouting for my bride. Little Clara, who at the time was just a skinny child, came out to meet me when I stepped into the courtyard, took me by the hand, and drew me silently toward the dining room. There was Rosa in the folds of the white satin lining of her white coffin, still intact three days after she had died, and a thousand times more beautiful than I remembered her, for in death Rosa had been subtly transformed into the mermaid she had always been in secret.

"Damn her! She slipped through my hands!" they say I shouted, falling to my knees beside her, scandalizing all the relatives, for no one could comprehend my frustration at having spent two years scratching the earth to make my fortune with no other goal than that of one day leading this girl to the altar, and death had stolen her away from me.

Moments later the carriage arrived, an enormous black, shiny coach drawn by six plumed chargers, as was used on those occasions, and driven by two coachmen in livery. It pulled away from the house in the middle of the afternoon beneath a light drizzle, followed by a procession of cars that carried family and friends and all the flowers. It was the custom then for women and children not to attend funerals, which were considered a male province, but at the last minute Clara managed to slip into the cortège to accompany her sister Rosa, and I felt the grip of her small gloved hand. She stayed by my side all along the way, a small, silent shadow who aroused an unknown tenderness in my soul. At that moment I hadn't been told that she hadn't spoken in two days; and three more were to pass before the family became alarmed by her silence.

Severo del Valle and his oldest sons bore Rosa's white coffin with the silver rivets, and they themselves laid it down in the open niche in the family tomb. They were dressed in black, silent and dry-eyed, as befits the norms of sadness in a country accustomed to the dignity of grief. After the gates to the mausoleum had been locked and the family, friends, and gravediggers had retired, I was left alone among the flowers that had escaped Barrabás's hunger and accompanied Rosa to the cemetery. Tall and thin as I was then, before Férula's curse came true and I began to shrink, I must have looked like some dark winter bird with the bottom of my jacket dancing in the wind. The sky was gray and it looked as if it might rain. I suppose it must have been quite cold, but I didn't feel it, because my rage was eating me alive. I couldn't take my eyes off the small marble rectangle where the name of Rosa the Beautiful had been engraved in tall Gothic letters, along with the dates that marked her brief sojourn in this world. I thought about how I had lost two years dreaming of Rosa, working for Rosa, writing to Rosa, wanting Rosa, and how in the end I wouldn't even have the consolation of being buried by her side. I thought about the years I still had left to live and decided that without her it wasn't worth it, for I would never find another woman with her green hair and underwater beauty. If anyone had told me then that I would live to be more than ninety, I would have put a gun to my head and pulled the trigger.

I didn't hear the footsteps of the caretaker as he approached me from behind; I jumped when he touched me on the shoulder.

"How dare you put your hands on me!" I roared.

The poor man jumped back in fright. A few drops of rain fell sadly on the flowers of the dead.

"Forgive me, señor," I think he must have said. "It's six o'clock and I have to lock up."

He tried to explain to me that the rules forbade anyone but employees from staying in the place after sundown, but I didn't let him finish. I thrust a few bills in his hand and pushed him away so he would leave me in peace. I saw him walk away looking back at me over his shoulder. He must have thought I was a madman, one of those crazed necrophiliacs who sometimes haunt cemeteries.

It was a long night, perhaps the longest in my life. I spent it sitting next to Rosa's tomb, speaking with her, accompanying her on the first part of her journey to the Hereafter, which is when it's hardest to detach yourself from earth and you need the love of those who have remained behind, so you can leave with at least the consolation of having planted something in someone else's heart. I remembered her perfect face and cursed my luck. I blamed Rosa for the years I had spent dreaming of her deep within the mine. I didn't tell her that I hadn't seen any other women all that time except for a handful of shriveled old prostitutes, who serviced the whole camp with more good will than ability.

But I did tell her that I had lived among rough, lawless men, that I had eaten chick-peas and drunk green water far from civilization, thinking of her night and day and bearing her image in my soul like a banner that gave me the strength to keep hacking at the mountain even if the lode was lost, even if I was sick to my stomach the whole year round, even if I was frozen to the bone at night and dazed by the sun during the day, all with the single goal of marrying her, but she goes and dies on me, betraying me before I can fulfill my dreams, and leaving me with this incurable despair. I told her she had mocked me, that we had never been completely alone together, that I had only been able to kiss her once. I had had to weave my love out of memories and cravings that were impossible to satisfy, out of letters that took forever to arrive and arrived faded, and that were incapable of reflecting the intensity of my feelings or the pain of her absence, because I have no gift for letter writing and much less for writing about my own emotions. I told her that those years in the mine were an irremediable loss, and that if I had known she wasn't long for this world I would have stolen the money that I needed to marry her and built her a palace studded with treasures from the ocean floor—with pearls and coral and walls of nacre. I would have kidnapped her and locked her up, and only I would have had the key. I would have loved her without interruption almost till infinity, for I was convinced that if she had been with me she would never have drunk the poison that was meant for her father and she would have lived a thousand years. I told her of the caresses I'd saved for her, the presents with which I'd planned to surprise her, the ways I would have loved her and made her happy. In short, I told her all the crazy things I never would have said if she could hear me and that I've never told a woman since.

That night I thought I had lost my ability to fall in love forever, that I would never laugh again or pursue an illusion. But never is a long time. I've learned that much in my long life.

I had a vision of anger spreading through me like a malignant tumor, sullying the best hours of my life and rendering me incapable of tenderness or mercy. But beyond confusion and rage, the strongest feeling I remember having that night was frustrated desire, because I would never be able to satisfy my need to run my hands over Rosa's body, to penetrate her secrets, to release the green fountain of her hair and plunge into its deepest waters. In desperation I summoned up the last image I had of her, outlined against the satin pleats in her virginal coffin, with her bride's blossoms in her hair and a rosary in her hands. I couldn't know that years later I would see her once again for a fleeting second just as she was then, with orange blossoms in her hair and a rosary in her hands.

With the first glints of dawn the caretaker appeared again. He must have felt sorry for the half-frozen madman who had spent the night among the livid ghosts of the graveyard. He held out his flask.

"Hot tea," he offered.

But I pushed it away and walked out with great furious strides, cursing, among the lines of tombs and cypresses.

The night that Dr. Cuevas and his assistant cut open Rosa's corpse in the kitchen to establish the cause of her death, Clara lay in bed with her eyes wide open, trembling in the dark. She was terrified that Rosa had died because she had said she would. She believed that just as the power of her mind could move the saltcellar on the table, she could also produce deaths, earthquakes, and other, even worse catastrophes. In vain her mother had explained that she could not bring about events, only see them somewhat in advance. She felt lonely and guilty, and it occurred to her that if only she could be with Rosa she would feel much happier. She got up in her nightshirt and walked barefoot to the bedroom she had shared with her older sister, but she was not in the bed where she had seen her for the last time. She went out to look for her. The house was dark and quiet. Her mother, drugged by Dr. Cuevas, was asleep, and her brothers and sisters and the servants were already in their rooms. She went through the sitting rooms, slipping along the walls, frightened and cold. The heavy furniture, the thick drapes, the paintings on the wall, the wallpaper with its flowers against a background of dark cloth, the low lamps flickering on the ceiling, and the potted ferns on their porcelain columns all looked menacing to her. She noticed a crack of light coming from under the drawing-room door, and she was on the verge of going in, but she was afraid she would run into her father and that he would send her back to bed. So she went toward the kitchen, thinking to comfort herself against Nana's breasts. She crossed the main courtyard, passed between the camellias and the miniature orange trees, went through the sitting rooms of the second wing of the house and the dark open corridors, where the faint gas lights were left burning every night in case there was an earthquake and to scare the bats away, and arrived in the third courtyard, where the service rooms and kitchen were. There the house lost its aristocratic bearing and the kennels, chicken coops, and servants' quarters began. Farther on was the stable where the old horses Nívea still rode were kept, even though Severo del Valle had been one of the first to buy an automobile. The kitchen door and shutters were closed, and so was the pantry. Instinct told Clara that something out of the ordinary was going on inside. She tried to see in but her nose didn't reach the window ledge. She had to fetch a wooden box and pull it to the window. She stood on tiptoe and looked through a crack between the wooden shutter and the window frame, which was warped with damp and age. Then she saw inside.

Dr. Cuevas, that kind, sweet, wonderful old man with the thick beard and ample paunch, who had helped her into this world and attended her through all the usual childhood illnesses and all her asthma attacks, had been transformed into a dark, fat vampire just like the ones in her Uncle Marcos's books. He was bent over the table where Nana prepared her meals. Next to him was a young man she had never seen before, pale as the moon, his shirt stained with blood and his eyes drunk with love. She saw her sister's snow-white legs and naked feet. Clara began to shake. At that moment Dr. Cuevas moved aside and she was able to see the dreadful spectacle of Rosa lying on her back on the marble slab, a deep gash forming a canal down the front of her body, with her intestines beside her on the salad platter. Rosa's head was twisted toward the window through which Clara was squinting, and her long green hair hung like a fern from the table onto the tiled floor, which was stained with blood. Her eyes were closed, but the little girl, because of the shadows, her own distance, and her imagination, thought she saw a supplicating and humiliated expression on her sister's face.

Stock-still on her wooden box, Clara could not keep from watching until the very end. She peered through the crack for a long time, until the two men had finished emptying Rosa out, injecting her veins with liquid, and bathing her inside and out with aromatic vinegar and essence of lavender. She stood there until they had filled her with mortician's paste and sewn her up with a curved upholsterer's needle. She stayed until Dr. Cuevas rinsed his hands in the sink and dried his tears, while the other one cleaned up the blood and the viscera. She stayed until the doctor left, putting on his black jacket with a gesture of infinite sadness. She stayed until the young man she had never seen before kissed Rosa on the lips, the neck, the breasts, and between the legs; until he wiped her with a sponge, dressed her in her embroidered nightgown, and, panting, rearranged her hair. She stayed until Nana and Dr. Cuevas came and dressed Rosa in her white gown and put on her hair the crown of orange blossoms that they'd kept wrapped in tissue paper for her wedding day. She stayed until the assistant took her in his arms with the same tenderness with which he would have picked her up and carried her across the threshold of his house if she had been his bride. She could not move until the first lights of dawn appeared. Only then did she slide back into her bed, feeling within her the silence of the entire world. Silence filled her utterly. She did not speak again until nine years later, when she opened her mouth to announce that she was planning to be married.

The Three Marías

Seated in their dining room among the battered, antiquated pieces that had been fine Victorian furniture long ago, Esteban Trueba and his sister Férula were eating the same greasy soup they had every day of the week, and the same tasteless fish they had for dinner every Friday. They were attended by the same servant who had taken care of them their whole lives, in the tradition of the paid slaves of the era. Stooped and half-blind, but still energetic, the old woman came and went between the kitchen and the dining room, bearing the enormous platters with the utmost solemnity. Doña Ester Trueba did not join her children at the table. She spent her mornings immobile in her chair, looking out the window at the bustle of the street, and observing the gradual decline of the neighborhood that in her youth had been so elegant. After breakfast she was put back into her bed, propped up in the half-seated position that was the only one her arthritis allowed, with no other company than her pious reading matter—books of miracles and lives of the saints. There she stayed until the following morning, when the same routine would be repeated. Her only outings were her weekly trips to Sunday mass at the Church of Saint Sebastián, which was two blocks from her house, whence she was conveyed in a wheelchair by Férula and the maid.

Esteban finished picking the whitish fish from the tangle of bones and laid his knife and fork across his plate. He sat as stiffly as he walked, straight as a pole, his head thrown slightly back and to one side, with a sidelong glance that held a mixture of pride, distrust, and myopia. His gesture would have been unpleasant if his eyes had not been so astonishingly sweet and bright. His tense posture would have suited a short stubby man who wanted to appear taller, but he himself was almost six feet tall and slender. All the lines of his body were vertical and swept upward, from his sharp aquiline nose and pointed eyebrows to his high forehead, which was crowned with a lion's mane of hair that he combed straight back. He was big-boned, with thick, spatulate fingers. He walked with a long stride, and moved with energy; he appeared to be very strong, although there was no lack of grace to his movements. He had a very agreeable face, despite his severe, somber demeanor and his frequently sour expression. His most salient trait was his moodiness and a tendency to grow violent and lose his head, a characteristic he had had since childhood, when he used to throw himself on the floor foaming at the mouth, so furious that he could scarcely breathe, and kicking like one possessed by the devil. He had to be plunged into freezing water to regain control. Later on he learned to manage these fits, but he was left with a short temper, which needed very little provocation to blossom into terrible attacks.

"I'm not returning to the mine," he said.

It was the first sentence he had exchanged at the table with his sister. He had made his mind up the night before, when he realized that it was senseless to continue leading a hermit's life while seeking for a quick fortune. He still had two years left on the concession to the mine, enough time to finish exploring the marvelous lode he had discovered, but he felt that even if the foreman robbed him a little or did not know how to work it as well as he himself might, that was no reason for him to bury himself alive in the desert. He had no wish to become rich by such a sacrifice. He had his whole life ahead of him to make money if he could, time enough to be bored and to await death, without Rosa.

"You'll have to work at something, Esteban," Férula replied. "It's true we spend almost nothing, but Mama's medicines are expensive."

Esteban looked at his sister. She was still a beautiful woman, with rich curves and the oval face of a Roman madonna, but already the ugliness of resignation could be glimpsed through her pale, peach-toned skin and her eyes full of shadows. Férula had accepted the role of her mother's nurse. She slept in the room that adjoined her mother's, ready at any moment to run in and administer her potions, hold her bedpan, or straighten her pillows. She was a tormented soul. She took pleasure in humiliation and in menial tasks, and since she believed that she would get to heaven by suffering terrible injustice, she was content to clean her mother's ulcerated legs, washing her and sinking deeply into her stench and wretchedness, even peering into her bedpan. And, much as she hated herself for these torturous and unconfessable pleasures, she hated her mother more for being their instrument. She waited on her without complaint, but she managed subtly to extract from her the price of her invalidism. Without anything being said openly, the fact remained that the daughter had sacrificed her life to care for the mother, and that she had become a spinster for that reason. Férula had turned down two suitors on the pretext of her mother's illness. She never spoke of it, but everyone knew about it. She moved thickly and awkwardly and had the same sour character as her brother, but life and the fact that she was a woman had forced her to overcome it and to clamp down on the bit. She seemed so perfect that word had spread she was a saint. She was cited as an example because of the devotion that she lavished on Doña Ester and because of the way she had raised her only brother when their mother became ill and their father died, leaving them in dire poverty. Férula had adored her brother Esteban when he was a child. She slept with him, bathed him, took him out for strolls, did other people's sewing from dawn to dusk to pay for his schooling, and wept with rage and helplessness the day Esteban took a job in a notary's office because they could not make ends meet with what she earned. She had taken care of him and waited on him as she now did her mother, and she had woven him too into her invisible net of guilt and unrepayable debts of gratitude.

The boy began to move away from her the day he first put on long pants. Esteban could recall the exact moment when he had realized that his sister was an ominous shadow in his life. It was when he had received his first wages. He had decided to save fifty centavos to fulfill a dream he had cherished ever since he was a child: to have a cup of Viennese coffee. Through the windows of the Hotel Francés he had seen the waiters pass with trays held high above their heads on which lay these treasures: tall glass goblets crowned with towers of whipped cream and adorned with beautiful glazed maraschino cherries. The day of his first paycheck, he had crossed back and forth outside the establishment before getting up the courage to go through the door.

Finally, beret in hand, he had stepped timidly across the threshold and entered the luxurious dining room, with its teardrop chandeliers and stylish furniture, convinced that everyone was staring at him, that their thousand eyes found his suit too tight and his shoes old. He sat down on the edge of the chair, his ears burning, and gave his order to the waiter with a mere thread of a voice. He waited impatiently, watching people come and go in the tall mirrors, tasting with anticipation that pleasure he had so often dreamed of. His Viennese coffee arrived, far more impressive than he had imagined—superb, delicious, and accompanied by three honey biscuits. He stared at it in fascination for a long while, until he finally dared to pick up the long-handled spoon and, with a sigh of ecstasy, plunge it into the cream. His mouth was watering. He wanted to make this moment last as long as possible, to stretch it all the way to infinity. He began to stir the spoon, observing the way the dark liquid of the cup slowly moved into the cream. He stirred and stirred and stirred . . . and suddenly the tip of the spoon knocked against the glass, opening a crack through which the coffee leapt, pouring onto his clothes. Horrified, Esteban watched the entire contents of the goblet spill onto his only suit before the amused glances of the occupants of the adjoining tables. Pale with frustration, he stood up and walked out of the Hotel Francés fifty centavos poorer, leaving a trail of Viennese coffee on the springy carpet. When he reached his house, he was soaked and furious, beside himself. When Férula found out what had happened, she told him acidly, "That's what you get for spending Mama's medicine money on your private little whims. God punished you." At that moment Esteban saw clearly the ways his sister used to keep him down and how she managed to make him feel guilty. He understood that he would have to escape. As he made moves to get out from under her tutelage, Férula began to dislike him. His freedom to come and go stung her like a reproach, like an injustice. When he fell in love with Rosa and Férula saw how desperate he was, like a little boy begging for her help, needing her, following her around the house pleading with her to intercede on his behalf with the del Valle family, that she speak to Rosa, that she bribe Nana, she again felt important to her brother. For a time they seemed to have been reconciled. But that rapprochement did not last long, and Férula was quick to realize that she had been used. She was happy when she saw her brother leave for the mine. From the time he had begun to work, when he was fifteen, Esteban had supported the household and had promised always to do so, but for Férula that had not been enough. It bothered her to have to stay locked up within these walls that stank of medicine and age, to be kept awake at night by the moans of her sick mother, always attentive to the clock so as to administer each dose at the proper time, bored, tired, and unhappy while her brother had no taste of such obligations. Before him lay a destiny that was bright, free, and full of promise. He could marry, have children, know what love was. The day she sent the telegram telling him of Rosa's death she had felt a strange shiver, almost of joy.

"You'll have to work at something," Férula repeated.

"You'll never lack for anything so long as I live," he said.

"That's easy to say," Férula replied, drawing a fish bone from between her teeth.

"I think I'm going to go to the country, maybe to Tres Marías."

"That place is in ruins, Esteban. I've always told you that the best thing you could do with it is sell it, but you're as stubborn as a mule."

"Land is something one should never sell. It's the only thing that's left when everything else is gone."

"I don't agree. Land is a romantic idea. What makes a man rich is a good eye for business," Férula insisted. "But you always said that one day you would go and live in the country."

"That day has arrived. I hate this city."

"Why don't you say it's because you hate this house?"

"That too," he answered brutally.

"I would like to have been born a man, so I could leave too," she said, full of hatred.

"And I would not have liked to be a woman," he said.

They finished eating in silence. The brother and sister had drifted apart, and the only thing that remained to unite them was the presence of their mother and the vague memory of the love they had had for each other as children. They had grown up in a ruined home, witness to the moral and economic deterioration of their father and then the slow illness of their mother. Doña Ester had begun to suffer from arthritis at an early age, becoming stiffer and stiffer until she could only move with the greatest difficulty, like a living corpse; finally, no long able to bend her knees, she had settled for good into her wheelchair, her widowhood, and her despair. Esteban remembered his childhood and adolescence, his tight-fitting suits, the rope of Saint Francis he was forced to tie around his waist as a sign of who only knew what vows his mother or his sister had made, his carefully mended shirts, and his loneliness. Férula, five years his senior, washed and starched his only two shirts every other day so that he would always look fresh and properly dressed, and reminded him that on their mother's side they were heir to the noblest and most highborn surname of the viceroyalty of Lima. Trueba had simply been a regrettable accident in the life of Doña Ester, who was destined to marry someone of her own class, but she had fallen hopelessly in love with that good-for-nothing immigrant, a first-generation settler who within a few short years had squandered first her dowry and then her inheritance.

But his blue-blood past was of no use to Esteban if there was not enough money in the house to pay the grocer and he had to go to school on foot because he did not have the fare for the streetcar. He recalled how they had packed him off to school with his chest and back lined with newspaper, because he had no woolen underclothes and his overcoat was in tatters, and how he had suffered at the thought that his schoolmates might be able to hear, as he could, the crunch of the paper as it moved against his skin. In winter, the only source of heat in the whole house was the brazier in his mother's bedroom, where the three of them huddled together to save on candles and coal. His had been a childhood of privations, discomfort, harshness, interminable nighttime rosaries, fear, and guilt. All that remained of those days was his fury and his outsized pride.

Two days later Esteban Trueba left for the country. Férula accompanied him to the train station. She kissed him a cold goodbye on the cheek and waited for him to board the train carrying his two leather suitcases with the bronze locks, the same ones he had bought when he left for the mine and that were supposed to last him the rest of his life, according to the salesman's promise. She told him to be sure to take care of himself and to try to visit them from time to time; she said she would miss him, but they both knew they were destined not to see each other for many years, and underneath it all they were both rather relieved.

"Let me know if Mother takes a turn for the worse!" Esteban shouted through the window as the train pulled out.

"Don't worry!" Férula replied, waving her handkerchief from the platform.

Esteban Trueba leaned back in the red velvet seat and felt deep gratitude to the British, who had had the foresight to build first-class cars in which one could travel like a gentleman, without having to put up with chickens, baskets, string-tied bundles, and the howls of other people's children. He congratulated himself for having decided on the more expensive ticket for the first time in his life, and observed that this was one of the details that marked the difference between a yokel and a gentleman. He decided that from that day on, no matter how tight his circumstances, he would always pay for the small comforts that made him feel rich.

"I don't plan to be poor ever again!" he decided, dreaming of the seam of gold.

Through the window of the train he watched the passing landscape of the central valley. Vast fields stretched from the foot of the mountain range, a fertile countryside filled with vineyards, wheatfields, alfalfa, and marigolds. He compared it with the sterile plateaus of the North, where he had spent two years stuck in a hole in the midst of a rough and lunar horizon whose terrifying beauty never ceased to interest him. He had been fascinated by the colors of the desert, the blues, the purples, the yellows of the minerals lying on the surface of the earth.

"My life is changing," he said softly. He closed his eyes and fell asleep.

He got off the train at the station of San Lucas. It was a wretched place. At that hour of the morning there was not a soul on the wooden platform, its roof eaten away by inclement weather and ants. From where he stood he could see the whole valley through an impalpable mist that rose from the earth the night rain had soaked. The distant mountains disappeared behind the clouds of a shrouded sky; only the snowy peak of the volcano could be seen in all its clarity, outlined against the landscape and lit by a timid winter sun. He looked around him. In his childhood, during the only happy time he could recall, before his father slid utterly into ruin and abandoned himself to alcohol and disgrace, the two of them had gone horseback riding in this part of the country. He remembered that he played during the summers at Tres Marías, but it was all so long ago that memory had almost erased it, and he did not recognize the place. He combed the landscape for the town of San Lucas, but was only able to make out a faroff hamlet that was faded in the dampness of the morning. He walked around the station. There was a padlock on the door to the only office. There was a penciled note tacked on it, but it was so smudged that he could not read it. He heard the train pull out behind him, leaving a column of white smoke. He was alone in the silent landscape. He picked up his bags and stepped out into the mud and stones of a path that led into the town. He walked for more than ten minutes, grateful that it was not raining, because it was only with great difficulty that he managed to advance along the path with his heavy suitcases, and he realized that the rain had rapidly converted it into an impassable mudhole. As he neared the hamlet, he saw smoke in several of the chimneys and breathed a sigh of relief, for it was so lonely and decayed, he had feared it was a ghost town.

He stopped at the edge of town and saw no one. Silence reigned on the only street, which was lined with modest adobe houses, and he felt as if he were walking in his sleep.

He approached the nearest house, which had no windows; the door was open. Leaving his bags on the sidewalk, he stepped inside, calling out in a loud voice. It was dark inside because the only source of light was the door, and it took his eyes several seconds to adjust. Then he was able to make out two children playing on the hard earth floor, staring at him with great, astonished eyes, and beyond them, in a court-yard, a woman walking toward him, wiping her hands on the edge of her apron. When she saw him, she made an instinctive motion to arrange a lock of hair that had fallen over her forehead. He greeted her and she replied, covering her mouth with her fingers as she spoke, to hide her tooth-less gums. Trueba explained that he needed to rent a cart, but she appeared not to understand him and only stood there, hiding the children in her apron, with a vacant expres-sion. He walked out the door, picked up his bags, and set out on his way again.

When he had walked nearly around the entire town without seeing anyone and was just beginning to grow desperate, he heard the hooves of a horse behind him. It was a rickety cart driven by a woodcutter. Trueba stood in front of it, forcing the driver to stop.

"Can you drive me to Tres Marías? I'll pay you hand-somely!" he shouted.

"What takes you there, sir?" the man replied. "That place is just a lawless heap of rocks, a no-man's-land."

But he agreed to take him, and helped him arrange his suitcases among the bundles of wood. Trueba sat down beside him on the coachman's seat. Here and there children darted out of doorways as they heard the wagon pass. Trueba felt lonelier than ever.

About five miles outside the town of San Lucas, along a ruined path overgrown with weeds and full of potholes, there was a wooden sign with the name of the property. It hung from a broken chain and the wind knocked it against the post with a muffled sound that made it echo like a funeral drum. A single glance was enough to make him understand that it would take a Hercules to rescue the place from desolation. The weeds had swallowed up the path, and wherever he looked all he saw were rocks, thick underbrush, and mountains. There was not even a suggestion of pasture or of the vineyards he remembered, and no one came out to greet him. The cart moved slowly, following the tracks that the passage of men and beasts had carved into the mass of weeds. After a moment he was able to make out the main house, which was still standing, although it looked like something from a nightmare, full of rubble, with chicken wire and garbage strewn across the floor. Half the tiles on the roof were broken, and a wild tangle of vines had grown through the windows and covered most of the outside wall. Around the house stood several windowless adobe huts. They had not been whitewashed and were black with soot. Two dogs were fighting ferociously in the courtyard.

The rattle of the cart wheels and the woodcutter's curses roused the inhabitants of the huts, who gradually emerged from their doorways. They stared at the new arrivals with amazement and mistrust. It had been fifteen years since they had seen an owner, and they had simply assumed that there no longer was one. They could not have recognized in this tall, imperious man the little boy with chestnut curls who had played in this same courtyard many years before. Esteban stared back at them and likewise remembered no one. They were a sorry lot. He saw various women of indecipherable age, their skin dry and cracked, some apparently pregnant, all of them barefoot and dressed in faded rags. He calculated that there must be at least a dozen children of all sizes and ages. The youngest ones were naked. Other faces peered from the doorways, too timid to come out. A few children scampered to hide behind the women.

Esteban stepped down from the cart, unloaded his two bags, and pressed a few coins into the woodcutter's hand.

"I'll wait for you if you like, *patrón,*" the man said.

"This is as far as I'm going."

He walked up to the house, gave the door a single forceful push, and went in. There was enough light inside because morning entered through the broken shutters and the chinks in the ceiling where the tiles had fallen through. The place was full of dust and spiderwebs, and looked thoroughly abandoned; clearly in all these years none of the tenant farmers had dared to leave his hut to move into the large, empty house of the absent owner. They had not touched the furniture; it was all as it had been when he was a child, each piece exactly where it had stood before, except uglier, and more lugubrious and rickety than he remembered. The entire house was carpeted with a thick layer of grass, dust, and dried-out leaves. It smelled like a tomb. A skeletal dog barked angrily at him, but Esteban Trueba paid him no attention until the dog, too tired to continue, lay down in a corner to scratch his fleas. Esteban put his bags on a table and set out to walk through the house, fighting off the sadness that was beginning to overwhelm him. He went from one room to another, noticing how time had worn everything away, and the poverty and dirt, and it seemed to him that this was a hole far worse than the mine. The kitchen was a wide filthy room, with a high ceiling and walls blackened with smoke from the wood and coal stoves, moldy and in ruins. The copper pots and pans that had not been used for fifteen years, apparently untouched in all that time, still hung from their nails. The bedrooms had the same beds and huge wardrobes with full-length glasses that his father had bought long ago, but the mattresses were a pile of rotten wool in which bugs had nested for generations. He heard the faint passage of the rats in the rafters. He could not tell if the floors were made of wood or tiles, because they were invisible, completely covered with grime. A layer of gray dust blurred the contours of the furniture. Where the drawing room had been he could still see the German piano, with one broken leg and yellow keys, which sounded like an untuned harpsichord.

On the shelves there were still a few illegible books, their pages chewed up by the damp, and on the floor there were the remnants of ancient magazines whose pages had been scattered by the wind. The armchairs sat with their springs sticking out, and there was a mouse nest in the wing chair where his mother had liked to knit before her illness turned her hands to claws.

When he finished his tour, Esteban had a clearer view of things. He knew that an immense task lay ahead of him, for if the house was in such bad repair, he could scarcely expect the rest of the property to be in any better condition. For a second he was tempted to pile his two bags back on the cart and return whence he had come, but he rejected that plan in a flash and resolved that if there was anything that could alleviate the grief and rage of Rosa's loss it would be breaking his back working in this ruined land. He took off his coat, drew a deep breath, and went out into the courtyard where the woodcutter was still waiting, not far from the tenants who had grouped themselves at a certain distance, with the shyness typical of country people. They looked at each other with curiosity. Trueba took two steps toward them and noticed a slight backward movement in the tiny cluster; he let his eyes wander over the shabby peasants and tried to force a friendly smile to the runny-nosed children, the bleary-eyed old people, and the women without hope, but it came out like a grimace.

"Where are the men?" he asked.

The only young man stepped forward. He was probably the same age as Esteban Trueba, but he looked older.

"They left," he said.

"What's your name?"

"Pedro Segundo García, sir," the man replied.

"I'm the *patrón* here now. The party's over. We're going to work. Anyone who doesn't like the idea should clear out immediately. Whoever stays won't lack for food, but he'll have to work good and hard. I don't want any deadbeats or smart-alecks around, you understand?"

They looked at one another in amazement. They had not understood half of what he said, but they could recognize their master's voice when they heard it.

"We understand, *patrón*," Pedro Segundo García said. "We have nowhere to go. We've always lived here. We'll stay."

A little boy squatted on the ground and began to defecate, and a mangy dog ran up to sniff him. Revolted, Esteban ordered them to take the child away, hose the courtyard down, and kill the dog. Thus began the new life that, in time, would make him forget Rosa.

No one's going to convince me that I wasn't a good *patrón*. Anyone who saw Tres Marías in decline and who could see it now, when it's a model estate, would have to agree with me. That's why I can't go along with my granddaughter's story about class struggle. Because when it comes right down to it, those poor peasants are a lot worse off today than they were fifty years ago. I was like a father to them. Agrarian reform ruined things for everyone.

I used all the money I had saved to marry Rosa, and everything the foreman sent me from the mine, to pull Tres Marías out of misery, but it wasn't money that saved the place, it was hard work and organization. The word went out that there was a new *patrón* at Tres Marías and that we were using mules to clear the land of stones and plow the fields to ready them for planting. In no time at all men began to arrive, offering their service as hired hands, because I paid well and gave them meals. I bought animals. Animals were sacred to me, and even if we had to go a year without eating meat, they were never killed. Thus our livestock prospered. I organized the men into different crews, and after they had finished working in the fields we set to work on restoring the main house. They weren't carpenters or masons, and I had to teach them everything from books I bought. We even did the plumbing. We fixed the roofs, whitewashed the house from top to bottom, and cleaned it inside and out until it sparkled. I distributed the furniture among the various tenants, except the dining-room table, which was still intact despite the worms that had got into everything, and the wrought-iron bed that had belonged to my parents. I continued living in the empty house, with no other furniture apart from those two pieces and a few wooden crates to sit on, until Férula sent me the new furniture I had ordered from the capital. They were large, heavy, ostentatious pieces that were built to last for generations and to withstand country life. The proof is that it took an earthquake to destroy them. I arranged them along the walls, with an eye more to convenience than aesthetics, and once the house was comfortable I felt happy and began to get used to the idea that I was going to spend many years—perhaps even my whole life—in Tres Marías.

The tenants' wives took turns as servants in the main house, and they also tended my orchard. I soon saw the first flowers in the garden I had planned out with my own hand and that, with a few minor changes, is the same one that's there today. In those days people worked without grumbling. I think my presence made them feel secure again. They saw the land gradually restored to prosperity. They were good, simple men, with no rebels among them. It's also true that they were very poor and very ignorant. Before I got there, they were just tilling their own small family plots, which provided them with the bare necessities to keep from starving to death—providing, of course, that they weren't struck by some catastrophe such as drought, frost, plague, ants, or snails, in which case things became very difficult indeed. But after I arrived all that changed. One by one we rescued the old fields. We rebuilt the chicken coops and stables and began to plan an irrigation system so the crops wouldn't have to depend on the weather. But it wasn't an easy life. It was very hard. Sometimes I would walk to town and return with a veterinarian who would check the cows and hens and, while he was at it, anybody who was sick. It's not true that I assumed that if the vet knew how to treat animals his training was good enough for people, as my granddaughter says when she wants to get me mad. The fact is, you couldn't get a doctor in a godforsaken place like that. The peasants went to an Indian *curandera* who knew all about the power of herbs and suggestion, and in whom they had great confidence. More than in the vet. Mothers gave birth with help from their neighbors, prayers, and a midwife who almost never arrived on time, because she had to make the trip by burro, but she was as good at delivering babies as she was at pulling calves from wall-eyed cows. Those who were gravely ill, whom no spell of the *curandera* or potion from the vet could help, were placed on a cart and taken by Pedro Segundo García or me to a hospital run by nuns, where there was frequently a doctor who helped them die. The dead and their bones ended up in a tiny graveyard next to the abandoned church, at the foot of the volcano, where there is now a proper cemetery. Once or twice a year I arranged for a priest to come and bless unions, animals, and machines, baptize children, and say a belated prayer for the dead. The only amusement then was castrating pigs and bulls, cockfights, hopscotch, and the incredible tales of old Pedro García, may he rest in peace. He was Pedro Segundo's father and he said his grandfather had fought in the ranks of the patriots who kicked the Spaniards out of America. He showed the children how to let themselves be stung by spiders and drink the urine of pregnant women as a form of immunization. He knew almost as many herbs as the *curandera*, but he would get confused when it came to deciding on their use, and he had committed some irreparable mistakes. Nonetheless, I have to say that he had an unbeatable method for pulling teeth, which had made him justly famous throughout the region. It was a combination of red wine and Our Fathers, which plunged the patient into a hypnotic trance. He pulled one of my molars, and if he were alive today he would be my dentist.

I soon felt at home in the country. My closest neighbors were a good horse ride away, but I wasn't interested in having a social life. I enjoyed my solitude, and besides I had a lot of work on my hands. I gradually became a savage. I began to forget words, my vocabulary grew smaller, and I became very demanding. Since I had no need to keep up appearances, the bad character I've always had only got worse. Everything made me angry. I got furious if I saw the children circling the kitchen to steal bread, if the hens were noisy in the courtyard, if sparrows invaded the cornfields. When my ill humor began to bother me and I felt uncomfortable in my own skin, I would go out hunting. I would wake up long before dawn and leave with my shotgun on my shoulder, with my game bag and my partridge hound. I liked to ride horseback in the dark, and I liked the cold air of those early hours, the long wait in the shadows, the silence, the smell of gunpowder and blood, the feel of the weapon drawn back against my shoulder with a dry knock, and the sight of the prey as it fell kicking. All this would calm me, and when I returned from hunting, with four wretched rabbits in my pouch, and a few partridges so full of holes that they couldn't even be cooked, half dead on my feet and covered with mud, I felt happy and relieved.

Whenever I think back on those days, I feel a great sadness. My life has gone by very fast. If I had it to do over again, there are a few mistakes I wouldn't make, but in general there's nothing I regret. Yes, I've been a good *patrón*; there's no doubt about it.

The first months, Esteban Trueba was so busy channeling water, digging wells, removing stones, clearing pastures, and repairing the chicken coops and stables that he had no time to think about anything. He went to bed thoroughly exhausted and woke at dawn, stopping just long enough to eat a meager breakfast in the kitchen before riding off to supervise the work in the fields. He did not return until sundown. Only then did he sit down to eat his one real meal of the day, alone at the dining-room table. The first months, he kept his promise to himself of always bathing and changing his clothes for dinner, as he had heard the British colonizers did in the most distant hamlets of Africa and Asia, so as not to lose their dignity and authority. He would put on his best clothes, shave, and play his favorite opera arias on the gramophone. But little by little he let himself be conquered by rusticity, and came to accept the fact that he had no calling as a dandy, especially since there was no one to appreciate his efforts. He stopped shaving, cut his hair only when it reached his shoulders, and continued to bathe once a day only because the habit was so ingrained in him, but he grew indifferent to his clothes and manners. He was slowly becoming a barbarian. Before going to sleep he would read for a while or play chess. He had developed the ability to compete against a book without cheating and had learned to lose matches without getting mad. Still, the exhaustion produced by so much hard work was not enough to suppress his robust and sensual nature. He began to have difficult nights in which the blankets seemed excessively heavy to him, the sheets too light. His horse played nasty tricks on him, suddenly becoming a formidable female, a hard, wild mountain of flesh, on which he rode until his bones ached. The warm, aromatic melons in his orchard looked to him like enormous breasts, and he was astonished to find himself burying his face in his saddle blanket, seeking in the sour smell of his horse's sweat the forbidden, distant scent of his first prostitutes. During the night, he sweated through nightmares of rotten shellfish, of enormous slabs of raw beef, of blood, semen, and tears. He would wake up tense, with his penis like an iron rod between his legs, angrier than ever. Hoping for relief, he would run out and plunge naked into the icy waters of the river until he couldn't breathe, but then he would feel invisible hands stroking his legs. Beaten, he would let himself float aimlessly, feeling the hug of the current, the kiss of the tadpoles, the lash of the rushes that grew along the banks. Soon his terrible need became notorious. Nothing could quench it, neither immersing himself in the river, nor cinnamon teas, nor placing a piece of flint beneath his mattress, not even those shameful manipulations that drove the boys in boarding school out of their minds, left them blind, and plunged them into eternal damnation. When he began to look with concupiscent eyes at the birds in the corral, the children playing naked in the orchard, and even at raw bread dough, he understood that his virility would not be soothed by priestly substitutes. His common sense told him that he would have to find a woman, and once he had made up his mind, the terrible anxiety that afflicted him began to ebb and his fury seemed to abate. That day he woke up smiling for the first time in months.

Pedro García, the old man, saw him whistling on his way to the stables, and shook his head in wonder.

All that day, the *patrón* was busy plowing a field that had just been cleared and that was slated to be planted with corn. Afterward he went with Pedro Segundo García to attend to a cow that was in the process of giving birth and whose calf was turned the wrong way around. He had to stick his arm in up to the elbow to turn the creature upside down and help it pull its head through. The cow died anyway, but he did not get upset about it. He ordered the calf bottle-fed, washed himself in a pail, and got back on his horse. Normally it would have been his dinnertime, but he was not hungry. He was in no hurry, for he had already made his choice.

He had seen the girl many times carrying her sniveling little brother on her hip, with a bag on her shoulder or a water jug on her head. He had watched her washing clothes, squatting on the flat stones of the river, her dark legs polished by the water, as she rubbed the faded rags with her rough peasant hands. She was big-boned and had an Indian face, with broad features, dark skin, and a sweet, peaceful expression. Her fleshy ample mouth still had all its teeth, and when she smiled her whole face lit up, but that did not happen very often. She had the beauty of early youth, although he could see that it would quickly fade, as it does with women who are born to have many children, work without rest, and bury their dead. Her name was Pancha García, and she was fifteen years old.

When Esteban Trueba went out to look for her, it was already late in the afternoon and the air was crisp. He rode his horse slowly through the long stretches of green that separated the pastures, asking after her as he went, until he spotted her on the path that led to her hut. She was doubled over beneath the weight of a sheaf of hawthorn for the kitchen hearth, barefoot, her head bowed. He looked at her from high in the saddle and immediately felt the urgent desire that had been tormenting him for so many months. He trotted up until he was right beside her. She heard him, but she continued walking without looking up, following the custom of all the women of her kind who bow their heads before the male. Esteban bent down and removed her burden, held it in the air for a moment, and then hurled it violently to the side of the path. He threw his arm around her waist, swept her up with an animal-like grunt, and placed her before him in the saddle. The girl did not resist. He kicked his heels in the stirrups and they took off at a gallop in the direction of the river. They dismounted without speaking and looked each other over. Esteban unfastened his broad leather belt and she stepped back, but he grabbed her with a single stroke of his hand. They fell arm in arm among the eucalyptus leaves.

Esteban did not remove his clothes. He attacked her savagely, thrusting himself into her without preamble, with unnecessary brutality. He realized too late, from the blood spattered on her dress, that the young girl was a virgin, but neither Pancha's humble origin nor the pressing demands of his desire allowed him to reconsider. Pancha García made no attempt to defend herself. She did not complain, nor did she shut her eyes. She lay on her back, staring at the sky with terror, until she felt the man drop to the ground beside her with a moan. She began to whimper softly. Before her, her mother—and before her, her grandmother—had suffered the same animal fate. Esteban Trueba adjusted his trousers, fastened his belt, helped her to her feet, and lifted her onto the haunches of his horse. They headed back. He was whistling. She continued to weep. Before dropping her off at her hut, the *patrón* kissed her on the lips.

"Starting tomorrow, I want you to work in the house," he said.

Pancha agreed without looking up. Her mother and her grandmother had also been servants in the main house.

That night, Esteban Trueba slept like an angel, without dreaming of Rosa. He woke the next morning full of energy, feeling taller and stronger. He set off for the fields humming, and when he returned Pancha was in the kitchen, busily stirring marmalade in a huge copper pot. That night he waited for her with impatience, and when the sounds of housework fell silent in the old adobe house and the nocturnal scampering of the rats began, he felt the girl's presence in the doorway of his room.

"Come, Pancha," he called. It was not an order, but an entreaty.

Now Esteban took the time to savor her fully and made sure that she felt pleasure too. He explored her slowly, learning by heart the smoky scent of her body and her clothes, which had been washed with ash and pressed with a coal-filled iron. He learned the texture of her straight, dark hair, of her skin that was soft in the most hidden places and rough and callused everywhere else, of her fresh lips, her tranquil sex, and her broad belly. He desired her calmly, initiating her into the most secret and most ancient of sciences. He was probably happy that night and the few nights after as the two of them cavorted like two puppies in the huge wrought-iron bed that had belonged to the first Trueba and was now somewhat wobbly, although it still withstood the thrusts of love.

Pancha García's breasts swelled and her hips filled out. Esteban Trueba's ill humor lifted for a while, and he took a certain interest in his tenants. He went to visit them in their wretched huts. In the shadows of one of them he came upon a box filled with newspaper, in which a newborn baby and a puppy lay in a shared sleep. In another he saw an old woman who had been slowly dying for the past four years, whose shoulder blades were jutting through the open wounds in her back. In a courtyard, moored to a post, he saw a teenaged idiot with a rope around his neck, drooling and babbling incoherently as he stood there naked, with a mule-sized penis that he beat incessantly against the ground. For the first time in his life, he realized that the worst abandonment of Tres Marías was not that of land and animals but of the people, who had lived unprotected ever since his father had gambled away his mother's dowry and inheritance. He decided it was time to bring a bit of civilization to this outpost hidden halfway between the mountains and the sea.

A fever of activity commenced that shook Tres Marías from its stupor. Esteban Trueba put people to work as they had never worked in their whole lives. Anxious to rescue in the course of a few months what had lain in ruins for years, the *patrón* hired every man, woman, old person, and child who could stand on his own two feet. He had a granary built, as well as larders for storing food in winter. He had horse meat salted and pork smoked, and set the women to making fruit preserves. He modernized the dairy, which was just an old shed filled with flies and manure, and forced the cows to produce enough milk to meet his needs. He began construction of a six-room schoolhouse, because he aspired to the day when all the children and adults of Tres Marías would know how to read, write, and do simple arithmetic, even though he was not in favor of their acquiring any additional learning, for fear they would fill their minds with ideas unsuited to their station and condition. Nonetheless, he was unable to obtain a teacher willing to work in such a remote area and, faced with the difficulty of luring the children to school with promises of lashings and caramels when he tried to teach them to read himself, he finally gave up his dream and relegated the school to other uses. His sister Férula sent him all the books he asked for from the city. They were practical texts, from which he learned to give injections by pricking himself in the leg, and to build a crystal radio set. He spent his first profits on rough cloth, a sewing machine, a box of homeopathic pills with an instruction booklet, an encyclopedia, and a shipment of readers, notebooks, and pencils. He cherished the idea of setting up a dining hall where every child would receive one full-course meal a day, so that they would grow up strong and healthy and be able to start work at a tender age, but he realized it was crazy to expect the children to arrive from all ends of the property just for a plate of food, so he transformed the project into a sewing workshop. Pancha García was chosen to decipher the mysteries of the sewing machine. At first she thought it was an instrument of the devil endowed with a life of its own, and refused to go anywhere near it, but Esteban was unyielding and in the end she mastered it. He also set up a modest general store where the tenants could buy whatever they needed without having to make the trip by oxcart all the way into San Lucas. The *patrón* would buy things wholesale and resell them at cost to his workers. He introduced a voucher system, which at first functioned as a form of credit, but gradually became a substitute for legal tender. With these slips of pink paper his tenants could buy everything in the general store; their wages were paid in them. In addition to the famous slips of paper, each worker also had the right to a small plot of land that he could cultivate in his free time, as well as six hens a year per family, a measure of seed, a share of the harvest to meet his basic needs, bread and milk for every day, and a bonus of fifty pesos that was distributed among the men at Christmas and on Independence Day. Even though they worked as equals with the men, the women did not receive this sum because, except for widows, they were not considered heads of family. Laundry soap, knitting wool, and a special syrup to strengthen the lungs were distributed free, for Trueba did not want anyone dirty, cold, or sick living on his land. One day he read in the encyclopedia about the advantages of a balanced diet, and so began his mania for vitamins, which was to last for the rest of his life. He had a tantrum whenever he saw any of the peasants giving their children only bread and feeding milk and eggs to the pigs. He began holding required meetings in the schoolhouse to inform them about vitamins and to let them know, in passing, whatever news he managed to pick up on his crystal set. He soon tired of chasing radio waves with his wire and ordered a short-wave radio with two enormous batteries. This apparatus enabled him to intercept a few coherent messages in the midst of a deafening roar from across the sea. Thus it was that he learned about the war in Europe and was able to follow the advances of the troops on a map he hung on the school blackboard, which he marked with pins. The tenants watched him in amazement, without the foggiest idea of why anyone would stick a pin in the color blue one day and move it to the color green the next. They could not imagine the world as the size of a piece of paper spread over a blackboard, in which whole armies were reduced to the head of a pin. In fact they cared not at all about the war, about scientific inventions, about the advance of industry, the price of gold, or the latest extravaganzas in the world of fashion. These were fairy tales, which did nothing to alter the narrowness of their existence. To that undaunted audience, the news on the radio was remote and alien, and the machine lost all its luster for them when it became evident that it was useless when it came to forecasting the weather. The only one who showed the slightest interest in the messages that came through was Pedro Segundo García.

Esteban Trueba spent many hours with him, first in front of the crystal set, and then, with the battery-operated radio, awaiting the miracle of the distant, anonymous voice that gave them contact with civilization. Even so, this did not bring the two men closer. Trueba knew that this unformed peasant was more intelligent than the others. He was the only one who knew how to read or carry on a conversation more than three sentences long. He was the closest thing to a friend that Trueba had within a radius of fifty miles, but his monumental pride prevented him from recognizing in the man any virtues beyond those that marked him as a good peon. Trueba was not one to encourage intimacy with his subordinates. Pedro Segundo hated him, even though he had never given a name to the tortured feeling that gripped his soul and filled him with confusion. It was a mixture of fear and resentful admiration. His intuition told him that he would never have the courage to confront him face to face, because he was the *patrón*. He would have to put up with his tantrums, his inconsiderate orders, and his self-importance for the rest of his life. During the years when Tres Marías had been abandoned, Pedro Segundo had naturally assumed command of the small tribe that had survived in these forsaken lands. He had grown used to being respected, to giving orders, to making decisions, and to having no more than the sky over his head. The *patrón's* arrival had changed all that, but he could not deny that they were better off now, for they no longer went hungry and they were better protected and safer. At times Trueba thought he caught a glimmer of murderous hatred in his eyes, but there was never cause to rebuke him for any insolence. Pedro Segundo obeyed without complaint and worked without grumbling. He was honest, and he seemed loyal enough. If he saw his sister Pancha in the hall of the main house, walking with the heavy gait of the satisfied woman, he bowed his head and was silent.

Pancha García was young and the *patrón* was strong. The predictable result of their alliance began to show within a few short months. The veins of the young girl's legs suddenly appeared like worms on her dark skin. Her movements slowed and her gaze grew distant. She lost all interest in the lusty thrashing in the wrought-iron bed, her waist swelled rapidly, and her breasts drooped with the weight of the new life that was growing inside her. Esteban was slow to notice, for he hardly looked at her anymore; his first enthusiasm having waned, he rarely caressed her either. He simply used her as a hygienic method for relieving the tensions of the day and obtaining a good night's sleep. But the moment came when Pancha's pregnancy was obvious even to him. He felt repulsed by her. He began to see her as an enormous container that held a formless, gelatinous mass that he was unable to view as his own child. Pancha left the main house and returned to her parents' hut, where no one asked her any questions. She continued working in the main-house kitchen, kneading dough and sewing on the sewing machine, daily growing more deformed by her maternity. She stopped serving Esteban at the table and avoided running into him, since they no longer had anything to say to one another. A week after she left his bed, he dreamt again of Rosa and awakened on wet sheets. He looked out the window and saw a slender little girl hanging up the wash on a wire. She could not have been more than thirteen or fourteen years old, but she was fully developed. Just then she turned and looked at him: she had the expression of a woman.

Pedro García saw his *patrón* whistling on his way to the stables and he shook his head in wonder.

In the course of the next ten years, Esteban Trueba became the most respected *patrón* in the region. He built brick houses for his workers, hired a teacher for the school, and raised the standard of living of everyone on his lands. Tres Marías was a good business that required no help from the seam of gold; on the contrary, it served as collateral for an extension on his concession to the mine. Trueba's bad temper became legend, and grew so exaggerated that it even made him uncomfortable. He forbade anyone to talk back to him and could tolerate no opposition; he viewed the slightest disagreement as a provocation. His concupiscence also intensified. Not a girl passed from puberty to adulthood that he did not subject to the woods, the riverbank, or the wrought-iron bed. When there were no more available women in Tres Marías, he began to chase after those from the neighboring haciendas, taking them in the wink of an eye, anywhere he could find a place in the fields, usually at dusk. He did not bother to hide, because he was afraid of no one. On a few occasions, a brother, father, husband, or employer showed up at Tres Marías to call him to account, but faced with his uncontrolled violence, these visits in the name of justice or revenge became less frequent. Word of his cruelty spread throughout the region, provoking jealous admiration among the men of his class. The peasants hid their daughters and clenched their fists helplessly because they could not confront him. Esteban Trueba was stronger, and he had impunity. Twice the bullet-riddled bodies of peasants from other haciendas were discovered. There was not the shadow of a doubt in anybody's mind that the guilty one was from Tres Marías, but the rural police simply recorded that bit of information in their record book with the tortured hand of the semi-literate, adding that the victims had been caught committing a theft. The matter never went any further. Trueba continued polishing his reputation as a rake, sowing the entire region with his bastard offspring, reaping hatred, and storing up sins that barely nicked him because he had hardened his soul and silenced his conscience with the excuse of progress. In vain, Pedro Segundo García and the old priest from the nuns' hospital tried to suggest to him that it was not little brick houses or pints of milk that made a man a good employer or an honest Christian, but rather giving his workers a decent salary instead of slips of pink paper, a workload that did not grind their bones to dust, and a little respect and dignity. Trueba would not listen to this sort of thing: it smacked, he said, of Communism.

"They're degenerate ideas," he muttered. "Bolshevik ideas designed to turn the tenants against me. What they don't realize is that these poor people are completely ignorant and uneducated. They're like children, they can't handle responsibility. How could *they* know what's best for them? Without me they'd be lost—if you don't believe me, just look what happens every time I turn my back. Everything goes to pieces and they start acting like a bunch of donkeys. They're very ignorant. My people have it fine now, what more do they need? They have everything they want. If they complain, it's out of sheer ingratitude. They have brick houses, I blow their kids' noses and cure their parasites, give them vaccinations and teach them how to read. Is there any other hacienda for miles around that has its own school? No! Whenever I can, I bring a priest in to say mass for them, so I don't see why the priest comes to talk to me about justice. He has no business butting in on matters he doesn't know anything about and that're outside of his duties. I'd like to see him try to run this property! I wonder if he'd be so high-minded then! You have to use a strong hand on these poor devils—that's the only language they understand. The minute you get soft, they lose their respect. I'm not denying that I've often been severe, but I've always been fair. I've had to teach them everything, even how to eat, because if it were up to them, all they'd eat is bread. If I don't keep an eye on them, they start giving their milk and eggs to the pigs. They don't know how to clean their asses and they want the right to vote! How are they supposed to know about politics when they don't even know where they live? They're capable of voting for the Communists, just like the miners in the North, who might push the whole country over the brink with their strikes—and now of all times, when the price of copper is at its peak. What I would do up there is send in the troops and let some bullets fly, to teach them once and for all. Unfortunately, the only thing that really works in these countries is the stick. This isn't Europe. What you need here is a strong government, with a strong man. It would be lovely if we were all created equal, but the fact is we're not. It couldn't be more obvious. The only one who knows how to work around here is me, and I defy you to prove otherwise. I'm the first one up and the last one to bed in this godforsaken place. If it was up to me, I'd send it all packing and go live like a prince in the capital, but I have to stay here, because if I were to leave for so much as a week, it would all collapse and these poor creatures would be starving to death again before you know it. Just remember what it was like when I arrived here years ago: a wasteland. It was a ruin filled with rocks and vultures. A no-man's-land. All the pastures were overgrown. No one had thought of channeling the water. They were satisfied to plant their dirty little lettuce plants in their front yards and let the rest of it sink into misery. I had to come in order for there to be law and order here, and work. How could I be anything but proud? I've worked so well that I've already bought up the two neighboring haciendas. This property is now the biggest and richest in the whole area—an example, the envy of everyone around, a model hacienda. And with the new highway going right alongside us its value has doubled. If I wanted to sell out, I could go to Europe and live off the interest, but I'm not going anywhere. This is where I plan to stay, killing myself. I'm doing it for them. If it weren't for me, they'd be lost. If we go to the heart of the matter, they're useless even for running errands. As I've always said, they're like children. There's not one of them can do what he's supposed to do without me there behind him driving him on. And then they start in on me with the story that we are all equal! It's enough to make you die laughing!"

To his mother and sister he sent crates of fruit, salted meat, hams, fresh eggs, hens both living and in brine, sacks of flour, rice, and other grains, huge wheels of country cheese, and all the money they might need, because he had plenty. Tres Marías and the mine were both producing as they should for the first time since God put them on this planet, as he liked to tell anyone who would listen. He sent Doña Ester and Férula all sorts of things they had never hoped for in this life, but in all those years he never found the time to visit them, not even if he was passing through on one of his trips to the North. He was so busy in the fields, with the new land he had bought and the various other businesses on which he had begun to cast his eye, that he had no time to waste at the bedside of an invalid. Besides, the mails kept them in touch and the train let him send them anything he felt like sending. He had no need to see them. You could say everything by letter. Everything except whatever he did not want them to know, such as the string of bastards that was springing up behind him as if by magic. It seemed that no sooner did he roll in the pasture with a girl than she became pregnant. It had to be the work of the devil. No one had ever seen such astonishing fertility and he was sure that at least half the infants were not his. That was why he decided that aside from Pancha García's son, who was called Esteban like himself and whose mother was definitely a virgin when he had possessed her, the rest of them might or might not be his. It was always better to think that they were not. Whenever a woman showed up at his door with a newborn baby in her arms asking for his surname or some other form of assistance, he would send her on her way with a few banknotes pressed into her hand and the warning that if she ever bothered him again he would send her flying with his whip, so that she would be cured of any wish to wiggle her tail at the first man she saw and then come accusing *him*. This was why he never knew the exact number of his children, and the fact of the matter was that he was not interested. He figured that when he was ready to have children he would find a woman of his own class, with the blessings of the Church, because the only ones who really counted were the ones who bore their father's surname; the others might just as well not have been born. And he would have none of that monstrous talk about everyone being born with the same rights and inheriting equally, because if that happened everybody would go to hell and civilization would be thrown back to the Stone Age. He remembered Nívea, Rosa's mother, who, after her husband had retired from politics, terrified by the poisoned brandy, had begun her own political campaign. She would chain herself with other ladies to the gates of Congress and the Supreme Court, setting off a degrading spectacle that made all their husbands look ridiculous. He knew that Nívea went out at night to hang suffragette posters on walls across the city and that she was capable of walking through the heart of the city in the plain light of day with a broom in her hand and a tricornered hat on her head, calling for women to have equal rights with men, to be allowed to vote and attend the university, and for all children, even bastards, to be granted the full protection of the law.

"That woman is sick in the head!" Trueba would proclaim. "It would go against nature. If women don't know that two and two are four, how are they going to be able to handle a scalpel? Their duty is motherhood and the home. At the rate they're going, the next thing you know they'll be asking to be deputies, judges—even President of the Republic! And in the meantime they're sowing confusion and disorder that could lead to disaster. They're printing obscene pamphlets, speaking on the radio, chaining themselves to public places till the police have to come with a blacksmith and cut them free, and they might even get arrested, which is what they should be. It's a crying shame that there's always some influential husband, some spineless judge or firebrand member of Congress to set them free. What these cases really need is a strong hand."

The war in Europe had ended and the railroad cars piled high with dead were a distant clamor, though it had not quieted down entirely. It was from there that subversive ideas were carried on the uncontrollable winds of the radio, the telegraph, and the steamers laden with immigrants who stepped ashore in a daze, fleeing the hunger back home, stunned by the roar of the bombs and the corpses rotting in the plowed fields. It was an election year and there was reason for concern over the turn of events. The country was waking up. The wave of discontent that was stirring the people was beginning to strike at the heart of that oligarchic society. In the countryside that year, everything happened: drought, snails, and hoof-and-mouth disease. There was unemployment in the North, and in the capital the effects of the distant war were still being felt. It was a year of poverty, a year in which the only thing missing to complete the sense of disaster was an earthquake.

The upper class, however, in whose hands were concentrated all the power and wealth, was unaware of the danger that threatened the fragile equilibrium of their position. The rich amused themselves by dancing the Charleston and the new rhythms of jazz, the fox-trot, and some Negro *cumbias* that were marvelously indecent. Steamer crossings to Europe were resumed, after being suspended during four years of war, and new routes, this time to North America, became the rage. Golf was a novelty, bringing the cream of society together around a tiny ball that was struck with a stick, just as the Indians had done two hundred years before in these same places. The ladies wore long strings of cultured pearls that hung down to their knees, and cloche hats that hid their eyebrows. They cut their hair like men, made themselves up to look like prostitutes, stopped wearing corsets, and smoked like chimneys. The men were in a state of shock from the American automobiles, which arrived in the country in the morning and were sold by afternoon, despite the fact that they cost a small fortune and were hardly more than an explosion of smoke and clanking screws flying at a suicidal rate along roads that had been built for horses and other natural beasts and most certainly not for these products of the imagination. Whole inheritances were played at gambling tables, along with the easy fortunes of the postwar years. Champagne was uncorked and cocaine was introduced for the more wicked and refined. The collective madness looked as if it would never end.

But in the countryside the new automobiles were as unreal as short dresses, and those who were just emerging from the invasion of snails and hoof-and-mouth disease simply viewed it as a good year. Esteban Trueba and the other landowners in the area gathered in their club to plan political strategy for the upcoming Presidential elections. The peasants were still living exactly as they had in colonial times, and had not heard of unions, or Sundays off, or the minimum wage; but now delegates from the new-formed parties of the left, disguised as evangelicals, were beginning to infiltrate the haciendas, with a Bible tucked under one armpit and Marxist pamphlets under the other, simultaneously preaching the abstemious life and revolution or death. Those conspiratorial lunches of the *patrones* would culminate in either Romanesque debauchery or cockfights, and by evening the men would take the Red Lantern by storm, where twelve-year-old prostitutes and Carmelo, the only homosexual in the brothel and the town, would dance to the strains of an antediluvian Victrola beneath the watchful eye of Sofía, who was too old to go chasing around herself, although she still had the energy to run her business with an iron hand and keep the police from barging in and the customers from taking liberties with the girls—screwing them and then refusing to pay. Of all of them, the one who danced the best was Tránsito Soto, who was also best at resisting the drunk men's attacks. She was indefatigable and never complained. It was as if she had the Tibetan gift of placing her skinny adolescent frame in her client's hands and transporting her soul to some distant place. Esteban Trueba liked her because she was not squeamish about new ideas and the brutalities of love, sang with the voice of a hoarse bird, and had once told him she was going to go far in life and he had found that amusing.

"I'm not going to spend my life in the Red Lantern," she had said. "I'm going to the capital, because I want to be rich and famous."

Esteban went to the brothel as it was the only source of entertainment in the town, but he was not a man for whores. He did not like to pay for something he could get by other means. Still, he enjoyed spending time with Tránsito Soto. She made him laugh.

One day, after making love, he was in a generous mood, something that hardly ever happened, and he asked Tránsito Soto if she would like him to give her a present.

"Lend me fifty pesos!" she requested instantly.

"That's a lot of money. Why so much?"

"For a train ticket, a red dress, high-heeled shoes, a bottle of perfume, and a permanent. That's everything I need to start. I'll pay you back someday. With interest."

Esteban gave her the fifty pesos because that morning he had sold five bulls and his pockets were full of bills, and also because the exhaustion of pleasure made him rather sentimental.

"I'm only sorry that I won't be seeing you again, Tránsito. I've grown accustomed to you."

"But we *will* see each other, *patrón*. Life is long and full of unexpected turns."

The immense meals in the club, the cockfights, and the afternoons in the brothel all culminated in a clever, although by no means original, plan for making sure that the peasants exercised their right to vote. The *patrones* threw them a big party with empanadas and lots of wine, barbecued a few cows specially slaughtered for the occasion, serenaded them with songs accompanied on the guitar, beat them over the head with a few political harangues, and promised them that if the conservative candidate won the election they would all receive a bonus, but that if he lost they would lose their jobs. In addition, they rigged the ballot boxes and bribed the police. At the end of the party they piled the peasants onto wooden carts and hauled them off to vote, under careful observation, amidst much joking and laughter. It was the one time in their lives they showed the peasants a trace of intimacy: pal this and pal that, don't worry, *patrón*, I'm on your team, you can count on me, that's the way I like it, pal, it's nice to see you have a patriotic conscience, you know the liberals and radicals are all a bunch of morons and the Communists are atheist bastards who eat little children.

On the day of the election everything went according to plan, in perfect order. The armed forces were there to up-hold the democratic process, and all was peaceful on a spring day more sprightly and sunny than usual.

"An example for this continent of Indians and Negroes who spend their time making revolutions to overthrow one dictator and install another. This is a different country. This country's a genuine republic. We have civic pride. Here the Conservative Party wins cleanly and openly, and we don't need a general to keep things orderly and calm, not like the neighboring dictatorships where they kill each other off while the gringos walk away with all their raw materials," Trueba declared in the club dining room, raising his wine-glass to offer a toast when the results of the elections were announced.

Three days later, when things were back to normal, the letter from Férula arrived at Tres Marías. The night before, Esteban Trueba had dreamt of Rosa. It had been a long time since that had happened. In the dream she had appeared with her weeping-willow hair hanging over her shoulders, like a botanical mantle that covered her down to her waist. Her skin was hard and cold, the color and texture of alabaster. She was naked and held a bundle in her arms, and she walked as people do in dreams, with the shimmering green halo floating out around her body. He saw her coming slowly toward him, and when he reached out to touch her, she hurled her package to the ground, shattering its contents at his feet. He knelt down and picked it up: it was a tiny girl without eyes, and she was calling him Papa. He awoke in a state of anxiety and was grumpy all morning. Because of the dream he was already uneasy, long before Férula's letter was delivered. As he did every morning, he went into the kitchen for his breakfast and saw a hen pecking crumbs from the floor. He gave it a kick that ripped its stomach open, leaving it to die in a pool of guts and feathers, flapping its wings. Instead of calming him down, this only increased his irritation, and he felt as if he were choking. He climbed up on his horse and galloped off to supervise the livestock that were being branded. He stopped first at the house of Pedro Segundo García, who had gone to the station in San Lucas to leave off a parcel and had passed through town to pick up the mail. Pedro had returned with Férula's letter.

The envelope lay all morning on the table in the entrance hall. When Esteban Trueba arrived home, he went straight in to take a bath; he was covered with sweat and dust and saturated with the unmistakable odor of frightened beasts. Only later did he sit down at his desk to do his accounts and order a meal brought in to him on a tray. He did not look at his sister's letter until nighttime, when he checked the house, as was his custom before going to bed, to be sure that all the lights were extinguished and all the doors were locked. Férula's letter looked like all the others she had sent him, but even before opening it he knew, as he held it in his hand, that its contents would change his life. He felt exactly as he had years earlier when he held his sister's telegram informing him of Rosa's death.

He opened it, his temples pulsing with foreboding. The letter said briefly that Doña Ester Trueba was dying, and that after so many years of taking care of her and waiting on her hand and foot, Férula now had to suffer with the torment of her mother not recognizing her and calling day and night for her son Esteban, because she did not want to die without seeing him. Esteban had never really loved his mother or felt at ease in her presence, but the news shook him nonetheless. He understood that the excuses he had always made to avoid seeing her would not avail him now, and that the time had come for him to travel to the capital and face for the last time this woman who was always present in his nightmares, with her rancid smell of medicine, her frail moans, and her interminable prayers, this suffering woman who had peopled his childhood with prohibitions and terrors and weighed his manhood with responsibilities and guilt.

He summoned Pedro Segundo García and explained the situation. He led him to the desk and showed him the ledgers and accounts of the general store. He handed him a bunch of keys with all except the key to his wine cellar, and announced that from that moment till the day he returned, Pedro would be responsible for everything that happened in Tres Marías, and that he would pay dearly for any mishaps that occurred. Pedro Segundo García took the keys, tucked the ledgers under his arm, and smiled without a trace of happiness.

"One does one's best, *patrón,*" he said, shrugging his shoulders.

The next day, for the first time in years, Esteban Trueba retraced the steps that had led him from his mother's house to the countryside. An oxcart took him and his suitcases as far as the station in San Lucas, where he took the first-class coach from the days of the British railway, and crossed once more the vast fields that lay at the feet of the *cordillera.*

He closed his eyes and tried to sleep, but the image of his mother haunted his dreams.

THREE

Clara the Clairvoyant

Clara was ten years old when she decided that speaking was pointless and locked herself in silence. Her life changed markedly. Fat, kindly Dr. Cuevas attempted to treat her with pills of his own devising, with vitamins in syrup and throat swabbings with borax honey, but all to no apparent effect. He soon realized that his remedies were useless and that his very presence induced a state of terror in the child. Whenever she saw him, Clara would begin to shriek, running for refuge to the farthest corner of the house, where she would huddle like a frightened animal; so he abandoned his treatments and suggested that Severo and Nívea take her to see a Rumanian named Rostipov, who was causing quite a sensation that season. Rostipov made his living as a magician in vaudeville shows and had achieved the incredible feat of stringing a wire from the pinnacle of the cathedral to the cupola of the Galician Brotherhood, on the other side of the plaza, which he walked across with only a frail stick for balance. Despite his more frivolous side, Rostipov had caused an uproar in scientific circles because he spent his free time curing hysteria with magic wands and hypnotic trances. Nívea and Severo took Clara to the consulting room that the Rumanian had improvised in his hotel. Rostipov carefully examined her. When he had finished, he declared that her case was not within his province to cure, since the child was silent because she did not feel like speaking, not because she was unable to. Nevertheless, at her parents' insistence, he concocted some lilac-colored sugar pills, which he prescribed with the warning that they were a Siberian remedy for deaf-mutes. But in this case the power of suggestion failed, and the second bottle of pills was swallowed by Barrabás in a moment of oversight that fortunately had no appreciable results. Severo and Nívea attempted to make her speak with household remedies, threatening and cajoling and even refusing to let her eat, to see if hunger would force her to open her mouth to ask for food, but that, too, was to no avail.

Nana had the idea that a good fright might make the child speak, and spent nine years inventing all sorts of desperate strategies for frightening Clara, the end result of which was to immunize the girl forever against terror and surprise. Soon Clara was afraid of nothing. She was unmoved by the sudden appearance of the most livid and undernourished monsters in her room, or by the knock of devils and vampires at her bedroom window. Nana dressed up as a headless pirate, as the executioner of the Tower of London, as a werewolf or a horned devil, depending on her inspiration of the moment and on the ideas she got while flipping through the pages of certain horror magazines, which she bought for this purpose and from which, although she was unable to read, she copied the illustrations. She had acquired the habit of gliding silently through the hallways and jumping at the child in the dark, howling through the doorways, and hiding live animals between her sheets, but none of this elicited so much as a peep from the little girl. At times Clara lost her patience. She would throw herself on the floor, kicking and shouting, but without pronouncing a single word in any recognizable tongue; or she would scrawl on the tiny blackboard that never left her side, setting down the worst insults she could think of to say to the poor woman, who would weep disconsolately in the kitchen.

"It's for your own good, my little angel!" Nana would sob, wrapped in a bloody sheet, her face blackened with burnt cork.

Nívea forbade her to continue frightening her daughter. She realized that the tension in the air increased Clara's mental powers and disturbed the spirits that were hovering around the child. Besides, that procession of terrifying figures was destroying Barrabás's nervous system. He had never had a well-developed sense of smell, and was incapable of recognizing Nana beneath her multiple disguises. The dog would begin to urinate on himself sitting down, leaving an immense puddle all around him, and frequently his teeth would chatter. But Nana took advantage of the slightest distraction on Nívea's part to persist in her attempts to cure the child's muteness with the same remedy she used for hiccups.

Clara was removed from the convent school at which all the del Valle sisters had been educated, and placed under the instruction of private tutors who came to the house. Severo brought in a special governess from England, Miss Agatha, who was tall and amber-colored, and had the large hands of a bricklayer, but she was no match for the climate, the spicy food, and the independent flights of the saltshaker across the dining-room table, and was forced to return to Liverpool. The next one was a Swiss girl, who fared no better, and then a French one, who arrived courtesy of the family's acquaintance with the ambassador of that country; but she was so rosy, round, and sweet that within a few short months she was with child. A brief investigation revealed the father to be Luis, Clara's older brother. Without asking their opinion, Severo made them marry, and, despite the predictions to the contrary of Nívea and her friends, they were very happy. After all these experiences, Nívea convinced her husband that the study of foreign languages was not important for a child with telepathic gifts, and that it would be far better for her to continue piano lessons and to learn how to sew.

Little Clara read all the time. Her interest in books was indiscriminate. She was as happy to read the magic books from her Uncle Marcos's enchanted trunks as she was to contemplate the Liberal Party documents her father kept in his study. She filled innumerable notebooks with her private observations, recording the events of those years, thanks to which they were not erased by the mists of forgetfulness and I can now use them to reclaim her memory.

Clara the Clairvoyant could interpret dreams. It was an inborn talent, requiring none of the trying cabalistic study to which her Uncle Marcos had applied himself with far more effort and far less effect. The first one to realize this was

Honorio, the gardener, who dreamt one night that there were snakes between his toes and that in order to get rid of them he had kicked and kicked until he had squashed nineteen. He told this to the little girl while he was pruning the rosebushes, simply to entertain her, because he adored her and it made him sad that she was mute. Clara took out her slate from her apron pocket and wrote down her interpretation of Honorio's dream: "You will have a lot of money, it will last only a short while, you will make it without effort, play number 19." Honorio did not know how to read, but Nívea read the message out to him amid joking and laughter. The gardener did everything Clara told him to do and won eighty pesos in an illegal numbers game that was held behind a coal store. He spent it on a new suit, an unforgettable drinking spree with all is friends, and a porcelain doll for Clara. From that day on, the child had more work than she could handle deciphering dreams behind her mother's back, for once Honorio's story made the rounds she was pursued by questions: what does it mean to fly above a tower with swans' wings; to float out to sea on a raft and hear a siren with a widow's voice; for someone to give birth to twins joined at the shoulder, each with a sword in his hand—and Clara would unhesitatingly write down on her little slate that the tower is death and whoever flies over it will be saved from an accidental death; that whoever is shipwrecked and hears the voice of a siren will lose his job and undergo great suffering, but he will be rescued by a woman with whom he will open a business; and that the twins are a husband and wife forced to share a single destiny, perpetually wounding one another with the blows of their swords.

Dreams were not the only thing that Clara read. She could also predict the future and recognize people's intentions, abilities that she maintained throughout her life and that increased with time. She announced the death of her godfather, Don Salomón Valdes, a broker at the stock exchange, who, convinced that he had lost everything he owned, hanged himself from the chandelier in his elegant office. There they found him, at Clara's insistence, looking every bit like a dejected sheep, exactly as she had described him on her slate. She predicted her father's hernia; all the earthquakes and other natural disturbances; the one and only time snow fell in the capital, freezing to death the poor people in their shantytowns and the rosebushes in the gardens of the rich; and the identity of the murderer of schoolgirls long before the police discovered the second corpse; but no one believed her, and Severo did not want her giving her opinion on matters concerning criminals who were not related to the family. With a single glance Clara realized that Getulio Armando was going to swindle her father in the business of the Australian sheep, because she read it in the color of his aura. She wrote it to her father, but he did not pay attention, and by the time he remembered her prediction he had already lost half his fortune and his partner was off in the Caribbean, newly wealthy, with a harem of big-bottomed mulattas and his own private boat for sunbathing.

Clara's ability to move objects without touching them did not disappear with the onset of menstruation, as Nana had predicted, but rather became more pronounced, until she was so accomplished that she could move the keys on the piano with the cover down, even though she never learned to move the instrument itself around the drawing room, as she wanted to. She spent the main part of her time and energy in these extravagant pursuits. She developed the capacity to guess an astonishing percentage of the cards in a deck, and invented games of fantasy to play with her brothers and sisters. Her father forbade her to read the future in cards and to invoke ghosts and mischievous spirits that annoyed the rest of the family and terrorized the servants, but Nívea understood that the more limitations and shocks her daughter was subjected to the madder she became, and decided to leave her in peace with her spiritualist tricks, her fortune-telling games and her cavernous silence, and did her best to love her unconditionally and accept her as she was. Clara grew like a wild plant, despite the recommendations of Dr. Cuevas, who had brought from Europe the novel idea of cold baths and electric shocks for the treatment of the insane.

Barrabás accompanied the child day and night, except during the normal periods of his sexual activity. He was always hovering around her like a gigantic shadow as silent as the little girl herself. He threw himself at her feet when she sat down and slept beside her every night, chugging like a locomotive. He became so attached to his mistress that when she sleepwalked through the house the dog followed imitating her posture. Whenever there was a full moon, they could be seen gliding down the corridors like two ghosts floating through the pale light. As the dog grew in size, his distractedness became more evident. He never comprehended, for example, the transparent nature of glass, and in moments of great emotion he would charge the windows at a gallop, with the innocent intention of catching a fly. He would fall through to the other side in a din of breaking glass, surprised and disappointed. In those days windowpanes were brought from France by ship and the animal's mania for crashing into them became a problem, until Clara thought of painting cats on the glass. When Barrabás became an adult, he stopped fornicating with the feet of the piano, as he had in his childhood, and his reproductive instinct declared itself only when he sniffed a bitch in heat in his close environs. On such occasions there was neither chain nor door that could hold him back. He would hurl himself onto the street, over-coming every obstacle in his path, and remain at large for two or three days. He always returned with the poor dog hanging off him, suspended in the air, impaled on his im-mense masculinity. The children had to be whisked out of the way so they would not see the horrendous spectacle of the gardener hosing the dogs down with freezing water until, many gallons and kicks and other indignities later, Barrabás became unstuck from his beloved, leaving her to die in the courtyard of the house, where Severo was obliged to finish her off with a coup de grâce.

Clara's adolescence passed calmly in her parents' large house with its three courtyards. She was spoiled to death by her older brothers, by Severo, who preferred her to all his other children, by Nívea, and by Nana, who alternated her sinister attacks disguised as a ghost with the most tender of attentions. Almost all her brothers and sisters had married or left—some to travel, others to work in the provinces—and the big house, which had contained such a large family, was almost empty, with many of its rooms locked. The child spent whatever free time her tutors left her in reading, moving numerous different objects without touching them, chasing Barrabás, practicing various techniques of prognosti-cation, and learning to knit, which was the only one of the domestic arts she ever mastered. Ever since the Holy Thursday on which Father Restrepo had accused her of being possessed, there had been a shadow over her head that the love of her parents and her siblings' discretion kept under control; still, word of her unlikely talents circulated by whispers in gatherings of local ladies. Nívea realized that people never invited her daughter to their home and that even her own cousins did everything they could to avoid her. She so successfully compensated for the lack of friends with her own total dedication, however, that Clara grew up happily and in later years would recall her childhood as a luminous part of her existence, despite her solitude and muteness. All her life she would remember the afternoons spent in the company of her mother in the sewing room, where Nívea sewed clothing for the poor on her machine and told stories and anecdotes about the family. She would point to the daguerrotypes on the wall and tell Clara of the past.

"You see that serious man with a pirate's beard? That's your Uncle Mateo, who went to Brazil on some scheme that had to do with emeralds, but a fiery mulatta gave him the evil eye. All his hair fell out, his nails dropped off, he lost his teeth, and he had to go to see a sorcerer, a voodoo priest, a dark Negro, who gave him an amulet; and then his teeth grew back, his nails came out again, and he got back his hair. Look at him, Clara: he's hairier than an Indian. He was the only bald man in the world who ever got a second head of hair."

Clara would smile without saying a word and Nívea would go on talking because she had grown used to her daughter's silence. In addition, she nourished the hope that if she kept putting ideas into Clara's head, sooner or later she would ask a question and regain her speech.

"And this," she would say, "is your Uncle Juan. I loved him very much. He once farted and that became his death sentence: a great disgrace. It was during a picnic lunch. All my cousins and I were out together on the most fragrant spring afternoon, with our muslin dresses and our hats full of flowers and ribbons, and the boys were wearing their Sunday best. Juan took off his white jacket—why, I can see him now! He rolled up his sleeves and swung gracefully from the branch of a tree, hoping that with his trapeze artist's skill he could win the admiration of Constanza Andrade, the Harvest Queen, with whom, from the moment he laid eyes on her, he had been desperately in love. Juan did two impeccable push-ups and one complete somersault, but on his next flip over he let go a loud burst of wind. Don't laugh, Clara! It was terrible. There was an embarrassed silence and the Harvest Queen began to laugh uncontrollably. Juan put on his jacket and grew very pale. He walked slowly away from the group and we never saw him again. They even looked for him in the Foreign Legion. They asked for him in all the consulates, but he was never heard of again. I think he must have become a missionary and gone to minister to the lepers out on Easter Island, which is as far away as a man can go to forget and be forgotten because it's not on the normal routes of navigation and isn't even shown on Dutch maps. From that day on, he was referred to as Juan of the Fart."

Nívea would take her daughter to the window and show her the dried-out trunk of the poplar tree.

"It was an enormous tree," she would say. "I had it cut before my oldest son was born. They say it was so tall that you could see the whole city from its top, but the only one who got that high had no eyes to see it with. It was a tradition in the del Valle family that when any of the young men wanted to wear long pants, he had to climb it to prove his valor. It was like an initiation rite. The tree was full of marks. I saw them with my own eyes when they knocked it down. From the first middle-sized branches, which were thick as chimneys, you could already see the marks left by the grandfathers, who had made the same ascent in their own youth. From the initials cut into the trunk you could tell who had climbed higher, who was the bravest, as well as who had stopped, too terrified to continue. One day it was the turn of Jerónimo, the blind cousin. He began the climb feeling his way up the branches without a moment's hesitation, for he couldn't see how high up he was and had no intuition of the void. He reached the top, but he wasn't able to complete the J of his initial, because he came unstuck like a gargoyle and plummeted headfirst to the ground, landing at the feet of his father and brothers. He was fifteen years old. They wrapped the body in a sheet and took it to his mother, who spat in all their faces and shouted at them with a sailor's insults and cursed the men who had induced her son to climb the tree, until finally the Sisters of Charity came to cart her off in a straitjacket. I knew that one day my sons would be expected to continue that barbarous tradition. That's why I had them cut it down. I didn't want Luis and the other children growing up in the shadow of that scaffold in the courtyard."

At times Clara would accompany her mother and two or three of her suffragette friends on their visits to factories, where they would stand on soapboxes and make speeches to the women who worked there while the foremen and bosses, snickering and hostile, observed them from a prudent distance. Despite her tender age and complete ignorance of matters of this world, Clara grasped the absurdity of the situation and wrote in her notebook about the contrast of her mother and her friends, in their fur coats and suède boots, speaking of oppression, equality, and rights to a sad, resigned group of hard-working women in denim aprons, their hands red with chilblains. From the factory the ladies would move on to the tearoom on the Plaza de Armas, where they would stop for tea and pastry and discuss the progress of their campaign, not for a moment letting this frivolous distraction divert them from their flaming ideals. At other times her mother would take her to the slums on the outskirts of the city or to the tenements, where they arrived with their car piled high with food and with clothes that Nívea and her friends sewed for the poor. On these occasions too, the child wrote with formidable intuition that charity had no effect on such monumental injustice. Her relationship to her mother was close and cheerful, and Nívea, despite having given birth to fifteen children, treated Clara as if she were an only child, creating a tie so strong that it continued into succeeding generations as a family tradition.

Nana had become an ageless woman still in full possession of all the strength of her younger years. She was still able to leap out of corners hoping to scare the child's muteness away, just as she could spend the entire day standing over the hellfire in the center of the third courtyard, pushing an enormous stick around in the copper pot where she bubbled the thick topaz-colored quince jam that, once cooled,

Nívea delivered in molds of all shapes and sizes to the poor. Accustomed to living surrounded by children, Nana turned all her tenderness to Clara after the others left home. Even though the child was by now too old for it, she bathed her as if she were a baby, dousing her in the enameled tub with water scented with jasmine and basil, rubbing her with a sponge, soaping her meticulously without missing the least chink of ear or foot, massaging her with cologne and powdering her with a swan's-down puff, and brushing her hair with infinite patience, until it was as soft and shiny as an underwater plant. She dressed her, put her to bed, brought her breakfast on a tray, and forced her to drink linden tea for her nerves, camomile for her stomach, lemon for translucent skin, rue for bile, and mint for her breath, until the child became a beautiful, angelic being who walked through the halls and patios wrapped in a scent of flowers, a rustling of starched petticoats, and a halo of curls and ribbons.

Clara's childhood came to an end and she entered her youth within the walls of her house in a world of terrifying stories and calm silences. It was a world in which time was not marked by calendars or watches and objects had a life of their own, in which apparitions sat at the table and conversed with human beings, the past and the future formed part of a single unit, and the reality of the present was a kaleidoscope of jumbled mirrors where everything and anything could happen. It is a delight for me to read her notebooks from those years, which describe a magic world that no longer exists. Clara lived in a universe of her own invention, protected from life's inclement weather, where the prosaic truth of material objects mingled with the tumultuous reality of dreams and the laws of physics and logic did not always apply. Clara spent this time wrapped in her fantasies, accompanied by the spirits of the air, the water, and the earth. For nine years she was so happy that she felt no need to speak. Everyone had lost all hope of ever hearing her voice again, when on her birthday, after blowing out the nineteen candles on her chocolate cake, she tried out the voice that she had kept in storage all those years, and that sounded like an untuned instrument.

"I'm going to be married soon," she said.

"To whom?" Severo asked.

"To Rosa's fiancé," Clara replied.

Only then did they realize she had spoken for the first time in all those years. The miracle shook the house to its foundations and set the whole family weeping. They called each other on the telephone, word went out across the city, and they summoned Dr. Cuevas, who could not believe the news. In the uproar about Clara's regaining her voice they all forgot what she had said, and they did not remember until two months later, when Esteban Trueba, whom they had not seen since Rosa's funeral, showed up at the door to ask for Clara's hand.

Esteban Trueba alighted in the station and carried his two suitcases himself. The iron cupola the British had built in imitation of Victoria Station in the days when they had the concession to the national railways had not changed at all since the last time he had been there several years before—the same dirty windows, the same little shoeshine boys, the same women selling biscuits and candies, and the same porters with their dark caps bearing the insignia of the British crown, which no one had thought to replace with the colors of the national flag. He hailed a carriage, and gave his mother's address. The city looked unfamiliar. There was a jumble of modernity; a myriad of women showing their bare calves, and men in vests and pleated pants; an uproar of workers drilling holes in the pavement, knocking down trees to make room for telephone poles, knocking down telephone poles to make room for buildings, knocking down buildings to plant trees; a blockade of itinerant vendors hawking the wonders of this grindstone, that toasted peanut, this little doll that dances by itself without a single wire or thread, look for yourself, run your hand over it; a whirlwind of garbage dumps, food stands, factories, cars hurtling into carriages and sweat-drawn trolleys, as they called the old horses that hauled the municipal transport; a heavy breathing of crowds, a sound of running, of scurrying this way and that, of impatience and schedules. Esteban felt oppressed by it. He hated the city much more than he had remembered. He recalled the open meadows of the countryside, days clocked by the fall of rain, the vast solitude of his fields, the cool quiet of the river and his silent house.

This city is a shithole, he concluded.

The carriage trotted toward the house where he had grown up. He shuddered at how badly the neighborhood had declined over the years, ever since the rich had decided to move their houses farther up the hill from everyone else and the city had expanded into the foothills of the *cordillera*. There was not a trace of the square where he had played as a little boy; it was now an empty lot filled with carts from the market that were parked among piles of garbage where stray dogs rummaged. His house was a ruin. He saw all the signs of the passage of time. On the rickety, old-fashioned stained-glass door, with its motifs of exotic birds, there was a bronze knocker in the shape of a woman's hand pressing on a ball. He knocked and waited what seemed like an interminable while until the door was opened with a tug on a string that ran from the door-knob to the top of the stairs. His mother lived on the second floor and rented out the first floor to a button factory. Esteban began to climb the creaky steps, which had not been waxed in a long time. An ancient servant, whose existence he had completely forgotten, stood waiting for him on the landing and embraced him tearfully, just as she had greeted him at fifteen when he came home from working at the notary office where he earned his living copying property transfers and powers of attorney. Nothing had changed, not even the placement of the furniture, but everything struck him as different: the hallways with their worn wood floors, the broken windowpanes patched with scraps of cardboard, the dusty ferns languishing in rusty tin cans and chipped ceramic pots, the fetid smells of urine mixed with food that turned his stomach. What poverty! Esteban thought. He wondered what on earth his sister did with all the money he sent her so that she could live in dignity.

Férula came out to meet him with a sad grimace of welcome. She was greatly changed. She was no longer the opulent woman he had left years ago. She had lost weight, and her nose seemed enormous on her angular face. She gave off an aura of melancholy and bewilderment, a scent of lavender and old clothes. They embraced in silence.

"How's Mama?" Esteban asked.

"Come see. She's waiting for you," Férula replied.

They walked down a corridor of connecting rooms, each identical to the next, dark and small, with tomblike walls, high ceilings, and narrow windows, their wallpaper of discolored flowers and languid maidens stained from the soot of the coal stoves and the patina of time and poverty. From far away they could hear the voice of a radio announcer singing the praises of Dr. Ross's pills, tiny but effective against constipation, insomnia, and bad breath. They stopped outside the closed door of the bedroom of Doña Ester Trueba.

"Here she is," said Férula.

Esteban opened the door. It was several seconds before he could see in the darkness. The smell of medicine and decay hit him in the face, a sweetish odor of sweat, dampness, confinement, and something else that at first he could not quite identify but that quickly stuck to him like a plague: the smell of decomposing flesh. A thread of light leaked through the window, which was ajar, and he was able to make out the wide bed in which his father had died and his mother had slept every night since she was married. It was carved in black wood, with a canopy of angels in relief and a few scraps of red brocade that were frayed with age. His mother was propped up in a half-seated position. She was a block of solid flesh, a monstrous pyramid of fat and rags that came to a point in a tiny bald head with a pair of eyes that were sweet, blue, innocent, and surprisingly alive. Arthritis had transformed her into a monolithic being. She could no longer bend any of her joints or turn her head. Her fingers were clawed like the feet of a fossil, and in order to sit up in bed she had to be supported by a pillow at her back held in place by a wooden beam that, in turn, was propped against the wall. The passage of time could be read by the marks the beam had cut into the plaster: a path of suffering, a trail of pain.

"Mama," Esteban murmured, and his voice broke in his chest, exploding into a contained sobbing that erased in a single stroke his sad memories, the rancid smells, frozen mornings, and greasy soup of his impoverished childhood, his invalid mother and absent father, and the rage that had been gnawing at him ever since the day he first learned how to think, so that he forgot everything except those rare, luminous moments in which this unknown woman who now lay before him in her bed had rocked him in her arms, felt his forehead for fever, sung him lullabies, bent over to read the pages of a favorite book with him, had wept with grief to see him leave for work so early in the morning when he was still a boy, wept with joy when he returned at night, had wept, Mother, for me.

Doña Ester reached out her hand, but not in greeting; the gesture was intended to hold him back.

"Don't come any closer, son," she said, and her voice was still intact, just as he remembered it, the healthy, songlike voice of a young girl.

"It's because of the smell," Férula said brusquely. "It clings."

Esteban pulled back the threadbare damask quilt and saw his mother's legs. They were two bruised, elephantine columns covered with open wounds in which the larvae of flies and worms had made their nests and were busy tunneling; two legs rotting alive, with two outsized, pale blue feet with no nails on the toes, full to bursting with the pus, the black blood, and the abominable animals that were feeding on her flesh, mother, in God's name, of my own flesh.

"The doctor wants to amputate them, darling," Doña Ester said in her calm little-girl voice, "but I'm too old for that. I'm tired of suffering. It's time for me to die. But I didn't want to die without seeing you again, because after all these years I began to think that you were dead, and that perhaps your sister was writing your letters to spare me that additional pain. Come into the light, son, so I can get a good look at you. My God! You look like a savage!"

"It's country life, Mama," he murmured.

"Finally! You still look strong. How old are you now?"

"Thirty-five."

"A good age to get married and settle down, so I can die in peace."

"You're not going to die, Mama!" Esteban begged.

"I want to know that I'll have grandchildren, someone to carry on our name, with our blood in his veins. Férula's given up all hope of marrying, but you must find yourself a wife. A decent, Christian woman. But first you'd better cut your hair and shave your beard. Do you hear me?"

Esteban nodded. He knelt beside his mother and buried his face in her swollen hand, but the stench threw him back. Férula took him by the arm and led him out of that afflicted room. Once outside he inhaled deeply, the smell still clinging to his nostrils, and it was then he felt the rage—the rage he knew so well—that rose to his head like a blazing wave, injecting his eyes and bringing a pirate's curses to his lips. Rage at all the time he had gone without thinking of his mother, rage at having let her go uncared for, at not having loved her and cared for her enough, at being a miserable son of a bitch, no, forgive me, Mother, that's not what I meant to say; Jesus, she's dying, she's an old woman and I can't do a damned thing, not even ease her pain, alleviate the decay, get rid of that terrifying stench, that death soup in which you are boiling alive, Mother.

Two days later, Doña Ester Trueba died in the bed of pain where she had spent the final years of her life. She was alone, because her daughter Férula had gone as she did every Friday to the tenements in the Misericordia District to say the rosary for the poor, the atheists, the prostitutes, and the orphans, who threw garbage at her, dumped chamber pots onto her, and spat on her while she, kneeling in the desolate slum alleyway, shouted an unbroken litany of Our Fathers and Hail Marys as she dripped with the slop of the poor, the spit of atheists, the garbage of prostitutes, and the refuse of orphans, weeping her lament of humiliation, begging forgiveness for those who know not what they do and feeling that her bones were turning to rubber, her legs to cotton, and that a summer heat was pressing sin between her thighs—take from me this chalice, Lord, that her groin was bursting into hellfire: flames of fear, of holiness, ay, Our Father, don't let me fall into temptation, Jesus.

Esteban was not with Doña Ester either when she died quietly in her bed of pain. He had gone to see the del Valle family to inquire if they might still have an unmarried daughter, because after so many years of absence and barbarism, he knew of nowhere else to begin to keep his promise to his mother of giving her legitimate grandchildren, and he concluded that if Severo and Nívea had accepted him as a prospective son-in-law back in the days of Rosa the Beautiful, there was no reason they should refuse him, especially now that he was a rich man and no longer needed to scrape the earth for gold and had everything he needed on deposit at the bank.

That night Esteban and Férula found their mother dead in bed. She was smiling peacefully, as if at the last moment of her life her illness had wished to spare her its familiar torture.

The day Esteban Trueba asked to be received, Severo and Nívea del Valle remembered the words with which Clara had broken her lengthy silence. Thus they were not the least surprised when their visitor asked if they had any daughters of marriageable age and condition. They tallied things up, telling him that Ana had become a nun, Teresa was very ill, and all the others were already married except for Clara, the youngest, who was still available, although she was a rather eccentric creature not particularly well suited to the duties of marriage and domestic life. With all due honesty, they told him of their daughter's traits, without omitting the fact that she had spent more than half her lifetime without speaking because she did not feel like it and not because she was unable to, as the Rumanian Rostipov had made quite clear and as Dr. Cuevas had confirmed after innumerable examinations. But Esteban Trueba was not the kind of man to let himself be scared away by tales of ghosts in hallways, objects that move of their own accord, or prognostications of bad luck, much less by Clara's prolonged silence, which he considered a virtue. He concluded that none of these things posed any obstacle to bringing healthy, legitimate children into the world, and he asked to be introduced to Clara. Nívea went out to fetch her daughter and the two men were left alone in the drawing room, an occasion that Trueba, with characteristic candor, took advantage of to present his economic position.

"Please, Esteban, one thing at a time!" Severo interrupted him. "First you have to see the girl and get to know her a little, and then we also have to consider Clara's wishes. Don't you think so?"

Nívea returned with Clara. The young girl entered the room with blazing cheeks and blackened nails; she had been outside helping the gardener plant dahlia bulbs, and just this once her clairvoyant faculties had failed her, leaving her unprepared to meet her visitor in more suitable attire. When he saw her, Esteban jumped to his feet in astonishment. He recalled her as a thin, asthmatic child without the least grace, but the young woman who stood before him was a delicate ivory medallion, with a sweet face and a mane of chestnut hair whose curls spilled from her coiffure, melancholy eyes that gave her a sparkling, half-mocking look when she laughed her frank, open laugh, her head gently thrown back. She greeted him with a strong handshake that showed no trace of shyness.

"I was expecting you," she said simply.

They spent a few hours in this formal visit, speaking of the opera season, trips to Europe, the political situation, and the winter chills, while they drank sweet wine and ate puff pastries. Esteban watched Clara with all the discretion he could muster, feeling himself gradually coming under the young girl's spell. He could not recall being this interested in anyone since the glorious day when he had first set eyes on Rosa the Beautiful buying licorice in the pastry shop on the Plaza de Armas. He compared the two sisters in his mind and concluded that Clara had the advantage when it came to charm, although there was no doubt that Rosa had been far more beautiful. Night fell and two maids came in to draw the curtains and light the lamps. Esteban realized that his visit had gone on too long. His manners left a great deal to be desired. He said a stiff good night to Severo and Nívea and asked permission to visit Clara again.

"I hope I don't bore you, Clara," he said, blushing. "I'm a simple country man, and I'm at least fifteen years older than you. I don't know how to act with a young girl like yourself. . . ."

"Do you want to marry me?" Clara asked, and he noticed an ironic gleam in her hazel eyes.

"My God, Clara!" exclaimed her mother, horrified. "Forgive her, Esteban, the child's always been impertinent."

"I want to know, Mama. I don't want to waste my time," Clara said.

"I also like things to be direct." Esteban smiled happily. "Yes, Clara, that's why I came."

Clara took him by the arm and accompanied him to the

gate. In the final glance they exchanged, Esteban understood
that she had accepted him. He was overcome with happiness.
As he got into his carriage, he was smiling, unable to believe
his good fortune and not understanding how such a charming girl as Clara could have accepted his proposal without
even being acquainted with him. He did not know that she
had seen her own destiny, that she had summoned him with
the power of her thought, and that she had already made up
her mind to marry without love.

Out of respect for Esteban Trueba's mourning, they
waited a few months, during which he courted Clara the
old-fashioned way, just as he had done with her sister Rosa,
without knowing that Clara hated licorice and that acrostics
made her laugh. At the end of the year, around Christmastime,
they officially announced their engagement in the newspaper
and exchanged rings in the presence of their closest friends,
more than a hundred all together, at a Pantagruelian banquet
that was an endless parade of stuffed turkey, sugar-cured
pork, fresh-water eel, lobster au gratin, raw oysters, the
Carmelite nuns' special orange and lemon pies, the Domini-
cans' walnut and almond tortes, the Clarisas' chocolate and
cream cakes, and cases of French champagne that were
brought courtesy of the consul, who took advantage of his
diplomatic privileges to traffic in contraband. All was served
and presented with the utmost simplicity by the old servants
of the house, who wore their everyday black aprons to give
the celebration the appearance of a simple family gathering,
because any display of extravagance was a sign of vulgarity
that would be condemned as a sin of vanity and bad taste,
according to the austere and somewhat lugubrious ancestry
of that society descended from hard-working Basque and
Spanish immigrants. Clara was a vision in white Chantilly
lace and natural camellias, as happy as a parrot after her nine
years of silence, dancing with her fiancé beneath the cano-
pies and lanterns, completely oblivious to the warnings of
the spirits that gestured desperately at her from the curtains,
because in the tumult and whirl she could not see them. The
ceremony of the rings had remained unchanged ever since
colonial times. At ten o'clock at night, one of the menser-
vants circulated among the guests ringing a tiny glass bell.
The music stopped and the guests gathered in the main hall

where a small, innocent priest, adorned with the vestments of high mass, read the complicated sermon he had written exalting confused and impracticable virtues. Clara did not listen to him, because when the din of the music had died down and the whirl of the dancers had subsided, she began to pay attention to the whispering spirits behind the curtains and she realized that it had been hours since she had last seen Barrabás. She looked everywhere for him, summoning all her senses, but her mother's elbow in her ribs brought her back to the pressing matter of the ceremony. The priest finished his speech and blessed the two gold rings. Esteban quickly put one on his bride-to-be and slipped the other on his own finger.

At that moment a scream of horror shook the guests. The crowd cleared to either side, making a path for Barrabás, who staggered out blacker and larger than ever with a butcher's knife stuck in his back clear to the hilt, bleeding to death like an ox, his long colt legs trembling, his muzzle dripping with threads of blood, his eyes clouded in agony; dragging one paw after the other, he traced the zigzag path of a wounded dinosaur. Clara fell back onto the French silk loveseat. The enormous dog approached her, laid his huge, millennial animal head in her lap, and looked up at her with lovesick eyes that gradually dimmed and grew blind, while the white Chantilly lace, the French silk of the sofa, the Persian carpet, and the parquet floor absorbed his blood. Barrabás was dying without any hurry, his eyes riveted on Clara, who stroked his ears and murmured words of comfort until finally, with a single rattle, the dog fell rigid at her feet. Suddenly it was as if they had all been wakened from a nightmare, and the sounds of panic spread through the room. The guests hurriedly said goodbye, stepping over the pools of blood and quickly gathering up their fur stoles, their top hats, their canes, their umbrellas, and their beaded evening bags. The only ones left in the parlor were Clara, with the animal on her lap, her parents, who were locked in terrified embrace at the thought of such an evil omen, and her fiancé, who could not comprehend such an uproar over a dead dog; but when he realized that Clara was transfixed, he picked her up in his arms and carried her half-conscious to her room, where Nana's ministrations and Dr. Cuevas's pills prevented her from falling back into her stupor and her muteness. Esteban Trueba asked the gardener to help him, and between the two of them they threw Barrabás's body into the car. Death had made him so heavy that it was nearly impossible to lift him.

The following year was spent preparing for the wedding. Nívea took charge of Clara's trousseau, since Clara did not show the slightest interest in the contents of the sandalwood trunks, and continued her experiments with the three-legged table and her divining cards. The sheets so carefully embroidered, the linen tablecloths and the underwear the nuns had sewn ten years ago for Rosa, with the intertwined initials of Trueba and del Valle, were now part of Clara's trousseau. Nívea ordered clothes from Buenos Aires, London, and Paris—travel dresses, country dresses, party dresses, stylish hats, matching shoes and purses of lizard and suède, and various assorted other things, which remained in their tissue-paper wrappings, preserved with lavender and camphor, without the young bride's ever giving them so much as one distracted look.

Esteban Trueba took charge of a team of bricklayers, carpenters, and plumbers who were engaged to construct the largest, sunniest, and sturdiest house imaginable, built to last a thousand years and lodge several generations of a bountiful family of legitimate Truebas. He hired a French architect and had part of the building materials imported from abroad, so that his would be the only house with German stained-glass windows, moldings carved in Austria, faucets of English bronze, Italian marble floors, and special locks ordered by catalogue from the United States, which arrived with the wrong instructions and no keys. Férula, horrified by the expense, tried to keep him from additional folly, from buying French furniture, teardrop chandeliers, and Turkish carpets, by arguing that this would quickly be their ruin and that they would find themselves repeating the story of the extravagant Trueba who had sired them, but Esteban countered that he was rich enough to give himself these luxuries and threatened to line the doors with silver if she went on bothering him. She replied that such wastefulness was certainly a mortal sin and that God would punish all of them for spending on nouveau riche vulgarities what they should be giving to the poor.

Despite the fact that Esteban Trueba was no great lover of innovation, and had, in fact, a deep mistrust of the dislocations of modernity, he decided that his house should be constructed like the new palaces of North America and Europe, with all the comforts but retaining a classical style. He wanted it to be as far removed as possible from the native architecture. He would hear nothing of three courtyards, corridors, rusty fountains, dark rooms, walls of whitewashed adobe, or dusty tiles on the roof; he wanted two or three heroic floors, rows of white columns, and a majestic staircase that would make a half-turn on itself and wind up in a hall of white marble, enormous, well-lit windows, and the overall appearance of order and peace, beauty and civilization, that was typical of foreign peoples and would be in tune with his new life. His house would be the reflection of himself, his family, and the prestige he planned to give the surname that his father had stained. He wanted the splendor to be visible from the street, and so he designed a French garden with topiaries fit for Versailles, deep wells of flowers, a smooth and perfect lawn, jets of water, and several statues of the gods of Olympus and perhaps one or two courageous Indians from the history of the Americas, naked and crowned with feathers, his one concession to patriotism. He could hardly guess that that solemn, cubic, dense, pompous house, which sat like a hat amid its green and geometric surroundings, would end up full of protuberances and incrustations, of twisted staircases that led to empty spaces, of turrets, of small windows that could not be opened, doors hanging in midair, crooked hallways, and portholes that linked the living quarters so that people could communicate during the siesta, all of which were Clara's inspiration. Every time a new guest arrived, she would have another room built in another part of the house, and if the spirits told her that there was a hidden treasure or an unburied body in the foundation, she would have a wall knocked down, until the mansion was transformed into an enchanted labyrinth that was impossible to clean and that defied any number of state and city laws. But when Trueba built the house that everybody called "the big house on the corner," it bore the stately seal with which he managed to stamp everything around him, as if in memory of his childhood privations. Clara never went to see the house during the time it was being built. She was as uninterested in it as she was in her trousseau, and she left all decisions in the hands of her fiancé and her future sister-in-law.

When her mother died, Férula found herself alone and with no useful purpose to her life, at an age when she could no longer hope to marry. For a time, she made daily visits to the slums as part of a frenzied charitable activity, which gave her chronic bronchitis and brought no peace to her tormented soul. Esteban wanted her to take a trip, buy herself some clothes, and enjoy herself for the first time in her melancholy life, but she already had the habit of austerity and had spent too much time cooped up in her house. She was afraid of everything. Her brother's marriage plunged her into uncertainty, because she feared that this would be yet another reason for Esteban to keep his distance, and he was her only comfort and support. She was afraid of ending her days crocheting in some nursing home for spinsters from good families; thus she was overjoyed to learn that Clara was incompetent when it came to the simplest domestic tasks and that whenever she had to make a decision she became distracted and vague. She's a bit on the stupid side, Férula concluded with delight. It was clear that Clara would be incapable of administering the mansion her brother was constructing and that she would need a lot of help. As subtly as she could, she made it known to Esteban that his future wife was completely helpless and that she, with her proven spirit of self-sacrifice, could help her out and was ready to do so. Esteban could never follow her conversations when they took this sort of turn. As the wedding date approached and she realized she would have to decide her own fate, Férula grew desperate. Convinced that her brother would never give her a clear answer, she waited for an opportunity to speak alone with Clara. She found it one Saturday afternoon at five o'clock when she saw her walking down the street. She invited her to the Hotel Francés for tea. The two women sat surrounded by cream puffs and Bavarian porcelain, while in the back of the tearoom an all-female ensemble played a melancholy string quartet. Férula quietly observed her future sister-in-law, who looked about fifteen and whose voice was still off-key as a result of all her years of silence, not knowing how to broach the subject. After a seemingly endless pause in which they ate a trayful of pastries and drank two cups of jasmine tea apiece, Clara straightened a wisp of hair that had fallen across her eyes, smiled, and gave a gentle tap to Férula's hand.

"Don't worry," she said. "You're going to live with us and the two of us will be just like sisters."

Férula was startled. She wondered if the rumors about Clara's talent for reading minds were true. Her first reaction was pride, and she would have refused the offer just because of the beauty of the gesture, but Clara did not give her time. She leaned across and kissed her on the cheek with such candor that Férula lost control and began to cry. It had been a long time since she had shed even a single tear and she was astonished to see how badly she had needed some sign of tenderness. She could not remember the last time anyone had spontaneously touched her. She wept for a long time, unburdening herself of many past sorrows and her loneliness, still holding on to Clara's hand. Clara helped her blow her nose and between sobs fed her forkfuls of pastry and sips of tea. They wept and talked until eight o'clock at night, and that afternoon in the Hotel Francés they sealed a pact of friendship that would last for many years.

As soon as the period of mourning for Doña Ester was over and the big house on the corner was finished, Esteban Trueba and Clara del Valle were married in a modest ceremony. Esteban gave his wife a set of diamond jewelry, which she thought beautiful. She packed it away in a shoe box and quickly forgot where she had put it. They spent their honeymoon in Italy and two days after they were on the boat. Esteban was as madly in love as an adolescent, despite the fact that the movement of the ship made Clara uncontrollably ill and the tight quarters gave her asthma. Seated by her side in the narrow cabin, pressing cold compresses to her forehead and holding her while she vomited, he felt profoundly happy and desired her with unjust intensity, considering the wretched state to which she was reduced. On the fourth day at sea, she woke up feeling better and they went out on deck to look at the sea. Seeing her with her wind-reddened nose, and laughing at the slightest provocation, Esteban swore that sooner or later she would come to love him as he needed to be loved, even if it meant he had to resort to extreme measures. He realized that Clara did not belong to him and that if she continued living in a world of apparitions, three-legged tables that moved of their own volition, and cards that spelled out the future, she probably never would. Clara's impudent and nonchalant sensuality was also not enough for him. He wanted far more than her body; he wanted control over that undefined and luminous material that lay within her and that escaped him even in those moments when she appeared to be dying of pleasure. His hands felt very heavy, his feet very big, his voice very hard, his beard very scratchy, and his habits of rape and whoring very deeply ingrained, but even if he had to turn himself inside out like a glove, he was prepared to do everything in his power to seduce her.

They returned from their honeymoon three months later. Férula was waiting for them in their new house, which still smelled of paint and fresh cement and was filled with flowers and platters heaped with fruit, just as Esteban had ordered. When they stepped across the threshold for the first time, Esteban lifted his wife in his arms. His sister was surprised not to feel jealousy and observed that Esteban looked rejuvenated.

"Getting married has done you a world of good," she said.

She showed Clara around the house. Clara ran her eyes over everything and found it all quite lovely, just as she had politely approved of a sunset on the high seas, the Piazza San Marco, and her diamond jewelry. When they came to the door of the room that was to be her own, Esteban asked her to shut her eyes and led her into it by the hand.

"You can open them now," he said.

Clara looked around. It was a large room with walls papered in blue silk, with English furniture, big windows and balconies that opened onto the garden, and a canopied bed with gauze curtains that looked like a sailboat on a sea of calm blue silken water.

"Very lovely," Clara said.

Then Esteban pointed to the place where Clara was standing. It was the special surprise he had prepared for her. Clara looked down and gave a frightful cry; she was standing on the black back of Barrabás, who lay there split down the middle, transformed into a rug. His head was still intact and his two glass eyes stared up at her with the helpless look that is the specialty of taxidermists. Her husband managed to catch her before she fell to the floor in a dead faint.

"I told you she wasn't going to like it," said Férula.

Barrabás's tanned hide was quickly removed from the bedroom and shoved in a corner of the basement, along with the magic books from Uncle Marcos's enchanted trunks and other treasures, where it resisted moths and neglect with a tenacity worthy of a better cause, until it was rescued by subsequent generations.

It soon became evident that Clara was pregnant. Férula's affection for her sister-in-law became a passion, a dedication to waiting on her and caring for her and an unlimited tolerance for her distractions and eccentricities. For Férula, who had spent her life taking care of an old lady who was slowly, irremediably rotting alive, looking after Clara was like being in heaven. She bathed her in jasmine and basil water, rubbed her with cologne, powdered her with a swan's-down puff, and brushed her hair until it was as soft and shiny as an underwater plant, just as Nana had done before.

Long before his newlywed impatience had died down, Esteban Trueba was forced to return to Tres Marías, where he had not set foot for more than a year and where, despite the vigilance of Pedro Segundo García, its owner's absence was sorely felt. The property, which had once seemed to him like paradise and had been his pride and joy, was now a nuisance. As he watched the expressionless cows chewing their cuds, the sluggish labors of the peasants repeating the same motions day after day throughout their lives, the unchanging background of the snowy *cordillera*, and the frail column of smoke rising from the volcano, he felt like a prisoner.

While he was in the countryside, life in the big house on the corner changed, making way for a gentle routine without men. Férula was the first out of bed in the morning, because she was still in the habit of rising early from the days when she watched over her invalid mother, but she let her sister-in-law sleep late. In midmorning she personally served her breakfast in bed, threw open the blue silk curtains to let the sun in, and filled the French porcelain bathtub that was painted with sea nymphs, giving Clara time to shake off her sleep as she greeted one by one the spirits in the room, brought the tray up to her chest, and dipped her toast in the thick hot chocolate. Then Férula drew her out of bed with a mother's gentle caresses, telling her the good news from the morning paper, which was less every day, so that she was forced to fill the gaps with gossip about the neighbors, domestic trivia, and made-up anecdotes that Clara found very lovely and forgot within five minutes; thus Férula could tell the same ones over and over and Clara always enjoyed herself just as if it were the first time she was hearing them.

Férula took her strolling in the sun, because it was good for the baby; shopping, so the child would lack for nothing when it was born and have the finest clothing in the world; for lunch at the golf club, "so everyone would see how beautiful you have become since marrying my brother"; to see her parents, "so they don't think you've forgotten them"; and to the theater, "so you don't spend the whole day shut inside the house." Clara let herself be shepherded around with a sweetness that was not stupidity but distraction, and she devoted all her powers of concentration to vain attempts to communicate with Esteban by telepathy—her messages did not arrive—and to perfecting her abilities as a clairvoyant.

For the first time she could remember, Férula felt happy. She was closer to Clara than she had ever been to anyone, even her own mother. Someone less original than Clara would have tired of her sister-in-law's excessive pampering and constant worry, or have succumbed to her domineering and meticulous nature. But Clara lived in another world. Férula abhorred the moment when her brother returned from the country and filled the house with his presence, breaking the harmony they had established while he was away. When he was in the house, she had to disappear into the shadows and be more prudent in the way she addressed the servants, as well as in the care she lavished on Clara. Every night, when the married couple retired to their rooms, she was overwhelmed by a peculiar hatred she could not explain, which filled her soul with regret. To take her mind off things, she reverted to her old habit of saying the rosary in the slums and confessing her sins to Father Antonio.

"Hail Mary, Full of Grace."

"Conceived without sin."

"I hear you, my child."

"Father, I don't know how to say this. I think I committed a sin."

"Of the flesh, my child?"

"My flesh is withered, Father, but not my spirit! The devil is tormenting me."

"The mercy of the Lord is infinite."

"You don't know the thoughts that can run through the mind of a single woman, Father, a virgin who has never been with a man, not for any lack of opportunities but because God sent my mother a protracted illness and I had to be her nurse."

"That sacrifice is recorded in heaven, my child."

"Even if I sinned in my thoughts?"

"Well, it depends on your thoughts. . . ."

"I can't sleep at night. I feel as if I'm choking. I get up and walk around the garden and then I walk inside the house. I go to my sister-in-law's room and put my ear to her door. Sometimes I tiptoe in and watch her while she sleeps. She looks like an angel. I want to climb into bed with her and feel the warmth of her skin and her gentle breathing."

"Pray, my child. Prayer helps."

"Wait, I'm not finished. I'm ashamed."

"You shouldn't be ashamed with me; I'm just an instrument of God."

"When my brother's back from the country, it's even worse, Father. My prayers are useless. I can't sleep, I sweat, I shake, and finally I get up and walk through the whole dark house, gliding down the corridors as carefully as possible so they don't squeak. I listen to them through their bedroom door and once I even saw them, because the door had been left ajar. I can't tell you what I saw, Father, but it must be a terrible sin. It's not Clara's fault, I know, because she's as innocent as a little child. It's my brother who leads her into it. I know he's damned."

"Only God can judge and damn, my child. What were they doing?"

Férula could spend half an hour on the details. She was a gifted narrator who knew exactly where to pause, how to measure her cadence, how to explain without too many gestures, painting a scene so true to life than her listener felt as if he were there. It was incredible how she could sense from the half-open door the quality of their trembling, the abundance of juices, the words whispered in the ear, the most secret smells—a veritable miracle. She unburdened herself of these agitated states of mind, returned to the house with her idol's mask, impassive and severe, and resumed giving orders—put this here, and it was done; change the flowers in the vases, and they were changed; wash the windows; hush those damn birds, their noise won't let Señora Clara sleep, and all that cackling is going to frighten the baby and who knows but it might be born with wings. Nothing escaped her watchful eye. She was always moving, unlike Clara, who found everything so lovely and who was as happy to eat truffles as she was to have leftover soup, to sleep in a featherbed as to sleep sitting up in a chair, or to bathe in scented water as not to bathe at all. As her pregnancy advanced, she seemed to be distractedly letting go of reality and turning inward in a secret, unceasing conversation with her baby.

Esteban wanted a son who would bear his name and pass his family name on down the generations.

"It's a little girl and her name is Blanca," Clara had said when she announced that she was pregnant.

And so it was.

Dr. Cuevas, whom Clara no longer feared, calculated that the birth would be sometime around the middle of October, but it was already the beginning of November and Clara was still swinging her enormous belly around, in a state of semi-somnambulance, ever more distracted, more exhausted, and more asthmatic, indifferent to everything around her, even her husband. From time to time she didn't even recognize him and would ask "May I help you?" when she noticed him standing by her side. Once the doctor had ruled out the possibility of a miscalculation in the date and it was evident to all that Clara had not the slightest intention of giving birth the normal way, he proceeded to open her belly and extract little Blanca, who proved to be an uglier, hairier child than usual. Esteban jumped when he saw her, convinced that destiny was playing a cruel joke on him and that instead of the legitimate Trueba he had promised his mother on her deathbed, he had sired a monster, and a female one to boot. He personally examined the child and verified that she had all the necessary parts in their correct locations, at least those that could be seen with the naked eye. Dr. Cuevas consoled him by explaining that the child's repulsive appearance was due to the fact that she had spent a longer time than usual in her mother's body, to the effects of the Caesarean, and to her own small, thin, dark, and somewhat hairy constitution. Clara, on the other hand, was delighted with her daughter. She seemed to have wakened from a protracted stupor and discovered the joy of being alive. She took the child in her arms and would not let her go. She went everywhere with her little girl clutched to her breast, nursing her constantly without a set schedule and without regard for manners or modesty, like an Indian. She did not want to swaddle her, cut her hair, pierce her ears, or hire a nursemaid to take care of her, and least of all to use milk manufactured in some laboratory, as all the ladies did who could afford such luxuries. Nor would she accept Nana's prescription for giving her cow's milk diluted with rice water, because, she said, if nature had wanted human beings to be raised on that, she would have made women's breasts capable of secreting it. Clara spoke to the child all the time, not in baby talk but in perfect Spanish, as if she were conversing with a grown-up, the same way she addressed plants and animals; she was convinced that if she had had such good results with flora and fauna, there was no reason why it should not work with her own child. The combination of mother's milk and conversation transformed Blanca into a healthy, almost pretty child who bore no resemblance at all to the armadillo she had been at birth.

A few weeks after Blanca's birth, Esteban Trueba was able to confirm, thanks to her lively kicks aboard the sailboat on the blue silk sea, that maternity had not diminished his wife's enthusiasm for making love—just the opposite. And Férula, too busy in caring for the child, who had formidable lungs, an impulsive nature, and a voracious appetite, had no time to say the rosary in the slums or attend confession with Father Antonio, much less to peek through the half-open door.

FOUR

器

The Time of the Spirits

At an age when most children are still in diapers, Blanca
looked like an intelligent midget. She stumbled when she
walked, but she kept her balance and she spoke correctly and
fed herself, all because her mother treated her like an adult.
She had all her teeth and was just beginning to open the big
wardrobes and wreak havoc on their contents when the
family decided to spend the summer at Tres Marías, a place
Clara had only heard about. At that moment in Blanca's life,
her curiosity was stronger than her instinct for survival, and
Férula was constantly chasing the child up and down the
hall, afraid she would fall from the second story, stick her
head in the oven, or swallow a bar of soap. The idea of
taking the child to the country seemed risky, exhausting, and
unnecessary, since Esteban could do everything he needed to
do by himself at Tres Marías while she and Clara enjoyed
their civilized existence in the capital. But Clara was enthusiastic. To her the country was a romantic idea—because she
had never been inside a stable, as Férula put it. The preparations for the trip kept the family busy for two weeks, and the
house became a clutter of trunks, steamer baskets, and va-
lises. They hired a special car on the train to accommodate
the unbelievable amount of baggage and servants Férula
thought they needed, not to mention the birds in their cages,
which Clara could not leave behind, and Blanca's toy chests,
which were filled with mechanical clowns, porcelain figu-
rines, stuffed animals, wind-up dancers, and dolls with real

human hair and movable joints, who traveled with their own clothing, carriages, and china dishes. At the sight of that disorganized, nervous crowd and that pandemonium of belongings, Esteban felt defeated for the first time in his life, especially when he discovered, in the midst of all the baggage, a life-size statue of Saint Anthony, cross-eyed and wearing embossed sandals. He stared at the surrounding chaos and regretted his decision to travel with his wife and daughter, wondering how it could be possible that he had only packed two bags for this foray into the outside world when they had amassed a carload of dishes and a parade of servants that had nothing to do with the purpose of the trip.

At San Lucas they took three carriages, which conveyed them to Tres Marías in a cloud of dust, like a bunch of gypsies. Waiting for them in the courtyard of the hacienda were all the tenants, under orders from the foreman, Pedro Segundo García. They were speechless at the sight of this traveling circus. At Férula's bidding they began to unload the carriages and take the things into the house. No one noticed a little boy of about Blanca's age who was standing there with a runny nose, his naked belly swollen with parasites. He had a pair of beautiful black eyes that looked out at the world with an old man's gaze. He was the foreman's son and, to differentiate him from his father and grandfather, had been named Pedro Tercero García. In the tumult of getting settled, exploring the house, snooping around the orchard, greeting everyone, setting up the altar of Saint Anthony, and shooing the chickens from the beds and the mice from the closets, Blanca pulled off her clothes and ran out naked to play with Pedro Tercero. They played among the packages, hid beneath the furniture, exchanged wet kisses, chewed the same bread, ate the same snot, and smeared themselves with the same filth until, wrapped in each other's arms, they finally fell asleep under the dining-room table. Clara found them there at ten o'clock at night. Everyone had spent hours looking for them with torches. Teams of tenants had gone up and down the riverbanks, the granaries, the fields, and the stables searching for them, and Férula had got down on her knees before the altar of Saint Anthony. Esteban was hoarse from calling their names and Clara had vainly tried to summon her ability to read the future. When they found them, the little boy was on his back on the floor and Blanca was curled up with her head on the round belly of her new friend. Many years later, they would be found in the same position, and a whole lifetime would not be long enough for their atonement.

From the very first day, Clara understood that there was a place for her in Tres Marías and, just as she recorded it in her notebooks, she felt that she had finally discovered her mission in life. She was not impressed by the brick houses, the school, and the abundant food, because her ability to see what was invisible immediately detected the workers' resentment, fear, and distrust; and the almost imperceptible noise that quieted whenever she turned her head enabled her to guess certain things about her husband's character and past. Still, the *patrón* had changed. Everyone could appreciate that he had stopped going to the Red Lantern. His nights on the town, his cockfights, his gambling, his violent tantrums, and, above all, his bad habit of tumbling girls in the wheatfields were a thing of the past. This they attributed to Clara. And Clara too had changed. From one day to the next, her listlessness had vanished, she had stopped finding everything "so lovely," and she seemed to have been cured of her habit of speaking with invisible spirits and moving the furniture by supernatural means. She rose at dawn with her husband and ate breakfast with him already dressed; then, while he went out to supervise the work in the fields, Férula took charge of the housework, the servants from the city, who could not adjust to the discomforts of the country and the flies, and Blanca. Clara divided her time between the sewing workshop, the general store, and the school, where she established her headquarters for treating mange and lice, untangling the mysteries of the alphabet, teaching the children to sing "I have a dairy cow, she's not just any cow," and the women to boil milk, cure diarrhea, and bleach clothes. At sundown, before the men came in from the fields, Férula gathered all the peasant women and children to say the rosary. They came more out of kindness than faith, giving the aging spinster a chance to recall her good old days in the tenements. Clara waited for her sister-in-law to finish the mystical litanies of Our Fathers and Hail Marys, then used the meetings to repeat the slogans she had heard her mother shout when she chained herself to the gates of Congress. The women listened with embarrassed smiles, for the same reason they prayed with Férula: so as not to displease the *patrón*'s wife. But those inflammatory cries only made them laugh. "Since when has a man not beaten his wife? If he doesn't beat her, it's either because he doesn't love her or because he isn't a real man. Since when is a man's paycheck or the fruit of the earth or what the chickens lay shared between them, when everybody knows he is the one in charge? Since when has a woman ever done the same things as a man? Besides, she was born with a wound between her legs and without balls, right, Señora Clara?" they would say. Clara was beside herself. The women nudged each other in the ribs and smiled shyly with their toothless mouths and their wrinkled eyes, their skin toughened by the sun and their unhealthy lives, knowing full well that if they took it into their heads to put Clara's ideas into practice, their husbands would beat them. And deservedly, to be sure, as Férula herself declared. Esteban soon found out about the second half of their prayer meetings and became enraged. It was the first time he had ever been angry with Clara and the first time she saw him have one of his famous tantrums. He shouted like a madman, pacing up and down the living room and slamming his fist against the furniture, arguing that if Clara intended to follow in her mother's footsteps she was going to come face to face with a real man, who would pull her pants down and give her a good spanking so she'd get it out of her damned head to go around haranguing people, and that he categorically forbade her to go to prayer meetings or any other kind and that he wasn't some ninny whose wife could go around making a fool of him. Clara let him scream his head off and bang on the furniture until he was exhausted. Then, inattentive as ever, she asked him if he knew how to wiggle his ears.

The vacation grew longer and the meetings in the school-house continued. Summer came to an end and autumn covered the fields with fire and gold, changing the landscape. The first cold days arrived with their rain and mud, but Clara did not show the least sign of wanting to return to the city, despite a sustained campaign on the part of Férula, who hated the countryside. During the summer, she had complained about the stifling evenings, which she spent shooing flies, about the dust clouds in the courtyard, which covered the house as if they were living in a mine shaft, about the dirty water in the bathtub, where her special perfumed salts became a Chinese soup, about the flying cockroaches that got between the sheets, about the burrows of the mice and ants, about the half-drowned spiders she found kicking in the glass of water on her night table each morning, about the insolent hens who laid their eggs in her shoes and shat on the lingerie in her dresser. When the weather changed, she had new calamities to complain about: the mud in the courtyard, the abbreviated days—it was dark at five and there was nothing to do but face the long, solitary night—the wind, and the winter colds, which she countered with eucalyptus plasters that were powerless to keep the family from infecting each other in an endless chain. She was tired of struggling against the elements with nothing to break the monotony but watching Blanca grow. The child looked like a cannibal, she said, playing with that dirty little boy, Pedro Tercero, and worst of all the child had no one of her own class to mix with; she was picking up bad manners, and went around with flushed cheeks and scabs on her knees: "Look how she talks, she sounds like an Indian. I'm tired of pulling lice out of her hair and putting blue methylene on her mange." Despite her muttering, she maintained her rigid dignity, her unchanged bun, her starched blouse, and the ring of keys that hung from her waist. She never perspired, never scratched herself, and always kept her faint scent of lavender and lemon. No one thought that anything could undermine her self-control, until one day she felt an itching on her back. It was such a strong itch that she could not refrain from discreetly scratching it, but nothing gave her any relief. Finally she went into the bathroom and took off her corset, which she always wore, even on the days when she had a lot of work. As she loosened the stays, a dazed mouse, which had spent the entire morning vainly trying to find an exit between the hard points of the corset and the oppressed flesh of its owner, fell to the floor. Férula had the first attack of nerves in her life. Everyone came running at her cries and found her standing in the tub, livid with terror and still half undressed, screaming like a maniac and pointing with a shaking finger at the tiny rodent, who was struggling to his feet and attempting to make his way to a safer place. Esteban said that it was menopause and that there was nothing anyone could do. They paid no more attention when she had the second spell. It was Esteban's birthday, and that Sunday morning dawned as sunny as anyone could want. There was a great commotion in the house, because there was going to be a party in Tres Marías for the first time since the forgotten days when Doña Ester was a girl. They invited various relatives and friends, who took the train out from the city, and all the landed gentry from the neighborhood, without overlooking the town notables. A week before the party, they prepared the banquet: half a steer roasted in the courtyard, kidney pie, chicken casserole, various corn dishes, eggfruit, and the best harvest wines. At noon the guests began to arrive by coach and horse, and the great adobe house filled with laughter and conversation. Férula excused herself for a moment and ran to the bathroom, one of those immense bathrooms where the toilet was placed in the middle of the room surrounded by a vast desert of white tiles. She was ensconced on that throne-like solitary seat when the door opened and in walked one of the guests, no less a personage than the mayor of the town, already unbuttoning his fly and slightly tipsy from his apéritif. When he saw the lady, he became paralyzed with confusion and surprise, and by the time he was able to react the only thing he could think of was to walk toward her with a twisted smile, crossing the entire room and extending his hand.

"Zorebabel Blanco Jamasmié, pleased to meet you," he introduced himself.

"For God's sake! It's impossible to live among such uncouth people! If the rest of you want to stay in this uncivilized purgatory, that's your prerogative, but I'm returning to the city. I want to live like a human being, the way I always have," Férula exclaimed when she was able to speak of the incident without bursting into tears. But she did not leave. She did not want to be separated from Clara. She had come to adore the very air Clara exhaled, and even though she no longer had occasion to give her baths and sleep in the same bed with her, she found a thousand ways to express her tender feelings, and to this she dedicated her existence. That woman who was so hard on herself and others could be sweet and smiling with Clara and at times, by extension, with Blanca. Only with Clara did she allow herself the luxury of giving in to her overwhelming desire to serve and be loved; with her, however slyly, she was able to express the secret, most delicate yearnings of her soul. The long years of solitude and unhappiness had distilled her emotions and purified her feelings down to a few terrible, magnificent passions, which possessed her totally. She had no gift for small perturbations, mean-spirited resentments, concealed envies, works of charity, faded endearments, ordinary friendly politeness, or day-to-day acts of kindness. She was one of those people who are born for the greatness of a single love, for exaggerated hatred, for apocalyptic vengeance, and for the most sublime forms of heroism, but she was unable to shape her fate to the dimensions of her amorous vocation, so it was lived out as something flat and gray trapped between her mother's sickroom walls, wretched tenements, and the tortured confessions with which this large, opulent, hot-blooded woman—made for maternity, abundance, action, and ardor—was consuming herself. She was about forty-five years old then, and her splendid breeding and distant Moorish ancestors kept her looking fit and polished, with black, silky hair and a single white lock on her forehead, a strong and slender body and the resolute step of the healthy. Still, the emptiness of her life made her look far older than she was. I have a photograph of Férula taken around that time, on one of Blanca's birthdays. It is an old sepia-toned picture, discolored with age, but you can still see how she looked. She was a regal matron, but with a bitter smile on her face that revealed her inner tragedy. Those years with Clara were probably the only happy period in her life, because only with Clara could she be herself. Clara was the one in whom she confided her most subtle feelings, and to her she consecrated her enormous capacity for sacrifice and veneration. She once was bold enough to tell her how she felt, and Clara wrote in her notebook that Férula loved her far more deeply than she deserved or than she could ever hope to repay. Because of that excessive love, Férula did not want to leave Tres Marías; not even after the plague of ants, which began with a humming in the pastures and quickly became a dark shadow that glided everywhere, devouring everything in its path—the corn, the wheat, the alfalfa, and the marigolds. The ants were sprinkled with gasoline and set on fire, but they reappeared, invigorated. The tree trunks were painted with quicklime, but the ants continued to climb, sparing neither pears, oranges, nor apples. They went into the garden and ate their way through the canteloupes. They entered the dairy, and at dawn the milk was sour and full of minuscule cadavers. They got into the chicken coops and ate the chickens alive, leaving behind a whirl of feathers and a pile of pathetic little bones. They cut paths right through the house, tunneled through the pipes, took over the pantry. Everything that was cooked had to be eaten immediately, because if it was left on the table for even a few minutes, they arrived in a procession and gobbled it up. Pedro Segundo García fought them with fire and water and buried sponges soaked in honey so that it would attract them all to the same place, where he could kill them by surprise, but it was all in vain. Esteban Trueba went into town and returned weighed down with pesticides in every form known to man—powders, liquids, and pills—which he sprayed and sprinkled everywhere. No one could eat any vegetables, because they would get stomach cramps. But the ants continued to appear and multiply, daily growing more impudent and more decisive. Esteban went back into town and sent a telegram to the city. Three days later Mr. Brown, a tiny gringo, arrived at the train station clutching a mysterious suitcase; Esteban introduced him as an agricultural technician specializing in insecticides. After cooling off with a glass of wine with fruit in it, he opened his suitcase on the table. He removed a whole arsenal of tools that none of them had ever seen before and proceeded to trap an ant and carefully observe it with his microscope.

"What are you looking for, mister? They're all the same," said Pedro Segundo García.

The gringo did not answer him. When he had finished identifying the species, its life-style, the location of its burrows, its habits, and even its most secret desires, a whole week had passed and the ants were beginning to crawl into the children's beds, had finished off the winter food reserve, and were starting to attack the cows and horses. So Mr.

Brown explained that they would have to be sprayed with one of his special products, which would make the males of the species sterile. Thus they would cease to reproduce. Then they had to be sprinkled with still another poison, also of his own invention, which would bring about a fatal illness in the females, and that, he promised, would put an end to the whole problem.

"How long will it take?" asked Esteban Trueba, whose patience was giving way to fury.

"One month," said Mr. Brown.

"By that time they'll have eaten all the people, Mr. Brown," said Pedro Segundo García. "If you'll allow me, *patrón*, I'm going to call in my father. For the past three weeks he's been telling me he has a cure for plagues. I'm sure it's just one of those old people's tales, but there's no harm trying."

They brought in old Pedro García, who shuffled in looking so dark, small, and toothless that Esteban was surprised at this sign of time's relentless passage. The old man listened with his hat in his hand, looking down at the ground and chewing the air with his empty gums. Then he asked for a white handkerchief, which Férula brought from Esteban's wardrobe, and went outside. He crossed through the courtyard and entered the orchard, followed by all the inhabitants of the house as well as the foreign midget, who was smiling scornfully, these poor savages, oh God! The old man squatted down with difficulty and began to collect ants. When he had a fistful, he put them in the handkerchief, knotted its four corners, and placed the little bundle in his hat.

"I'm going to show you the way out, ants, so you get out of here and take the rest of them with you."

The old man climbed up onto a horse and ambled slowly, mumbling advice and recommendations, prayers of wisdom and enchanted formulas, to the ants. The others saw him disappearing off the edge of the property. The gringo sat down on the ground and laughed like a madman, until Pedro Segundo García grabbed him and shook him.

"Go laugh at your grandmother, mister. That old man is my father," he warned.

Pedro García returned at dusk. He slowly dismounted, told the *patrón* he had led the ants to the edge of the highway, and went into his house. He was tired. The next morning there were no ants in the kitchen, none in the pantry, the granary, the stable, the chicken coops, the pastures. The family and the tenants went all the way to the river, checking everywhere along the way, and found not a single ant, not even one to use as a sample. The expert was furious.

"You have to show me how to do that!" he shouted.

"By talking to them, mister. Tell them to go, that they're a nuisance here. They understand," explained old Pedro García.

Clara was the only one to whom the procedure seemed completely normal. Férula latched on to it as proof that they were living in a hole, an inhuman region in which neither God's laws nor scientific progress seemed to have made inroads, and that any day now they were all going to be traveling by broom; but Esteban Trueba told her to be still, because he did not want anyone putting any new ideas into his wife's head. In the past few days Clara had reverted to her visionary tasks, speaking with apparitions and spending hours writing in her notebooks. When she lost all interest in the schoolhouse, the sewing workshop, and the women's meetings and once again found everything ever so lovely, they knew that she was pregnant again.

"And it's your fault!" Férula shouted at her brother.

"I hope so," he replied.

It was soon evident that Clara was in no condition to spend her pregnancy in the country and give birth in the village, so they began getting ready to return to the city. This was of some consolation to Férula, who took Clara's pregnancy as a personal affront. She traveled ahead with most of the baggage and servants, to open the big house on the corner and prepare for Clara's arrival. Several days later, Esteban accompanied his wife and daughter back to the city, leaving Tres Marías once again in the hands of Pedro Segundo García, whose responsibilities as foreman had brought him no more privileges, but only more work.

The trip from Tres Marías to the city used up all of Clara's remaining strength. I saw her grow paler and more asthmatic, with dark rings under her eyes. With the jouncing up and down first of the horses and then the train, the dust of the road, and her natural inclination to get queasy, she was losing energy before my very eyes. There wasn't much I could do to help her, because when she felt ill she didn't like anyone to talk to her. When we got out in the station, I had to hold her up because her legs were giving out.

"I think I'm going to elevate," she said.

"Not here!" I shouted, terrified at the idea of Clara flying over the heads of the passengers along the track.

But she wasn't talking about physical levitation; she meant she wanted to rise to a level that would allow her to leave behind the discomfort and heaviness of pregnancy and the deep fatigue that had begun to seep into her bones. She entered one of her long periods of silence—I think it lasted several months—during which she used her little slate, as she had in her days of muteness. This time I wasn't worried, since I expected she would return to normal just as she had after Blanca was born. Besides, I had come to understand that silence was my wife's last refuge, not a mental illness as Dr. Cuevas said it was. Férula looked after her as obsessively as if she had been an invalid. She refused to leave her alone and completely neglected Blanca, who cried all day long because she wanted to return to Tres Marías. Clara walked around the house like a silent, overweight shadow, with a Buddhistic indifference toward everything around her. She didn't even look at me. She walked right by me as if I were a piece of furniture, and whenever I spoke to her she acted as if she were on the moon, as if she hadn't heard me or didn't know who I was. We hadn't resumed sleeping in the same bed. The lazy, empty days in the city and the irrational atmosphere in the house set my nerves on edge. I managed to keep myself busy, but it wasn't enough: I was always in a bad mood. I went out every day to check on my business affairs. It was around that time that I began speculating in the stock market, and I spent hours studying the ups and downs of international finance. I devoted myself to investing money, starting new companies, and importing. I spent a lot of time in my club. I also began to get involved in politics, and even joined a gym where a gigantic trainer forced me to exercise certain muscles I hadn't even known I had. I had been advised to have massages, but I never liked them: I hate to be touched by mercenary hands. But none of this was enough to fill my days. I was uncomfortable and bored. I wanted to return to the country, but I didn't dare leave my house, where there was clearly need for a man among so many hysterical women. Besides, Clara was putting on too much weight. Her belly was so huge that it could barely be supported by her fragile frame. She was embarrassed to be seen undressed, but she was my wife and I couldn't allow her to be ashamed in front of me. I helped her bathe and dress—if Férula didn't beat me to it—and I felt infinitely sorry for her, so tiny and thin with that monstrous belly, as the moment of delivery approached. I lay awake at night thinking that she could die giving birth, and I would closet myself with Dr. Cuevas trying to figure out the best way to help her. We had agreed that if things didn't look good it was better to do another Caesarean, but I didn't want her to be sent to a hospital, and he refused to do another operation like the first one in the house. He said we didn't have the proper facilities, but in those days hospitals were a major source of infection, and more people died in them than were saved.

One day a short time before her delivery date, Clara came down from her Brahmanic refuge without warning and began to speak again. She asked for a cup of hot chocolate and then asked me to take her out for a walk. My heart skipped a beat. The whole house was filled with joy. We opened a bottle of champagne, I had fresh flowers put in all the vases, ordered camellias, her favorite flower, and carpeted her room with them until they began to give her asthma and we had to remove them in a hurry. I ran to buy her a diamond brooch on the street of the Jewish jewelers. Clara thanked me effusively and found it ever so lovely, but she never put it on. I suppose she must have locked it up in some unlikely place and then forgotten all about it, like almost all the other jewels I bought for her over the years we spent together. I called Dr. Cuevas, who came over on the pretext of having tea but was really there to examine Clara. He took her to her room and then told Férula and myself that even though she seemed to have recovered from her mental crisis, we would have to expect a difficult delivery because the child was very big. Just then Clara stepped into the sitting room. She must have heard his final sentence.

"Everything will turn out fine," she said. "There's no need for you to worry."

"I hope this time it will be a boy so we can give him my name," I joked.

"It's not one, it's two," Clara replied. "The twins will be called Jaime and Nicolás, respectively," she added.

That was too much for me. I suppose I blew my stack from all the pressure I'd been under the preceding months. I got furious, arguing that those were names for foreign merchants, that no one in my family or hers had ever had such names, that at least one of them should be called Esteban, like myself and my father, but Clara explained that repeating the same name just caused confusion in her notebooks that bore witness to life. Her decision was inflexible. To frighten her, I smashed a porcelain jar that, I believe, was the last vestige of the splendid days of my great-grandfather, but she was unmoved. Dr. Cuevas smiled from behind his teacup, which only made me more indignant. I slammed the door behind me and went to the club.

That night I got drunk. Partly because I needed to and partly for vengeance, I went to the best-known brothel in the city, which had a historic name. Now I want to make it clear that I'm not a man for whores and that I've only resorted to them during periods when I've been forced to live alone. I don't know what got into me on that particular day. I was annoyed with Clara, I was in a bad mood, I had excess energy, I was tempted. In those days, the Christopher Columbus was flourishing, but it hadn't yet acquired the international reputation it attained when it appeared on the navigational charts of the British shipping companies and in all the guidebooks, and when they showed it on television. I stepped into a sitting room with French provincial furniture, the type with twisted claws, where I was received by a native matron who did a perfect imitation of a Parisian accent; she reeled off the price list, and asked me if I had anything special in mind. I told her that my experience was limited to the Red Lantern and a few wretched miners' whorehouses in the North, so that any young, clean woman would be fine with me.

"I like you, monsieur," she said. "I'm going to bring you the best in the house."

At her summons, a woman appeared sheathed in a black satin dress that was far too tight and could barely contain her exuberant femininity. Her hair was combed over one ear, a hairstyle I've never liked, and as she walked she gave off a terrible musky scent that floated on the air, as insistent as a moan.

"I'm glad to see you, *patrón*," she said, and it was then I recognized her, because her voice was the only thing that hadn't changed about Tránsito Soto.

She led me by the hand to a room shut like a tomb, its windows covered with dark curtains, in which the light of day could not have entered in eons but which was nonetheless a palace compared to the sordid quarters of the Red Lantern. There I personally undressed Tránsito, undid her dreadful hairdo, and was able to observe that with the years she had grown taller, put on weight, and become more beautiful.

"I see you've made some progress," I said.

"Thanks to your fifty pesos, *patrón*," she replied. "They helped me get started. Now I can return them to you readjusted, because with inflation they're not worth what they once were."

"I'd rather have you owe me a favor, Tránsito," I said, laughing.

I finished taking off her petticoats and verified that there was almost nothing left of the slender girl with jutting knees and elbows who had worked in the Red Lantern, except for her tireless sensual appetite and her voice that sounded like a hoarse bird. Her body was hairless and her skin had been rubbed with lemon and cream of witch hazel, as she explained to me, which made it as soft as a baby's. Her nails were painted red and she had a snake tattooed around her navel, which could move in circles while the rest of her body remained absolutely still. While she was demonstrating her skill at making the serpent wiggle, she told me the story of her life.

"What would have become of me if I had stayed at the Red Lantern, *patrón*? I would have lost my teeth. I'd be an old woman now. You get used up fast in this profession, you have to look out for yourself. And I'm not even a streetwalker! I've never liked that—it's very dangerous. To work the street, you have to have a pimp; otherwise it's too risky. Nobody respects you. But why give a man something it's so hard to earn? In that respect women are really thick. They're the daughters of rigidity. They need a man to feel secure but they don't realize that the one thing they should be afraid of is men. They don't know how to run their lives. They have to sacrifice themselves for the sake of someone else. Whores are the worst, *patrón*, believe me. They throw their lives away working for some pimp, smile when he beats them, feel proud when he's well dressed, with his gold teeth and rings on his fingers, and when he goes off and takes up with a woman half their age they forgive him everything because 'he's a man.' No, sir, I'm not like that. No one's ever supported me and that's why you'll never find me supporting someone else. I work for myself, and whatever I earn I spend as I see fit. It's been a struggle, believe me—don't think I've had an easy time of it, because the madams of these places don't like to deal with women. They prefer pimps. They don't help you out. They have no consideration."

"But it looks as if they really appreciate you here, Tránsito. They told me you're the best in the house."

"I am. But this business would fall on its face if not for me, because I work like a horse. The rest of the girls are like a bunch of dishrags. All we get now are old men; it's not the way it used to be. We ought to modernize the whole business, bring in civil servants, who have nothing to do in the middle of the day, and young people, and students. We ought to get better furnishings, liven the place up, and clean it. Clean the whole place! That way the customers would feel more trusting and they wouldn't go around worrying about catching some venereal disease, right? This place is a pigsty. They never clean. Look, pick up the pillow and I guarantee you a tick will come hopping out. I've told the madam, but she doesn't listen. She doesn't have a head for business."

"And you do?"

"Of course, *patrón*! I have a million ideas for improving the Christopher Columbus. I bring enthusiasm to this profession. I'm not like those girls who go around complaining all the time and blaming their bad luck when things go wrong. Can't you see how far I've come? I'm the best now.

If I put my mind to it, I could have the best house in the country. I guarantee you."

I was enjoying myself. I could really appreciate her, because I had stared at ambition so many times in the mirror when I was shaving in the mornings that I was able to recognize whenever I encountered it in others.

"I think that's an excellent idea, Tránsito," I told her. "Why don't you open your own business? I'll advance you the money," I said, fascinated at the idea of broadening my commercial interests in that direction. I must have really been drunk!

"No thanks, *patrón*," Tránsito replied, caressing her snake with a lacquered fingernail. "There's no point in trading one capitalist for another. The thing to do is form a cooperative and tell the madam to go to hell. Haven't you ever heard of that? You better be careful. If your tenants set up a cooperative, you'd really be finished. What I want is a whores' cooperative. Or whores and fags, to make it more encompassing. We'll lay out everything, the money and the work. What do we need a *patrón* for?"

We made love with a violence and ferocity I had almost forgotten after so much sailing in the ship of the gentle blue silk sea. In that chaos of sheets and pillows, clasped in the living knot of desire, screwed into each other to the point of fainting, I felt I was twenty again, and happy to be holding in my arms this bold, swarthy woman who didn't fall apart when you got on top of her, a strong mare you could ride on without giving it a second thought, who didn't make your hands feel heavy, your voice hard, your feet gigantic, or your beard too scratchy, but someone like yourself, who could take a string of bad words in her ear and didn't need to be rocked with tender arguments or coaxed with flattery. Afterward, sleepy and happy, I rested awhile by her side, admiring the solid curve of her hips and the shudder of her snake.

"We'll see each other again, Tránsito," I told her, giving her a tip.

"That's what I said before, *patrón*. Remember?" she replied with a final flip of her serpent.

The truth was I had no intention of ever seeing her again. In fact I planned to forget all about her.

I wouldn't have mentioned this episode if Tránsito Soto hadn't played such an important role in my life a long time later, because, as I said earlier, I'm not a man for whores. But this story could not have been written if she hadn't intervened to rescue us and, in the process, our memories.

A few days later, while Dr. Cuevas was making preparations before opening Clara's belly up again, Severo and Nívea del Valle died, leaving behind numerous children and forty-seven living grandchildren. Clara found out in a dream before everybody else, but she told no one except Férula, who managed to calm her down by explaining that pregnancy produces a state of jumpiness in which bad dreams frequently occur. She redoubled her attentions, rubbing Clara's stomach with sweet almond oil to keep her from getting stretch marks, and her breasts with honey so her nipples would not split. She fed her powdered eggshell so her milk would be good and her teeth strong, and recited the prayers of Bethlehem for a healthy delivery. Two days after her dream, Esteban Trueba came home earlier than was his custom, pale and disheveled, grabbed his sister Férula by the arm, and led her into the library.

"My in-laws were killed in an accident," he told her curtly. "I don't want Clara to find out until after she's given birth. We have to build a wall of censorship around her: no newspapers, no radio, no visitors—nothing! Keep an eye on the servants and make sure no one tells her."

But his good intentions were shattered by the strength of Clara's premonitions. That night she dreamt that her parents were walking through a field of onions and that Nívea had no head, so she knew exactly what had happened without needing to read about it or hear it on the radio. She woke up very agitated and asked Férula to help her dress because she had to go find her mother's head. Férula ran to Esteban and he called Dr. Cuevas, who, even at the risk of harming the twins, gave her a potion for madness that should have put her to sleep for two days but that had not the slightest effect on her.

Señor and Señora del Valle had died exactly as Clara dreamed, and exactly as Nívea, joking, had frequently announced that they would die.

"One of these days we're going to kill ourselves in this damned machine," she would say, pointing at her husband's ancient Sunbeam.

From his youth Severo del Valle had had a weakness for modern inventions. The automobile was no exception. In a time when everybody else still traveled by foot, by horse-drawn carriage, or by bicycle, he bought the first car to arrive in the country, which was on display as a curiosity in a downtown shopwindow. It was a mechanical wonder that moved at the suicidal speed of fifteen or even twenty kilometers an hour, to the astonishment of the pedestrians and the curses of those who were splattered with mud or covered with dust as it went by. At first people fought it as a public hazard. Eminent scientists explained in the newspaper that the human organism was not made to withstand moving about at twenty kilometers an hour and that the new ingredient called gasoline could catch fire and cause a chain reaction that would consume the entire city. Even the Church became involved. Father Restrepo, who had kept a watchful eye on the del Valle family ever since the disturbing affair with Clara that Holy Thursday during mass, became the self-proclaimed guardian of morality and railed in his Galician accent against the "amicis rerum novarum," the friends of new things such as these satanic machines, which he compared to the chariot of fire in which the prophet Elias disappeared on his way to heaven. But Severo ignored the scandal and in a short time several other gentlemen followed his example, until the sight of an automobile ceased to be such a novelty. He used it for more than ten years, refusing to change models when the city swelled with modern cars that were more efficient and safer, for the same reason that his wife refused to get rid of the dray horses until they died peacefully of old age. Inside, the Sunbeam had lace curtains and two glass vases, which Nívea kept full of fresh-cut flowers. It was lined with polished wood and Russian leather and its bronze hardware gleamed like gold. Despite its British origin, it had been baptized with the very Indian name of Covadonga. It was perfect, to tell the truth, except that its brakes never worked very well. Still, Severo was proud of his mechanical abilities. He took the car apart several times trying to fix it and then he entrusted it to the Big Cuckold, an Italian mechanic who was the best in the country. He had acquired his nickname from a tragedy that had cast its shadow over his life. People said that his wife, sick and tired of betraying him without his noticing, abandoned him one stormy night, and before she left him she took a bunch of rams' horns she had got at the butcher's and tied them to the points of the fence around his garage. The next day, when the Italian arrived at work, he found a knot of children and neighbors making fun of him. That scene, however, in no way undermined his professional reputation, although he too was unable to fix Covadonga's brakes. Severo opted for traveling with a large rock in his car. Whenever he parked on an incline, one passenger would hold his foot on the brake and another would jump out quickly and place the stone in front of the wheels. This system usually worked, but on that fatal Sunday, appointed by destiny to be their last, it did not. The del Valles motored out into the suburbs as they always did on a clear day. Suddenly the brakes gave out completely, and before Nívea could jump out with the rock or Severo could alter its course, the car took off downhill. Severo tried to swerve and then he tried to stop, but the devil had taken charge of the machine, which flew out of control and smashed into a cart loaded with construction iron. One of the plates came through the windshield and decapitated Nívea. It was a clean cut. Her head shot out of the car and, despite a search by the police, the forest rangers, and a swarm of neighbors who searched for it with bloodhounds, after two days they had failed to find any trace of it. By the third day, the bodies had begun to stink and they had to be buried incomplete in a magnificent funeral that was attended by the whole del Valle tribe and an incredible number of friends and acquaintances, not to mention the delegations of women who went to pay their last respects to the remains of Nívea, who was considered the first feminist in the country. Her enemies said of her that if she had lost her head during her lifetime there was no reason why she should find it in death. Clara, locked in her house, surrounded by the servants who took care of her, with Férula as her guard, and drugged by Dr. Cuevas, did not attend. Out of consideration for everyone who had tried to spare her this additional suffering, she said nothing that would indicate she knew about the hair-raising affair of the lost head. But once the funeral was over and life appeared to return to normal again, Clara convinced Férula to go with her to look for it, and there was no use in her sister-in-law's giving her more pills and potions, because she was firm in her determination. Defeated, Férula understood that it was no longer possible to say that the image of the lost head was a bad dream, and that it would be best if she helped Clara with her plans before her anxiety completely unhinged her. They waited for Esteban Trueba to leave the house. Férula helped her dress and called for a hired carriage. Clara's instructions to the driver were rather imprecise.

"Go straight. I'll tell you the route," she said, guided by her instincts for seeing what was invisible.

They left the city and came into the open country where the houses were far apart and the hills and gentle valleys began. At Clara's command they turned onto a service road and continued among birches and onion fields until she ordered the driver to pull up along a clump of underbrush.

"It's here," she said.

"But that's impossible! We're much too far from where the accident occurred!" said Férula.

"It's here!" Clara insisted, getting out of the car with difficulty, holding up her enormous belly. She was followed by her sister-in-law, who was muttering prayers, and by the driver, who did not have the foggiest idea of the purpose of their trip. She tried to make her way through the brush, but the twins made it impossible.

"Do me a favor, señor," she said to the driver. "Step through here and hand me that woman's head you'll see lying on the ground."

He inched his way beneath the thorny brush until he came upon Nívea's head, which looked like a lonely melon. He picked it up by the hair and took it with him, crawling on all fours. While the man leaned against a tree and vomited, Férula and Clara cleaned the dirt and pebbles that had got into Nívea's ears, nose, and mouth, and arranged her hair, which had become rather unkempt, but they were unable to close her eyes. They wrapped the head in a shawl and returned to the car.

"Hurry, señor," Clara told the driver. "I think I'm giving birth!"

They arrived at the house just in time to get the mother into bed. Férula fluttered about with all the necessary preparations while a servant went to fetch Dr. Cuevas and the midwife. With the bouncing of the car, the emotions of the past few days, and the doctor's potions, Clara had acquired a skill at giving birth that she did not have the first time around. She clenched her teeth, grabbed on to the mizzen and foremast of the sailboat, and gave herself fully to the task of bringing forth onto the calm blue silken sea the twins Jaime and Nicolás, who came sailing out under the gaze of their grandmother staring open-eyed at them from the bureau. Férula grabbed each of them by the lock of wet hair at their napes and helped to pull them out with the experience she had acquired watching the birth of colts and calves at Tres Marías. Before the doctor and midwife could arrive, she hid Nívea's head beneath the bed, to avoid having to invent awkward explanations. When they finally arrived, there was precious little for them to do, because the mother was resting comfortably and the babies, as tiny as seven-month-olds but with all their parts and in good condition, were sleeping in the arms of their debilitated aunt.

Nívea's head became a problem, because there was no place to put it where it would not be seen. Finally, Férula wrapped it in a cloth and placed it in a leather hatbox. They discussed the possibility of giving it a proper burial, but it would have required interminable paperwork to have the tomb unsealed in order to include the missing part. Besides, there would have been an uproar if word had got out about how Clara had found the head where the bloodhounds had failed. Esteban Trueba, ever fearful of public ridicule, opted for a solution that would not provide material for malicious tongues, because he knew that his wife's strange behavior was the target of local gossips. It had gone beyond Clara's skill at moving objects without touching them and at predicting the impossible. Someone had uncovered the story of Clara's childhood muteness and the curse of Father Restrepo— that saintly man who the Church was hoping would become the first in the country to attain beatitude. The two years in

Tres Marías had helped to quell the rumors, and people had begun to forget, but Trueba knew that it would take a mere trifle, such as the affair of his mother-in-law's head, for the whispers to start up again. For this reason, and not out of neglect, as was later said, the hatbox was stowed away in the basement, where it awaited a more propitious moment to be given a Christian burial.

Clara recovered quickly from the double birth. She entrusted the care of the children to her sister-in-law and to Nana, who came to work in the Trueba household after the death of her employers, "to continue working for the same blood," as she put it. She had been born to cradle other people's children, wear their hand-me-down clothing, eat their leftovers, live on borrowed happiness and grief, grow old beneath other people's roofs, die one day in her miserable little room in the far courtyard in a bed that did not belong to her, and be buried in a common grave in the public cemetery. She was nearly seventy, but her zeal was unbending. She was still tireless in her comings and goings, untouched by time, still able to dress up as a ghost and jump on Clara in the nooks and crannies of the house whenever she had another of her spells of muteness, still strong enough to fight with the twins and softhearted enough to spoil Blanca, just as she had spoiled her mother and grandmother before her. She had acquired the habit of constantly mumbling prayers under her breath, because when she realized that no one in the house believed in God, she took it upon herself to pray for all the living members of the family—as well as, of course, for the dead, for whom her devotions were simply an extension of the service she had rendered while they were alive. In her old age she forgot whom she was praying for, but she kept up the habit, convinced that it would be of use to someone. Her piety was the only thing she shared with Férula. In everything else they were rivals.

One Friday afternoon, three translucent ladies knocked at the door to the big house on the corner. They had eyes like sea mist, covered their heads with old-fashioned flowered hats, and were bathed in a strong scent of wild violets, which infiltrated all the rooms and left the house smelling of flowers for days after their visit. They were the three Mora sisters. Clara was in the garden and appeared to have been waiting for them all that afternoon. She greeted them with a baby at each breast, and Blanca playing at her feet. They looked at each other, recognized each other, smiled at each other. It was the beginning of a passionate spiritual relationship that was to last the remainder of their lives and, if their predictions have come true, must still be flourishing in the Hereafter.

The three Mora sisters were students of spiritualism and supernatural phenomena. Thanks to a photograph that showed the three of them around a table with a misty, winged ectoplasm flying overhead, which some unbelievers attributed to a stain from the developer and others to a simple photographic trick, they were the only people who possessed irrefutable proof that souls can take on physical form. Via mysterious connections available only to initiates, they learned of Clara's existence, established telepathic contact with her, and immediately realized they were astral sisters. By way of a series of discreet inquiries, they managed to obtain her earthly address and arrived at her door with decks of cards impregnated with beneficent liquids, several sets of geometrical figures and mysterious tools of their own invention for unmasking fake parapsychologists, and a tray of ordinary pastries as a gift for Clara. They became intimate friends, and from that day on they met every Friday to summon spirits and exchange recipes and premonitions. They discovered a way to transmit mental energy from the big house on the corner to the other extreme of the city, where the Moras lived in an old mill they had converted into their singular abode, and also in the opposite direction, which enabled them to give each other moral support in difficult moments of their daily lives. The Moras knew many people, almost all of them interested in such matters, who gradually began to attend the Friday meetings, to which they brought their knowledge and their magnetic fluids. Esteban Trueba would see them crossing through his house and insisted on these few conditions: that they respect his library, that they not use the children for psychic experiments, and that they be discreet, because he did not want any public scandal.

Férula disapproved of these activities of Clara's; to her they seemed at odds with religion and good manners. She observed their sessions from a prudent distance, without participating, but watching from the corner of her eye while she crocheted, ever ready to intervene in case Clara went too far in one of her trances. She had noticed that her sister-in-law was always exhausted at the end of the sessions where she served as medium, and she would begin to speak in pagan tongues, and in a voice that was not her own. Nana also kept her eye out, on the pretext of serving little cups of coffee, startling the spirits with her starched petticoats and the click of her whispered prayers and loose teeth—not to protect Clara from her own excesses, but rather to make sure no one stole the ashtrays. In vain Clara explained to her that her guests were not interested in ashtrays, primarily because none of them smoked; but Nana had already made up her mind that they were all, with the exception of the three enchanting Mora sisters, a bunch of evangelical scoundrels.

Nana and Férula despised each other. They squabbled over the children's affection and fought for the right to care for Clara in her rantings and ravings; their silent, continuous war was conducted in the kitchens, the courtyards, the hallways, but never near Clara, because the two of them had agreed to spare her that particular anguish. Férula had come to love Clara with a jealous passion that resembled that of a demanding husband more than it did that of a sister-in-law. With time she lost her prudence and began to let her adoration show in many ways that did not go unobserved by Esteban. Whenever he returned from the country, Férula would manage to persuade him that Clara was in what she called "one of her bad spells," so that he could not sleep in the same bed with her and would enter her room rarely, and then only briefly. She would buttress her argument with recommendations from Dr. Cuevas, which later, when he was asked point-blank, turned out to have been made up. She found a thousand ways to come between the husband and wife and, if all else failed, she would encourage the children to beg their father to take them on an outing, their mother to read them a book, or both parents to watch over them because they had a fever or to play with them. "Poor things," she would say. "They need their father and their mother. They spend the whole day with that ignorant old woman who fills their heads with outmoded ideas; she's making them into imbeciles with her superstition. What we should do with Nana is put her away. People say the Handmaidens of God have a marvelous asylum for old housekeepers. They treat them like real ladies. They don't have to work, there's good food—that's the most humane thing we could do. Poor Nana, she's all used up." Without being able to pinpoint the cause, Esteban began to feel uncomfortable in his own house. His wife had grown increasingly remote, strange, and inaccessible. There was no way for him to reach her, not even with presents. His timid show of affection did not work, nor did the unbridled passion that always overcame him in her presence. In all that time his love for her had grown to the point where it had become an obsession. He wanted Clara to think of nothing but him, and he could not bear for her to have a life outside that did not include him. He wanted her to tell him everything and to own nothing he had not given her with his own two hands. He wanted her to be completely dependent.

But reality was different. Clara seemed to be flying in an airplane, like her Uncle Marcos, unmoored from land, seeking God through Tibetan sciences, consulting spirits with a three-legged table that gave little jolts—two for yes, three for no—deciphering messages from other worlds that could even give her the forecast for rain. Once they announced that there was a hidden treasure beneath the chimney. First she had the wall knocked down and then, when it was not found, the staircase and half of the main sitting room. Still nothing. Finally it turned out that the spirit, confused by the architectural alterations she had made to the house, was unable to detect that the hiding place of the gold doubloons was not in the Trueba mansion but across the street at the house of the Ugartes, who refused to demolish their dining room because they did not believe the story about the Spanish ghost. Clara was incapable of braiding Blanca's hair for school, a task she entrusted to Férula or Nana, but she had a wonderful relationship with her based on the same principles as the relationship she had had with

Nívea. They told each other stories, read the magic books from the enchanted trunks, consulted family portraits, told anecdotes about uncles who let fly great amounts of wind, and others, blind, who fell like gargoyles from poplar trees; they went out to look at the *cordillera* and count the clouds, and spoke in a made-up language with no t's and with r's instead of l's, so that they sounded just like the man in the Chinese laundry. Meanwhile, Jaime and Nicolás were growing up apart from the feminine dyad, adhering to the then common belief that "we have to become men." The twins grew strong and cruel in the games typical of their age. They chased lizards to slice off their tails, mice to make them run races, and butterflies to wipe the powder from their wings; then, when they were older, they punched and kicked each other on instructions from that Chinese laundryman, who was ahead of his time and had been the first to introduce the country to the millennial practice of the martial arts. But no one had paid any attention when he demonstrated how he could split bricks in two with his hand and had tried to open his own academy, so he had ended up washing other people's clothes. Years later, the twins put the finishing touches on their manhood by escaping from school and diving into the empty lot behind the garbage dump, where they traded some of their mother's silverware for a few minutes of forbidden love with an enormous woman who cradled both of them in breasts like those of a Dutch cow, drowning them in the soft wetness of her armpits, crushing them with her elephantine thighs and sending them both to heaven with the dark, hot, juicy cavern of her sex. But that was not until much later, and Clara never knew about it, so she could not write it in her notebooks that bore witness to life, for me to read one day. I found out from other sources.

Clara had no interest in domestic matters. She wandered from one room to the next without ever being the least surprised to find everything in perfect order and sparklingly clean. She sat down to eat without ever wondering who had cooked the food or where it had come from, just as she was oblivious to the person serving it. She forgot the names of the servants and even of her own children, yet she always managed to be present, like a cheerful, beneficent spirit, at whose slightest footfall clocks began to wind themselves. She dressed in white, because she had decided that it was the only color that did not change her aura, in simple dresses that Férula made for her on the sewing machine and that she preferred to the ruffled, sequined gowns her husband bought with the aim of showing her off in the latest fashions.

Esteban had bouts of despair because Clara treated him with the same kindness she displayed toward everybody else. She spoke to him in the same cajoling tones she used to address her cats, and was incapable of telling whether he was tired, sad, euphoric, or eager to make love. However, from the color of his rays she knew at a glance whether he was hatching a swindle, and she could defuse one of his tantrums with a few simple, mocking words. It exasperated him that Clara never seemed truly grateful for anything and never seemed to need anything that he could give her. She was as distracted and as smiling in bed as she was in everything else; relaxed and simple, but absent. He knew that her body was his to engage in all the acrobatics he had learned in the books he kept hidden in a corner of his library, but with Clara even the most abominable contortions were like the thrashings of a newborn; it was impossible to spice them up with the salt of evil or the pepper of submission. In a rage, Trueba sometimes reverted to his former sins, rolling with some robust peasant woman in the tall rushes of the riverbank while Clara stayed behind with the children in the city and he had to tend to the hacienda in the country, but instead of relieving him these episodes only left a bitter taste in his mouth. They brought no lasting pleasure, particularly since he knew that if he told his wife about them she would be appalled by his mistreatment of the other woman but not by his infidelity to her. Jealousy, like many other typical human reactions, was simply not part of Clara's vocabulary. He also went to the Red Lantern a few times, but he stopped going because he could not perform anymore with prostitutes and he had to swallow his humiliation by stammering various excuses: he had drunk too much wine, had eaten too much at lunch, had been walking around with a cold for several days. Nor did he return to Tránsito Soto, because he sensed that she embodied the real danger of addiction. He felt a terrible desire boiling up within him, a fire impossible to quench, a thirst for Clara that would never, even on the longest and most passionate nights, be satisfied. He fell asleep exhausted, his heart on the verge of bursting in his chest, but even in his dreams he was aware that the woman sleeping by his side was not really there: she was in some unknown, other dimension where he could never reach her. At times he would lose his patience and furiously shake her awake, shouting the worst accusations he could think of, but then he would end up weeping in her lap and begging her forgiveness for his cruelty. Clara understood, but there was nothing she could do. Esteban Trueba's exaggerated love for her was without a doubt the most powerful emotion of his life, greater by far than his rage and pride. Half a century later, he would still be speaking of it with the same shudder and the same sense of urgency. In his old man's bed, he would continue to call her name until the day he died.

Férula's comments increased Esteban's anxiety. Every obstacle his sister placed between himself and Clara drove him out of his mind. He even came to hate his own children for taking all their mother's time. He took Clara on a second honeymoon to the same places where they had spent the first, and on weekend escapades to a hotel, but it was all useless. He was convinced that Férula was entirely to blame, that she had planted an evil seed in his wife to prevent her from loving him, and that she was stealing forbidden kisses that properly belonged to him. He would grow livid with anger when he came upon Férula giving Clara her bath. He grabbed the sponge from her hands, thrust her out of the room, and pulled Clara from the tub practically in midair. He gave her a good shaking and forbade her to let herself be bathed again, because at her age it was a vice, and he dried her off himself, wrapping her in her robe and leading her to the bed, feeling all the while that he was acting like a fool. If Férula tried to serve his wife a cup of chocolate, he grabbed it from her hands on the pretext that she was treating her like an invalid; if she kissed her good night, he pulled her away with a sweep of his hand, saying that it was not right for them to kiss; if she chose the best portions for her from the serving tray, he rose from the table in a temper. Brother and sister became rivals, each scrutinizing the other with eyes full of hatred, concocting fine-edged arguments to disqualify each other in Clara's eyes, spying on each other, and growing ever more jealous. Esteban stopped going to the country and put Pedro Segundo García in charge of everything, including his imported cows. He stopped going out with his friends, stopped going to the golf course, stopped working, so as to watch his sister day and night and block her path every time she tried to get near Clara. The atmosphere of the house became dense, dark, and unbreathable. Even Nana walked around like someone haunted. The only one who continued completely unaffected was Clara, who in her distraction and innocence had no idea of what was going on.

Esteban's and Férula's hatred for each other took a long time to explode. It began with a concealed uneasiness and a desire to offend each other in small details, but it grew until it filled the house. That summer Esteban had to go to Tres Marías because exactly at harvest time Pedro Segundo García fell off a horse and ended up in the hospital with a cracked skull. As soon as the foreman had recovered, Esteban returned to the city without telling anyone. On the train he felt a terrible foreboding and an unspoken desire that something dramatic should take place, but he did not know that the drama had already begun when he desired it. He arrived back in the city in the middle of the afternoon, but went directly to his club, where he played a few hands of poker and dined, without successfully quelling his anxiety and impatience. During dinner, there was a slight earthquake. The crystal chandeliers swayed with their usual tinkling, but no one so much as looked up. Everyone continued eating and the musicians continued playing without missing a single note, but Esteban Trueba jumped up as if it were an omen. He finished his meal in a hurry, then asked for his check and left.

Férula, who usually had her nerves well under control, had never got used to earthquakes. She had conquered her fear of the ghosts Clara would invoke and the mice in the countryside, but earthquakes shook her to her bones and long after they had passed she was still trembling. That night she had not yet gone to bed, and she came running into Clara's room. Clara had drunk her evening tea and was sleeping peacefully. In search of a little company and warmth, Férula climbed into bed beside her, careful not to wake her up and whispering silent prayers so that the tremors would not become a fullblown quake. Esteban Trueba found her there. He entered the house as silently as a thief, went up to Clara's room without turning on the lights, and appeared like a tornado before the two sleeping women, who thought he was in Tres Marías. He leaned over his sister with the same rage he would have felt if she were his wife's seducer. He pulled her from the bed, dragged her down the hall, pushed her down the stairs, and thrust her into the library while Clara shouted from her bedroom doorway, not understanding what was going on. Alone with Férula, Esteban vented all his fury as an unhappy husband, shouting things at her he never should have said, calling her everything from a dyke to a whore and accusing her of perverting his wife with her spinster caresses and of driving her crazy, distracted, mute, and spiritualist with her arsenal of lesbian arts. He accused her of taking her pleasure with Clara while he was away, and of besmirching the names of the children, the honor of the house, and the memory of their dear departed mother, and told her he was sick and tired of her evil tricks and that he was throwing her out of the house. She should leave immediately and he never wanted to set eyes on her again. He forbade her to come near his wife and children and promised that she would never want for money; as long as he lived, he would see to it that she had enough to live on decently, as he had once promised her, but that if he ever caught her prowling around his family he would kill her on the spot, and she should get that through her head. "I swear to you in the name of our mother that I'll kill you!"

"I set my curse on you, Esteban!" Férula shouted back. "You will always be alone! Your body and soul will shrivel up and you'll die like a dog!"

And she left the big house on the corner forever, dressed only in her nightgown, taking nothing with her.

The next day, Esteban Trueba went to see Father Antonio and told him what had happened, without going into detail. The priest listened passively, with the bland expression of one who has heard it all before.

"What do you want from me, my son?" he asked when Esteban had finished speaking.

"That once a month you make sure my sister receives a certain envelope I'm going to deliver to you. I don't want her to have any financial worries. And I must explain that I'm not doing this out of kindness but because of a promise."

Father Antonio took the first envelope with a sigh and sketched the sign of benediction with his hands, but Esteban had already turned to leave. He gave Clara no explanation of what had come between his sister and himself. He told her he had thrown her out of the house and that he strictly forbade her to mention his sister's name in his presence, suggesting that if she had a shred of decency she would also refrain from mentioning it behind his back. He had all Férula's clothing and any objects that might serve as reminders of her removed from the house and resolved that as far as he was concerned his sister was dead.

Clara understood that there was no point in asking any questions. She went to the sewing room to look for her pendulum. Then she spread a map of the city on the floor and held the pendulum a foot and a half above it, waiting for the oscillations to tell her her sister-in-law's address, but after trying all afternoon she realized that the system would not work unless Férula had a fixed address. The pendulum having failed, she went out to look for her by carriage, hoping that her instinct would guide her in her search, but that method also was unsuccessful. She consulted her three-legged table, but no spiritual guide showed up to lead her through the city to Férula. She called her with her mind and consulted her tarot cards, but it was all to no avail. Finally she decided to resort to more traditional techniques. She began to look for her through friends and by asking the various delivery men who came to the house and might have come across her, but no one had seen a trace of her. Eventually her investigation led her to Father Antonio's door.

"Don't look for her," the priest told her. "She doesn't want to see you."

Clara realized that that was why none of her infallible methods of divining had worked.

"The Mora sisters were right," she said to herself. "You can't find someone who doesn't want to be found."

• • • •

Esteban Trueba entered a very prosperous period. His business deals seemed to have been touched by a magic wand. He felt pleased with life, and he was rich, just as he had once set out to be. He had acquired the concessions for other mines, was exporting fruit to foreign countries, had founded a construction firm, and Tres Marías, which had greatly expanded, was now the best hacienda in the area. He had been untouched by the economic crisis that convulsed the rest of the country. In the northern provinces, the collapse of the nitrate fields had left thousands of workers destitute. Hungry tribes of unemployed workers and their families— women, children, and old people—had taken to the roads in search of work and, as they approached the capital, were slowly forming a belt of misery around it. They settled in any way they could, under planks of wood and pieces of cardboard, in the midst of garbage and despair. They wandered the streets begging for a chance to work, but there were no jobs and slowly but surely the rugged workers, thin with hunger, shrunken with cold, ragged and desolate, stopped asking for work and asked for alms instead. The city filled with beggars, and then with thieves. Never had there been such terrible frosts as there were that year. There was snow in the capital city, an unaccustomed spectacle that remained on the front page of all the newspapers, touted as a festive decoration, while in the impoverished shantytowns on the city's outskirts the blue, frozen bodies of small children were discovered every morning. There was not enough charity for so many poor, defenseless people.

That was the year of exanthemic typhus. It began like any other calamity that strikes the poor but quickly took on the characteristics of a divine punishment. It was born in the poorest quarters of the city, because of the harsh winter, the malnutrition, and the dirty water, and it joined forces with the unemployment and spread in every direction. The hospitals could not cope. The sick wandered through the streets with missing eyes, picking the lice from their hair and throwing them at the healthy. The plague spread to every house, infecting schools and factories, so that no one felt secure. Everyone lived in fear, inspecting themselves for the first signs of the dread disease. Those who caught it began to shake with an icy cold that lodged in their bones, and gradually fell prey to a deep lethargy. They were left gazing like madmen to be eaten alive by their own fever, filling with sores, shitting blood, hallucinating scenes of fire and drowning, falling to the ground with bones like wool, legs like rags, and a taste of bile in their mouths. Their bodies became raw meat, with a red pustule next to a blue one next to a yellow one next to a black one, as they vomited up their own intestines and cried out to God for mercy, begging Him to let them die for they could not go on, their heads were bursting and their souls escaping in a blur of shit and fear.

Esteban proposed to take his whole family to the countryside to protect them from the infection, but Clara would not hear of it. She was busy tending to the poor in a task that had neither beginning nor end. She left the house early in the morning and at times returned close to midnight. She emptied the wardrobes of the house, taking the children's clothes, the blankets from the beds, her husband's jackets. She packed up food from the pantry and established a shipping system with Pedro Segundo García, who sent cheese, eggs, smoked meat, fruit, and chicken from Tres Marías for her to distribute among the poor. She lost weight and looked emaciated. She began to walk in her sleep again.

Férula's absence was a cataclysm in the house. Even Nana, who had always wished for this moment, was upset. When spring came and Clara was able to get some rest, her tendency to escape reality and lose herself in daydreams became more pronounced. Even though she could no longer rely on her sister-in-law's impeccable skills for ordering the chaos of the big house on the corner, she still paid no attention to domestic matters. She left everything in the hands of Nana and the other servants, and immersed herself in the world of apparitions and psychic experiments. Her notebooks that bore witness to life grew confused, and her calligraphy lost its convent elegance, degenerating into a series of mangled scribbles that were sometimes so tiny they were impossible to read and sometimes so large that three words would fill a page.

In the years that followed, a group of Gurdjieff students, Rosicrucians, spiritualists, and sleepless bohemians gathered around Clara and the three Mora sisters. They ate three meals a day in the house and spent their time alternating between urgent consultations with the spirits of the three-legged table and reading the verses of the latest mystic poet to land in Clara's lap. Esteban allowed this invasion of grotesqueries because he had long ago realized that it was pointless to interfere in his wife's life. But he was determined that at least his sons would be kept at a safe distance from her magic, so Jaime and Nicolás were sent to a Victorian English boarding school, where any excuse sufficed for pulling down a student's pants and caning his buttocks. This happened especially to Jaime, who made fun of the British royal family and at the age of twelve displayed an interest in reading Marx, a Jew who was spreading revolution around the world. Nicolás inherited the adventurous spirit of his great-uncle Marcos and his mother's propensity for making up astrological charts and reading the future, but this did not constitute a major crime in the rigid code of the school, only an eccentricity, so he fared far better there than his brother.

Blanca's case was a different matter, because her father did not interfere with her education. He believed that her destiny was marriage and a brilliant life in society, where the ability to converse with the dead, if kept on a frivolous level, could be an asset. He maintained that magic, like cooking and religion, was a particularly feminine affair; for this rason, perhaps, he was able to feel a certain sympathy for the three Mora sisters, while he despised male spiritualists almost as much as he did priests. As for Clara, she went everywhere with her daughter hanging from her skirts. She included her in the Friday sessions and raised her in the greatest intimacy with spirits, with the members of secret societies, and with the impoverished artists whose patroness she was. Just as she had gone with her mother in the days when she was mute, she now took Blanca with her on her visits to the poor, weighed down with gifts and comfort.

"This is to assuage our conscience, darling," she would explain to Blanca. "But it doesn't help the poor. They don't need charity; they need justice."

This was the point on which she had her worst arguments with Esteban, who was of a different opinion on the subject.

"Justice! Is it just for everyone to have the same amount? The lazy the same as those who work? The foolish the same as the intelligent? Even animals don't live like that! It's not a matter of rich and poor, it's a matter of strong and weak. I agree that we should all have the same opportunities, but those people don't even try. It's very easy to stretch out your hand and beg for alms! But I believe in effort and reward. Thanks to that, I've been able to achieve what I've achieved. I've never asked anybody for a favor and I've never been dishonest, which goes to prove that anyone can do it. I was destined to be a poor, unhappy notary's assistant. That's why I won't have these Bolshevik ideas brought into my house. Go do your charitable work in the slums, for all I care! It's all well and good: good for building the character of young ladies. But don't start coming in here with the same half-cocked ideas as Pedro Tercero García, because I won't stand for it!"

It was true that Pedro Tercero García was talking about justice in Tres Marías. He was the only one who dared to speak back to the *patrón*, despite the beatings his father gave him every time he caught him in the act. Since he was a child, the boy had been making surreptitious journeys into town to borrow books, read the newspapers, and converse with the local schoolteacher, a fervent Communist who years later would be shot dead by a bullet between the eyes. He also stole away at night to the bar in San Lucas, where he met with certain union leaders who had a passion for fixing the world's troubles between sips of beer, or with the huge, magnificent Father Jose Dulce María, a Spanish priest with a head full of revolutionary ideas that had earned him the honor of being relegated by the Society of Jesus to that hidden corner of the world, although that didn't keep him from transforming biblical parables into Socialist propaganda. The day Esteban Trueba discovered that the son of his administrator was slipping subversive pamphlets to his tenants, he summoned him to his office and, in the presence of his father, gave him a lashing with his snakeskin whip.

"This is the first warning, you insolent little shit!" he

said without raising his voice and staring at him with fire in his eyes. "But the next time I catch you bothering people, I'm going to lock you up. I don't want rebels on my land, you hear, because I'm the one in charge here and I have the right to surround myself with people I like. And I don't like you, and now you know it. I put up with you because of your father, who's served me faithfully for all these years, but you'd better watch out, because things could turn out very bad for you. Now get out of here!"

Pedro Tercero García closely resembled his father. He was dark-skinned, and had the same hard features that looked as if they had been sculpted in stone, the same big sad eyes, and the same dark, stiff hair that stood up like a brush. He had only two loves, his father and the *patrón*'s daughter, whom he had loved from the day they slept together naked beneath the dining-room table, back in his early childhood. Nor had Blanca escaped the same fate. Every time she went on vacation to the country and arrived at Tres Marías in the whirl of dust that always preceded the coaches piled high with their chaotic baggage, her heart would pound with impatience and longing, like an African drum. She was always the first to jump down from the carriage and run toward the house, and she always found Pedro Tercero García in the place where they had seen each other for the first time, standing barefoot in the doorway, half hidden by the shadow of the door, timid and sullen in his worn pants, his old man's eyes scanning the horizon as he awaited her arrival. The two ran to each other, hugging, kissing, laughing, and affectionately punching each other and rolling on the ground as they pulled each other's hair and shouted with joy.

"That's enough, young lady! Let go of that raggedy child!" Nana would shriek, trying to pull them apart.

"Let them be, Nana," Clara would say, for she knew better. "They're only children, and they like each other."

The children ran off to hide and tell each other everything that they had stored up during the long months of separation. Pedro blushingly handed her some whittled animals he had made for her, and Blanca gave him the gifts she had brought for him: a penknife that opened like a flower, a tiny magnet that magically picked up rusty nails from the ground. The summer she arrived with half the contents of the trunk of magic books that had belonged to Uncle Marcos, she was nearly ten years old. Pedro Tercero still had trouble reading, but his curiosity and desire accomplished what his schoolmistress had been unable to do with all her canings. They spent that summer reading among the rushes by the river, the pine trees in the forest, and the sprouting stalks of the wheatfields, discussing the virtues of Sinbad and Robin Hood, the bad luck of the Black Pirate, the true and edifying stories from the *Treasury of Youth*, the worst meanings of the words that did not appear in the dictionary of the Spanish Royal Academy, the cardiovascular system in illustrated plates where you could see a man with no skin and all his veins and arteries exposed for all to see, but wearing underpants. Within a few weeks, the boy had learned to read voraciously. They entered the wide, deep world of impossible stories, gnomes, fairies, men stranded on islands who eat their comrades after casting their fate at dice, tigers who let themselves be tamed for love, fascinating inventions, geographical and zoological curiosities, Oriental countries with genies in bottles, dragons in caves, and princesses held prisoner in towers. They often went to see old Pedro García, whose senses had been worn away by time. He had gradually grown blind; his eyes slowly filled with a sky-blue film of which he said, "The clouds are taking over my sight." He was grateful for the visits from Blanca and Pedro, who was his grandson, although he had already forgotten that fact. He listened to the stories they had chosen from the magic books, which they had to shout into his ear, because also he said that the wind was invading his ears and making him deaf. In return he showed them how to protect themselves from the stings of poisonous insects and demonstrated the effectiveness of his antidote by placing a live scorpion on his arm. He taught them how to search for water. You have to hold a dry stick in your two hands and walk tapping the ground, in silence, thinking only of water and the thirst of the stick, until suddenly, sensing the presence of moisture, the stick began to tremble. That's where you have to dig, the old man said, but he explained that this was not the system he used for digging wells around Tres Marías, because he needed no stick. His bones were so thirsty that whenever he walked on top of underground water, no matter how far down, his own skeleton told him where it was. He taught them about the different grasses and herbs that grew in the fields, and made them smell them and taste them, even caress them, until they were able to identify them one by one according to their healing properties: this one to calm the mind, that one to get rid of diabolic influence, this one to make the eyes shine, that one to strengthen the stomach, this to stimulate the flow of blood. In this realm his knowledge was so vast that the doctor from the nuns' hospital used to come and ask his advice. Nevertheless, all his knowledge was powerless to cure the chicken fever of his daughter Pancha, which had dispatched her to the Hereafter. He had made her eat cow dung, and when that did not produce results he gave her horse manure, wrapped her in blankets, and made her sweat up her illness until there was nothing left of her but skin and bones. Then he massaged her with brandy and gunpowder, but it was all useless; Pancha's life ebbed away in an interminable case of diarrhea that destroyed her body and left her with an insatiable thirst. Defeated, Pedro García asked the *patrón* for permission to take her into town on a cart. The two children went with them. The doctor in the nuns' hospital carefully examined Pancha and told the old man there was nothing he could do, that if he had brought her earlier and not induced the sweating, he would have been able to treat her, but now her body could hold no liquid. She was just like a plant when its roots have gone completely dry. Pedro García took offense at that, and continued to deny his failure even when he returned to the hacienda with his daughter's body wrapped in a blanket, accompanied by the two frightened children, and unloaded her in the courtyard of Tres Marías grumbling about the doctor's ignorance. They buried her in a special plot in the tiny graveyard alongside the abandoned church, at the foot of the volcano, because she had been the *patrón*'s wife, in a manner of speaking, since she had given him the only son who bore his name, though not his surname, and a grandson, the strange Esteban García, who was destined to play a terrible role in the history of the family.

One day the old man Pedro García told Blanca and

Pedro Tercero the story of the hens who joined forces to confront a fox who came into the chicken coop every night to steal eggs and eat the baby chicks. The hens decided they had had enough of the fox's abuse. They waited for him in a group, and when he entered the chicken coop they blocked his path, surrounded him, and pecked him half to death before he knew what had happened.

"And that fox escaped with his tail between his legs, with all the hens chasing after him," the old man finished.

Blanca laughed at the story and said it was impossible, because hens are born stupid and weak and foxes are born astute and strong, but Pedro Tercero did not laugh. He spent the whole evening absorbed in thought, ruminating on the story of the fox and the hens, and perhaps that was the night the boy began to become a man.

❦

FIVE

The Lovers

Blanca's childhood went by without any major surprises. The hot summers at Tres Marías, where she discovered the strength of a love that grew as she did, alternating with the routine of the city, was not unlike that of other girls of her age and class, although Clara's presence added a note of eccentricity to her life. Every morning Nana would appear with the breakfast tray to shake her from her sleep, watch as she put on her uniform, stretch her socks for her, place her hat just so, help her into her gloves, arrange her handkerchief, and make sure she had all her books, all the while mumbling prayers for the souls of the dead and loudly advising Clara not to be deceived by the nuns.

"Those women are all depraved," she warned her. "They choose the prettiest, smartest girls from the best families to be sent to the convent. They shave the heads of the novitiates, poor girls, and set them up for a lifetime of baking cakes and taking care of other people's old folks."

The chauffeur took the little girl to school, where the first activity of the day was mass and obligatory communion. Kneeling in her pew, Blanca would inhale the intense smell of the virgin's incense and lilies, suffering the combined torment of nausea, guilt, and boredom. It was the only thing she disliked about the school. She loved the high-vaulted stone corridors, the immaculate cleanliness of the marble floors, the naked white walls, and the iron Christ who stood watch in the vestibule. She was a romantic, sentimental child, with a preference for solitude, few friends, and a propensity to be moved to tears when the roses in the garden bloomed, when she smelled the rags and soap the nuns used as they bent over their tasks, and when she stayed behind to experience the melancholy stillness of the empty classrooms. She was considered timid and morose. Only in the country, her skin tanned by the sun and her belly full of ripe fruit, running through the fields with Pedro Tercero, was she smiling and happy. Her mother said that that was the real Blanca, and that the other one, the one back in the city, was a Blanca in hibernation.

Because of the constant agitation that reigned in the big house on the corner, no one, except Nana, noticed that Blanca was becoming a woman. She entered adolescence overnight. She had inherited the Truebas' Spanish and Arab blood, their regal bearing and haughty grin, and the olive skin and dark eyes of her Mediterranean genes, all colored by her mother's heritage, from which she drew a sweetness no Trueba had ever known. She was a tranquil soul who entertained herself, studied hard, played with her dolls, and showed not the slightest inclination for her mother's spiritualism or her father's fits of rage. The family jokingly said that she was the only normal person for many generations, and it was true she was a miracle of equilibrium and serenity. At around thirteen she began to develop breasts; she lost weight, her waist thinned out, and she shot up like a transplanted tree. Nana pulled her hair back in a bun and took her to buy her first corset, her first pair of silk stockings, her first grown-up dress, and a collection of miniature towels for what she continued to call "demonstration." Meanwhile, her mother continued making chairs dance through the house, playing Chopin with the lid of the piano shut, and declaiming the beautiful verses of a young poet she had taken under her wing—a poet who was beginning to be talked about everywhere—never noticing the split seams of the schoolgirl's uniform or seeing that the apple face of her daughter was subtly changing into the face of a grown woman, because Clara paid more attention to auras and fluids than she did to pounds and inches. One day she saw her walk into the sewing room in her party dress and was astonished to discover that that tall, dark lady was her little Blanca. She put her arms around her, covered her with kisses, and warned her that she would soon begin to menstruate.

"Sit down and let me tell you what it is," Clara said.

"Don't worry, Mama, I've already had it once a month for the past year," her daughter said, laughing.

The relationship between them underwent no major changes with the girl's development, because it was based on the solid principle of mutual acceptance and the ability to laugh together at almost everything.

That year summer arrived early, with a sultry heat that covered the city with its nightmare glare. The family decided to advance their departure for Tres Marías by two weeks. As always, Blanca eagerly awaited the moment of seeing Pedro Tercero again, and as she had every year, the first thing she did on climbing down from the coach was run to look for him with her eyes glued to where she knew he would be standing. She saw his hidden shadow in the doorway and jumped from the vehicle, hurtling toward him with the eagerness of all her months of anticipation, but to her surprise the boy turned on his heel and fled.

All that afternoon Blanca went to each of their special meeting spots, asking for him, shouting his name, even looking for him at the house of old Pedro García, his grandfather. Finally at sundown she went to bed defeated, without eating supper. In her huge brass bed, shocked and hurt, she buried her face in the pillow and cried inconsolably. Nana brought her a glass of milk and honey, understanding in a flash the reason for her grief.

"It's about time!" she said with a twisted smile. "You're too old to be playing with that flea-ridden brat."

Half an hour later, her mother came in to kiss her good night and found her sobbing the last gasps of a melodramatic sorrow. For a moment Clara ceased to be a distracted angel and came to stand beside a simple mortal who suffered, at fourteen, the first torments of love. She wanted to inquire, but Blanca was very proud or already too much of a woman and would tell her nothing, so Clara just stood beside her bed and caressed her till she calmed down.

That night Blanca slept fitfully and woke at dawn surrounded by the shadows of her large bedroom. She lay in bed staring up at the coffered ceiling until she heard the first rooster crow. Then she got up, opened the curtains, and let the soft morning light and the first sounds of the world enter the room. She walked over to the mirror on the wardrobe and stared at herself for a long time. She took off her nightgown and, for the first time in her life looked at her body in detail, and as she did so she realized that it was because of all these changes that her friend had run away. She smiled a new, delicate smile, the smile of a woman. She put on her old clothes from the preceding summer, which were almost too small, wrapped herself in a shawl, and tiptoed out so as not to wake the rest of the family. Outside, the fields were shaking off their sleep and the first rays of sunlight were cutting the peaks of the *cordillera* like the thrusts of a saber, warming up the earth and evaporating the dew into a fine white foam that blurred the edges of things and turned the landscape into an enchanted dream. Blanca set off in the direction of the river. Everything was still quiet. Her footsteps crushed the fallen leaves and the dry branches, producing a light crunching sound, the only noise in that vast sleeping space. She felt that the shaggy meadows, the golden wheatfields, and the far-off purple mountains disappearing in the clear morning sky were part of some ancient memory, something she had seen before exactly like this, as if she had already lived this moment in some previous life. The delicate rain of the night had soaked the earth and trees, and her clothing felt slightly damp, her shoes cold. She inhaled the perfume of the drenched earth, the rotten leaves, and the humus, which awakened an unknown pleasure in all her senses.

Blanca arrived at the river and found her childhood friend sitting at the spot where they had met so many times. That year Pedro Tercero had not grown as much as she had; he was the same thin, dark child as always, with the same protruding belly and the old man's expression in his black eyes. When he saw her he stood up, and she guessed that she was at least half a head taller than he. They looked at each other disconcertedly, feeling for the first time in their lives that they were practically strangers. For what seemed like an infinite time they stood immobile, adjusting to the changes and the new distances, but then a sparrow trilled and everything reverted to the way it had been the preceding summer. Once again, they were two children running, hugging, laughing, falling to the ground and rolling over and over, crashing against the pebbles, murmuring each other's names, elated to be back together. Finally they calmed down. Her hair was full of dry leaves, which he removed one by one.

"Come here, I want to show you something," said Pedro Tercero.

He took her by the hand. They walked along savoring that reawakening of the world, dragging their feet through the mud, picking tender green stalks to suck out their sap, looking at each other and smiling, without speaking, until they reached a distant field. The sun was just appearing over the volcano, but the day had not settled in yet and the earth was still yawning. Pedro told her to throw herself flat on the ground and be very quiet. They crawled along, coming close to some clumps of underbrush, made a short detour, and suddenly Blanca saw it. It was a beautiful bay mare in the process of giving birth alone on the hillside. The children did not move, trying to keep even their breath silent; they watched her pant and push until they saw the colt's head appear and then, after a while, the rest of its body. The little animal fell to the ground and the mother began to lick it, leaving it as clean and shiny as waxed wood, coaxing it with her muzzle to stand up. The colt tried to get up on its feet, but its fragile newborn legs folded under it and it fell down, looking helplessly up at its mother who neighed a greeting to the morning sun. Blanca felt her breast shoot with joy, and tears came to her eyes.

"When I grow up, I'm going to marry you and we're going to live here in Tres Marías," she whispered.

Pedro stared at her with his sad old man's look and shook his head. He was still much more of a child than she, but he already knew his place in the world. He also knew that he would love this girl as long as he lived, that this dawn would live in his memory, and that it would be the last thing he would see before he died.

They spent that summer oscillating between childhood, which still held them in its clasp, and their awakening as man and woman. There were times when they ran like little children, stirring up the chickens and exciting the cows, drinking their fill of fresh milk and winding up with foam mustaches, stealing fresh-baked bread straight from the oven and clambering up trees to build secret houses. At other times they hid in the forest's thickest, most secret recesses, making beds of leaves and pretending they were married, caressing each other until they fell asleep exhausted. They were still innocent enough to remove their clothes without a trace of curiosity and swim naked in the river, as they always had, diving into the cold water and letting the current pull them down against the shiny stones. But there were certain things they could no longer share. They learned to feel shame in each other's presence. They no longer competed to see who could make the biggest puddle when they urinated, and Blanca did not tell him of the dark matter that stained her underwear once a month. Without anyone telling them, they realized that they could not act so freely in front of others. When Blanca dressed up as a young lady and sat on the terrace sipping lemonade with her family each afternoon, Pedro Tercero would watch her from afar, without coming closer. They began to hide when they wanted to play. They stopped walking hand in hand within sight of the adults, and they ignored each other so as not to attract attention. Nana gave a sigh of relief, but Clara started watching them more carefully.

The vacation was over and the Truebas returned to the city laden with jars of candy, preserves, boxes of fruit, cheese, pickled chicken and rabbit, and baskets full of eggs. While everything was being packed away in the cars that would take them to the train, Blanca and Pedro Tercero hid in the granary to say their goodbyes. In those three months they had come to love each other with the ecstatic passion that would torment them for the rest of their lives. With time their love became more persistent and invulnerable, but it already had the depth and certainty that characterized it later on. Atop a pile of grain, breathing in the pungent dust of the granary in the diffuse, golden morning light that filtered through the chinks, they kissed, licked, bit, and sucked each other, sobbed and drank each other's tears, swore eternal love and drew up a secret code that would allow them to communicate during the coming months of separation.

• • •

Everyone who witnessed the moment agrees that it was almost eight o'clock at night when Férula appeared without the slightest warning. They all saw her in her starched blouse, with her ring of keys at her waist and her old maid's bun, exactly as they had always seen her in the house. She entered the dining room just as Esteban was beginning to carve the roast, and they recognized her immediately, even though it had been six years since they last saw her and she looked very pale and a great deal older. It was a Saturday and the twins, Jaime and Nicolás, had come home from school for the weekend, so they too were at the table. Their testimony is very important, because they were the only members of the family who lived completely removed from the three-legged table, protected from magic and spiritualism by their rigid English boarding school. First they felt a sudden draft in the dining room and Clara ordered the windows shut because she thought it was the wind. Then they heard the tinkling of the keys and the door burst open and Férula appeared, silent and with a distant expression on her face, at the exact same moment that Nana came in from the kitchen carrying the salad platter. Esteban Trueba stopped with the carving knife and fork suspended in midair, paralyzed with surprise, and the three children cried, "Aunt Férula!" almost in unison. Blanca managed to rise to her feet to greet her, but Clara, who was seated beside her, reached out her hand and held her back. Clara was actually the only one to realize on first glance what was going on, despite the fact that nothing in her sister-in-law's appearance in any way betrayed her state. Férula stopped three feet from the table, looked at everyone with her empty, indifferent eyes, and advanced toward Clara, who stood up but made no effort to go any closer, and only closing her eyes and breathing rapidly as if she were about to have one of her asthma attacks. Ferula approached her, put a hand on each shoulder, and kissed her on the forehead. All that could be heard in the dining room was Clara's labored breathing and the metallic clang of the keys at Férula's waist. After kissing her sister-in-law, Férula walked around her and went out the way she had come in, closing the door gently behind her. The family sat frozen in the dining room, as if they were in the middle of a nightmare. Suddenly Nana began to shake so hard that the salad spoons fell off the platter. The sound of the silver as it hit the floor made everybody jump. Clara opened her eyes. She was still having difficulty breathing, and tears were running down her cheeks and neck, staining her blouse.

"Férula is dead," she announced.

Esteban Trueba dropped the carving implements on the tablecloth and ran out of the room and into the street, calling his sister's name into the night, but there was no trace of her. Meanwhile Clara ordered one of the servants to fetch their coats, and by the time her husband returned, she was halfway into hers and holding the car keys in her hand.

"Let's go to Father Antonio," she said.

They rode in silence. Esteban was at the wheel, his heart contracted, as they searched for Father Antonio's old church in the poor quarters of the city where he hadn't been in years. The priest was sewing a button on his threadbare cassock when they arrived with the news of Férula's death.

"But that's impossible!" he exclaimed. "I was with her two days ago and she was in good spirits."

"Please, Father, take us to her house," Clara begged. "I know what I'm saying. She's dead."

At Clara's insistence, Father Antonio accompanied them. He led Esteban down one narrow street after another until they came to where Férula lived. Through all those years of solitude she had lived in one of the tenements where she used to say the rosary against the wishes of its intended beneficiaries in the days of her youth. Esteban had to park the car several blocks away, because the streets had got narrower and narrower until they were only for bicycles and people on foot. They walked deeper into the neighborhood, avoiding the puddles of dirty water that overflowed from the gutters and dodging the piles of garbage in which cats were digging like silent shadows. The tenement was a long passageway of ruined houses, all exactly the same: small, impoverished dwellings built of cement, each with a single door and two windows. They were painted in drab colors and their peeling walls, half eaten by the damp, were linked across the narrow passageway by wires hung from side to side, which by day were used for laundry but this late at night swung empty in the dark. In the center of the little alley there was a single fountain, which was the only source of water for all the families who lived there, and only two lanterns lit the way between the houses. Father Antonio greeted an old woman who was standing by the fountain waiting for her pail to fill with the pathetic output of the faucet.

"Have you seen Señorita Férula?" he asked her.

"She should be in her house, Father. I haven't seen her these past few days," the old woman replied.

Father Antonio pointed to one of the houses. It was just like all the others, sad, flayed, and dirty, but there were two pots hanging by the door in which grew a few small tufts of geraniums, the flower of the poor. The priest knocked at the door.

"Go on in!" the old woman shouted from the fountain. "The señorita never locks her door. There's nothing to steal in there anyway!"

Esteban Trueba called his sister's name, but he didn't dare go in. Clara was the first one across the threshold. It was dark inside and they were immediately met by the unmistakable aroma of lavender and lemon. Father Antonio lit a match. The weak flame cut a circle of light in the shadows, but before they could take a single step the match went out.

"Wait here," he said. "I know the house."

He groped his way, and a moment later lit a candle. His figure stood out grotesquely and his face, deformed by the light from below, floated halfway to the ceiling, while his giant shadow danced against the walls. Clara described this scene in her notebooks that bore witness to life in minute detail: the two dark rooms, their walls stained with damp, the small dirty bathroom without running water, the kitchen in which there were only a few dry crusts of bread and a jar with a little tea in it. The rest of Férula's quarters seemed to Clara to fit precisely with the nightmare that had begun when her sister-in-law appeared in the dining room of the big house on the corner to say goodbye. It reminded her of a used-clothing store or the dressing room of a struggling theater company. Hanging from a few nails on the wall were old dresses, feather boas, squalid bits of fur, imitation rhinestone necklaces, hats that had gone out of style fifty years before, stained petticoats with threadbare lace, dresses that were once flashy and whose sheen had long since disappeared, inexplicable admirals' jackets and bishops' chasubles, all thrown together in grotesque fraternity, in which the dust of years had made its nest. On the floor there was a jumble of satin shoes, débutante's handbags, belts studded with fake stones, suspenders, and even the shining sword of a military cadet. She saw dreary wigs, pots of rouge, empty flasks, and an unruly collection of impossible objects scattered everywhere.

A narrow door divided the only two rooms of the house. In the other room, Férula lay on the bed. Festooned like an Austrian queen, she wore a moth-eaten velvet dress and petticoats of yellow taffeta. On her head, firmly jammed down around her ears, shone the incredible curly wig of an opera star. No one was with her, no one had known she was dying, and they calculated that she must have been dead for many hours, because the mice were already beginning to nibble her feet and eat her fingers. She was magnificent in her queenly desolation, and on her face was an expression of sweetness and serenity she never had in her grievous life.

"She liked to wear used clothing that she bought in secondhand shops or picked from the garbage," explained Father Antonio. "She would make herself up and put on these wigs, but she never hurt a fly. On the contrary, until her last she always said the rosary for the salvation of sinners."

"Leave me alone with her," Clara said firmly.

The two men went out into the alleyway, where neighbors were beginning to gather. Clara took off her white wool coat and rolled up her sleeves. She went up to her sister-in-law, gently removed the wig, and saw that she was nearly bald: aged and helpless. She kissed her on the forehead, just as Férula had kissed her only a few hours earlier in her own dining room, and then she calmly proceeded to improvise the rites of the dead. She undressed her, washed her, meticulously soaping her without missing a single crevice, rubbed her with cologne, dusted her with powder, lovingly brushed her four remaining strands of hair, dressed her in the most eccentric and elegant rags that she could find, and put back her soprano's wig, returning to her in death the infinite attentions that Férula had given her in life. While she worked, fighting off her asthma, she told her about Blanca, who was a young lady now, about the twins, about the big house on the corner, and about the country, "and if you only knew how much we missed you, Férula, how I've needed your help to look after the family, you know I'm no good at domestic matters, the boys are terrible but Blanca is a lovely child, and the hydrangeas that you planted with your own two hands in Tres Marías turned out beautiful, some are blue because I put some copper coins in the fertilizer, it's a secret of nature, and every time I arrange them in a vase I think of you, but I also think of you when there aren't any hydrangeas, I always think of you, Férula, because the truth is that since you left me no one has ever loved me as you did."

She finished arranging her, stayed a few minutes talking to her and caressing her, and finally called in her husband and Father Antonio to make the burial arrangements. In a cookie tin they found the unopened envelopes of money Esteban had sent his sister once a month for all those years. Clara gave them to the priest for charitable works, sure that would be what Férula would have wanted.

The priest stayed with the dead woman so that the mice wouldn't treat her disrespectfully. It was almost midnight when they left. Férula's neighbors had gathered in the doorway to discuss the news of her death. Esteban and Clara had to make their way through the huddle of curious faces and shoo away the dogs that were sniffing among the crowd. Esteban walked quickly with his big strides, practically dragging Clara behind him, without noticing the dirty water that was spattering his impeccable gray trousers from the English tailor. He was furious because his sister, even now that she was dead, could still manage to make him feel guilty, just as she had when he was a boy. He recalled his childhood, when she surrounded him with dark solicitude, wrapping him in debts of gratitude so huge that as long as he lived he would never be able to pay them back. Once again he felt the sense of indignity that had frequently tormented him when he was with her. He despised her spirit of sacrifice, her severity, her vocation for poverty, and her unshakable chastity, which he felt as a reproach toward his own egotistical, sensual, power-hungry nature. Go to hell, bitch! he thought, refusing to admit even in the farthest corner of his heart that his wife had ceased belonging to him ever since he threw Férula out of his house.

"Why did she have to live like this when she had more than enough money?" Esteban shouted.

"Because she didn't have anything else," Clara answered gently.

During the months that they were separated, Blanca and Pedro Tercero exchanged burning letters, which he signed with a woman's name and which she hid as soon as they arrived. Nana managed to intercept one or two, but she did not know how to read, and even if she had she would not have been able to break their secret code—fortunately for her, because her heart would not have withstood the shock. Blanca spent the winter knitting a sweater made of Scottish wool in her sewing class at school, with the boy's measurements in mind. At night she slept with her arms around the sweater, inhaling the scent of the wool and dreaming that it was he who spent the night beside her. Pedro Tercero, meanwhile, spent his winter writing songs on the guitar that he would sing to Blanca and whittling her likeness on any scrap of wood he could lay his hands on, unable to separate his angelic memories of the girl from the storms that were raging in his blood, turning his bones to pulp, lowering his voice, and causing hair to appear on his face. He was torn between the demands of his body, which was becoming that of a man, and the sweetness of a feeling that was still tinged with the innocent games of childhood. Both young people awaited the coming of summer with aching impatience. When it finally arrived and they met once again, the sweater Blanca had knit for Pedro didn't fit over his head, because in the intervening months he had left his childhood behind and acquired the dimensions of a man, and the tender songs he had composed now sounded ridiculous to her, because she had a woman's bearing and a woman's needs.

Pedro Tercero was still thin, and still had his stiff hair and sad eyes, but his voice had acquired a hoarse, passionate timbre that would one day make him famous, when he would sing songs of revolution. He seldom spoke and was rough and awkward in his social dealings, but gentle and delicate with his hands. He had the long fingers of an artist, which he used for whittling, for pulling laments from the strings of his guitar, and for drawing, just as easily as he used them to hold the reins of a horse or to raise an axe for chopping wood or to guide a plow. He was the only one in all Tres Marías who dared to confront the *patrón*. His father, Pedro Segundo, told him a thousand times not to look Esteban in the eye, not to answer back, and not to argue with him, and in his desire to protect him he had more than once given him a sound beating to knock some sense into his head. But his son was a born rebel. At the age of ten he already knew as much as his teacher in the school of Tres Marías, and at twelve he insisted on making the trip into town to attend the high school there. Rain or shine, he would leave his small brick house at five o'clock in the morning, by horse or on foot. He read and reread a thousand times the magic books from Uncle Marcos's enchanted trunks, and cotinued to nourish himself with other volumes lent to him by the union organizers at the bar and by Father José Dulce María, who taught him how to cultivate his natural poetic gifts and to translate his ideas into songs.

"My son, the Holy Church is on the right, but Jesus Christ was always on the left," he would say enigmatically between sips of the wine he used at mass, which he served to celebrate Pedro's visits.

And so it was that one day Esteban Trueba, who was resting on the terrace after lunch, heard the boy sing about a bunch of hens who had organized to defeat a fox. He called him over.

"I want to hear that," he said. "Go on, sing!"

Pedro Tercero lovingly picked up his guitar, rested his foot on a chair, and began to strum. His eyes did not leave the *patrón*'s face while his velvet voice rose passionately above the soporific air of the siesta. Esteban Trueba was no fool and immediately understood the defiance.

"So," he said, "the stupidest things can be set to music. You'd be better off learning love songs."

"I like this, *patrón*. In union there is strength, as Father José Dulce María says. If the hens can overcome the fox, what about human beings?"

He picked up his guitar and shuffled out without giving Esteban time to think of anything to say, even though anger had reached his lips and his tension was rising. From that day on, Esteban Trueba kept his eye on him and did not trust him. He tried to prevent him from continuing his schooling, inventing all sorts of tasks for him to do, men's work, but the boy simply rose earlier and went to sleep later in order to finish the work. That was the year Esteban whipped him before his father because he brought the tenants the new ideas that were circulating among the unionists in town—ideas like Sundays off, a minimum wage, retirement and health plans, maternity leave for women, elections without coercion, and, most serious of all, a peasant organization that would confront the owners.

That summer, when Blanca went to spend her vacation at Tres Marías, she almost failed to recognize him; he had grown six inches and had left behind the potbellied little boy with whom she had spent her childhood summers. She got down from the car, smoothed her skirt, and for the first time in her life did not run to meet him, but simply nodded her head in greeting, although her eyes told him what could not be said in front of everyone—and anyway she had already told him in her unbridled letters in code. Nana watched it all from the corner of her eye and laughed mockingly. When she walked in front of Pedro Tercero, she sneered at him.

"It's time you learned to stay with your own class instead of nosing around señoritas," she said between clenched teeth.

That night Blanca ate with the rest of the family in the dining room. They were served the chicken casserole that always welcomed them to Tres Marías, and she showed no sign of her usual restlessness during the extended afterdinner conversation, while her father sipped his cognac and talked about imported cows and gold mines. She waited for her mother to signal to her that she was excused. Then she calmly stood up, wished everyone good night, and went to her room. For the first time in her life she locked it. She sat down on her bed without removing her clothes and waited in the dark until the twins' raucous shouts in the room next door and the servants' footsteps had subsided, and the doors, the locks, and the whole house had settled into sleep. Then she opened the window and jumped out, falling onto the hydrangea bushes that her Aunt Férula had planted long ago. It was a clear night, and she could hear the crickets and the frogs. She took a deep breath and the air brought her the sweet scent of peaches that were drying in the courtyard to be used in preserves. She waited for her eyes to adjust to the darkness and then began to walk, but she was unable to continue because she heard the furious barking of the guard dogs that were left unleashed at night. They were four mastiffs that had been raised tied to chains and spent the daytime locked in a cage. She had never seen them up close and she was sure they would not recognize her. For a moment she was swept by panic and about to scream, but then she remembered that old Pedro García had once told her that thieves never wear clothes so dogs will not attack them. Without a moment's hesitation she pulled off her clothes as fast as she could, threw them over her arm and continued walking calmly forward, praying that the animals wouldn't smell her fear. She saw them spring forward, barking, and continued without losing rhythm. The dogs came closer, growling with suspicion, but she did not stop. One of them, bolder than the others, came close to sniff her. She felt his warm breath against her back, but she paid no attention. They continued to bark and growl for a long while, accompanied her part of the way, and then, frustrated, went away. Blanca gave a sigh of relief and realized that she was covered with sweat and shaking. She had to lean against a tree and wait until the exhaustion that had turned her knees to jelly passed. Then she quickly put her clothes on and ran toward the river.

Pedro Tercero was waiting for her in the place where they had met the summer before and where, years earlier, Esteban Trueba had stolen Pancha García's humble virginity. When she saw him, Blanca blushed violently. During the months of separation, he had been toughened by the hard job of becoming a man, while she had been shut within the walls of her house and her convent school, preserved from the wear and tear of life and nursing her romantic fantasies while she knit with Scottish wool, but the image of her dreams had nothing to do with this tall young man who was walking toward her murmuring her name. Pedro Tercero reached out his hand and touched her neck by her ear. Blanca felt something hot run through her bones, loosening her limbs. She closed her eyes and surrendered to it. He pulled her gently toward him and wrapped his arms around her. She pressed her face against the chest of this man she did not know, so different from the scrawny boy with whom she had exchanged such passionate caresses only months before. She inhaled his new scent, rubbed herself against his bristly skin, ran her hands over his lean, strong body, and felt a full, all-encompassing sense of peace that had nothing at all to do with the state of agitation that had taken possession of him. They sought each other with their tongues, as they always did, even though it seemed like a new invention, and fell kneeling as they kissed in desperation. Then they rolled onto the soft bed of damp earth. They were discovering each other for the first time and there was no need for words. The moon crossed the whole horizon, but they did not see it; they were too busy exploring their deepest intimacy, insatiably entering each other's skins.

From that night on, Blanca and Pedro Tercero met every night in the same place, at the same time. By day she embroidered, read, or painted insipid watercolors around the house, under Nana's approving glance, now that she could finally sleep in peace. But Clara sensed that something strange was going on, because she could see a new color in her daughter's aura, and she felt sure that she knew why. Pedro Tercero performed his usual tasks in the field and continued to go into town to see his friends. By nightfall he was dead with fatigue, but the idea of seeing Blanca gave him back his strength. It was not for nothing he was fifteen years old. Thus the summer passed, and years later they would both recall those passionate nights as the happiest time of their lives.

Meanwhile, Jaime and Nicolás used their vacations to do all the things that were forbidden in their British boarding school. They shouted until they were hoarse, fought at the slightest provocation, and came to resemble two filthy little urchins with scabby knees and heads full of lice, replete with warm freshly picked fruit, sun, and freedom. They left early in the morning and came home at sundown, spending their days hunting rabbits with their slingshots, riding horseback until they were worn out, and spying on the women who were washing clothes down by the river.

•   •   •

And so three years went by, until the earthquake changed things. After that vacation, the twins returned to the city ahead of the rest of the family, accompanied by Nana, the city servants, and most of the baggage. The boys went straight to their boarding school, while Nana and the other employees readied the big house on the corner for the arrival of the owners.

Blanca stayed behind in the country with her parents for a few more days. It was then that Clara began having nightmares, walking in her sleep, and waking up screaming. During the day, she went about half in a dream, seeing premonitions in the animals' behavior: the hens were not laying their daily eggs, the cows were acting frightened, the dogs were howling to death, the rats, spiders, and worms were coming out of their hiding places, the birds were leaving their nests and flying off in great formations, while her pigeons were screaming with hunger in the treetops. She stared obsessively at the frail column of white smoke that was issuing from the volcano, and peered at the changes in the color of the sky. Blanca made her all sorts of soothing teas and warm baths, and Esteban resorted to the old box of homeopathic pills to calm her down, but her nightmares continued.

"There's going to be an earthquake!" Clara announced, daily growing paler and more agitated.

"For God's sake, Clara, there are always quakes!" Esteban replied.

"This time it's going to be different. There will be ten thousand dead."

"There aren't even that many people in the whole country," he said, laughing.

The cataclysm began at four o'clock in the morning. Clara woke a little before it, having had an apocalyptic nightmare of exploded horses, cows hurled into the sea, people crawling under stones, and gaping caverns in the earth into which whole houses were falling. She rose livid with terror and ran to Blanca's room. But, as she did every night, Blanca had locked her door and slipped out the window in the direction of the river. The last few days before returning to the city, her summer passion took on a dramatic quality, and with a new separation imminent, the two young people seized every possible opportunity to give free rein to their desires. They spent the nights at the river, immune to their weariness and the cold, thrashing with the strength of their desperation, and only as the first glimpse of dawn came through the clouds did Blanca return to the house and climb through her bedroom window, falling into bed just as the first cocks crowed. Clara arrived at her daughter's door and tried to open it, but it was bolted. She knocked, and when no one opened it she turned and ran outside the house, where she saw the window wide open and Ferula's hydrangeas trampled. In a flash she understood the color of Blanca's aura, the bags under her eyes, her listlessness, her silence, her morning sleepiness, and her afternoon watercolors. And in that instant the earthquake began.

Clara felt the ground shake and was unable to keep her footing. She fell to her knees. The tiles on the roof gave way and crashed around her with a deafening roar. She saw the adobe walls of the house crumple as if they had been chopped with an axe, and then the earth opened just as she had seen it in her dream and an enormous crevice formed before her, swallowing the chicken coops, the laundry troughs, and part of the stable. The water tank swayed from side to side and smashed to the ground, spilling a thousand gallons of water on the few surviving hens, who flapped their wings desperately. In the distance the volcano began to shoot flames and smoke like a furious dragon. The dogs broke loose from their chains and raced madly up and down; the horses that had survived the collapse of the stable stomped the air and neighed in terror before bolting off into the open fields; the poplars teetered like drunks and fell with their roots in the air, crushing the swallows' nests. Most terrible of all was the roar coming from the center of the earth, that hard-breathing giant that was heard at length, filling the air with fear. Clara tried to drag herself toward the house calling Blanca's name, but the death-rattling shudders of the earth prevented her from moving. She saw the peasants running out of their houses terrified, imploring heaven, throwing their arms around each other, pulling their children, kicking their dogs, pushing their old people, and trying to salvage their few poor belongings in that din of brick and tile flying from the very bowels of the earth, like an interminable noise of the end of the world.

Esteban Trueba appeared in the doorway at the very instant when the house snapped in half like an eggshell and collapsed in a cloud of dust, flattening him beneath a pile of rubble. Clara pulled herself to where he was, shouting his name, but there was no reply.

The first tremor of the earthquake lasted nearly a minute and was the strongest that had ever been recorded in that country of catastrophes. It leveled almost everything that stood, and whatever was left was finished off in the string of secondary tremors that continued to shake the world until the sun came up. At Tres Marías they waited till daybreak to count the dead and dig out those who had been buried alive beneath the avalanche, many of whom were still moaning, among them Esteban Trueba, whose location was known to everyone although no one expected him to be alive. It took four men under Pedro Segundo's guidance to remove the hill of dust, tile, and adobe that had fallen on top of him. Clara had lost her angelic distraction and was helping to remove the stones with the strength of a man.

"We have to get him out! He's still alive and he can hear us!" Clara assured them, and that gave them the courage to continue.

Blanca and Pedro Tercero appeared at first light, unhurt. Clara hurled herself at her daughter and slapped her on the face, but then she embraced her tearfully, relieved to know she was alive and to have her by her side.

"Your father's in there!" Clara cried, pointing.

The young people joined in, and after an hour, when the sun was already shining on that anguished landscape, they lifted the *patrón* from his tomb. He had so many broken bones that they could not be counted, but he was alive and his eyes were open.

"We have to take him into town to see a doctor," said Pedro Segundo.

They were discussing how to transport him without his bones popping through his skin like a broken bag, when old Pedro García came up; thanks to his blindness and his age, he had survived the earthquake without getting upset. He bent down beside the wounded man, feeling him with his hands, looking with his ancient fingers, until there was not an inch he had not covered or a bone he had not felt.

"If you move him, he'll die," he concluded.

Esteban Trueba was still conscious and he heard the words quite clearly. He remembered the ant plague and decided that the old man was his only hope.

"He knows what he's doing," he stammered.

Pedro García had a blanket brought and, between his son and his grandson, they laid the *patrón* on it, lifted him carefully, and raised him onto an improvised table that they had set up in what was formerly the courtyard but was now no more than a small clearing in that nightmare of debris, animal corpses, crying children, moaning dogs, and praying women. They had rescued a wineskin from among the ruins, which Pedro García divided three ways: a third to wash the injured man's body, a third for Esteban to drink, and the other third he drank parsimoniously himself before beginning to set Esteban's bones, one by one, patiently and calmly, pulling here, adjusting there, putting each one back in its proper place, splinting them, wrapping them in strips of sheet to keep them immobile, mumbling litanies to the healing saints, invoking good luck and the Virgin Mary, and putting up with the screams and blasphemies of Esteban Trueba, without ever altering his beatific blind man's expression. By touch he restored the body so perfectly that the doctors who examined Trueba afterward could not believe such a thing was possible.

"I wouldn't even have tried," said Dr. Cuevas when he heard what had happened.

The destruction from the earthquake plunged the country into a long period of mourning. It was not enough that the earth shook until everything was flung to the ground; the sea drew back for several miles and returned in a single gigantic wave that sent boats to the top of mountains far from the coast, removed whole villages, roads, and animals, and submerged a number of southern islands more than a foot below the surface. Buildings fell like wounded dinosaurs; others collapsed like a house of cards. The dead numbered in the thousands and there was not a single family that had not lost one of its own. The salt water from the sea ruined the crops, and fires razed whole regions of cities and

towns. Finally lava began to flow, and as a crowning punishment, ash fell on the villages close to the volcano. People
stopped sleeping in their houses, terrified at the thought that
such a disaster could recur, improvising tents in open spaces
or sleeping in the middle of squares and streets. Soldiers had
to take control of the chaos. They shot anyone they caught
stealing, because while the faithful crowded into the churches
begging forgiveness for their sins and beseeching God to
stay his fury, thieves were running through the ruins slicing
off ears with earrings and fingers with rings, not stopping to
ascertain whether the victims were dead or only trapped in
the cave-in. A wave of germs was unleashed, causing all
sorts of epidemics across the country. The rest of the world,
too busy with another war, barely noticed that nature had
gone berserk in that remote corner of the globe, but even so
shiploads of medicine, blankets, food, and building material
arrived, all of which disappeared in the mysterious labyrinths
of various bureaucracies and were still available for purchase
years later, when canned vegetables from the United States
and powdered milk from Europe could be bought in the
most exclusive stores at the same price as any other gourmet
food.

Esteban Trueba spent four months wrapped in bandages, stiff as a board from splints, patches, and hooks, in a
dreadful torment of itching and immobility, and consumed
by impatience. His character deteriorated to the point where
no one could stand him. Clara stayed in the country to look
after him, and when communication was restored and things
began to return to order, they sent Blanca to her convent
school as a boarder, because her mother could not be responsible for her.

In the capital, the earthquake caught Nana in her bed,
and even though it was not as strong as in the South, the
fright killed her just the same. The big house on the corner
creaked like a walnut, its walls filled with cracks, and the
huge crystal chandelier in the dining room fell to the floor
ringing like a thousand bells, breaking to smithereens. Aside
from that, the only serious effect was the death of Nana.
When the fear of the first moment had passed, the rest of the
servants realized that the old woman had not run out into
the street with the others. They went in to look for her and

found her in her cot, her eyes popped out and the little hair she had left standing on end in sheer terror. Because of the ensuing chaos, they were unable to give her a proper funeral, as she would have wished, and were forced to bury her in a hurry, without speeches or tears. None of the many children she had raised with so much love attended her funeral.

The earthquake signaled such an important change in the life of the Trueba family that from then on they divided all events into before and after that day. In Tres Marías, Pedro Segundo García once again assumed the post of foreman, since the owner was unable to get out of bed. To him fell the job of organizing the workers, restoring order, and reconstructing the wreckage of the entire property. They began by burying their dead in the graveyard at the foot of the volcano, which had miraculously escaped the wave of lava that had run down the sides of the evil mountain. The new tombs gave a festive air to the pathetic little graveyard, and they planted rows of birches so there would be shade for those who came to visit their dead. They rebuilt the little brick houses one by one, exactly as they were before, along with the stables, the dairy, and the granary. Then they prepared the earth for planting, thankful that the lava and ash had fallen on the other side, sparing the property. Pedro Tercero had to give up his excursions into town because his father needed him to help in the work. He came unwillingly, letting his father know that he was breaking his back to restore the *patrón*'s wealth while the rest of them would remain as poor as they had been before.

"That's the way it's always been, son. You can't change the law of God," his father would reply.

"Yes, you can, Papa. There are people doing it right now, but we don't even get the news here. Important things are happening in the world," Pedro Tercero countered, following up with the speech of the Communist teacher or Father José Dulce María.

Pedro Segundo did not reply and continued working without pause. He looked the other way when his son, taking advantage of the *patrón*'s injury, broke the grip of censorship and introduced into Tres Marías the forbidden pamphlets of the unionists, the teacher's political newspapers, and the strange biblical interpretations of the Spanish priest.

On orders from Esteban Trueba, his foreman began to reconstruct the main house exactly as it had been before. The old men did not even change the adobe walls for modern bricks, or modify the narrow windows. The only improvement was the addition of hot water in the bathrooms and the replacement of the old wood stove by a kerosene device, to which, however, no cook ever managed to adjust and which ended up in the middle of the courtyard as a plaything for the hens. While the house was being built, they erected a shelter of wooden planks with a zinc roof, where they settled Esteban in his sickbed. From there, through a window, he could watch the work progressing and shout his instructions, boiling with rage at his protracted immobility.

Clara changed enormously during those months. She had to work closely with Pedro Segundo García at the task of saving what they could. For the first time in her life she took charge of material things, without any help, for she could no longer rely on her husband, on Férula, or on Nana. She awoke from a long childhood in which she had always been protected and surrounded by attention and comforts, with no responsibilities. Esteban Trueba became convinced that everything he ate disagreed with him, except what she prepared for him herself, so she spent a good part of the day standing in the kitchen plucking chickens to make invalid soup and kneading bread. She had to be his nurse, washing him with a sponge, changing his bandages, removing his bedpans. Every day, he grew more irate and despotic, ordering her put my pillow here, no, higher up, bring me wine, no, I said white wine, open the window, close it, this hurts, I'm hungry, I'm hot, scratch my shoulder, lower. Clara came to fear him far more than she had when he was a healthy, strong man who disrupted her peaceful life with his scent of the eager male, his hurricane voice, his relentless warfare, and his pompous airs, imposing his will and shattering his whims against the delicate balance she tried to keep between the spirits of the Hereafter and the needy souls of the Here-and-Now. She came to despise him. As soon as his bones knit and he could be moved a little, Esteban felt the torturous desire to embrace her. Every time she stood beside him, he grabbed at her, confusing her, in his invalid's disturbed state of mind, with the robust peasant women who in his early days had served him in both kitchen and bed. Clara felt that she was too old for that sort of thing. Misfortune had spiritualized her, and age and her lack of love for her husband had led her to think of sex as a rather crude form of amusement that made her joints ache and knocked the furniture around. Within a few hours, the earthquake had brought her face to face with violence, death, and vulgarity and had put her in touch with the basic needs to which she had been oblivious. Her three-legged table and her capacity to read tea leaves were useless in protecting the tenants from epidemics and disorder, the earth from drought and snails, the cows from foot-and-mouth disease, the chickens from distemper, the clothing from moths, her children from abandonment, and her husband from death and his own rage. Clara was tired. She felt alone and confused, and when it came to time to make decisions, the only person she could turn to was Pedro Segundo García. That loyal, silent man was always there, within reach of her voice, providing a certain stability in the midst of the catastrophe that had shaken her life. At the end of the afternoon, Clara would often look for him to give him a cup of tea. They sat beneath the eaves in wicker chairs, waiting for night to come and relieve the tension of the day. They watched the darkness fall softly and the first stars begin to twinkle in the sky, listened to the croaking of the frogs, and kept their silence. They had much to say to each other, many problems to resolve, many agreements pending, but they both understood that that half hour spent in silence was a well-deserved reward. They sipped their tea slowly, to make it last, and each thought of the other's life. They had known each other for more than fifteen years, and had spent their summers in proximity, but in all that time they had exchanged only a handful of sentences. He had seen her as a luminous summer apparition, removed from the brutal demands of the world, different from all other women he had known. Even then, with her hands sunk in the dough or her apron bloody from the chicken to be served at lunch, she struck him as a sort of ghost in the reverberation of the day. Only at dusk, in the calm of those moments shared over a cup of tea, could he see her human side. He had secretly sworn her his loyalty and, like an adolescent, there were times when he fantasized about giving his life for her. He valued her as much as he detested Esteban Trueba.

When the men came to install a telephone, the house still had a long way to go before it could be lived in. Esteban Trueba had been fighting to get one for four years, and they delivered it just when he did not even have a roof to protect it from inclement weather. The apparatus did not last very long, but it was useful for calling the twins and listening to them talk as if they were in another galaxy, amid the deafening roar and the interruptions of the operator in town, who participated in their conversations. By telephone they learned that Blanca was ill and that the nuns did not want to be responsible for her. She had a persistent cough and frequent attacks of fever. The dread of tuberculosis was in every home then, because there was not a family that had not lost one of its members to consumption, so Clara decided to go and fetch her. The same day Clara was leaving, Esteban Trueba smashed the phone to bits with his cane because it was ringing and though he shouted that he was coming, that it should be still, the machine continued ringing, and in a fit of rage he fell on top of it, showering it with blows and in the process breaking the clavicle that old Pedro García had taken so much trouble to restore.

It was the first time Clara had ever traveled by herself. She had made the same trip year after year, but always inattentively because there was someone else to worry about the mundane details while she dreamily watched the landscape out the window. Pedro Segundo García took her to the station and helped her to her seat. When she said goodbye, she leaned over, kissed him gently on the cheek, and smiled. He pressed his hand to his face to protect that fleeting kiss and he did not smile, because he was filled with sadness.

Guided more by her intuition than by her knowledge of things or by logic, Clara managed to reach her daughter's school without mishap. The Mother Superior received her in her Spartan office, where there was an immense, bloody Christ on the wall and an incongruous spray of red roses on the table.

"We've sent for the doctor, Señora Trueba," she said.

"There's nothing wrong with the child's lungs, but nevertheless you'd better take her. The country air will do her good. We simply can't assume responsibility for her. I'm sure you understand."

The nun rang a little bell and Blanca appeared in the doorway. She looked thinner and paler, with violet rings around her eyes that would have been enough to startle any mother, but Clara quickly understood that her daughter's illness was not in her body, but in her soul. The hideous gray uniform made her look much younger than she really was, despite the fact that her womanly curves showed through the design. Blanca was surprised to see her mother, whom she remembered as a lighthearted, absent-minded angel dressed in white, transformed into an efficient woman with callused hands and two deep lines at the corners of her mouth.

They went to see the twins at school. It was the first time they had all been together since the earthquake, and they were surprised to find that the only part of the country unscathed by the disaster was that ancient institution, where the event had been ignored completely. The country's ten thousand dead had gone unmourned and uneulogized while the boys went on singing English songs and playing cricket, moved only by reports that reached them, three weeks late, from the British Isles. The women were astonished to discover that these two boys whose veins flowed with Moorish and Spanish blood, and who were born in the farthest depths of the Americas, now spoke Spanish with an Oxford accent, and that the only emotion they were capable of expressing was surprise, raising their left eyebrows. They had nothing in common with the two energetic, lice-infested boys who spent their summers in the country. "I hope all that Anglo-Saxon phlegm doesn't turn you into morons," Clara said as she bade her sons goodbye.

The death of Nana, who despite her age was in charge of the big house on the corner when the owners were away, sent the remaining servants into disarray. Without her vigilance, they neglected their duties and began to spend their time in an orgy of siestas and gossip, while the plants went dry for lack of watering and spiders filled the dusty corners of the house. The deterioration was so obvious that Clara decided to shut the house and dismiss everyone. Then she and Blanca set about the task of covering all the furniture in sheets and blanketing the house with mothballs. One by one they opened the bird cages, and the sky filled with parakeets, canaries, lovebirds, and finches, which flew around in circles, blinded by their sudden freedom, and finally took off in every direction. Blanca noticed that in the course of all these chores not a single ghost appeared from behind the curtains, not a single Rosicrucian arrived on a tip from his sixth sense, nor did any starving poet come running in summoned by necessity. Her mother seemed to have become an ordinary down-to-earth woman.

"You've changed, Mama," Blanca said.

"It's not me who's changed," her mother replied. "It's the world."

Before they left, they went to Nana's room in the servants' quarters. Clara opened her drawers, removed the cardboard suitcase that the good woman had used for fifty years, and went through her wardrobe. There was just a handful of clothing, a few old sandals, and boxes of every shape and size tied with bits of ribbon or elastic, in which she kept engraved announcements of First Communions and baptisms, locks of hair, fingernails, discolored photographs, and a few pairs of well-worn baby shoes. They were her souvenirs of all the del Valle and Trueba children she had cradled in her arms. Under the bed they found a bundle that contained the costumes Nana had used to frighten Clara in her years of silence. Seated on the cot with these treasures in her lap, Clara wept for a long time for this woman who had devoted her entire life to making that of others more agreeable, and who had died alone.

"After trying so hard to frighten me to death, she's the one who died of fright," Clara observed.

They had the body transferred to the del Valle family tomb, in the Catholic cemetery, because they knew she would not have liked being buried among Protestants and Jews and that in death she would have wanted to remain side by side with those she had served in life. They placed a spray of flowers by her grave and left for the station, where they would catch the train back to Tres Marías.

During the train ride, Clara brought her daughter up to date on the state of the family and her father's health, expecting that Blanca would ask the one question she knew she wanted to ask, but Blanca did not mention Pedro Tercero García, and Clara was not bold enough to do so herself. She believed that by giving problems a name they tended to manifest themselves, and then it was impossible to ignore them; whereas if they remained in the limbo of unspoken words, they could disappear by themselves, with the passage of time. Pedro Segundo was waiting for them at the station with the car, and Blanca was surprised to hear him whistling all the way to Tres Marías, because he had such a taciturn reputation.

They found Esteban Trueba sitting in a chair upholstered with blue felt, to which a set of bicycle wheels had been attached while he waited for the arrival of the wheelchair that they had ordered from the city and that Clara had brought with her luggage. He was running the house with energetic stabs of his cane and his usual panoply of insults, and was so absorbed in his duties that when they arrived he greeted them with an indifferent kiss and forgot to ask after his daughter's health.

That night they dined at a rustic table made of planks, their meal lit by a kerosene lamp. Blanca saw her mother serve the food on plates of handcrafted clay, such as was used for making bricks, since all the dishes had perished in the quake. Without Nana to run the kitchen, things had been simplified to the point of frugality; their meal consisted of lentil soup, bread, cheese, and quince jelly, which was less than Blanca ate at school on meatless Fridays. Esteban said that as soon as he could stand on his two feet he would go in person to the city to buy better, more refined furnishings for the new house; he was sick and tired of living like a peasant just because of the wild hysterical character of this godforsaken country of theirs. All Blanca remembered of the conversation was that he had fired Pedro Tercero García with the warning that he not set foot on the property again, because he had caught him spreading Communist ideas among the tenants. The girl went pale when she heard this, spilling the contents of her spoon on the tablecloth. Clara was the only one to notice the change in her expression, since Esteban was absorbed in his usual monologue about the ingrates who bite the hand that feeds them, "all because of those goddam politicians like that new Socialist candidate, a real nincompoop who has the nerve to ride up and down the country in his shabby little train, stirring the people up with his Bolshevik ideas, he'd better keep away from here if he knows what's good for him because we'll make mincemeat of him, we're ready and waiting, there's not an owner for miles around who doesn't feel the same way I do, we're not letting anyone in here to start preaching against honest work, the reward for work well done, the reward for those who meet life head-on, you can't expect the weak to have the same as those of us who've worked from sunup to sundown and know how to invest our money, run risks, and take on responsibilities, because when you get right down to it the land belongs to those who work it, which is going to boomerang on them because the only one who knows how to work around here is me, without me this place would have been a wreck and stayed one, not even Jesus Christ said we have to share the fruits of our labor with the lazy, and that little shit Pedro Tercero dares to say that on my land, the only reason I didn't shoot him through the eyes is because I respect his father and because you could say I owe my life to his grandfather, but I warned him that if I caught him prowling around here I'd blow his brains out."

Clara took no part in the conversation. She was too busy putting things on the table and taking them away, and keeping an eye on her daughter, but as she removed the soup bowl with the leftover lentils she caught the final words of her husband's harangue.

"You can't keep the world from changing, Esteban," she said. "If it's not Pedro Tercero García, someone else will bring new ideas to Tres Marías."

Esteban Trueba brought his cane down on the soup tureen his wife had in her hands and knocked it to the floor, splattering its contents. Blanca jumped to her feet in horror. It was the first time she had seen her father's temper turned against her mother. She expected Clara to enter one of her moonstruck trances and exit through the window, but nothing of the sort took place. Clara picked up the broken pieces of tureen with her usual aplomb, not showing any sign that she was listening to the stream of curses issuing from Esteban's lips. She waited for him to finish, wished him good night with a gentle kiss on the cheek, and left the room, taking Blanca by the hand.

Blanca did not let Pedro Tercero's absence disturb her. She went to the river every day and waited. She knew that sooner or later word of her return to Tres Marías would reach the boy and that the call of love would overtake him no matter where he was. And so it happened. On the fifth day she saw a tramp in a winter poncho and a broad-brimmed hat coming toward her, pulling a burro weighed down with kitchen utensils, pewter pots, copper teapots, huge enameled casseroles, and ladles of all shapes and sizes, with a jangle of tin cans that heralded his arrival ten minutes in advance. She did not recognize him. He looked like an impoverished old man, one of those sad wandering souls who travel the provinces hawking their wares from door to door. He stopped in front of her and took off his hat, and then she saw the beautiful black eyes shining between a disheveled head of hair and a rough beard. The burro continued nibbling grass with its burden of noisy pots and pans, while Blanca and Pedro Tercero slaked the accumulated hunger and thirst of the long months of silence and separation, rolling among the rocks and brush and moaning passionately. Afterward they sat embracing among the rushes on the riverbank. Amid the buzz of the dragonflies and the croaking of the frogs, she told him how she had put banana peels and blotting paper in her shoes so she would develop a fever and had drunk ground chalk until she got a genuine cough, to convince the nuns that her lack of appetite and her pallor were the unmistakable symptoms of tuberculosis.

"I wanted to be with you!" she said, kissing him on the neck.

Pedro Tercero talked to her about what was going on in the rest of the world and in the country, about the distant war that had sent half of humanity into a hail of shrapnel, and an agony of concentration camps, and produced a flood of widows and orphans. He spoke of the workers of Europe and the United States, whose rights were respected because the slaughter of organizers and Socialists of the preceding decades had led to laws that were more just and republics that were governed properly, where the rulers did not steal powdered milk sent from abroad to the victims of disasters.

"The peasants are always the last to understand. We don't know what's going on in other parts of the world," he said. "They hate your father here. But they're so afraid of him that they can't organize. You understand, Blanca?"

She understood, but right then she was interested in inhaling his scent of fresh grain, kissing his ears, running her fingers through his thick beard, and listening to his enamored moans. She was also afraid for him. She knew that not only would her father shoot the promised bullet into his head, but that any of the owners in the region would gladly do the same. Blanca reminded Pedro Tercero of the story of the Socialist leader who a few years earlier had bicycled across the province, distributing pamphlets on the haciendas and organizing the tenants until the Sánchez brothers caught him, beat him to death, and hanged him from a telephone pole at the intersection of two roads, where everyone could see him. There he had hung for a day and a half, swinging against the sky, until the mounted police arrived and cut him down. To cover up the affair, they accused the Indians on the reservation, even though everybody knew that they were peaceful and that anyone afraid to kill a chicken would hardly kill a man. But the Sánchez brothers dug him up from the cemetery and hauled the body out into full view, and then it was too much to attribute to the Indians. Still, despite the evidence, the law would not intervene, and the death of the Socialist was quickly forgotten.

"They could kill you," Blanca pleaded, embracing him.

"I'm careful," Pedro Tercero assured her. "I don't stay too long in the same place. That's why I won't be able to see you every day. Wait for me right here. I'll come whenever I can."

"I love you," she told him, weeping.

"I love you, too."

They hugged with the insatiable passion of their youth, while the burro went on chewing grass.

Blanca managed not to be sent back to school by making herself nauseated with hot brine, giving herself diarrhea from eating green plums, and bringing herself to the point of exhaustion by tightly fastening a horse's girth around her waist, until she had acquired a reputation of sickliness, which was precisely what she wanted. She had learned to imitate the symptoms of various illnesses so well that she could have fooled a whole committee of physicians. She even convinced herself that she had a most delicate constitution. Every morning, as soon as she woke up, she ran her mind over her body, to see where she hurt and what new afflictions she had developed. She learned to take advantage of the slightest excuse for feeling ill, from a change in temperature to a shift in the pollen count, and to transform the least ache or pain into a full-blown agony. In Clara's view, the best thing for one's health was to keep one's hands busy, so she kept her daughter's illnesses in line by making her work. The girl had to awaken early like everybody else, take a cold bath, and do her chores, which included teaching in the schoolhouse, sewing in the workshop, and seeing to all the work of the infirmary, from giving enemas to suturing wounds with a needle and thread from the sewing basket, with no reprieve when she fainted at the sight of blood or broke out in a cold sweat when she had to wipe up someone's vomit. Old Pedro García, who was nearly ninety and could barely drag his bones from one place to another, shared Clara's notion that hands were meant to be used. This is why one day, when Blanca was complaining of a terrible migraine, he called her and without warning dropped a ball of clay into her lap. He spent that afternoon teaching her how to shape the clay into pieces of kitchen crockery, and the girl forgot all about her pains. The old man could not know that he was giving Blanca something that would later be her only means of survival, as well as her sole comfort in the sad hours to come. He taught her how to move the wheel with her foot while her hands flew across the moistened clay to make vases and jugs. But Blanca soon discovered that she was bored making utilitarian objects, and that it was far more amusing to make statues of animals and people. In time she created a whole miniature world of household animals and people engaged in every trade: carpenters, laundresses, cooks, each with his or her own tiny tools and furniture.

"This isn't good for anything!" Esteban Trueba said when he saw his daughter's output.

"Let's find a use for it," Clara suggested.

Thus was born the idea of the crèches. Blanca began to

create tiny figures for the family's Christmas manger, not only the Three Kings and the shepherds, but a whole crowd of every kind of people and every type of animal—African camels and zebras, American iguanas and Asian tigers—without worrying about the exact fauna of Bethlehem. Afterward she added imaginary animals, gluing half an elephant to half a crocodile, without realizing that she was doing in clay what her Aunt Rosa, whom she never knew, had done with thread on her enormous tablecloth. Clara decided that if craziness can repeat itself in a family, then there must be a genetic memory that prevents it from being swallowed by oblivion. Blanca's multitudinous crèches became a tourist attraction. She had to train two girls to help her, because she was unable to keep up with the orders. That year everybody wanted one of her crèches, especially since she did not charge for them. Esteban Trueba concluded that her mania for clay was fine as a form of amusement for a proper young lady, but that if it became a business, the name of Trueba would be brought down to the level of those merchants who sold nails in the hardware stores and fried fish in the market.

Blanca's meetings with Pedro Tercero became infrequent, but for that very reason they were all the more intense. During those years, she grew accustomed to sudden starts and protracted waits. She resigned herself to the idea that they would always have to make love on the sly and she stopped nursing the dream of getting married and living in one of her father's small brick houses. Often whole weeks went by without her having any news of him, but then suddenly a mailman on a bicycle would appear at the hacienda, or a Protestant preacher with a Bible tucked under his arm, or a gypsy speaking some half-pagan tongue, all of them so inoffensive that they entered the grounds without arousing the suspicion of the ever-watchful eye of the owner. She recognized Pedro Tercero by his pitch-black eyes. Nor was she the only one; the tenants at Tres Marías and many peasants from haciendas across the region also waited for him. Ever since the young man had been chased away by the owner, he had become a hero. Everyone wanted the honor of hiding him for the night; the women wove him ponchos and winter socks and the men saved him their best brandy and the best dried beef of the season. His father, Pedro

Segundo García, suspected that his son was breaking Trueba's prohibition, and could well imagine the tracks he left behind. He was torn between his love for his son and his role as guardian of the hacienda. He was also afraid he might recognize him and that Esteban Trueba would read it on his face, but he secretly rejoiced at the thought that his son was behind some of the unusual things that were taking place throughout the countryside. The only thing that never crossed his mind was that his son's visits might have something to do with Blanca Trueba's outings by the river, because that possibility was simply not within the natural scheme of things. He never spoke of his son except within the privacy of his own family, but he was proud of him and preferred to see him as a fugitive than as one more of the peasants, planting potatoes and harvesting poverty like everybody else. When he heard other people humming the song about the hens and fox, he would smile at the thought that his son had made more converts with his subversive ballads than with the Socialist Party pamphlets he so tirelessly distributed.

SIX

Revenge

A year and a half after the earthquake, Tres Marías was once again the model estate it had been before. The main house was the equal of the old one, but it was sturdier and had hot water in the bathrooms. The water was like light chocolate, and sometimes there were even tadpoles in it, but it poured out in a strong, cheerful gush—the German pump was a wonder. I went everywhere with only a thick silver cane for support, the same one I use today. My granddaughter says I don't need it. She says I only use it to emphasize my words. My long illness damaged my body and worsened my disposition. I admit that by the end even Clara couldn't stop my tantrums. Anyone else would have been left an invalid by that accident, but desperation gave me strength. I would think of my mother sitting in her wheelchair and rotting alive, and that gave me the tenacity to stand up and start walking, even if it was with the aid of curses. I think people were afraid of me. Even Clara, who had never dreaded my temper, partly because I was careful not to turn it against her, walked around half terrified. And seeing her that way made me frantic.

Slowly but surely Clara changed. She looked tired, and I could see that she was pulling away from me. She had no compassion for my suffering, and I realized that she was avoiding me. I would even venture to say that at the time she felt more comfortable milking the cows with Pedro Segundo than keeping me company in the sitting room. The more distant Clara became, the more I needed her love. The desire I had for her when we married had not diminished; I wanted to possess her absolutely, down to her last thought, but that diaphanous woman would float by me like a breath of air, and even if I held her down with my hands and embraced her with all my strength, I could never make her mine. Her spirit wasn't with me. When she was afraid of me, our life became a torment. During the day, we went about our business. We both had a lot to do. We met only at mealtimes, and I was the one who wound up doing all the talking, because she was always in the clouds. She spoke very little, and had lost that fresh, brazen laughter that was the first thing I had liked about her. She no longer threw her head back and laughed with all her teeth showing. She barely even smiled. I thought that my age and the accident were driving us apart and that she was bored with married life, something that happens to all couples; then, too, I was never a gentle lover, the type that brings flowers home and says a lot of sweet words. But I did what I could to get close to her. God knows I tried! I would come into her room when she was busy writing in her notebooks or working with her three-legged table. I tried to share those aspects of her life, but she didn't like anyone to read her notebooks that bore witness to life, and my presence interfered with her concentration when she was talking with her spirits, so I had to stop. I also gave up the idea of establishing a good relationship with Blanca. Ever since she was a child, my daughter had been rather strange; she was never the loving, gentle girl I would have liked to have. As a matter of fact, she was more like an armadillo. From the very beginning she was surly with me, and she didn't have to worry about getting over any Electra complex, because she never had one. But now she was a young lady; she was intelligent and mature for her age, very close to her mother. I thought she might be able to help me, and I attempted to enlist her as an ally, buying her presents and trying to joke with her, but she eluded me, too. Now that I'm very old and can talk about it without losing my head, I think her love for Pedro Tercero García was to blame. Blanca could not be blackmailed. She never asked for anything. She spoke even less than her mother, and if I ever forced her to kiss me she did it so reluctantly that it hurt me like a slap across the face. "Everything will change when we return to the city and start living like civilized people again," I would tell myself back then, but neither Clara nor Blanca showed the slightest interest in leaving Tres Marías; on the contrary, every time I raised the matter, Blanca said that country life had restored her health but that she still didn't feel strong enough, and Clara reminded me that there was still a lot to do on the hacienda, that things weren't at a point where we could leave them. My wife didn't miss the refinements she had been accustomed to, and the day the shipment of furniture and household goods I had ordered to surprise her arrived at the door, all she said was how "lovely" it was. I myself had to figure out where everything should go; she didn't seem to care at all. The new house was decked out with a luxury unrivaled even in those magnificent days before the place was passed down to my father, who left it a ruin. Huge colonial pieces made of blond oak and walnut arrived, along with heavy wool carpets, and lamps of hammered iron and copper. I ordered a set of hand-painted English china worthy of an embassy, a full set of glassware, four chests stuffed with decorations, linen sheets and tablecloths, and a whole collection of classical and popular records with their own modern Victrola. Any other woman would have been delighted with all this and would have had her work cut out for her for months to come, but not Clara, who was impervious to these things. All she managed to do was train a couple of cooks and the daughters of two of our tenants to help around the house, and as soon as she was free of brooms and saucepans she returned to her notebooks and her tarot cards. She spent most of her day busy with the sewing workshop, the infirmary, and the schoolhouse. I left her alone, because those chores made her whole existence worthwhile. She was a charitable and generous woman, eager to make those around her happy—everyone except me. After the house collapsed we rebuilt the grocery store, and just to please her I stopped using the slips of pink paper and began to pay my tenants with real money; Clara said that way they could also shop in town and put a little aside if they wanted. But that wasn't true. All it was good for was for the men to go get themselves dead drunk in the bar at San Lucas and for the women and children to go hungry.

We had a lot of fights about that sort of thing. The tenants were the cause of all our fights. Well, not all. We also talked about the war. I used to follow the progress of the Nazi troops on a map I had hung on the drawing-room wall, while Clara knitted socks for the Allied soldiers. Blanca would hold her head in her hands, not understanding how we could get so excited about a war that had nothing to do with us and that was taking place across the ocean. I suppose we also had misunderstandings for other reasons. Actually, we hardly ever agreed on anything. I don't think my bad disposition was to blame for all of it, because I was a good husband, nothing like the hothead I had been when I was a bachelor. She was the only woman for me. She still is.

One day, Clara had a bolt installed on her bedroom door and after that she never let me in her bed again, except when I forced myself on her and when to have said no would have meant the end of our marriage. At first I thought that she had one of those strange ailments women get from time to time, or else her menopause, but when it persisted for several weeks I decided we'd better have a talk. She calmly explained that our marriage had deteriorated and that she had lost her natural inclination for the pleasures of the flesh. She had concluded that if we had nothing to say to each other, we would also be unable to share a bed, and she seemed surprised that I could spend all day being furious at her and then wish to spend the night making love. I tried to make her see that in this respect men and women are very different, and that despite all my bad habits I still adored her, but it was no use. At the time, I was in better shape than she was even with my accident and though she was much younger. I had lost weight as I got older and I didn't have an ounce of fat on me. I was as strong and as healthy as I'd been as a young man. I could spend the whole day horseback riding, sleep anywhere, and eat anything I felt like without having to worry about my bladder, my liver, or any of the other organs people talk about incessantly. I'll admit, my bones ached. On chilly evenings or humid nights, the pain in the bones that had been crushed in the earthquake became so unbearable that I would have to bite my pillow to keep people from hearing my screams. When I couldn't take another minute, I knocked back a big swig of brandy and two aspirins, but it didn't help. The funny part of it is that although my sexuality had got more selective over time, I was almost as easily aroused as in my youth. I liked looking at women; I still do. It's an aesthetic pleasure, almost spiritual. But only Clara awakened any real desire in me, because through all the years of life together we had learned to know each other, and we each had the exact geography of the other at our fingertips. She knew exactly where my most sensitive places were, and she could tell me exactly what I wanted to hear. At an age when most men are bored with their wives and need the stimulation of other women, I was convinced that only with Clara could I make love the way I had on my honeymoon: tirelessly. I wasn't tempted to look for anyone else.

I remember starting to hound her as soon as the sun went down. In the evenings she would sit and write and I'd pretend to be sucking on my pipe, but actually I was looking at her from the corner of my eye. As soon as she began getting ready to go to bed—she would clean her pen and shut her notebooks—I'd begin. I limped out to the bathroom, spruced myself up, and put on the plush ecclesiastic dressing gown I had bought to seduce her in, but she never seemed to notice. Then I pressed my ear to the door and waited. When I heard her coming down the hall, I jumped out ahead of her. I tried everything from showering her with praise and gifts to threatening to knock down her door and beat her to a pulp, but none of these effects was enough to bridge the gap between us. I suppose it was useless for me to expect her to forget my sour temper of the daytime with all sorts of amorous attentions in the evening. Clara eluded me with that distracted attitude of hers I came to despise. I can't understand what it was about her that attracted me so much. She was a middle-aged woman, without a trace of flirtatiousness, who walked with a slight shuffle and had lost the unwarranted gaiety that had made her so appealing in her youth. Clara was neither affectionate nor seductive with me. I'm convinced she didn't love me. There was no reason for me to desire her so outrageously and to let myself get so carried away by her refusal. But I couldn't help it. Her slightest gesture, her faint scent of fresh laundry and soap, the light in her eyes and the grace of her delicate neck crowned with untamable curls—I loved everything about her. Her fragility made me feel the most unbearable tenderness toward her. I wanted to protect her, to clasp her in my arms, to make her laugh like in the old days; I wanted to sleep with her beside me, her head on my shoulder, her legs tucked under mine, so small and warm, so vulnerable and precious, with her hand on my chest. At times I would decide I was going to punish her by feigning indifference, but after a few days I gave up because she seemed more relaxed when I ignored her. I drilled a hole in the bathroom wall so I could watch her naked, but it got me so excited I decided to plaster it over. To hurt her feelings, I pretended I was going to the Red Lantern, but all she said was that it was a lot better than raping peasant girls, which surprised me, because I didn't think she knew about that. As a result of her comments, I tried rape again, just to see if it would get a rise out of her, but time and the earthquake had taken their toll on my virility. I no longer had the strength to grab a sturdy peasant girl by the waist and swing her up onto my saddle, much less rip her clothes off and enter her against her will. I was of an age when you need help and tenderness if you're going to make love. I was old, damn it.

He was the only one to notice that he was shrinking. He could tell from his clothes. It was not just that things fit loosely; his sleeves and his pant legs were suddenly too long. He asked Blanca to fix his clothing on her sewing machine, on the pretext that he had lost some weight, but he wondered whether old Pedro García had set his bones backward and whether that's why he was shrinking. But he did not tell a soul, just as he never talked about his pain, because it was a matter of pride.

The country was getting ready for the Presidential elections. At a dinner of conservative politicians in town, Esteban Trueba made the acquaintance of Count Jean de Satigny. He wore kidskin shoes and jackets of raw linen, did not perspire the way other mortals did, smelled of English cologne, and was always perfectly tanned from his habit of knocking a ball through a little hoop with a stick in the midday sun; when he spoke, he drew out the final syllables of words and swallowed his r's. He was the only man Esteban had ever met who polished his fingernails and put blue eyewash in his eyes. He had calling cards with his family crest on them and respected all the known rules of urbanity as well as some of his own invention, such as eating artichokes with tongs, which provoked general stupefaction. Men made fun of him behind his back, but it was soon clear that they were imitating his elegance, his kidskin shoes, his indifference, and his civilized manner. The title of count put him on a different footing from the other immigrants who had arrived from Central Europe fleeing the plagues of the preceding century, from Spain escaping the war, from the Middle East with their Turkish bazaars, and from Armenia with their typical food and their trinkets. The Count de Satigny did not have to work for a living, as he let everyone know. His chinchilla business was just a hobby.

Esteban Trueba had seen chinchillas prowling on his land. He had shot at them to keep them from devouring his crops, but it had never occurred to him that those insignificant rodents could be turned into ladies' coats. Jean de Satigny was looking for a partner to put up the capital, the work, and the stock houses; someone who would run all the risks and divide the profits fifty-fifty. Esteban Trueba was no adventurer, but the French count had the winged grace and ingenuity to seduce him, so he spent many sleepless nights mulling over the idea of the chinchilla farm and working out the figures. Meanwhile, Monsieur de Satigny spent long periods at Tres Marías as an honored guest. He played with his little ball in the noonday sun, drank enormous quantities of unsweetened melon juice, and delicately poked around Blanca's ceramics. He even suggested that she export her work to other places, where there was a guaranteed market for indigenous crafts. Blanca tried to disabuse him of his error, explaining that neither she nor her work contained a drop of Indian blood, but the language barrier prevented him from understanding her point of view. The count was a social acquisition for the Trueba family; from the moment he arrived at the hacienda, they were showered with invitations to neighboring properties, to meetings with the local political authorities, and to all the cultural and social events in the area. People wanted to get close to the Frenchman, hoping that some of his refinement would rub off on them. Young girls sighed at the thought of meeting him and mothers longing to have him as their son-in-law fought for the honor of having the family as their guest. Men envied Esteban Trueba, who had been chosen for the chinchilla farm. Clara was the only one who was not impressed by him or carried away by his manner of peeling an orange with a knife and fork, never touching it with his fingers, and cutting the peel in the shape of a flower, or by his skill at quoting poets and philosophers in his native language. Clara had to ask his name every time she saw him and was always disconcerted to find him in his silk robe in the bathroom of her house. But Blanca enjoyed herself with him and was glad for a chance to dress up in her finest clothes, arrange her hair especially for him, and set the table with the English china and the silver candlesticks.

"At least he's civilizing us," she said.

Esteban Trueba was less impressed by the nobleman's bragging than he was by the chinchillas. He wondered why in God's name he had not thought of tanning their skins himself, instead of wasting so much time raising all those stupid chickens that died of diarrhea at the drop of a hat, and all those cows that had to chew through acres of pasture and a whole box of vitamins for one lousy quart of milk and were always covered with shit and flies. But Clara and Pedro Segundo García did not share Esteban's enthusiasm for the rodents, she for humanitarian reasons, since she thought it was horrendous to raise them just so you could skin them, and he because he had never heard of keeping rats in special houses.

One night the count went out to smoke one of his Oriental cigarettes, specially imported from Lebanon—wherever that was, as Trueba always said—and to inhale the scent of the flowers, which rose in great mouthfuls from the garden, filling every room in the house. He walked up and down the terrace, taking in the expanse of the land around the house, sighing aloud at the thought of that exuberant nature which could assemble, in the most godforsaken country on the planet, mountains and sea, valleys and sky-scraping peaks, rivers of crystalline water, and a peaceful fauna that allowed you to wander tranquilly without having to worry about poisonous snakes or starving beasts. And, completing his idea of perfection, there were no resentful Negroes or wild Indians. He was fed up with traveling through exotic countries selling shark-fin aphrodisiacs, ginseng to cure all ills, carved Eskimo statues, stuffed Amazonian piranhas, and chinchillas for ladies' coats. He was thirty-eight years old, at least that is what he admitted to, and he felt that he had finally found paradise on earth, where he could settle into some sort of easygoing business with a few ingenuous partners. He sat down on a log to smoke in the darkness. Suddenly he saw a shadow moving. For a fleeting second he thought it might be a thief, but then he discounted that, because robbers in a place like this were as unlikely as wild animals. He approached cautiously and saw that it was Blanca, who was letting her legs out the window and slipping down the wall like a cat, falling noiselessly onto the hydrangeas below. She was dressed like a man, because by now the dogs knew her and she no longer needed to go naked. Jean de Satigny observed her walk off under the eaves of the house and in the shadow of the trees; he was going to follow her, but then he thought better of it. He was frightened of the dogs, and he realized that he did not need to follow her to know where a young girl would be going who escaped through her bedroom window in the dead of night. But he was worried, because what he had just seen jeopardized the scheme he had in mind.

The next day the count asked for Blanca Trueba's hand in marriage. Esteban, who had not had a chance to get to know his daughter, mistook her placid amiability and her eagerness to set the table with the silver candlesticks for love. He was delighted that his daughter, so bored and in such bad health, should have managed to land the most sought-after bachelor in the area. What could he have seen in her? he wondered, taken aback. He told the count that he would have to discuss it with his daughter, but that he was sure there would be no objection and that, as for himself, he was overjoyed to welcome him into his family. He summoned his daughter, who was giving a geography class in the school, and locked himself in his office with her. Five minutes later the door swung open and the count saw the young girl exit with her cheeks aflame. She shot him a murderous look and turned her face away. Someone less tenacious would have packed his bags and gone to stay in the only hotel in town, but the count told Esteban that he was sure of winning the girl's love if they only gave him enough time. Esteban Trueba told him he was welcome to stay in Tres Marías for as long as he thought necessary. Blanca said nothing, but from that day on she refused to join them at the table and missed no opportunity to make the Frenchman feel unwanted. She put away her party dresses and the silver candlesticks and carefully avoided him. She told her father that if he ever mentioned marriage again, she would take the first train out of town and return to her convent as a novice.

"You'll change your mind!" Esteban Trueba roared.

"I doubt it," she replied.

The arrival of the twins at Tres Marías that year was a great relief. They brought a gust of freshness and vitality to the oppressed atmosphere of the hacienda. Neither of the two brothers appreciated the Frenchman's charms, despite his discreet attempts to win their favor. Jaime and Nicolás made fun of his fine manners, his effeminate shoes, and his foreign name, but Jean de Satigny did not seem to mind. His good humor disarmed them in the end, and they wound up spending the remainder of the summer on good terms. They even joined forces with him to lure Blanca out of her determined obstinacy.

"You're already twenty-four, sister. Do you want to end up saying rosaries for the poor?"

They tried to convince her to cut her hair and copy the dresses that were all the rage in the fashion magazines, but she had no interest in those exotic styles, which would not have had a prayer of surviving the dustbowl of the countryside.

The twins were so different they did not even look like brothers. Jaime was tall, robust, timid, and studious. Since his school required it, he had managed to develop an athletic build in gym, but he viewed sports as a dull and useless pastime. He could not understand how Jean de Satigny could spend the whole morning hitting a ball with a stick just to knock it through a metal hoop when it was so much easier to put it in with your hand. Jaime had various strange habits that became evident around that time and grew more pronounced over the course of his life. He did not like anyone to breathe too close to him, shake his hand, ask him personal questions, ask to borrow books, or write him letters. This made his dealings with people difficult, but it did not isolate him, because within five minutes of meeting him it was clear that, despite his peevish attitude, he was generous and candid and had a tremendous capacity for kindness, which he tried in vain to cover up because it embarrassed him. He was much more interested in others than he let on, and it was easy to move him. The tenants of Tres Marías called him "the little *patrón*," and he was the one they turned to whenever they needed something. Jaime would listen to them without saying a word, respond in monosyllables, and then turn his back on them, but he would not rest until he had solved their problem. He was unsociable, and his mother said that even as a child he would not let anybody touch him. From the time he was a little boy he had had outlandish habits. He would take his clothes off and give them to someone else. Affection and the expression of emotions struck him as signs of inferiority. Only with animals did he relax his exaggerated modesty; he rolled on the ground with them, ran his hands over them, fed them directly in the mouth, and slept curled up with the dogs. He would do the same with very young children, provided no one was watching; when there were other people around, he preferred to play the strong, solitary man. His twelve years of British schooling had failed to give him spleen, which was considered a gentleman's most attractive trait. He was incorrigibly sentimental. This was why he had become interested in politics and decided not to be a lawyer, as his father wished, but a doctor who would help the needy, as his mother, who knew him better, had suggested. Jaime had played with Pedro Tercero García throughout his childhood, but not until that year did he come to admire him. Blanca had to forgo two of their meetings by the river in order for the young men to meet. They talked of justice, of equality, of the peasant movement and of Socialism, while Blanca listened with impatience, wishing they would hurry up and finish their discussion so she could be alone with her lover. This friendship linked the two boys until death, without Esteban Trueba's ever finding out.

Nicolás was as pretty as a girl. He had inherited his mother's delicate, transparent skin, and was small, astute, and fleet-footed as a fox. He was blindingly intelligent, and effortlessly surpassed his brother in everything they undertook together. He had invented a game to torture him with: he would take the opposing side on any argument, and would argue so well and so persuasively that he always ended convincing Jaime that he was wrong, forcing him to admit his error.

"Are you sure I'm right?" Nicolás would finally ask his brother.

"Yes, you're right," Jaime would grudgingly admit with a rectitude that prevented him from arguing in bad faith.

"Good!" Nicolás would exclaim. "Because now I'm going to prove that you're right and I'm wrong. I'm going to give you the arguments you would have given me if you were smarter."

Jaime would lose patience and start beating up his brother but he would quickly regret it, because he was much stronger than Nicolás and his own strength made him feel guilty. At school, Nicolás used his intelligence to pester others, and whenever he found himself faced with a violent situation he would call in his brother to defend him while he egged him on from behind. Jaime got used to standing in for Nicolás, and it seemed perfectly normal to him to be punished instead of his brother, to do his homework and cover up his lies. Apart from girls, Nicolás's primary interest in that period of his life was to cultivate Clara's capacity for predicting the future. He bought books about secret societies, about horoscopes, and anything that had to do with the supernatural. That year he also took to exposing miracles. He bought a popular edition of *The Lives of the Saints* and spent the summer looking for ordinary explanations of the most extraordinary spiritual feats. His mother made fun of him.

"If you can't understand how the telephone works," she would say, "how do you expect to understand miracles?"

Nicolás's interest in supernatural things had begun a few years earlier. On the weekends when he was allowed to leave his boarding school, he would visit the three Mora sisters in their old mill to study various occult sciences. But it soon became abundantly clear that he had not the slightest talent for clairvoyance or telekinesis, and he was forced to be content with the mechanics of astrological charts, tarot cards, and the *I Ching*. And since one thing always leads to another, at the house of the Mora sisters he met a beautiful young woman named Amanda, somewhat older than himself, who initiated him into yogic meditation and acupuncture, sciences that Nicolás later used to treat rheumatism and other minor pains, which was more than his brother would be able to do with traditional medicine after seven years of school. But that was all much later. That summer he was twenty-one and he was bored in the country. His brother kept close watch to prevent him from giving the girls a hard time, for Jaime had proclaimed himself the protector of the maidenly virtues of Tres Marías; despite this, Nicolás managed to seduce almost all the adolescent girls around, using acts of gallantry never seen before in those parts. The rest of his time Nicholás spent investigating miracles, trying to learn the tricks his mother used to move saltcellars with her mind, and writing passionate stanzas to Amanda, who sent them back by return mail, corrected and improved, without deterring her admirer in the least.

Old Pedro García died a few days before the Presidential elections. The nation was convulsed by the campaign; special trains crossed the country from north to south, the candidates appearing at the rear with their retinue of proselytes, greeting everyone exactly the same way, promising exactly the same things, festooned with banners and roaring with a choral society and loudspeakers that shattered the tranquil landscape and stunned the cattle. The old man had lived so long that he was nothing more than a pile of glass bones covered by a yellow skin. His face was a latticework of wrinkles. He clacked as he walked, rattling like a pair of castanets, and since he had no teeth he was forced to eat baby food. Though he was blind and deaf, he never failed to recognize things and his memory of the past and the immediate present was remarkable. He died sitting in his wicker chair at dusk. He liked to sit in the doorway of his little house and feel the sun go down, which he could sense from the subtle change in temperature, the sounds in the courtyard, the haste of the cooks, and the silence of the hens. It was there that death found him. At his feet was his great-grandson Esteban García, who was by that time almost ten, driving a nail through the eyes of a chicken. He was the son of Esteban García, the only bastard offspring of the *patrón* named for him. No one knew his origin, or the reason he had that name, except himself, because his grandmother, Pancha García, had managed before she died to poison his childhood with the story that if only his father had been born in place of Blanca, Jaime, or Nicolás, he would have inherited Tres Marías, and could even have been President of the Republic if he wanted. In that part of the country, which was littered with illegitimate children and even legitimate ones who had never met their fathers, he was probably the only one to grow up hating his last name. He hated Esteban Trueba, his seduced grandmother, his bastard father, and his own inexorable peasant fate. Esteban Trueba did not treat him any differently from any of the other children around the property. He was simply one more in the pile of creatures who sang the national anthem in the schoolhouse and stood in line to receive their Christmas presents. Trueba had forgotten all about Pancha García and the fact that he had had a child with her, much less the sullen little grandson who despised him but watched him from afar to imitate his gestures and his speech. The child would lie awake at night imagining all sorts of dreadful illnesses and accidents that could put an end to the life of the *patrón* and his children so that he could inherit the property. Tres Marías would become his kingdom. He nursed these fantasies throughout his life, even long after it was evident that he would receive nothing by way of inheritance. He always reproached Trueba for the dark existence he had forged for him, and he felt constantly punished, even in the days when he had reached the height of his power and had them all in his fist.

The child noticed that something in the old man had changed. He went up to him and touched him, and the whole body swayed. Pedro García fell to the ground like a bag of bones. His eyes were covered by the milky film that had slowly screened out all light over the course of a quarter century. Esteban García picked up his nail and was just about to stick it in his grandfather's eye when Blanca arrived and shoved him away, never suspecting that this evil, dark-skinned creature was her nephew and that he would one day be the instrument of a tragedy that would befall her family.

"Oh God, he's dead," she sobbed, leaning over the body of the old man who had filled her childhood with stories and protected her clandestine love affair.

Old Pedro García was buried following a three-day wake for which, on instructions from Esteban Trueba, no expense was spared. They placed his body in a coffin of rough pine and laid him out in his Sunday suit, the same one he had worn at his wedding and whenever he went to vote or lined up for his fifty pesos at Christmas. They dressed him in his one white shirt, which was very loose around the neck because he had shrunk with age, and his mourning tie, with a red carnation in his lapel, as on all festive occasions. They held his jaw in place with a handkerchief and placed his black hat on his head, because he had repeatedly declared that he wanted to take it off when he said hello to God. He had no shoes, so Clara took a pair that belonged to Esteban Trueba, for everyone to see that he would not go barefoot to heaven.

Jean de Satigny was excited about the funeral. He showed up with a camera and tripod he had extracted from his belongings, and took so many portraits of the dead man that his relatives were afraid he might steal his soul, so they destroyed the plates. The wake was attended by peasants from throughout the region, because over the course of his century-long lifetime Pedro García had become related to many of the local farmers. The *curandera* arrived along with several Indians from her tribe, who began to weep for the deceased when she gave the order, and did not stop until the reveling was over three days later. People gathered outside the old man's house to drink wine, play the guitar, and keep an eye on the steers that were being roasted. Two priests on bicycles also arrived to bless the mortal remains of Pedro García and oversee the funeral rites. One of them was a rubicund giant with a strong Spanish accent, Father José Dulce María, whose name was familiar to Esteban Trueba. He was just about to forbid him to set foot on the property when Clara convinced him that this was hardly the time to place his political enmities before the peasants' Christian fervor. "At least he'll bring a little order to matters of the spirit," she said. So in the end Esteban Trueba welcomed him and invited him to stay in the house with his lay brother, who did not open his mouth and kept his eyes on the ground, his head bowed, and his hands joined. The *patrón* was moved by the death of the old man who had saved the crops from the plague of ants, and his life as well, and he wanted everyone to remember this funeral as a major event.

The priests assembled the tenants and the visitors in the little schoolhouse to read through the forgotten gospels and say a mass for the eternal rest of the soul of Pedro García. Afterward they withdrew to the room that had been reserved for them in the main house, while everybody else resumed the rowdy celebration that had been interrupted by their arrival. That night Blanca waited for the guitars and the Indians' lament to quiet down and for everyone to go to bed before she jumped out her bedroom window and took off in her usual direction, protected by the shadows. She continued to do so for the next three nights, until the priests departed. Everyone except her parents knew that Blanca was meeting one of them down by the river. It was Pedro Tercero García, who hadn't wanted to miss his grandfather's funeral and took advantage of the borrowed cassock to harangue the workers house by house, explaining that the coming elections were their chance to shake off the yoke under which they had always lived. They listened in surprise and confusion. For them, time was measured in seasons, and thought by generations. They were slow and cautious. Only the very young ones, those who had radios and listened to the news, those who sometimes went to town and talked with the union men, were able to follow his train of thought. The others listened to him because he was the hero the owners were after, but they were convinced that he was talking nonsense.

"If the *patrón* finds out we're voting Socialist, we're done for," they said.

"There's no way he can know! The ballots are secret," the false priest argued back.

"That's what you think," replied his father, Pedro Segundo. "They say they're secret, but afterward they always know exactly who we voted for. Besides, if your party wins they'll throw us out. We'll lose our jobs. I've always lived here. What would I do?"

"They can't throw you all out, because the owner loses more than you do if you go!" countered Pedro Tercero.

"It makes no difference who we vote for—they always win anyway."

"They change the ballots," said Blanca, who was at the meeting, sitting on the ground among the peasants.

"This time they can't," said Pedro Tercero. "We'll be sending people from the party to watch the polling places and make sure they seal the ballot boxes."

But the peasants did not trust him. Experience had taught them that in the end the fox always eats the hens, despite the subversive ballads that were traveling from mouth to mouth preaching just the opposite. Therefore, when a train came through carrying the new candidate of the Socialist Party, a charismatic, nearsighted doctor who could move huge crowds with his passionate speeches, they watched him from the station, observed in turn by the owners, who formed a fence around them, armed with shotguns and clubs. They listened respectfully to what the candidate had to say, but they were afraid to make the least gesture of greeting—except for a few farmhands who, armed with picks and shovels, rushed to surround him and cheered until they were hoarse, because they had nothing to lose. They were nomads who wandered the countryside without regular work, without families, without masters, and without fear.

Shortly after the death and memorable interment of Pedro García, Blanca began to lose her apple-colored freshness and to suffer from a natural fatigue that was not the result of holding her breath and from morning nausea that was not the result of drinking heated brine. She thought it was from eating too much food; it was the season of golden peaches, apricots, and young corn cooked with basil in clay casseroles. It was the season for making marmalade and jam for winter. But neither fasting, camomile, purgatives, nor rest could cure her. She lost her enthusiasm for the school, the infirmary, and even her ceramic crèches. She grew weak and somnolent, could spend hours lying in the shade looking up at the sun, uninterested in anything else. The only activity she kept up were her nocturnal escapes out the window when she had a rendezvous with Pedro Tercero down by the river.

Jean de Satigny, who had not admitted defeat in his romantic siege, observed her closely. Out of discretion, he had spent several periods in the hotel in town and made a few brief journeys to the capital, from which he would return weighed down with brochures about chinchillas, their hutches, their feeding, their sicknesses, their reproductive habits, the method for tanning their skins, and everything else that had to do with those tiny beasts who were destined to be converted into stoles. The count spent most of the summer as a guest at Tres Marías. He was a delightful visitor—well educated, lighthearted, and calm. He always had a friendly word on the tip of his tongue and was as ready to celebrate the cooking as he was to entertain his hosts by playing the piano in the sitting room, where his execution of the Chopin nocturnes rivaled Clara's. He was an inexhaustible source of anecdotes. He woke up late in the morning and devoted an hour or two to the care of his own person. First he would do his exercises and run around the house, oblivious to the taunts of the hardy peasants looking on. Next he would soak himself in a hot bath, and then he would take his time selecting his clothing for every occasion in the day. This last activity was a wasted one, because no one appreciated his elegance and often the only thing he achieved with his British riding outfits, his velvet jackets, and his Tyrolean hats with their little feathers was that Clara, with the best intentions, would offer him clothing more appropriate for the country. Jean did not lose his good humor. He accepted the ironic smiles of the owner of the house, Blanca's grimaces, and the perennial distraction of Clara, who, even after a year, was still asking him his name. He knew how to prepare a few French dishes, perfectly seasoned and magnificently presented, which were his contribution whenever there were guests for dinner. It was the first time any of them had seen a man interested in cooking, but they supposed it must be a European custom and did not dare make fun of him for fear of seeming ignorant. Besides the material on chinchillas, he also brought from the capital the popular wartime booklets that had been created to propagate the image of the heroic soldier, and sentimental novels he had bought for Blanca. In afterdinner conversation, he sometimes referred, in a tone of utter boredom, to summers spent with the European nobility in the castles of Liechtenstein or the Côte d'Azur. He never missed an opportunity to say how happy he was to have traded all that for the enchantment of America. Blanca would ask him why he had not chosen the Caribbean, or at least a country with mulattas, coconut palms and drums if what he was after was the exotic, but he maintained that there was no place on earth as pleasant as this half-forgotten country at the end of the earth. The Frenchman never spoke of his private life, except to slip in certain subtle hints that would enable an astute observer to recognize his splendid past, his incalculable fortune, and his noble origins. There was no consensus on his civil status, his age, his family, or the region of France he came from. Clara felt that so much mystery was dangerous and tried to penetrate it with her tarot cards, but Jean would not permit his fortune to be told or the lines of his hands to be read. Nor did they know his astrological sign.

Esteban Trueba was not the slightest bit concerned about any of this. For him it was enough that the count was willing to join him in a game of chess or dominoes, that he was clever and friendly and never asked to borrow money. Ever since Jean de Satigny had begun to visit them, the boredom of the countryside, where after five o'clock in the afternoon there was nothing left to do, had become less oppressive. Besides, he liked the idea that his neighbors envied him for having this distinguished guest at Tres Marías.

Word had got out that Jean was wooing Blanca, but that did not prevent his remaining the favorite of all the matchmaking mothers of the area. As for Blanca, she gradually adjusted to his presence. He was so discreet and gentle that she finally forgot about his proposal; she even thought it might have been some sort of joke on the count's part. She took the silver candlesticks from the cupboard again, set the table with the English china, and once more wore her city dresses to the family's late-afternoon gatherings. Jean often invited her into town or asked her to accompany him on his numerous social engagements. On such occasions Clara had to go with them, because Esteban Trueba was unyielding when it came to this: he did not want his daughter to be seen alone with the Frenchman. He would, however, allow them to walk unchaperoned around the property, provided that they did not go too far and that they returned before dark. Clara said that if the point was to protect their daughter's virginity, that was a lot more dangerous than letting her go to tea at the Uzcategui family hacienda, but Esteban was confident that there was nothing to worry about with Jean, since his intentions were noble enough, and that they only had to watch out for malicious gossips, who could easily destroy their daughter's reputation. Jean and Blanca's country walks consolidated their friendship. They did, after all, get along well. They both liked to go horseback riding in the middle of the morning, with a picnic basket and an array of canvas and leather bags containing Jean's belongings. At every stop the count posed Blanca against the landscape and took her picture, although she put up a certain resistance because she felt rather ridiculous. This feeling was borne out when they saw the developed photographs, where Blanca appeared with a smile that was not her own, standing in an uncomfortable position and with an unhappy look that according to Jean was due to her inability to pose naturally, and according to Blanca to the fact that he forced her to stand all twisted and to hold her breath for endless seconds until the plate had absorbed the image. They usually picked a shady place beneath the trees, where they spread a blanket on the grass and settled in for a few hours. They spoke of Europe, of books, of anecdotes from Blanca's family, or of Jean's voyages. She gave him a book by the Poet, and he was so excited by it that he memorized long sections of it and could recite them perfectly. He said it was the best poetry ever written, and that even in French, the language of the arts, there was nothing to compare it to. They never talked about their feelings. Jean was solicitous, but he was not pleading or insistent; if anything, he was fraternal and lighthearted. If he kissed her hand, it was to bid her good night; he did it with a schoolboy look on his face that drained all romanticism from the gesture. If he admired a dress she was wearing, a dish she had prepared, or one of her crèche figures, his tone had an ironic touch to it that allowed her to interpret his words in many ways. If he gathered flowers for her or helped her down from her horse, he did it with a casualness that transformed his chivalry into a simple act of friendship. In any case, just to be on the safe side, every time she had an opportunity Blanca let him know that she would never marry him, not even if her life depended on it. Jean de Satigny would smile his sparkling, seductive smile without saying a word, and Blanca could not help noticing that he was a lot more handsome than Pedro Tercero.

Blanca did not know that Jean was spying on her. He had seen her slip out the window in men's clothing many times. He would follow her part of the way, but he always turned back, afraid that the dogs would attack him in the dark. But from the way she was headed, he knew she always went to the river.

Meanwhile, Trueba still had not made up his mind about the chinchillas. As a sort of test, he had agreed to set up a cage with a few pairs of the rodents, imitating on a reduced scale the enterprise under consideration. It was the one and only time anyone saw Jean de Satigny with his sleeves rolled up for work. Nonetheless, the chinchillas came down with a disease peculiar to rats, and they were all dead within two weeks. He could not even tan their skins, because their fur turned dark and fell from the hide as easily as feathers from the skin of a boiled fowl. Jean stared in horror at the bald cadavers, with their stiff little feet and empty eyes, his hopes dashed of convincing Esteban Trueba, who lost all interest in the fur trade at the sight of such extensive loss of life.

"If this had hit a whole factory, I would have been completely ruined," Trueba concluded.

Between the plague of the chinchillas and Blanca's escapades, the count wasted several months of his time. He was growing weary of all the negotiations, and he could see that Blanca was never going to notice his charms. He could also see that the rodent farm would never be a reality, so he decided that he had better hasten things along before some clever fellow won the heiress. Besides, he was beginning to like Blanca, now that she was more robust and had acquired that languor that was smoothing away her rough, peasant edges. He preferred women who were placid and well rounded, and the sight of Blanca stretched out on cushions looking up at the sky during their siesta reminded him of his mother. At times she even moved him. From a host of small details imperceptible to others, Jean learned to guess when she was planning one of her nocturnal excursions to the river. She would sit through the evening meal without eating, on the pretext that she had a headache, and ask to be excused early from the table; there would be a strange gleam in her eyes and an impatience and eagerness in her motions that he had come to recognize. One night he decided to follow her all the way, to put an end to a situation that threatened to continue indefinitely. He was sure that Blanca had a lover, but he did not think it could be anything serious. Personally, Jean de Satigny had no particular fixation on virginity, and he had not raised the issue when he asked her hand in marriage. What interested him in her were other things, which could not be lost in a moment of pleasure at the river's edge.

After Blanca retired to her room and the rest of the family had left for theirs, Jean de Satigny remained behind in the dark drawing room, his ear cocked to the sounds of the house, until he calculated that she would be climbing out the window. He went out into the courtyard and stood under the trees to wait for her. He squatted in the shadows for more than half an hour, with nothing out of the ordinary disturbing the peace of the evening. Bored with waiting, he was just getting ready to go to bed when he noticed that Blanca's window was wide open. He realized that she must have leapt before he had positioned himself in the garden to observe her.

"Merde," he muttered.

Hoping that the dogs would not alert the entire household with their barking and that they would not jump him, he began walking toward the river, taking the path he had seen Blanca take many times before. He was not used to walking the plowed earth in his elegant shoes, or jumping over stones and sidestepping puddles, but the night was very bright, with a beautiful full moon that lit the sky with a phantasmagoric splendor. As soon as he had overcome his fear of the dogs, he was able to appreciate the beauty of the moment. He walked for at least a quarter of an hour before glimpsing the first beds of rushes along the riverbanks. He redoubled his caution and walked even more quietly, being careful not to give himself away by stepping on any branches. The moon was reflected in the water with a glassy brilliance, and the breeze gently stirred the rushes and the treetops. Absolute silence reigned, and for a moment he had the illusion that he was in the dream of a sleepwalker, in which he walked and walked without getting anywhere, always remaining in the same enchanted place, where time had stopped and where if you tried to touch the trees, which looked within hand's reach, you found only empty space. He had to make an effort to recover his usual state of mind, which was realistic and pragmatic. In a bend of the river, between huge gray rocks lit by the moon, he saw them, so close that he could almost touch them. They were naked. The man had his back to him, but he had no difficulty recognizing the Jesuit priest who had helped officiate at the funeral mass of old Pedro García. This surprised him. Blanca slept with her head resting on the smooth brown stomach of her lover. The frail light of the moon threw metallic rays across their bodies, and Jean de Satigny shivered at the sight of Blanca, who at that moment seemed to him the image of perfection.

It took the elegant French count nearly a minute to come out of the dreamlike state into which he had been swept by the sight of the lovers, the moon, and the silence of the surrounding fields, and to realize that the situation was far more serious than he had imagined. In the lovers' postures he could see the abandon typical of those who have known each other for a long time. What he was looking at did not at all resemble an erotic summer idyll, as he had supposed, but rather a marriage of body and soul. Jean de Satigny could not have known that Blanca and Pedro Tercero had slept this way the first day they met, and that they had continued doing so every time they could over all these years. Still, he knew it instinctively.

Trying not to make even the slightest sound, he turned and began walking back to the main house, wondering how to handle the situation. When he reached the house, he had already decided to tell Blanca's father, because Esteban Trueba's ever-ready anger seemed to him to be the best means for solving the problem. Let the natives work it out among themselves, he thought.

Jean de Satigny did not wait for morning. He knocked on his host's door, and before Trueba had shaken off his sleep, he hurled his version of the story at him. He said he had been unable to sleep because of the heat and that he had gone out for air, wandered down toward the river, and come upon the depressing spectacle of his future bride sleeping in the arms of the bearded priest, naked in the moonlight. For just a moment, this threw Trueba off course, because he could not imagine his daughter going to bed with Father José Dulce María, but he quickly realized what had happened, and understood the joke that had been played on him during the old man's funeral, realizing that his daughter's seducer was none other than Pedro Tercero García, that son of a bitch who would pay for this the rest of his life. He hitched up his pants, pulled on his boots, threw his rifle over his shoulder, and grabbed his riding whip from the wall.

"Wait here for me, *Don*," he ordered the Frenchman, who in any case had no intention of accompanying him.

Esteban Trueba ran to the stable and mounted his horse without bothering to saddle it. He was panting with indignation, his bones locked in position and feeling the effort, his heart pounding in his chest. "I'm going to kill them both," he muttered over and over, like a litany. He followed the road in the direction the Frenchman had indicated, but he had no need to ride all the way to the river, because halfway there he ran into Blanca, who was returning to the house, humming as she walked, her hair disheveled, her clothing dirty, with the happy look of those who have nothing else to ask from life. When he saw his daughter, Esteban Trueba was unable to restrain his evil character and he charged her with his horse, whip in the air, beating her mercilessly, lash upon lash, until the girl fell flat and rigid to the ground. Her father jumped down from his horse, shook her until she came to, and shouted every insult known to man plus others he made up in the heat of the moment.

"Who is it? Tell me who it is or I'll kill you!"

"I'll never tell," she sobbed.

Then Esteban Trueba understood that this was not the way to get something from his daughter, who had inherited his own stubbornness. He realized that, as always, he had got carried away with his punishment. He put her up on the horse and they returned to the house. Either instinct or the barking of the dogs had alerted Clara and the servants, who were waiting in the doorway with all the lights blazing. The only person not to be found anywhere was the count, who had taken advantage of the tumult to pack his bags, yoke the horses to his carriage, and leave discreetly for the hotel in town.

"My God, Esteban! What have you done?" Clara exclaimed at the sight of her daughter, who was covered with mud and blood.

Clara and Pedro Segundo García carried Blanca to her bed. The foreman had grown deathly pale, but he said nothing. Clara washed her daughter, applied cold compresses to her bruises, and rocked her until she had calmed down. After the girl was asleep, she went to confront her husband, who had locked himself in his study and was pacing furiously up and down, beating the walls with his whip, cursing and kicking all the furniture. When he saw her, Esteban vented his rage on Clara. He accused her of having raised Blanca without morals, without religion, without principles, like a libertine atheist, even worse, without a sense of her own class, because you could understand if she wanted to do it with someone from a decent family, but not with this hick, this simpleton, this hothead, this lazy good-for-nothing son of a bitch.

"I should have killed him when I said I would! Sleeping with my daughter! I swear I'm going to find him and when I lay my hands on him I'm going to cut his balls off if it's the last thing I ever do. I swear on my mother's soul he's going to regret that he was ever born!"

"Pedro Tercero García hasn't done a thing you haven't done yourself," Clara said when she could interrupt him. "You also slept with unmarried women not of your own class. The only difference is that he did it for love. And so did Blanca."

Trueba stared at her, paralyzed with surprise. For a second his fury seemed to deflate, and he felt as if she were making fun of him, but a wave of blood immediately rushed to his brain. He lost control and struck her in the face, knocking her against the wall. Clara fell to the floor without a sound. Esteban seemed to awaken from a trance. He knelt by her side, crying and begging her forgiveness, trying to explain, calling her by all the special names he used only when they were in bed, not understanding how he could have raised his hand against her, the only human being he really cared about and for whom he had never, not even in the worst moments of their common life, lost respect. He picked her up in his arms, seated her lovingly in an armchair, wet a handkerchief to put on her forehead, and tried to make her drink a little water. Finally, Clara opened her eyes. Blood was flowing from her nose. When she opened her mouth, she spat out several teeth, which fell to the floor, and a thread of bloody saliva trickled down her chin and neck.

As soon as Clara was able to move, she pushed Esteban out of her way, rose with great difficulty, and left the study, trying to walk as erect as she could. At the other side of the door was Pedro Segundo García, who managed to grab her just as she stumbled. Sensing him beside her, Clara collapsed. She pressed her swollen face against the shoulder of this man who had stood beside her through all the worst moments of her life, and she began to cry. Pedro Segundo Garcia's shirt was stained with blood.

Clara never spoke to her husband again. She stopped using her married name and removed the fine gold wedding ring that he had placed on her finger twenty years before, on that memorable night when Barrabás was assassinated with a butcher's knife.

Two days later, Clara and Blanca left Tres Marías and returned to the capital. Esteban, humiliated and furious, remained with the sensation that something in his life had been destroyed forever.

Pedro Segundo drove his mistress and her daughter to the station. After that night he was never again to see them, and he was silent and withdrawn. He helped them to their seats on the train and then stood with his hat in his hand and his eyes lowered, not knowing how to say goodbye. Clara hugged him. At first he was stiff and somewhat taken aback, but his own emotions quickly triumphed and he timidly encircled her with his arms and left an imperceptible kiss on her cheek. They looked at each other through the window for the last time and their eyes filled with tears. The faithful administrator returned to his small brick house, made a bundle of all his personal belongings, wrapped the small amount of money he had managed to accumulate over the years in a handkerchief, and left. Trueba saw him say good-bye to the other tenants and climb up on his horse. He tried to stop him, explaining that what had happened had nothing to do with him, and that it was not right that he should lose his job, his friends, his house, and his security because of his son.

"I don't want to be here when you find my son, *patrón*," were the last words Pedro Segundo García spoke before trotting off in the direction of the highway.

I felt so alone after that! I didn't know then that loneliness would never leave me, and that the only person I would ever have close to me the rest of my life would be an eccentric, bohemian granddaughter with green hair like Rosa's. But that was still many years ahead of me.

After Clara left, I looked around and noticed many new faces at Tres Marías. My old friends had either died or gone away. I had lost my wife and my daughter. My contact with my sons was minimal. My mother, my sister, dear old Nana, and old Pedro García were all dead. Even Rosa returned to haunt me like an unforgettable grief, and I could no longer count on Pedro Segundo García, who had stood beside me for thirty-five years. I couldn't stop crying. The tears would run down my face and I would brush them off with my hand, but they were followed by others. "Why don't you all go to hell!" I would roar into the far corners of the house. I wandered through the empty rooms, went into Clara's bed-room and rifled her wardrobe and her dresser in the hope of finding something she had worn—anything, so I could hold it to my nose and retrieve, even for a fleeting instant, that sweet, clean smell of hers. I would lie down on her bed, bury my face in her pillow, caress the objects she had left on her night table, and feel completely desolate.

Pedro Tercero García was the one to blame for every-thing that had happened. Because of him Blanca had left me; because of him I had fought with Clara; because of him Pedro Segundo had left the hacienda and the tenants looked at me with hatred in their eyes and whispered behind my back. He had always been a troublemaker. What I should

have done was kick him out at the very beginning. But out
of respect for his father and grandfather I let things go, and
the upshot was that the insolent trash took what I most
loved in the whole world. I went to the police station in
town and bribed the guardsmen to help me look for him. I
ordered them not to lock him up, but to turn him over to me
without any fuss. In the bar, the barbershop, the club, and at
the Red Lantern, I let it be known that there would be a
reward for anyone who delivered him to me.

"Watch out, *patrón*. Don't start taking the law into your
own hands," they warned me. "Things have changed a lot
since the days of the Sánchez brothers." But I didn't want to
listen. What would the law have done in a case like this?
Nothing.

A couple of weeks went by without incident. I rode out
to inspect my lands, paid a few visits to the neighboring
haciendas, kept my eye on the tenants. I was convinced they
were hiding the boy from me. I raised the amount of the
reward and threatened to have the guardsmen dismissed for
incompetence, but all to no avail. With each passing hour
my anger grew. I began to drink as I never had before, not
even when I was a bachelor. I slept badly and dreamt again
of Rosa. One night I dreamt I was beating her the way I had
Clara, and that her teeth also fell out on the floor. I woke up
screaming, but I was all alone, and there was no one to hear
me. I was so depressed I even stopped shaving, didn't change
my clothes, and I don't think I bathed either. Everything I
ate tasted sour to me. I had a taste of bile in my mouth. I
broke my knuckles banging on the walls, and rode a horse to
death galloping off the fury that was eating me alive. No one
came near me in those days; the maids' hands shook when
they served my food, which only made me madder.

One day I was in the hallway smoking a cigarette just
before the siesta when a dark little boy appeared in front of
me and stood there silently. His name was Esteban García.
He was my grandson, but I didn't know it. Only now, with
all the terrible things that happened at his hand, have I
learned how we were related. He was also the grandson of
Pancha García, a sister of Pedro Segundo, whom I have to
admit I don't remember.

"What do you want, kid?" I asked him.

"I know where Pedro Tercero García is," he told me.

I gave such a jump that I upset the wicker chair I had been sitting in. I grabbed the boy by the shoulders and shook him.

"Where? Where is the bastard?" I shouted.

"Are you going to give me the reward?" the child stammered, frightened to death.

"Don't worry," I answered. "But first I want to be sure that you're not lying. Let's go. Take me to where that worm is hiding."

I went to get my rifle and we left the house. The child told me we would have to go on horseback, because Pedro Tercero was hidden in the Lebus' sawmill, several miles from Tres Marías. How could I have failed to think of that? It was a perfect hideout. The Germans' sawmill was always shut at that time of year, and it was hard to reach from all the main roads.

"How did you find out that Pedro Tercero García is hiding there?"

"Everybody knows but you, sir," he replied.

We took off at a trot, because in that terrain you couldn't gallop. The sawmill is set into a mountainside, where a horse can't go fast. With the effort of the climb, the horses' hooves struck sparks from the stones. I think the noise of their hooves was the only sound for miles around on that sultry, quiet afternoon. When we came into the forest, the landscape changed and it grew cooler; the trees rose up before us in narrow rows that barely let the sun in. The ground was a soft, reddish carpet into which the horses' feet gently sank. We were surrounded by silence. The boy rode ahead of me, bareback on his horse, as close to the animal as if they were a single body, and I was behind, taciturn, brooding over my rage. At moments sadness swept over me, stronger than the fury I had been hatching all this time, stronger than the hatred I felt for Pedro Tercero García. It must have been two hours before we glimpsed the low sheds of the sawmill, arranged in a half circle in a clearing in the woods. The smell of wood and pine was so intense that for a moment I was distracted from the business at hand. I was overcome by the landscape, the forest, the silence. But that momentary weakness lasted only a second.

"Wait here and look after the horses. Don't move!"

I dismounted. The boy took the reins and I began to walk in a crouch, my rifle in my hands. I didn't feel my sixty years or the pain in my old crushed bones. I was propelled forward by the thought of revenge. A frail column of smoke was rising from the roof of one of the sheds, and I saw a horse tied to the door. I deduced that that was where Pedro Tercero must be hiding, so I headed toward that shed. My teeth were chattering with impatience. I had decided not to kill him with the first shot, because that would be too quick and all my pleasure would be gone in only a minute. I had waited so long for this moment that I wanted to savor it, but I also didn't want to give him a chance to escape. He was much younger than I, and if I didn't take him by surprise I was done for. My shirt was soaked with sweat and was clinging to my body. A veil had descended over my eyes, but I felt twenty years old and had the strength of a bull. I crept silently into the shed, my heart pounding like a drum. I found myself inside a large warehouse whose floor was covered with sawdust. There were huge stacks of wood, and some machines covered with green canvas to protect them from the dust. I continued inching forward, hiding behind the woodpiles, until suddenly I saw him. Pedro Tercero García was stretched out on the floor, his head on a folded blanket. He was sound asleep. Next to him was a small fire and a crock for boiling water. I stopped short, taken aback, and stared at him with all the hatred in the world, trying to fix in my memory forever that dark face with the almost childlike features, on which the beard looked like part of a disguise, and I could not understand what my daughter had seen in that ordinary-looking longhair. He must have been about twenty-five, but asleep he looked like a boy. I had to make an enormous effort to stop the shaking in my hands and teeth. I raised my gun and took a few steps forward. I was so close to him that I could have blown his head off without even aiming, but I decided to wait a few seconds for my pulse to quiet down. That moment was my downfall. I believe the habit of hiding must have sharpened Pedro Tercero García's hearing, and instinct told him that he was in danger. In a split second he must have waked up, but his eyes remained closed. He alerted all his muscles and concentrated all his energy into a single unbelievable leap that left him standing three feet away from where my bullet landed. I had no chance to aim again, for he crouched down, picked up a piece of wood, and hurled it at me, striking my gun, which flew out of my hand. I remember feeling a wave of panic at being suddenly unarmed, but then I realized that he was more scared than I was. We looked at each other in silence, panting, each awaiting the next move of the other. Then I saw the axe. It was so close to me that I could reach it by hardly extending my arm, which is what I did without a second thought. I took the axe and, with a wild scream that rose from my guts, I rushed forward, prepared to rip him down the middle with a single stroke. The axe gleamed in the air and fell on Pedro Tercero García. A shower of blood hit me in the face.

At the very last second he raised his arms to stop the axe and the edge of the tool sliced off three fingers of his right hand. The force of the blow thrust me forward and I fell on my knees. He held his hand to his chest and ran out the door, leaping over the woodpiles and the logs on the floor. He reached his horse, jumped into the saddle, and disappeared with a terrifying scream into the shadows of the pine trees. He left a trail of blood behind him.

I remained on all fours, crouching and gasping for breath. It took me several minutes to calm down and realize that I hadn't killed him. My first reaction was one of relief, because the feel of his warm blood on my face had quickly taken the edge off my hatred, and I had to make a real effort to remember how badly I had wanted to kill him to explain the violence that was suffocating me, making my chest nearly burst, my ears buzz, and my eyes cloud over. I opened my mouth in desperation, trying to get some air into my lungs, and managed to rise to my feet, but I began to shake. I took two steps and then I fell, landing on top of a pile of boards, sick to my stomach and unable to catch my breath. I thought I was going to faint. My heart was leaping in my chest like a machine gone wild. A long time must have passed. I don't know. Finally I looked up. I rose to my feet again and picked up my gun.

The child Esteban García was by my side, staring at me silently. He had picked up the sliced-off fingers and was holding them like a bouquet of bloody asparagus. I couldn't keep from retching then. My mouth filled with saliva, and I vomited all over my boots while the boy smiled impassively.

"Drop that, you filthy brat!" I shouted, striking him in the hand.

The fingers fell onto the sawdust, staining it red.

I picked up my gun and walked trembling toward the door. The cool evening air and the overwhelming scent of pine hit me in the face, bringing me back to reality. I inhaled eagerly, gulping the air. With great difficulty I made my way to my horse. My whole body ached and my hands were numb. The boy followed me.

We returned to Tres Marías, groping our way in the dark, which fell quickly once the sun had set. The trees made it difficult to advance; the horses tripped on the stones and brush; branches whipped us in the face. I was in another world, confused and terrified at my own violence, grateful that Pedro Tercero had escaped, because I knew that if he had fallen to the floor I would have continued striking with the axe till I killed him, destroyed him, cut him into little pieces with the same determination that had made me want to shoot him between the eyes.

I know what people say about me. Among other things they say that I've killed several men. They've accused me of murdering some peasants. It isn't true. If it were, I wouldn't mind admitting it, because at my age you can say those things with impunity. I don't have long to go before I'll be in the ground. I've never killed anyone, and the closest I came to doing so was the day I picked up an axe and threw myself on Pedro Tercero García.

It was night when we got home. I eased down from the horse and walked toward the terrace. I had completely forgotten about the little boy who had accompanied me, because the whole trip back he hadn't said a word, so I was surprised to feel him tugging at my sleeve.

"Now can I have the reward, sir?" he asked.

I sent him packing with a slap.

"There's no reward for traitors!" I snarled. "And furthermore, I forbid you to tell anyone about what happened! You understand?"

I entered the house and went directly to the liquor

cabinet. The brandy burned my throat and restored a bit of warmth to my body. Then I lay down on the sofa, breathing hard. My heart was still throbbing and I felt dizzy. With the back of my hand I wiped off the tears that were running down my cheeks.

Outside, Esteban García stood before the bolted door. Like me, he was weeping with rage.

SEVEN

♛

The Brothers

Clara and Blanca arrived in the city looking like disaster victims. Both had swollen faces, eyes red from crying, and rumpled clothes from the long train ride. Blanca, weaker than her mother although she was taller, younger, and heavier, sighed when she was awake and sobbed while she slept, in an uninterrupted lament that had begun the day of the beating. But Clara had no patience with misfortune, so when they reached the big house on the corner, which was as empty and lugubrious as a mausoleum, she decided that there had been enough weeping and moaning and that the time had come to bring some joy into their lives. She insisted that her daughter help her in hiring new servants, opening the shutters, removing the sheets that had been draped over the furniture and lampshades, unlocking the padlocks on the doors, shaking off the dust, and letting in light and air. They were in the middle of doing all this when the unmistakable aroma of wild violets invaded the house, alerting them to the arrival of the three Mora sisters, who, whether out of telepathy or sheer affection, had come to visit. Their happy chatter, cold compresses, spiritual counsel, and personal charm restored the bruised bodies and grieving souls of both mother and daughter.

"We'll have to buy some new birds," Clara said, looking out the window at the empty cages and at the weed-choked garden where the statues of the Olympian gods stood naked and covered with pigeon droppings.

"I don't understand how you can think about birds when you don't even have your teeth, Mama," said Blanca, who was still not used to her mother's new, toothless expression.

Clara saw to everything. Within two weeks the cages were filled with new birds and she had ordered a porcelain bridge that could be attached to her remaining molars, but the thing turned out to be so uncomfortable that she preferred wearing her denture on a ribbon around her neck. She put it in only to eat and, on occasion, for social gatherings. Clara brought life back to the house. She ordered the cook to keep a stove always lit and told her she should be prepared to feed a large number of guests at a moment's notice. She knew why she said it. Within a few days her spiritualist friends, the Rosicrucians, the Theosophists, the acupuncturists, the telepathists, the rainmakers, the peripatetics, the Seventh-Day Adventists, and the hungry or otherwise needy artists began to appear—all those who had habitually been part of Clara's court. Clara reigned over them like a small, happy, toothless queen. It was then that she began her first serious attempts to communicate with extraterrestrial beings and that, as she herself noted, she began to have her first doubts regarding the spiritual messages she received from the pendulum and the three-legged table. She often said that perhaps it was not the souls of the dead, wandering in another dimension, but rather beings from other planets who were trying to establish a relationship with earthlings but who, because they were made of an intangible matter, could easily be confused with souls. That scientific explanation enchanted Nicolás, but it did not enjoy the same reception with the Mora sisters, who were extremely conservative.

Blanca lived wholly apart from all these doubts. To her, beings from other planets belonged in the same category as souls, and therefore she could not fathom her mother's passionate interest in identifying them. She was very busy with the house, because Clara had once more turned her back on all the household chores, claiming that she had never had an aptitude for them. Keeping up the big house on the corner required an army of servants, and her mother's entourage forced them to maintain twenty-four-hour shifts in the kitchen. Grains and grasses had to be prepared for some, vegetables and raw fish for others, fruit and sour milk for the three Mora sisters, and succulent meat dishes, desserts, and other poisons for Jaime and Nicolás, who had insatiable appetites and still had not developed their own favorite dishes. In time, both of them would know hunger: Jaime out of solidarity with the poor, and Nicolás to purify his soul. But in those days they were still two robust youngsters eager to enjoy life's pleasures.

Jaime had begun at the university and Nicolás was wandering about in search of his destiny. They owned a prehistoric car, which they had bought with the proceeds from the silver platters they had stolen from their parents' house. They called it Covadonga, in memory of their del Valle grandparents. Covadonga had been taken apart and put back together with other pieces so many times that it barely ran. It moved with a deafening roar from its rusty motor, spewing smoke and bolts from its exhaust pipe. The brothers shared it solomonically: on even days it belonged to Jaime, and on odd to Nicolás.

Clara was very happy to be living with her sons and was determined to establish a friendly relationship with them. She had had very little contact with them when they were small, and in her haste to see them "become men," she had lost the best hours with her sons and been forced to keep all her tender feelings to herself. Now that they had attained adult proportions and were finally grown, she could give herself the pleasure of spoiling them as she should have when they were small, but it was too late, for the twins had been raised without her caresses, and they no longer needed them. Clara realized that her sons did not belong to her. She did not lose her head over this or her optimistic frame of mind. She accepted the young men as they were and was prepared to enjoy their company without expecting anything in return.

Blanca, however, grumbled because her brothers had transformed the house into a pigsty. In their wake they left a trail of destruction, damage, and noise. The young woman was gaining weight before everybody's eyes and daily grew more languid and ill-tempered. Jaime noticed his sister's belly and went to see his mother.

"Mama, I think Blanca's pregnant," he said without beating around the bush.

"I thought so myself, dear," his mother said, sighing.

Blanca did not deny it, and once the news was confirmed, Clara wrote it down in her notebooks that bore witness to life. Nicolás raised his eyes from his study of Chinese horoscopes and suggested that they ought to tell their father, because within a few more weeks it would be impossible to conceal the matter and everybody would find out.

"I'll never tell who the father is!" Blanca said with determination.

"I'm not talking about the father of the child, I'm talking about *our* father," said her brother. "Papa has the right to hear it from us, before someone else tells him."

"Send a telegram to the countryside," Clara suggested sadly. She realized that when Esteban Trueba found out, Blanca's baby would become a tragedy.

Nicolás composed the message with the same cryptographic spirit he employed in writing poems to Amanda, so that the local telegraph operator would not understand the message and start spreading gossip: "Blanca expecting send instructions. Stop." Esteban Trueba was as mystified as the telegraph operator, and was forced to call his family in the city to understand what they had meant. It fell to Jaime to explain the matter, and he added that the pregnancy was so advanced that there was nothing to be done. There was a long, terrible silence at the other end of the phone, and then his father hung up the receiver. In Tres Marías, livid with anger and surprise, Esteban Trueba picked up his cane and destroyed his telephone for the second time. It had never crossed his mind that a daughter of his could commit such a monstrous folly. Knowing who the father was, it took him only a fraction of a second to regret he had not shot him in the head when he had the chance. He knew that the scandal would be the same whether she gave birth to a bastard child or married the son of a peasant: society would condemn her in either case.

Esteban Trueba spent several hours pacing back and forth in his house, smashing his cane against the furniture and the walls, muttering curses between his teeth, and concocting ridiculous plans that ranged from sending Blanca to a convent in Extremadura to beating her to death. Finally, after he calmed down a bit, a miraculous idea occurred to him. He had his horse saddled, and galloped off in the direction of the town.

He found Jean de Satigny, whom he had not seen since the disastrous night when he had awakened him to tell him about Blanca's amorous adventures, sipping unsweetened melon juice in the only pastry shop in town. He was accompanied by the son of Indalecio Aguirrazábal, a dandified weakling with a high-pitched voice who was reciting the poetry of Rubén Darío. Without a trace of respect, Trueba lifted the French count by the lapels of his impeccable Scottish jacket and carried him straight out of the tearoom, practically dangling in midair, before the astonished stares of the other customers. He set him down in the middle of the sidewalk.

"You've given me enough problems, young man," he said. "First the business with your damned chinchillas and then my daughter. I've had enough. Go get your things, because you're coming with me to the city. You're going to marry Blanca."

He did not give him time to recover from the shock. He accompanied him to the local hotel, where he waited with his whip in one hand and his cane in the other while Jean de Satigny packed his bags. Afterward he took him directly to the station and unceremoniously loaded him onto the train. During the trip, the count tried to explain that he had nothing to do with all of this and that he had never so much as touched Blanca Trueba, and that probably the one responsible for what had happened was that bearded priest Blanca met down by the river every night. Esteban Trueba seared him with his fiercest look.

"I don't know what you're talking about, son. You must have dreamt that."

Trueba proceeded to explain to him the various clauses of the marriage contract, which did a great deal to assuage the Frenchman's fears. Blanca's dowry, her monthly income, and the prospect of inheriting a considerable fortune eventually brought him around.

"As you can see, this is a better proposition than the

chinchillas," concluded his future father-in-law without noticing the young man's nervous whimpering.

So it was that on Saturday Esteban Trueba arrived at
the big house on the corner with a husband for his deflow-
ered daughter and a father for the little bastard. Esteban was
shooting sparks of rage. With a sweep of his hand he
knocked over the pot of chrysanthemums in the entryway
and slapped Nicolás, who attempted to intercede and explain
things, and he announced that he did not want to see Blanca,
who was to remain locked up until her wedding day. Clara
did not come out to greet him. She stayed in her room and
did not open her door even after he broke his silver cane in
two trying to break it down.

The house entered a whirlwind of activity and quarrels.
The atmosphere seemed unbreathable, and even the birds fell
silent in their cages. The servants ran about on orders from
their brusque, anxious *patrón,* who allowed for no delays in
the execution of his wishes. Clara continued with her life,
ignoring her husband and refusing to speak to him. The
groom, a virtual prisoner of his future father-in-law, was
settled into one of the numerous guest rooms, where he
spent his time pacing the floor with nothing to do, without
seeing Blanca, and not understanding how he had ended up
in this melodrama. He did not know whether to feel sorry
for himself for having fallen victim to these savage aborigi-
nes, or to rejoice at being on the verge of fulfilling his dream
of marrying a rich, young, beautiful South American heiress.
As he was of an optimistic bent and endowed with the
common sense typical of all his countrymen, he opted for
the second interpretation, and by the end of the week he had
begun to relax.

Esteban Trueba set the date of the wedding for two
weeks hence. He decided that the best way to avoid a scandal
was to go out and meet it by throwing a spectacular affair.
He wanted to see his daughter married by the bishop, in a
white gown, with an eighteen-foot train held aloft by pages
and flower girls. He wanted her photograph to appear in the
society pages of the local papers, and he wanted there to be a
Caligulaesque party with sufficient fanfare and expense that
no one would notice the belly of the bride. The only one
who agreed with all his plans was Jean de Satigny.

The day Esteban Trueba summoned his daughter to take her to the dressmaker and try on her wedding gown was the first time he had seen her since the night of the beating. He was shocked to see how fat she had become and that her face was covered with blotches.

"I'm not getting married, Papa," she said.

"Be quiet!" he roared. "You're getting married. I don't want any bastards in the family, do you hear me?"

"I thought we already had several," Blanca replied.

"Don't talk back to me! I want you to know that Pedro Tercero García is dead. I killed him with my own hands, so you might as well forget about him and try to be a good wife to the man who's going to lead you to the altar."

Blanca began to cry and continued to weep inconsolably in the days to come.

The wedding Blanca had not wanted was held in the cathedral, with the blessings of the bishop and a train fit for a queen, sewn by the best tailor in the country, who had performed nothing short of a miracle by disguising the prominent stomach of the bride with layers of flowers and Greco-Roman pleats. The wedding culminated in a spectacular party, with five hundred guests in evening dress who invaded the big house on the corner, enlivened by an orchestra of hired musicians, with a scandalous number of whole steers grilled with herbs, fresh seafood, Baltic caviar, Norwegian salmon, birds stuffed with truffles, a torrent of exotic liquors, a flood of champagne, and an extravagance of desserts: ladyfingers, millefeuilles, éclairs, sugar cookies, huge glass goblets of glazed fruits, Argentine strawberries, Brazilian coconuts, Chilean papayas, Cuban pineapple, and other delicacies impossible to remember, all arrayed on a long table that ran the length of the garden, terminating in a colossal three-story wedding cake designed by an Italian artist born in Naples. This man, a friend of Jean de Satigny, had transformed his humble raw materials—flour, eggs, and sugar—into a replica of the Acropolis crowned with a cloud of meringue on which rested two mythological lovers, Venus and Adonis, fashioned out of almond paste colored to imitate the rosy tones of their flesh, their blond hair, and the cobalt blue of their eyes; with them was a pudgy Cupid, also edible, which was sliced in half with a silver knife by the proud groom and the dejected bride.

Clara, who from the very start had objected to the idea of marrying Blanca off against her will, decided not to attend the party. She stayed in the sewing room, spinning out dire predictions for the newlyweds, every one of which was borne out to the letter, as all concerned were later able to verify. Finally her husband came to beg her to change her clothes and make an appearance in the garden, even if only for ten minutes, to quell the rumors of the guests. She did so unwillingly, but out of love for her daughter she put in her teeth and managed to smile at the assembled guests.

Jaime arrived at the end of the party because he had stayed late working in the clinic for the poor where he was undergoing his first training as a medical student. Nicolás showed up with the lovely Amanda, who had just discovered Sartre and had adopted the dire look of the European existentialists, dressed all in black, pale-faced, her Arab eyes lined with kohl, her dark hair hanging to her waist, and a jangle of bracelets, necklaces, and earrings that caused a stir wherever she went. As for Nicolás, he was dressed in white, like a doctor, with amulets around his neck. His father came out to greet him, took him by the arm, and pushed him into a bathroom, where without a word he proceeded to pull off all his talismans.

"Go to your room and put on a decent tie! Go back to the party and behave like a proper gentleman! Don't let me catch you preaching some heretical religion among the guests! And tell that witch you've brought along to button up her neckline!" Esteban shouted at his son.

Nicolás obeyed him in the worst possible mood. On principle, he was a teetotaler, but he was so furious that he had a few drinks, lost his head, and jumped fully dressed into the garden fountain, from which he had to be rescued with his dignity thoroughly soaked.

Blanca spent the entire evening sitting in a chair staring at the cake with a dazed expression, tears running down her face. Meanwhile, her new husband fluttered among the diners attributing his mother-in-law's absence to a sudden attack of asthma and his bride's tears to the emotions of the occasion. No one believed him. Jean de Satigny kept kissing

Blanca on the neck, clasping her hands in his, and consoling her with sips of wine and bites of lobster, which he placed directly in her mouth, but it was all in vain: she continued to cry. Despite everything, the party was a great success, just as Esteban Trueba had hoped it would be. The guests ate and drank sumptuously, and watched the sun rise as they danced to the strains of the orchestra, while downtown, in the center of the city, groups of unemployed workers huddled around tiny bonfires, gangs of young men in dark shirts marched around raising their arms in stiff salute, imitating the figures they had seen in German movies, and in the headquarters of the various political parties the final touches were being put on campaign strategies for the upcoming elections.

"The Socialists are going to win," Jaime had said. After spending so much time living with the proletariat in the hospital where he worked, he had lost his reason.

"No, Jaime, the ones who always win are going to win again," Clara had replied, for she had seen it in the cards and her common sense had confirmed it.

After the party, Esteban Trueba took his son-in-law into the library and handed him a check. It was his wedding present. He had made all the arrangements for the couple to go to the North, where Jean de Satigny hoped to settle down to a comfortable life supported by his wife's income, far away from the comments of astute observers who would not be insensible to the size of his wife's belly. He was thinking about starting a little business of Incan pottery and mummies.

Before the newlyweds left the party, they went to say goodbye to Blanca's mother. Clara took Blanca aside and spoke to her in private. The girl still had not stopped crying.

"Stop crying, child," she told her. "Too many tears will hurt the baby, and only make it unhappy."

Blanca replied with another sob.

"Pedro Tercero García is alive," Clara added.

Blanca swallowed her hiccups and blew her nose.

"How do you know, Mama?" she asked.

"Because I dreamt it," Clara replied.

That was enough to reassure Blanca completely. She dried her tears, straightened her head, and didn't weep again until the day her mother died, seven years later, although it was not for lack of suffering, loneliness, and other causes.

Separated from her daughter, with whom she had always been very close, Clara entered another of her confused, depressed periods. Her life went on as before. The big house was always open and full of people, but she had lost her ability to laugh easily and was often to be seen staring straight ahead, lost in thought. She attempted to establish a system of communication with Blanca that would allow them to circumvent the terrible delays of the postal system, but telepathy did not always work and she was never sure how the message would be received. She could tell that her communiqués were being distorted by influences beyond her control and that the message received never resembled the one she had sent. Besides, Blanca was not given to psychic experiments; even though she had always been extremely close to her mother, she had never shown the slightest curiosity for mental phenomena. She was a practical, worldly, diffident woman, and her modern, pragmatic character was a serious obstacle to telepathy. Clara had to resign herself to more conventional methods. Mother and daughter wrote each other almost daily, and for several months their abundant correspondence took the place of Clara's notebooks that bore witness to life. Thus Blanca was kept abreast of everything that happened in the big house on the corner, and could entertain the illusion that she was still with her family and that her marriage was only a bad dream.

That year the paths of Jaime and Nicolás separated for good, because their differences had become irreconcilable. Nicolás had discovered flamenco dancing, which he said he had learned from the gypsies in the caves of Granada, even though he had never left the country; such was the strength of his conviction that even his own family began to wonder. He offered demonstrations on the slightest pretext. He would leap up on the dining-room table, the enormous oak table that had served as Rosa's bier so many years before and that Clara had inherited, and begin to beat his palms like a madman, tap his shoes spastically, and jump and shout so piercingly that he would attract all the inhabitants of the house as well as several neighbors and, on one occasion, even the police, who arrived with their nightsticks in hand, tracking mud across the carpets with their boots, but who wound up clapping their hands and shouting *Olé!* like everyone else. The table resisted heroically, although by the end of a week it looked like a butcher's table that had been used to slaughter calves. Flamenco dancing had no practical application in the closed society prevailing in the capital back then, but Nicolás ran a discreet announcement in the paper offering his services as a teacher of that fiery art. The next day he had a female student, and by the end of the week word of his charms had got out. Young girls flocked to him in droves. At first they were ashamed and timid, but he would begin twirling them around, tapping loudly while his arm encircled their waists and giving them his most seductive smile, and soon they were enthusiastic. His classes were a great success. The dining-room table was on the verge of splintering, Clara was complaining of migraines, and Jaime was locked in his room with wax in his ears, trying to concentrate on his studies. When Esteban Trueba found out what was going on in his house during his absence, he was justly and terrifyingly enraged, and forbade his son to use the house as an academy of Spanish dance or any other thing. Nicolás was forced to give up his contortions, but the whole experience made him the most popular young man of the season, the king of all the parties and of all the young girls' hearts, because while everybody else was busy studying, dressing in gray checked suits, and trying to grow a mustache to the rhythm of boleros, he was preaching free love, quoting Freud, drinking Pernod, and dancing flamenco. His social triumph did not, however, diminish his interest in his mother's psychic talents. He tried in vain to imitate her. He studied vehemently, practiced until his health was in jeopardy, and attended the Friday-night sessions with the three Mora sisters, despite his father's express orders to the contrary; for Esteban Trueba persisted in believing that these were not suitable matters for men. Clara tried to console him for his failures.

"You can't learn these things or inherit them," she would tell him when she saw him going cross-eyed with concentration in his strenuous efforts to move the saltshaker without touching it.

The three Mora sisters loved the boy very much. They lent him their secret books and helped him decipher the mysteries of horoscopes and divining cards. They would form a ring around him, holding each other by the hand, trying to suffuse him with their healing fluids, but that too failed to endow Nicolás with mental powers. They encouraged his love for Amanda. At first the young woman seemed to be fascinated by the three-legged table and the long-haired artists who flocked to Nicolás's house, but she soon tired of summoning spirits and reciting the Poet's verses, so she took a job as a newspaper reporter.

"That's a crooked profession," Esteban Trueba declared when he found out.

Trueba did not care for her. He did not even like to see her in his house. He thought she was a bad influence on his son and believed that her long hair, heavily made-up eyes, and glass beads were symptoms of some hidden vice, and that her tendency to kick her shoes off and sit cross-legged on the floor like an aborigine was mannish behavior.

Amanda had a very pessimistic view of the world, and to get through her depressions she smoked hashish. Nicolás joined her. Clara noticed that her son often had bad moments, but even her prodigious intuition did not allow her to make the connection between the Oriental pipes Nicolás smoked, his strange deliriums, his periodic drowsiness, and his attacks of sudden happiness, because she had never heard of that or any other drug. "It must be his age," she would tell herself whenever Nicolás was acting strangely. "He'll get over it." She had forgotten that Jaime had been born on the same day and did not have such fits.

Jaime's madness took a very different form. He had a calling for both sacrifice and austerity. There were only two pairs of pants and three shirts in his closet. Clara spent the winters rapidly knitting all sorts of woolen clothes to keep him warm, but he wore them only until someone who needed them more than he did crossed his path. All the money his father gave him ended up in the pockets of the impoverished people he cared for in the hospital. Whenever some emaciated dog followed him in the street, he brought it home, and whenever he heard about an abandoned child, unwed mother, or an old woman who needed his help, he brought the poor ones home so his mother could take care of their problems. Clara became an expert in social benefits. She was acquainted with all the services the state and the church provided for taking care of the disadvantaged. When all else failed, she took them into her own house. Her friends grew afraid of her, for every time she showed up on a visit it was because she needed something. The network of Clara and Jaime's protégés expanded, to the point where they lost count of how many people they were caring for; they were surprised whenever somebody appeared at the door to thank them for a favor they could not recall. Jaime approached the study of medicine as if it were a religious calling. Any diversion that took him away from his books or used up his time was a betrayal of the people he had sworn to serve. "This boy should have become a priest," Clara declared. For Jaime, who would not have been the least disturbed by the priestly vows of humility, poverty, and chastity, religion was the cause of half the world's misfortunes, so when his mother would make this comment he would become furious. He felt that Christianity, like almost all forms of superstition, made men weaker and more resigned, and that the point was not to await some reward in the sky but to fight for one's rights on earth. These were things he discussed in private with his mother; it was impossible to do so with Esteban Trueba, who quickly lost patience and ended up shouting and slamming doors because, as he put it, he was up to here with living among a bunch of lunatics and all he wanted was a little normality, but he had had the misfortune of marrying an eccentric and siring three good-for-nothing crazies who were ruining his life. Jaime didn't argue with his father. He was like a shadow in the house, giving his mother a distracted kiss whenever he saw her on his way to the kitchen, where, standing up, he would eat everyone else's leftovers before returning to his room and locking himself up to read or study. His bedroom was a tunnel of books, the walls covered from floor to ceiling with shelves full of volumes no one ever dusted because he always locked his door; they made a perfect nest for spiders and mice. In the center of the room was his bed, actually an army cot, which was lit by a naked light bulb hanging from the ceiling directly above his pillow. During an earthquake that Clara neglected to predict, they heard a roar like that of a derailed train, and when they were able to open the door they saw that the bed had been buried beneath an avalanche of books. The bookshelves had come loose from the walls, and Jaime had been squashed beneath them. They pulled him out without a scratch. While Clara was removing the books, she remembered the great earthquake, and it seemed to her that she had already lived this moment. The event was an opportunity to sweep the dust from Jaime's lair and chase away the insects and cobwebs with a broom.

The only time Jaime ever bothered to focus on the reality of his house was when he saw Amanda walking hand in hand with Nicolás. He rarely spoke to her and blushed violently whenever she spoke to him. He distrusted her exotic appearance and was convinced that if she wore her hair like other women and wiped the makeup off her eyes she would look like a very thin, greenish rat. Still, he could not keep his eyes off her. The rattle of bracelets that always accompanied her distracted him from his studies, and he had to make an enormous effort not to follow her around the house like a hypnotized chicken. Alone on his bed, unable to concentrate on what he was reading, he would imagine how Amanda looked naked, wrapped in her long black hair with all her noisy adornments, like an idol. Jaime was a recluse. He had been a reticent child, and later became a timid man. He did not love himself and perhaps for that reason felt that he did not deserve the love of others. The least manifestation of affection or gratitude toward him made him terribly embarrassed. Amanda represented the essence of everything feminine and, since she was Nicolás's girlfriend, of everything forbidden. The young woman's free, affectionate, adventurous personality fascinated him, and her appearance of a disguised rat aroused in him a tortured eagerness to protect her. He desired her with all his heart, but he would not go so far as to admit it, not even in his most hidden thoughts.

In that period Amanda was often at the Truebas'. She had a flexible schedule at the newspaper, and whenever she could she arrived at the big house on the corner with her brother Miguel. Their presence went practically unnoticed in that immense mansion always filled with people and activity. Miguel must have been five years old then. He was quiet and clean, caused no special stir, and was able to blend in with the design of the wallpaper and the furniture; he played alone in the garden and followed Clara from one end of the house to the other, always calling her Mama. For this reason, and also because he called Jaime Papa, everyone assumed that Amanda and Miguel were orphans. Amanda took her brother everywhere, even to work. He learned to eat anything, at any time of day, and to sleep in the most uncomfortable places. She swathed him in her passionate and violent love, scratched him like a puppy, shouted at him when she got angry, and ran to hug him when she regretted it. She would not let anyone reprimand him or tell him what to do, refused to listen when people commented on the strange life to which she was subjecting him, and defended him like a lioness, even though no one was planning to attack him. The only one allowed to give an opinion on Miguel's education was Clara, who managed to convince her that he should be sent to school, unless she wanted him to grow up to be an illiterate hermit. Clara was not especially keen on regular education, but she thought that in Miguel's case it was imperative that he be given a few hours of discipline every day and the opportunity to be with children his own age. She offered to enroll him herself and buy his school supplies and a uniform, and she went along with Amanda on the first day of class. Amanda and Miguel embraced tearfully in the doorway of the school, and the teacher was unable to loosen the little boy from his sister's skirt to which he clung tooth and nail, shrieking and kicking anyone who came near him. Finally, with Clara's help, the teacher managed to drag the child into the building and closed the door of the school behind her. Amanda spent the entire morning sitting outside on the sidewalk. Clara stayed with her, because she felt guilty for having caused so much grief and had begun to doubt the wisdom of her enterprise. At noon the bell rang and the gate swung open. They saw a herd of pupils, and in their midst, silent and tearless, in his proper place, with a pencil smear on his nose and his socks deep in his shoes, was little Miguel, who in these few short hours had learned to fend for himself without always holding on to his sister's hand. Amanda clasped him to her breast frenetically. She said in a moment of inspiration, "I'd give my life for you, Miguel." She did not know then that one day she would have to.

Meanwhile, Esteban Trueba daily felt more lonely and furious. He had resigned himself to the idea that his wife would never speak to him again. Tired of pursuing her up and down the house, begging her with his eyes and drilling holes in the bathroom wall, he decided to devote himself to politics. Just as Clara had predicted, those who always win won the elections, but by such a small margin that the entire country was put on notice. In Trueba's opinion, the time had arrived for him to come out in defense of the national interest and of the Conservative Party, since no one better personified the honest, uncontaminated politician, as he himself declared, adding that he had pulled himself up by his own bootstraps, and not only that, had created jobs and a decent life for all his workers and owned the only hacienda with little brick houses. He respected the law, the nation, and tradition, and no one could accuse him of any greater offense than tax evasion. He hired a foreman to replace Pedro Segundo García and put him in charge of the brood hens and imported cattle at Tres Marías and settled in the capital for good. He spent several months devoting himself to his campaign, drawing on the support of the Conservative Party, as well as his own fortune, which he placed at the disposal of the cause. The house filled with political propaganda and with the members of his party, who practically took it by storm, blending in with the hallway ghosts, the Rosicrucians, and the three Mora sisters. Clara's retinue was gradually pushed into the back rooms of the house, and an invisible border arose between the parts of the house occupied by Esteban Trueba and those occupied by his wife. In response to Clara's imagination and the requirements of the moment, the noble, seignorial architecture began sprouting all sorts of extra little rooms, staircases, turrets, and terraces. Each time a new guest arrived, the bricklayers would arrive and build another addition to the house. The big house on the corner soon came to resemble a labyrinth.

"Someday this house will make a good hotel," Nicolás declared.

"Or a little hospital," added Jaime, who was beginning

to cherish the idea of bringing his poor patients to the High District.

The façade of the house underwent no alterations. In front there were still the same heroic columns and the Versaillesesque garden, but in the back the style gradually disappeared. The rear garden was a tangled jungle in which every type of plant and flower had proliferated and where Clara's birds kept up a steady din, along with many generations of cats and dogs. Among that entire domestic fauna, the only one to have any importance in the collective memory of the family was a rabbit Miguel had once brought home, a poor ordinary rabbit that the dogs had constantly licked until all its hair fell out and it became the only bald member of its species, boasting an iridescent coat that gave it the appearance of a large-eared reptile.

As the day of the elections drew near, Esteban Trueba grew increasingly nervous. He had risked everything on this political adventure. One night he could not bear it anymore and went to knock on Clara's bedroom door. She opened it. She was in her nightgown, and had put her teeth in because she liked to nibble crackers while she wrote in her diary. To Esteban she looked as young and beautiful as the day he had first brought her to this blue-silk–papered bedroom and stood her on Barrabás's pelt. He smiled at the memory.

"Forgive me, Clara," he said, blushing like a schoolboy. "I feel lonely and worried. I'd like to stay here for a while if you don't mind."

Clara also smiled, but she did not speak. She pointed to the armchair and Esteban sat down. They remained silent for a while, sharing the plate of crackers and looking at each other in surprise, for they had been living under the same roof a long time without seeing each other.

"I suppose you know what's tormenting me," Esteban Trueba said finally.

Clara nodded.

"Do you think I'm going to win?"

Clara nodded again, and Trueba felt completely relieved, exactly as if she had given him a written guarantee. He gave a loud, joyous guffaw. Then he stood up, put his hands on her shoulders, and kissed her on the forehead.

"You're fantastic, Clara!" he exclaimed. "If you say so, I'll be senator."

After that evening, the hostility between them seemed to ebb. Clara still said nothing, but he ignored her silence and spoke normally to her, interpreting her slightest gestures as replies. When it was necessary, Clara used the servants or her children to send him messages. She worried about her husband's well-being, helped him with his work, and accompanied him when he asked her to. Sometimes she smiled at him.

Ten days later, Esteban Trueba was elected Senator of the Republic, just as Clara had predicted. He celebrated the event by throwing a party for all his friends and coreligionists, giving a cash bonus to his employees and to the tenants at Tres Marías, and leaving an emerald necklace on Clara's bed beside a bunch of violets. Clara began to attend social receptions and political events, where her presence was required so her husband could project the image of the simple family man that both the public and the Conservative Party found so appealing. On such occasions, Clara put in her teeth and wore some of the jewelry Esteban had given her. She was considered the most elegant, discreet, and charming lady of their social circle and no one would have dreamt that the distinguished couple never spoke.

With Esteban Trueba's new position, there were even more people to attend to in the big house on the corner. Clara had lost count of the number of mouths she fed and the expenses of the house. The bills were sent directly to Senator Trueba's office in Congress, where they were paid with no questions asked, for Esteban had discovered that the more he spent the more his fortune seemed to grow; he had concluded that Clara, with her indiscriminate hospitality and charity works, was not about to ruin him. At first, political power was like a new toy to him. In middle age he was the wealthy, respected man he had wanted to be when he was a struggling adolescent without godfathers and with no greater capital than his pride and ambition. But he soon realized that he was as alone as ever. His two sons eluded him and he had had no further contact with his daughter Blanca. All he knew about her was what her brothers told him, and he simply mailed her a check once a month, faithful to the promise he had made to Jean de Satigny. He was so out of touch with his sons that every conversation he had with them ended in a shouting match. Trueba learned of Nicolás's follies much too late, which is to say, after everyone else was already talking about them. Nor did he know anything of Jaime's life. If it had ever occurred to him that Jaime met frequently with Pedro Tercero García, for whom he had developed a brotherly affection, Trueba would certainly have had a stroke, but Jaime was very careful not to discuss such matters with his father.

Pedro Tercero García had left the countryside. After his terrible encounter with his *patrón*, he was taken in by Father José Dulce María in the parish house. The priest treated his hand. But the boy was deeply depressed and spoke constantly of the meaninglessness of life now that he had lost Blanca and could no longer play the guitar, which had been his one consolation. Father José Dulce María waited for the boy's strong constitution to heal his severed fingers. Then he put him on a cart and took him to the Indian reservation, where he introduced him to a century-old blind woman whose hands were clawed from rheumatism but who was still strong-willed enough to make baskets with her feet. "If she can make baskets with her toes, you can play the guitar without your fingers," he told him. And then the Jesuit told the boy his own story.

"I was also in love when I was your age," he said. "My girlfriend was the most beautiful girl in our village. We were going to get married and she had begun to embroider her trousseau and I had started saving money to build us a little house when I was called up for military service. When I returned, she had married the butcher and become a fat, matronly woman. I was about to throw myself into the river with a heavy stone tied to my feet, but then I decided to become a priest. A year after I took my vows, she became a widow and began to come to church and stare at me with languid eyes." The frank laughter of the gigantic Jesuit lifted Pedro Tercero's spirits and brought a smile to his lips for the first time in three weeks. "So you see, my child," the priest concluded, "there's no reason to lose hope. You'll see Blanca again, the day you least expect to."

Healed in both body and soul, Pedro Tercero García

made his way to the capital with a bundle of clothes and a few coins the priest had taken from the poor box. He had also given him the address of a Socialist leader, who took him in and gave him a place to sleep his first few nights in the city and then found him a job singing folk songs in a bohemian café. The young man settled in a working-class neighborhood, in a wooden shack that seemed like a palace to him. His only furniture was a box spring, a mattress, a chair, and two crates for a table. From there he preached Socialism and mulled over his disgust at Blanca's having married someone else, refusing to accept Jaime's explanations and consolation. He soon mastered his right hand and expanded his use of the two fingers that remained, continuing to compose songs about hens and hunted foxes. One day he was invited to appear on a radio program, which was the beginning of a giddy popularity he had never expected. His voice began to be heard often on the radio and his name became known. But Senator Trueba never heard it, because he did not allow radios in his house. He viewed them as instruments for the uneducated, and purveyors of sinister influences and vulgar ideas. No one was further removed from popular music than he was; the only melody he could stand to listen to was the sound of opera during the season and the zarzuela company that came from Spain each winter.

The day Jaime came home with the news that he wanted to change his last name because ever since his father had been a senator in the Conservative Party his fellow students at the university had been harassing him and the poor people in the Misericordia District no longer trusted him, Esteban Trueba lost his temper and was about to slap him when he realized that this time his son would not tolerate it.

"I married so I would have legitimate sons to bear my name, not bastards with their mother's!" he roared, livid with rage.

Two weeks later it was whispered in the corridors of Congress and the sitting rooms of the club that his son Jaime had pulled off his pants in the middle of the Plaza Brasil to give them to a beggar, and had walked the fifteen blocks back to his house in his underwear, followed by a bevy of children and curious observers who cheered him on. Tired of defending his honor from ridicule and gossip, Esteban allowed his son to take whatever name he wanted, provided that it not be his own. That day, locked in his study, he wept with disappointment and rage. He tried to tell himself that his son's eccentricities would disappear with age, and that sooner or later he would become a well-adjusted man who would join him in his business and become his support in his old age. With his other son he had given up hope. Nicolás went from one fantastic enterprise to another. His chief ambition at this point was to cross the *cordillera* in an unusual form of transportation, just as his Uncle Marcos had tried to do many years before. He had chosen to rise in a balloon, convinced that the spectacle of a gigantic balloon suspended in the clouds would be an irresistible form of publicity for almost any carbonated drink. He copied the model of a prewar German zeppelin, which lifted off by means of a hot-air system and could accommodate one or more passengers endowed with adventurous temperaments. His zeal to construct that enormous, inflatable sausage and to learn all its secret mechanisms, as well as to study wind currents, the predictions of his cards, and the laws of aerodynamics, kept him busy for quite some time. Weeks passed and he forgot all about the Friday spiritualist sessions with his mother and the three Mora sisters, and did not even notice that Amanda had stopped coming to the house. Once his flying ship was finished, he found himself face to face with an unexpected obstacle: the manager of the soda company, a gringo from Arkansas, refused to finance his project, arguing that if Nicolás was killed in his machine, sales of his beverage would decline. Nicolás tried to find other sponsors, but no one was interested. That did not dissuade him from his enterprise. He decided to go up anyway, even if his trip was unpaid for. On the appointed day, Clara continued her knitting unperturbed, without noticing her son's preparations, even though her family, friends, and neighbors were all horrified at the insane plan of crossing the mountains in that outlandish contraption.

"I have a hunch it isn't going to take off," said Clara without looking up from her knitting.

And she was right. At the last minute a truckful of policemen drove up beside the public park that Nicolás had chosen as his airfield. They demanded a city permit, which, of course, he did not have. Nor was he able to obtain one. He spent four days rushing from one office to the next, in a series of desperate maneuvers that all ran up against the same wall of bureaucratic incomprehension. He never found out that behind the police truck and the interminable paperwork was his father's influence, because his father was damned if he was going to permit such an adventure. Weary of fighting the timidity of the soda company and the aerial bureaucracy, Nicolás became convinced that the balloon would never rise, unless he did it surreptitiously, which was impossible given the dimensions of his ship. He suffered an anxiety attack, from which his mother rescued him by suggesting that in order not to lose his investment he try to think of some practical use for the material he had used to build his balloon. It was then that Nicolás had the idea of the sandwich factory. His plan was to make chicken sandwiches, wrap them in the pieces of the balloon's skin, and sell them to office workers. The large kitchen of his house seemed to him ideal for this purpose. The gardens soon filled with birds whose legs had been laced together, waiting their turn to be decapitated by the two butchers specially hired for that purpose. The courtyard filled with feathers and the Olympian statues were splattered with blood. The smell of consommé had made everyone nauseated, and the table used to gut the birds had begun to fill the whole neighborhood with flies when Clara brought an end to the slaughter with an attack of nerves that almost thrust her back to her days of muteness. This second commercial failure was less important to Nicolás, whose stomach and conscience had also been upset by the slaughter. He resigned himself to losing whatever he had invested in these schemes and locked himself in his room to plan new ways to make money and amuse himself.

"It's been a while since I've seen Amanda around here," Jaime said when he could no longer stand the impatience of his heart.

Then Nicolás remembered Amanda and realized that he had not seen her in the house for at least three weeks and that she had not been present at either the failed balloon attempt or the inauguration of the domestic production of bread with chicken. He went to ask Clara, but his mother also knew nothing of the girl and had begun to forget her. She had been forced to accept the fact that her house was now a way station and, as she put it, she did not have soul enough to worry about all the people who were absent. Nicolás decided to go look for her, because he realized that he missed the anxious butterfly of her presence and her silent, suffocating embraces in the empty rooms of the big house on the corner, where they thrashed about like puppies every time Clara let her guard down and Miguel was off playing or asleep in some corner.

The pension where Amanda lived with her little brother turned out to be a moldering old house that fifty years earlier had probably boasted some ostentatious splendor but had lost it as the city gradually expanded to the foothills of the *cordillera*. At first it had been occupied by Arab merchants who encrusted it with pink friezes; later, when the Arabs moved their business to the Turkish Quarter, the owner had turned it into a boardinghouse, subdividing it into poorly lit, sad, uncomfortable, and awkwardly constructed rooms for tenants of little means. It had an impossible labyrinth of dark, narrow halls, in which the stink of cauliflower soup and cabbage stew reigned eternally. The owner of the place came out to open the door in person. She was an immense mountain of a woman endowed with a majestic triple chin and tiny Oriental eyes sunk in folds congealed with grease; she wore rings on all her fingers, and used the affected gestures of a novice.

"We don't accept visitors of the opposite sex," she told Nicolás.

But Nicolás unfurled his irresistible seducer's smile, kissed her on the hand without jumping back at the sight of her filthy chipped vermilion fingernails, went into ecstasies over her rings, and passed himself off as a first cousin of Amanda's until the woman, defeated and twisting her mouth into flirtatious smiles and elephantine contortions, led him up the dusty stairs to the third floor and pointed to Amanda's door. Nicolás found the young girl in her bed, wrapped in a discolored shawl, playing checkers with her brother Miguel. She was so green and slight that it was hard for him to recognize her. Amanda stared at him without smiling and made no sign of welcome. Miguel, however, stood in front of him with his hands on his hips.

"You finally came," the child said.

Nicolás walked to the bed and tried to recall the dark, supple Amanda, the fruity, sinuous Amanda of their encounters in the darkness of the locked rooms, but between the caked wool of the shawl and the gray sheets there was a strange woman with huge, lost eyes who was staring at him with inexplicable harshness. "Amanda," he murmured, taking her by the hand. Without its silver rings and bracelets, the hand looked as weak as the leg of a dying bird. Amanda called her brother. Miguel went to the bed and she whispered something in his ear. The boy walked slowly toward the door. From the threshold he shot Nicolás a furious departing look and walked out, shutting the door noiselessly behind him.

"Forgive me, Amanda," Nicolás said. "I was very busy. Why didn't you tell me you were sick?"

"I'm not sick," she replied. "I'm pregnant."

That word hit Nicolás like a slap. He stepped back until he felt the glass of the window behind his shoulders. From the very first time he had undressed Amanda, fumbling his way in the darkness, tangled in the rags of her existentialist disguise, trembling with anticipation as he felt the protuberances and interstices that he had so often imagined without ever knowing them in all their splendid nakedness, he had assumed that she had sufficient experience to avoid making him a father at twenty-one and herself an unwed mother at twenty-five. Amanda had had other loves before, and had been the first person to speak to him of free love. She insisted on her unequivocal determination for them to remain together only so long as they were friends, without constraints or promises for the future, just like Sartre and Beauvoir. This agreement, which to Nicolás had first seemed like a shocking sign of coldness and distance, turned out to be to his advantage. Relaxed and happy as he was about everything in life, he let himself fall in love without thinking of the consequences.

"Now what are we going to do!" he exclaimed.

"An abortion, of course," she replied.

A wave of relief broke over Nicolás. He had sidestepped

the abyss yet one more time. As always happened when he was playing alongside a precipice, someone stronger than himself had risen up beside him to take charge of things— just like the times at school when he would taunt the other boys until they jumped on top of him and then, at the very last possible minute, when he was paralyzed with terror, Jaime would appear and stand in front of him, changing his panic to euphoria and allowing him to run for cover behind the pillars of the courtyard and shout insults from his refuge, while his brother bled from his nose and delivered punches with the silent tenacity of a machine. Now Amanda was taking responsibility for him.

"We can get married, Amanda—if—you want," he stammered to save face.

"No!" she answered without hesitation. "I don't love you enough for that, Nicolás."

His feelings immediately swerved, for that possibility had not occurred to him. Up until that point he had never felt rejected or abandoned, and in each of his affairs he had had to resort to all his tact to disengage himself without hurting the girl. He thought about the difficult situation Amanda now faced—poor, alone, and expecting a child. One word from him could change her fate, converting her into the respectable wife of a Trueba. These calculations flashed through his mind in a fraction of a second, but he immediately felt ashamed, and blushed at catching himself in such thoughts. Suddenly, Amanda looked magnificent to him. He remembered all the wonderful moments they had shared, the times they had lain on the floor smoking the same pipe to get high together, laughing at that grass that tasted like dry dung and had hardly any hallucinogenic effect but did activate the power of suggestion; the yoga exercises and meditations they had performed as a couple, seated face to face in complete relaxation, staring into each other's eyes and murmuring Sanskrit words that could send them all the way to nirvana but that generally had the opposite effect, and they would wind up slipping out of other people's sight, stretched out beneath the tall reeds in the garden, desperately making love; the books they had read by candlelight, drowning in passion and smoke; the interminable gatherings during which they discussed the pessimistic postwar philosophers or concentrated on trying to move the three-legged table—two taps for yes, three for no—while Clara laughed at them. He fell to his knees beside the bed, begging Amanda not to leave him, to forgive him, to let them go on as if nothing had happened, because this was simply an unfortunate accident that could not affect the untouchable essence of their relationship. But she seemed not to listen. She was caressing his hair with a maternal, distracted air.

"It's no use, Nicolás," she said. "Can't you see my soul is very old and you're still a child? You'll always be a child."

They continued to caress each other without desire, torturing themselves with pleas and memories. They were savoring the bitterness of a parting that they could already sense but could still confuse with a reconciliation. She got up from bed to prepare them both some tea, and Nicolás saw that she was using an old slip as a nightgown. She had lost weight, and her skinny calves invited his pity. She walked barefoot in the room, with the shawl over her shoulders and her hair unkempt, hovering over the little kerosene stove she kept perched on the single table that served as her dining-room table, her desk, and her kitchen table. He saw the disorder Amanda lived in and realized that until then he had known almost nothing about her. He had assumed that she had no other family besides her brother, and that she lived on a small salary, but he had never imagined her actual situation. Poverty to him was an abstract, distant concept, applicable to the tenants at Tres Marías and the indigent patients his brother Jaime helped; he had never had any direct contact with it himself. Amanda, his Amanda so close and so well known, suddenly became a stranger. He glanced at her clothes, which looked like the garments of a queen when she had them on, but now, hanging from their nails on the wall, seemed like the sad rags of a beggar. He looked at her toothbrush in a glass above the rusty sink, Miguel's school shoes that had been blackened and reblackened so many times they had lost their shape, at the old typewriter beside the stove, the books lying among the coffee cups, the broken window patched with newspaper. It was another world. A world whose existence he had not even suspected. Until that moment there had been a dividing line on one side of which stood the solemn poor and on the other people like himself, among whom he had classed Amanda. He knew nothing of that silent middle class that struggled between genteel poverty and the impossible desire of emulating the golden canaille to which he himself belonged. He felt confused and embarrassed, thinking of the many occasions in the past when she must have had to use witchcraft to keep her poverty from being noticed at the Truebas' and he, in his complete innocence, hadn't helped her. He remembered his father's stories about his poor childhood and how at Nicolás's age he was already out working to support his mother and sister. For the first time in his life, he managed to link those didactic anecdotes with a reality he could see. He thought Amanda's life must be like that.

They shared a cup of tea sitting on the bed, because there was only one chair. Amanda told him about her past, her family, her alcoholic father who had been a teacher in one of the northern provinces, her sad, overworked mother who had to support six children and how, as soon as she was able to stand on her own two feet, she had run away from home. She had reached the capital when she was only fifteen, arriving at the house of a generous godmother who helped her for a while. Later, when her mother died, she had gone to bury her and bring back Miguel, who was still in diapers. She had been his mother ever since. She had no idea what had become of her father and her other brothers and sisters. Nicolás felt a rising desire to protect her and take care of her, to make up for everything. He had never loved her more.

At dusk Miguel arrived with ruddy cheeks, squirming in silent amusement to hide the present he was holding behind his back. It was a paper sack of bread for his sister. He put it on the bed, kissed her tenderly, smoothed her hair with his tiny hand, and straightened the pillows. Nicolás shuddered. There was more tenderness and love in the gestures of that little boy than in all the caresses he had showered on any woman in his life. Only then did he understand what Amanda had meant. "I have a lot to learn," he murmured. He leaned his forehead against the greasy pane of the window, wondering whether he would ever be able to give as much as he hoped to receive.

"How are we going to do it?" he asked, not daring to pronounce the terrible word.

"Ask your brother Jaime for help," Amanda suggested.

Jaime received his brother in his tunnel of books, lying on his cot in the light of the solitary bulb that hung directly above him from the ceiling. He was reading the love sonnets of the Poet, who was by now a world-renowned figure, as Clara had predicted the first time she heard him recite in his telluric voice at one of her literary soirées. He wondered whether the sonnets might not have been inspired by Amanda's presence in the Trueba garden, where the Poet liked to sit at teatime and talk about songs of despair, during the period when he had been an assiduous visitor at the big house on the corner. He was surprised to see Nicolás, because since they had finished school, he and his brother had daily grown further apart. Most recently they had had nothing to say to each other, and on the rare occasions when they met on the doorstep, they had merely exchanged nods. Jaime had given up on his idea of drawing Nicolás into transcendental matters of existence.

He still took his brother's frivolous activities as a personal affront, for he could not accept the fact that Nicolás could waste his time and energy on balloon rides and the slaughter of chickens when there was so much work to be done in the Misericordia District. But he no longer tried to drag him to the hospital to make him look at suffering up close, hoping aginst hope that the pain of others might move his bird-of-passage heart, and he had stopped inviting him to the Socialist meetings at Pedro Tercero García's house, on the last street of the working-class district, where they all gathered every Thursday under the eye of the police. Nicolás made fun of his social concerns, arguing that only a fool with the calling of an apostle would go out into the world seeking misery and ugliness with the stump of a candle. Now Jaime's brother stood before him, staring at him with the guilty, pleading look he had used so many times to enlist his affection.

"Amanda's pregnant," Nicolás said without preamble.

He had to repeat himself, because Jaime did not move, remaining as unresponsive as ever, without the slightest gesture to show that he had heard his brother's words. But inside his frustration was choking him. Silently, he called Amanda's name, clutching the sweet echo of the word in order not to lose control. So fierce was his need to hold on to his illusions that he had managed to convince himself that the love between Amanda and his brother was completely juvenile and limited to innocent strolls on which they walked hand in hand, to discussions over a bottle of absinthe, and to the few fleeting kisses he had glimpsed over the years.

He had refused to admit the painful truth that was now confronting him.

"Don't tell me about it. It's no business of mine," he replied as soon as he was able to speak.

Nicolás collapsed onto the end of the bed, burying his face in his hands.

"Please, you've got to help her!" he begged.

Jaime closed his eyes and inhaled with difficulty, forcing himself to contain the wild feelings that made him want to kill his brother, to run and marry Amanda himself, to weep in impotence and disappointment. He had an image of her in his mind, the same image that appeared to him whenever he was racked by feelings of love. He saw her entering and leaving the house like a gust of fresh air, leading her little brother by the hand. He heard her laughter on the terrace and smelled the sweet, subtle aroma of her skin and hair when she walked past him in the midday sun. He saw her as he imagined her in all the idle hours he spent dreaming of her. Above all, he thought of her at the precise moment when she entered his bedroom and they were alone together in the intimacy of his refuge. She entered without knocking, while he was reading in bed, filling his burrow with the flutter of her long hair and her undulating arms. She touched his books without the slightest sign of reverence, and even dared to take them from their sacred shelves; she blew the dust off their covers without the least respect and tossed them onto the bed, chatting all the while as he trembled with desire and surprise, unable to extract from his whole encyclopedic vocabulary a single word to hold her there, until she finally took leave of him with a kiss on the cheek that continued to burn: a single, terrible kiss on which he built a labyrinth of dreams where the two of them were a prince and princess hopelessly in love.

"You know about medicine, Jaime," Nicolás pleaded. "You've got to do something."

"I'm only a student. I have a long way to go before I'm a doctor. I don't know anything about all that. And I've seen a lot of women die because some ignoramus got his hands on them."

"She trusts you. She says you're the only one who can help her," Nicolás replied.

Jaime grabbed his brother by the lapels and lifted him off the floor, shaking him like a puppet and hurling every insult he could think of at him, until his own sobs obliged him to set him down. Nicolás whimpered in relief. He knew his brother, and his intuition told him that, as always, he had decided to accept the role of protector.

"Thank you, Jaime!"

Jaime gave him a listless slap on the back and pushed him out of his room. He turned his key in the lock and lay face down on his cot, shaken by the hoarse, terrible moans with which men weep for love.

They waited until Sunday. Jaime agreed to see them in the clinic of the Misericordia District, where he was taking his training as a doctor. He had the key because he was always the last to leave, so he could get in with ease, but he felt like a thief because he would not be able to explain his presence there at such a time. For the previous three days, he had done nothing but study every step of the operation he was about to perform. He could repeat each word of the book in perfect order, but that did not bolster his confidence. He was shaking like a leaf. He tried not to think of all the women he had seen in the emergency room, those he had helped to save in this very examining room, and those who had died in these very beds, white as sheets, with a river of blood flowing between their legs and his science powerless to stop their life from running out of that open faucet. He had seen this drama close up, but until this moment he had never had to face the moral conflict of helping a desperate woman. Much less Amanda. He turned on the lights, donned the white tunic of his profession, and prepared his instruments, repeating aloud every detail he had memorized. He prayed for some monumental disaster to occur, some cataclysm that would shake the planet to its core, so that he would not have to do what he was about to do. But nothing happened until the appointed hour.

Meanwhile Nicolás had gone to fetch Amanda in old Covadonga, which still ran, though it barely sputtered along on its remaining nuts and bolts, lost in a black cloud of burning oil. She was waiting for him seated in her chair, holding Miguel's hand, the two of them deep in a mutual complicity from which, as always, Nicolás felt excluded. Amanda looked pale and emaciated after all the ups and downs of the last uncertain weeks, but she was calmer than Nicolás, who was practically incoherent and could not keep still, trying to cheer her with a false hilarity and pointless jokes. He had brought her an old ring with garnets and diamonds that he had taken from his mother's room, knowing full well that she would never miss it and that, even if she saw it on Amanda's hand, she would never recognize it because Clara could not keep track of things like that. Amanda gently returned it.

"You see, Nicolás?" she said, unsmiling. "You're still a child."

When it came time to leave, little Miguel put on a poncho and held tight to his sister's hand. Nicolás had to use all his charm and then brute strength to deposit him with the owner of the house, who in the past few days had been completely won over by the supposed cousin of her tenant and had, much against her will, agreed to look after the child for the evening.

They drove in silence, each lost in his own fear. To Nicolás, Amanda's hostility was like a pestilence that had descended between them. In the past few days she had begun to dwell on the idea of death, which she feared less than the pain and humiliation she would have to face that night. He steered Covadonga through an unfamiliar section of the city, down dark back streets in which garbage was piled against the walls of factories, in a forest of smokestacks that shut out the sky. Stray dogs sniffed at the grime, and beggars wrapped in newspaper slept in the doorways. He was startled that this should be the scene of his brother's daily activities.

• • •

Jaime was waiting for them in front of the clinic. His white smock and his own anxiety made him look much older than he was. He led them through a labyrinth of icy corridors to the room he had prepared, doing his best to distract Amanda from the ugliness of the place. He did not want her to notice the bins full of yellowed towels waiting to be washed on Monday, the graffiti on the walls, the loose tiles, and the rusty pipes that dripped continuously. Amanda stopped with a look of horror when they came to the door of the operating room: she had seen the instruments and the gynecological table. What until then had been an abstraction, a mere flirtation with the possibility of death, suddenly materialized before her. Nicolás was pale, but Jaime took them both by the arm and led them through the door.

"Don't look, Amanda!" he told her. "I'm going to put you to sleep."

He had never administered anesthesia or performed a surgical operation. As a student, his work was confined to administrative tasks, record-keeping, and providing assistance in treatment, suturing, and other minor tasks. He was even more afraid than Amanda, but to make her think this was all routine, he adopted the relaxed, pompous air he had seen doctors use. To spare her the embarrassment of undressing before him and to spare himself the pain of seeing her in the nude, he helped her lie down fully dressed on the operating table. While he washed his hands and showed Nicolás how to wash his too, he tried to distract her with the anecdote about the Spanish ghost that had appeared to Clara during one of the Friday-evening sessions, bringing word of a treasure buried in the foundations of the house; and he told her about his family: a collection of eccentric lunatics for several generations, whom even ghosts made fun of. But Amanda was not listening. She was as white as a sheet, and her teeth were chattering.

"What are these straps for?" she asked. "I don't want to be tied down."

"I'm not going to tie you down. Nicolás is going to give you the ether. Breathe normally, don't get frightened, and when you wake up it will be all over," Jaime told her, his eyes smiling above his mask.

Nicolás brought the anesthesia mask over to Amanda.

The last thing she saw before slipping into darkness was Jaime looking at her with such love in his eyes that she thought she must be dreaming. Nicolás removed her clothes and strapped her to the table, aware that this was even worse than rape, while his brother waited with gloved hands, trying not to see in her the woman of his dreams but only a body like so many others that crossed this table every day with screams of pain. He began to work slowly and carefully, telling himself again exactly what he had to do, mumbling the words he had learned by heart as the sweat poured down onto his eyes. He was keenly aware of the girl's breathing, the color of her skin, the rhythm of her heart, so that he could signal to his brother to increase the ether every time she moaned, praying that no complications would arise as he probed deeply into her most secret parts, never for a moment ceasing to curse his brother in his thoughts. For if this child had been his instead of Nicolás's, it would have been born healthy and intact, instead of exiting in bits and pieces in this sewer of a clinic. He would have cradled it and protected it instead of extracting it from its nest with a scoop. Twenty-five minutes later he was finished. He ordered Nicolás to help him with her until the effects of the ether had worn off, but when he looked up, he saw that his brother was slumped against the wall, retching violently.

"Idiot!" Jaime roared. "Go to the bathroom, and when you've finished puking up your guilt wait for me outside, because we still have a long way to go!"

Nicolás staggered out, and Jaime took off his mask and gloves and proceeded to loosen Amanda's straps, gently slip on her clothes, hide the bloody traces of his work, and remove the instruments of torture from her sight. Then he lifted her in his arms, treasuring this moment in which he could clasp her to his chest, and carried her to a bed he had already made up with clean sheets, which was more than the women who usually came for help received. He covered her and sat down beside her. For the first time in his life he was able to observe her at his leisure. She was smaller and sweeter than she looked when she was running around in her fortune-teller's costume and her armfuls of bracelets; and as he had imagined, the bones in her slender body were barely hinted at between the tiny hills and smooth alleys of her femininity. Without her scandalous mane of hair and her sphinx eyes, she looked fifteen. To Jaime, her vulnerability was more seductive than anything that had attracted him before. He felt twice as large, twice as heavy, and a thousand times stronger, but he knew he was defeated from the start because of the tenderness he felt and his desire to protect her. He cursed his invincible sentimentality and tried to see her as his brother's lover, a woman on whom he had just performed an abortion, but he immediately realized how impossible that was and surrendered to the pleasure and suffering of loving her. He stroked her transparent hands, her slender fingers, the shells of her ears, and ran his hands over her neck, listening to the imperceptible sound of the life inside her veins. He moved his mouth close to her lips and eagerly inhaled the scent of anesthesia, but he was not bold enough to touch them.

Amanda slowly emerged from sleep. First she felt cold and then she was seized by a fit of retching. Jaime comforted her by speaking to her in the same secret language he reserved for animals and for the smallest children in the hospital, until she gradually relaxed. She began to cry and he continued to caress her. They remained silent as she wavered between sleep, nausea, anxiety, and the pain that was beginning to grip her womb, and he fervently wished that this night would never end.

"Do you think I'll be able to have children?" she finally asked.

"I suppose so," he replied. "But try to find them a responsible father."

They both smiled with relief. Amanda searched Jaime's dark face, which was leaning over her, for signs of some resemblance to Nicolás, but found none. For the first time in her nomadic existence she felt protected and safe. She gave a sigh of contentment and forgot all about the sordid surroundings, the peeling walls, the cold metal cupboards, the dreadful instruments, the smell of disinfectant, and even that raucous pain that had settled inside her.

"Please lie down next to me and hold me," she said.

He lay down timidly on the narrow bed, wrapping his arms around her. He concentrated on being as still as he could so as not to disturb her and not to fall. He had the awkward tenderness of someone who has never been loved and is forced to improvise. Amanda closed her eyes and smiled. They lay there breathing together in utter calm, like brother and sister, until day began to break and the light from the window became stronger than the light of the lamp. Then Jaime helped her to her feet, put her coat around her shoulders, and led her by the arm to the waiting room, where Nicolás had spent the night sleeping in a chair.

"Wake up!" Jaime said. "We're going to take her home so Mama can look after her. It's better for her not to be alone for a few days."

"I knew we could count on you," Nicolás replied, his voice breaking with gratitude.

"I didn't do it for you, creep, I did it for her," Jaime growled, turning his back on his brother.

Clara let them into the big house on the corner without asking any questions. Or perhaps she had already asked them of her cards or the spirits. They had had to wake her, because the sun was just coming up and everyone was still asleep.

"Mama, you have to help Amanda," Jaime pleaded, with the certainty that came from their complicity in matters such as this. "She's sick and she needs to stay here a few days."

"What about little Miguel?" Amanda asked.

"I'll go get him," Nicolás replied, and he left.

They prepared one of the guest rooms and Amanda got into bed. Jaime took her temperature and said she ought to rest. He started to go out, but remained in the doorway, leaning against the frame, still undecided. Just then Clara returned with a tray of coffee for the three of them.

"I suppose we owe you an explanation, Mama," Jaime murmured as they drank their coffee.

"No, son," Clara answered gaily. "If it's a sin, I'd rather not know about it. Let's use the occasion to pamper Amanda. She needs it."

Her son followed her out. Jaime looked at his mother a few paces ahead of him in the hallway, barefoot, her loose hair hanging down her back, and wrapped in her white bathrobe, and he realized that she was not as tall and strong as she had seemed to him in childhood. He reached out and took her by the shoulder. She turned around and smiled, and

Jaime hugged her compulsively, clasping her to his chest and scratching her forehead with his chin, whose impossible beard was already clamoring for a shave. It was the first time he had embraced her spontaneously since he was a tiny baby rooted to her breast by need, and Clara was astonished to see how big her son had become; he had the thorax of a weight lifter and a pair of arms like hammers that could crush her with a terrifying force. Stirred and happy, she wondered how it was possible that this hairy giant with the strength of a bear and the candor of a novitiate could have ever lain inside her belly, especially as one of two.

During the next few days, Amanda ran a fever. Shaken, Jaime kept constant watch and gave her sulfa drugs. Clara tended her. She couldn't fail to notice that Nicolás discreetly asked about her but made no attempt to visit her. Jaime, on the other hand, lent her his favorite books and walked around like someone in a trance, babbling incoherently and crisscrossing the house as he had never done before. On Thursday night he forgot his Socialist meeting.

Thus, for a little while, Amanda became a member of the family, and Miguel, through exceptional circumstances, was present, hidden in a wardrobe, the day Alba was born in the Trueba house. He never forgot the grandiose, terrible sight of that tiny child entering the world, coated with all her bloody membranes, between the shrieks of her mother and the cries of the women bustling around her.

Meanwhile, Esteban Trueba had left on a trip to the United States. Tired of the pain in his bones and the secret illness that only he perceived, he had decided it was time to be examined by foreign doctors; he had reached the premature conclusion that Latin doctors were all charlatans who were closer to sorcerers than scientists. His shrinking was so infinitesimal, so slow and so sly, that no one other than himself had noticed it. He had to buy shoes one size smaller, shorten his trousers, and have a tuck taken in his shirtsleeves. One day he put on the black hat he had not worn all summer and it covered his ears completely, which led him to deduce that if his brain was shrinking, his ideas were also probably withering away. The gringo doctors measured his body, weighed each piece of him separately, interrogated him in English, injected liquids into him with one needle and extracted them with another, photographed him, turned him inside out like a glove, and even stuck a light up his anus. In the end, they concluded that it was all in his mind, that there was no reason for him to believe that he was shrinking, that he had always been the same size, but that perhaps he had dreamt that he was once six feet tall and wore a size-twelve shoe. Esteban Trueba lost patience and returned to his country prepared to ignore the problem of his height, since all great politicians in history had been small, from Napoleon to Hitler. When he arrived at his house, he saw Miguel playing in the garden and Amanda, thinner and with deep bags under her eyes, stripped of her makeup and her bracelets, sitting with Jaime on the terrace. He asked no questions, for he was accustomed to seeing total strangers living under his roof.

EIGHT

The Count

Had it not been for the letters Clara and Blanca exchanged, that entire period would have remained submerged in a jumble of faded, timeworn memories. Their abundant correspondence salvaged events from the mists of improbable facts. From the very first letter she received from her daughter after her wedding, Clara could tell that her separation from Blanca would not last long. Without saying a word to anyone, she prepared one of the largest, sunniest rooms in the house. In it she placed the bronze cradle in which her own three children had slept.

Blanca was never able to explain to her mother why she had agreed to marry, because she herself did not know. Analyzing her past when she had reached middle age, she decided that the main reason was her fear of her father. Ever since she was a child, she had been familiar with the irrational strength of his anger, and she was used to obeying him. In the end, her pregnancy and the news of Pedro Tercero's death decided her. Still, from the moment she accepted the liaison with Jean de Satigny, she knew that she would never consummate the marriage. She would invent every possible argument for postponing their union, at first relying on the discomforts peculiar to her state and afterward finding additional excuses, because she was convinced that it would be far easier to manage a husband like the count, who wore kidskin shoes, polished his fingernails, and was willing to marry a woman pregnant with someone else's child, than to oppose a father like Esteban Trueba. Of two evils, she chose the one that struck her as the lesser. She realized that there was a commercial arrangement between the French count and her father in which she had no say. In exchange for a surname for his grandchild, Trueba gave Jean de Satigny a rich dowry and the promise that he would eventually receive an inheritance. Blanca lent herself to their negotiations, but she was not prepared to surrender either her love or her intimacy to her husband, because she was still in love with Pedro Tercero, more out of force of habit than out of any hope of ever seeing him again.

Blanca and her new husband spent their wedding night in the honeymoon suite of the best hotel in the capital, which Trueba had filled with flowers in the hope of winning his daughter's forgiveness for the string of assaults to which he had subjected her during the preceding months. To her great surprise, there was no need for her to feign a migraine. As soon as they were alone together, Jean shed his role as the eager suitor who had planted furtive kisses on her neck and who had chosen the finest shrimp to put into her mouth one by one. It was as if he had thoroughly forgotten his seductive, silent-movie-idol manner, and become instead the brother he had been to her in the days of their country strolls, when they would spread their picnic lunch on the ground and take photographs and read aloud in French. Jean disappeared into the bathroom, where he stayed so long that by the time he returned to the bedroom Blanca was half asleep. She thought she must be dreaming when she saw that her husband had changed out of his wedding suit into black silk pajamas and a velvet Pompeian bathrobe. He had put a net over his impeccably waved hair and reeked of eau de cologne. He seemed to have no great amatory impatience. He sat down beside her on the bed and began to stroke her cheek with the same half-mocking touch he had used on earlier occasions. Then, in his affected, r-less Spanish, he proceeded to explain that he had no particular inclination for married life, being in love only with the arts, literature, and scientific curiosities, and therefore had no intention of disturbing her with the usual demands of a husband; they could live together, but not entwined, in perfect harmony and decorum. Relieved, Blanca threw her arms around his neck and kissed him on both cheeks.

"Thank you, Jean!" she exclaimed.

"You're welcome," he replied courteously.

They settled into the large Empire-style bed, talking about the wedding party and making plans for their future life.

"Don't you want to know who the father of my child is?" Blanca asked.

"I am," Jean replied, kissing her on the forehead.

They each slept on their own side of the bed, back to back. At five o'clock in the morning, Blanca awoke with an upset stomach from the cloyingly sweet smell of the flowers with which her father had adorned the nuptial chamber. Jean de Satigny helped her to the bathroom, supported her while she leaned over the toilet, led her back to bed, and put the flowers out in the hall. Afterward he was unable to fall back to sleep, and spent the rest of the night reading *La Philosophie dans le boudoir,* of the Marquis de Sade, while Blanca sighed through her dreams that it was marvelous to be married to an intellectual.

The next day, Jean went to the bank to cash a check from his father-in-law and spent nearly the whole day going from one store to another buying the attire he considered appropriate to his new economic position. Meanwhile, bored with waiting for him in the hotel lobby, Blanca decided to pay a visit to her mother. She put on her best morning hat and took a cab to the big house on the corner, where the rest of her family was eating in silence, still irritable and tired from the upheaval of the wedding and the aftereffects of their recent fights. When he saw her enter the dining room, her father gave a shout of horror.

"What are you doing here!" he roared.

"Nothing ... I've come to see you," Blanca murmured, terrified.

"You're out of your mind! Don't you realize that if anybody sees you they're going to say that your husband sent you home in the middle of your honeymoon? They'll think you weren't a virgin!"

"But I wasn't, Papa."

Esteban was about to strike her in the face, but Jaime

stood between them with such firmness that Esteban resigned himself to insulting her for her stupidity. Clara, unshakable, led Blanca to a chair and served her a plate of cold fish with caper sauce. While Esteban continued screaming and Nicolás went to get the car to return her to her husband, the two women whispered just like in old times.

That same afternoon Blanca and Jean took the train to the port, where they boarded an English ocean liner. He was wearing white linen trousers with a blue jacket styled like a sailor's, which went beautifully with the blue skirt and white jacket of his wife's tailored suit. Four days later, the vessel deposited them in the farthest province of the North, where their elegant travel attire and crocodile bags went unnoticed in the dry, suffocating heat of the siesta. Jean de Satigny settled his wife provisionally in a hotel and turned his attention to the task of finding them lodgings worthy of his new status. Within twenty-four hours the small provincial society world knew that an authentic count had arrived in their midst. This did much to advance Jean's cause. He was able to rent an ancient mansion that had belonged to one of the great saltpeter fortunes before they invented the synthetic substitute that had shot the whole industry to hell. The house was somewhat musty and abandoned, like everything in sight, and needed a number of repairs, but its former dignity and *fin de siècle* charms were intact. The count decorated it according to his personal taste, with a decadent, ambiguous refinement that startled Blanca, accustomed as she was to country life and her father's classical sobriety. Jean brought in suspicious Chinese porcelain vases that, instead of flowers, held dyed ostrich feathers, damask curtains with pleats and tassels, cushions with fringe and pompons, furniture of every style, gold room dividers, and screens and several incredible standing lamps held aloft by life-sized ceramic statues of half-naked Abyssinian Negroes wearing turbans and slippers with upturned toes. The curtains were almost always drawn, leaving the house in a tenuous darkness that kept the cruel desert light at bay. In the corners, Jean had placed Oriental incense burners in which he burnt special perfumed herbs and sticks of incense that at first turned Blanca's stomach but to which she quickly became accustomed. He hired several Indians to work for him, in

addition to a monumentally fat woman cook, whom he
taught to make the spicy sauces that he was so fond of, and a
lame, illiterate maid to wait on Blanca. They were all outfit-
ted with showy uniforms that looked like costumes from an
operetta, but he was unable to make them wear shoes,
because they were accustomed to going barefoot and could
not adjust. Blanca was uncomfortable in the house. She did
not trust the expressionless Indians who waited on her with
such evident ill will and seemed to make fun of her behind
her back. They moved around her like ghosts, gliding sound-
lessly through the rooms, almost always bored and empty-
handed. They never answered when she spoke to them, as if
they did not understand Spanish, and when they spoke
among themselves they always whispered or used one of the
mountain dialects. Whenever Blanca told her husband the
strange things she had observed among the servants, he
replied that they were Indian customs to which she should
pay no heed. Clara gave her the same answer in a letter after
Blanca wrote that one day she had seen one of the Indians
standing in a pair of astonishing antique shoes with twisted
heels and velvet laces, in which the man's broad, callused
feet had got stuck. "The heat of the desert, your pregnancy,
and your unconscious desire to live like a countess, in accordance with your husband's lineage, are making you see
things, darling," Clara wrote in jest, adding that the best
cure for Louis XV shoes was a cold shower and a cup of
camomile tea. Another time, Blanca found a small dead lizard
on her plate, which she was about to put in her mouth.
When she recovered from the shock and managed to regain
her voice, she called for the cook and pointed to the plate
with a trembling finger. The cook approached, her moun-
tainous fat and her braids swaying, and picked up the plate
without a word. But as she turned around, Blanca could have
sworn she caught a wink of complicity between her husband
and the cook. That night she lay awake very late, wondering
about what she had seen, until she finally concluded that she
had imagined it. Her mother was right: the heat and her
pregnancy were affecting her mind.

The farthest rooms in the house were allocated to Jean's
mania for photography. In them he set up his lights, his
tripods, and his various machines. He begged Blanca never

to enter what he called his "laboratory" without permission, because, he explained, the plates could be destroyed by natural light. He installed a lock on the door and carried the key everywhere he went on a gold watch chain, a completely useless precaution since his wife had practically no interest in her surroundings, much less in the art of photography.

The larger she grew, the deeper Blanca sank into an Oriental placidity that dashed all her husband's attempts to introduce her into society. He wanted to take her to parties, to drive her around by car, and to involve her in the decoration of her new home, but Blanca, heavy, torpid, solitary, and the victim of an unshakable fatigue, took refuge in her knitting and embroidery. She slept most of the day, and spent her few waking hours sewing tiny articles of clothing for a complete pink wardrobe, for she was convinced that her baby would be a girl. As her mother had done with her, she developed a whole system for communicating with the infant that was growing inside her, turning in on herself in a silent, uninterrupted dialogue. Her letters described her secluded, melancholy life, and she referred to her husband with blind sympathy, as a fine, discreet, considerate man. Thus, without ever setting out to do so, she set in motion the myth that Jean de Satigny was practically a prince, never mentioning the fact that he spent his afternoons inhaling cocaine and smoking opium, because she was sure her parents would not understand. She had a whole wing of the house to herself. There she had arranged her headquarters and begun to pile up all the things she was preparing for her daughter's arrival. Jean said that fifty children would not be able to wear all the clothes and play with all those toys, but Blanca's only amusement was to scour the paltry downtown stores, where she purchased every pink baby item she could find. She spent her days embroidering infants' dresses, knitting woolen booties, decorating little baskets, arranging the stacks of tiny blouses, bibs, and diapers, and ironing the sheets she had embroidered. After the siesta she would write her mother and sometimes her brother Jaime, and when the sun began to set and the air grew cooler she would go for a walk around the property to shake the numbness from her legs. In the evening she joined her husband in the enormous dining room, whose bordello lighting was supplied by the ceramic

Negroes standing in the corners. They sat at opposite ends of the table, which was set with a long tablecloth, a full service of china and glassware, and adorned with artificial flowers, because no real ones grew in that inhospitable region. They were always attended by the same impassive, silent Indian, who constantly sucked a green ball of coca leaves that was his chief sustenance. He was a peculiar servant, and had no specific duties within the domestic hierarchy. Waiting on table was certainly not his forte; he had still to master platters and serving implements, and would fling the food down however he could. One time, Blanca had to remind him please not to grab the potatoes with his hand and put them on her plate. But Jean de Satigny held him in mysterious regard and was training him to be his assistant in the laboratory.

"If he can't talk like a human being, how do you expect him to take pictures?" Blanca observed when Jean told her his plan.

This was the Indian Blanca thought she had seen in Louis XV heels.

Her first months as a wife were peaceful and boring. Blanca's natural tendency to isolation and solitude became accentuated. Since she refused to partake of the local social life, Jean de Satigny was forced to go alone to the numerous events to which they were invited. Later, returning home, he regaled Blanca with accounts of the vulgarity of these stale, out-of-date families, whose daughters were still chaperoned and whose gentlemen wore scapulars. Blanca led the idle life that was her true vocation, while her husband gave himself to those small pleasures that only money can buy and that he had denied himself for such a long time. Every night he went to the casino. His wife calculated that he must be losing huge sums of money, because at the end of the month there was invariably a long line of creditors at their door. Jean had very strange ideas about their household finances. He bought himself the most up-to-date automobile, with leopard-skin upholstery and golden fittings worthy of an Arab prince, the largest, most ostentatious car ever seen in those parts. He established a network of mysterious contacts that enabled him to buy antiques, particularly baroque French porcelain, for which he had a weakness. He also imported crates of fine liqueurs that were cleared through customs without incident. His contraband entered the house through the service door and exited through the front door on its way to other destinations, where Jean consumed it in secret revels or sold it at exorbitant prices. They never invited people to their house, and within weeks the ladies of the neighborhood had stopped inviting Blanca. Rumor had it she was proud, arrogant, and ill, which only increased the general sympathy for the count, who gained a reputation as a patient, long-suffering husband.

Blanca got along well with him. The only times they argued were when she tried to look into their finances. She could not understand how Jean could buy porcelain and drive that spotted car when he did not have enough money to pay the Chinese man in the general store or the salaries of their numerous servants. Jean refused to discuss the matter, on the assumption that it was a man's business and that she had no need to fill her sparrow's brain with problems she could not understand. Blanca supposed that Jean de Satigny's account with Esteban Trueba gave him unlimited amounts of money, and since it was impossible to reach an understanding with him, she ended up pretending to be ignorant of such matters. In this house embedded in sand and inhabited by strange Indians who seemed to exist in some other dimension, she vegetated like a flower from another climate, frequently coming across certain small details that made her question her own sanity. Reality seemed blurred to her, as if the same implacable sun that erased all colors had also deformed the world around her, transforming even people into silent shadows.

In the soporific heat of those months Blanca, protected by the creature that was growing inside her, forgot about the magnitude of her disgrace. She stopped thinking about Pedro Tercero García with the terrible urgency she had felt before and took refuge in the sweet, faded memories she could always conjure up at will. Her sensuality was dormant, and on the rare occasions when she brooded over her unfortunate fate, she had a pleasant vision of herself floating in a nebula, without suffering or joy, far away from the cruelties of life, with her daughter as her sole companion. She came to believe that she had lost her capacity to love, and that the burning desire of her flesh had been quelled forever. She spent interminable hours staring at the pallid landscape that stretched out before her window. The house was on the very edge of the city, and was ringed by a few rickety trees that had managed to withstand the onslaught of the desert. To the north, the wind had destroyed all vegetation, and she could see the immense plains of dunes and distant hills quivering in the sweltering light. During the day, she was overcome by the suffocation of that leaden sun, and at night she shivered in her bed, protecting herself from chills with hot-water bottles and woolen shawls. She stared at the limpid, naked sky looking for traces of a cloud, hoping that sooner or later a drop of rain would fall to break the unbearable harshness of that lunar valley. The months rolled by unchanging, with no other distraction than her mother's letters, which told of her father's political campaign, Nicolás's madness, and the excesses of Jaime, who lived like a priest but walked around with lovesick eyes. In one of her letters Clara suggested that to keep her hands busy she go back to making crèches. She tried. She ordered some of the special clay she had used at Tres Marías, set up a studio in the back of the kitchen, and had a couple of Indians build her an oven for firing her pieces. But Jean de Satigny made fun of her artistic impulse, saying that if she wanted to do something with her hands she would be better off knitting booties and learning to make pastry. She finally abandoned her work, not so much because of her husband's sarcasm, but because it seemed impossible to compete with the ancient pottery of the Indians.

Jean had organized his business with the same tenacity he had formerly brought to the idea of the chinchillas, but this time with more success. Aside from a German priest who had spent thirty years ranging across the area digging up the Inca past, no one else had bothered with those relics, since they were thought to be of little or no value. The government forbade any trafficking in Indian antiquities and had given the priest a general concession, authorizing him to catalogue whatever he found and hand it over to the museum. Jean saw them for the first time in the dusty display cases of the museum. He spent two days with the German. Happy after all these years to discover someone interested in his work, the priest had no misgivings about revealing his vast knowledge. Thus Jean learned how to determine the exact amount of time the relics had lain in the ground, how to differentiate the various styles and epochs, and how to locate burial grounds in the desert by means of signs invisible to civilized eyes. Finally, he decided that even if these shards lacked the golden splendor of Egyptian tombs, they nonetheless had a certain historical value. Once he obtained all the information that he needed, he organized teams of Indians to dig up whatever might have escaped the priest's zealous archaeological notice.

Magnificent ceramic jars, green with the patina of time, began to arrive at his house disguised in Indians' bundles and llama saddlebags, quickly filling the secret places that had been set aside for them. Blanca watched them piling up in the rooms and was astonished by their shapes. She held them in her hands, caressing them as if hypnotized, and whenever they were wrapped in straw and paper to be shipped to far-off, unknown destinations, she was grief-stricken. This pottery was just too beautiful. She felt that the monsters from her crèches did not belong under the same roof. For this reason, more than for any other, she abandoned her workshop.

The business of the Indian excavations was completely secret, since they were part of the historical heritage of the nation. Various teams of Indians who had slipped across the twisted passes of the border undetected were working for Jean de Satigny. They had no documents that proved they were human beings, and they were silent, stubborn, and inscrutable. Every time Blanca asked where these people who would suddenly appear in her courtyard came from, she was told they were cousins of the servant who waited on them in the dining room; and it was true, they all looked alike. They did not stay long, however. Most of the time they were in the desert, with only a shovel to dig the sand and a wad of coca in their mouths to keep them alive. Occasionally they were fortunate enough to unearth the half-buried remains of an Incan village, and in no time at all the house would fill with all the objects they had stolen from the site. The search, transport, and selling of this merchandise was conducted in such a cautious fashion that Blanca had no doubt that there was something highly illegal behind her husband's activities. Jean explained to her that the government was very interested in filthy pots and scrawny necklaces from the desert, and that in order to avoid the endless paperwork required by the official bureaucracy, he preferred to negotiate matters on his own. He shipped his items in boxes sealed with apple labels, thanks to the interested cooperation of certain customs inspectors.

None of this worried Blanca very much. The only thing that truly distressed her were the mummies. She was well acquainted with the dead, having spent much of her life in contact with them by means of her mother's three-legged table. She was used to seeing their transparent silhouettes gliding down the hallways of her parents' house, making noise in the wardrobes and appearing in people's dreams to predict calamities or lottery prizes. But the mummies were another matter. Those shrunken beings wrapped in rags that were decaying into dusty threads, with their wasted, yellow heads, their wrinkled hands, their sewn eyelids, the sparse hairs on their napes, their eternal, terrible, lipless smiles, their rancid odor, and that sad, impoverished aura of ancient corpses, made her sick in her soul. They were very rare. Only once in a great while did the Indians arrive with one in tow. Slow and immutable, they appeared at the door carrying an enormous vessel sealed with clay. Jean would carefully remove the lid in a room with all its doors and windows closed so that the first breath of air did not turn it to dust. Inside its jar, shrunken into a fetal position, wrapped in tatters, and accompanied by its wretched necklaces of teeth and a handful of rag dolls, the mummy looked like the pit of some exotic fruit. They were far more highly prized than any other objects that were brought out of the tombs, because private collectors and a few foreign museums paid very handsomely for them. Blanca wondered what sort of people collected the dead and where they put them. She could not imagine a mummy as part of the decoration in a drawing room, but Jean de Satigny told her that, displayed in a glass urn, they were even more valuable to European millionaires than works of art. It was not easy to get mummies onto the market, let alone through customs, which meant that there were times when they remained in the house for several weeks, awaiting their turn to embark on the long trip abroad. Blanca dreamt about them. She also had hallucinations, imagining that they were walking down the halls on tiptoe—tiny, cunning, furtive gnomes. She would close her bedroom door and put her head under the blankets, and there she would remain for hours at a time, trembling, praying, and calling for her mother with the power of thought. She told Clara about it in her letters, and her mother replied that there was no reason to fear the dead, only the living, because, despite their bad reputation, there was no evidence that mummies had ever attacked anyone; if anything, they were naturally timid. Emboldened by her mother's advice, Blanca decided to spy on them. She waited for them silently, watching through the half-open doorway of her bedroom. It was not long before she was convinced that they were walking up and down in the house, dragging their tiny feet across the carpets, whispering like schoolchildren, pushing and shoving their way in little groups of two and three, always moving toward the darkroom of Jean de Satigny. At times she thought she heard distant otherworldly moans, and she would fall prey to uncontrollable fits of terror, shouting for her husband, but no one came and she was too afraid to walk to the other side of the house to look for him. With the first rays of sunlight, Blanca would regain her good sense and control of her nerves. She realized that her nighttime anxiety was the fruit of the feverish imagination she had inherited from her mother, and this thought would console her until darkness began to fall again and the cycle of dread resumed. One day she simply could not stand the rising tension as night drew near, and she decided to tell Jean about the mummies. They were having dinner. When she told him about their nightly promenades, their whispers, and their suffocated cries, Jean de Satigny was rooted to his chair, his fork frozen in midair and his mouth locked open. The Indian who was just entering the dining room with the serving tray stumbled, and the roast chicken rolled under a chair. Jean employed all his charm, firmness, and reason to convince her that her nerves were playing tricks on her and that none of what she thought was really happening; that it was all the product of her unbridled fantasy. Blanca pretended to accept his explanation, but her husband's vehemence struck her as suspicious,

since he normally paid no attention to her problems. So did
the servant's face, which with its popped-out eyes had finally
lost the impassive gaze of an Incan idol. She decided to
embark on an investigation of the nomadic mummies. That
night she excused herself early after telling her husband that
she was going to take a tranquilizer to be sure of falling
asleep. But instead she drank a large cup of black coffee and
stationed herself behind her door, prepared to spend many
hours waiting.

She heard the first footsteps close to midnight. She
opened the door with the utmost caution and stuck her head
out just as a tiny crouched figure was moving down the hall.
This time she was positive she had not dreamt it, but because of the weight of her unborn child it took her almost a
minute to reach the corridor. It was a chilly night and the
desert breeze was blowing, making the old wooden ceilings
creak and the curtains swell like black sails on the high seas.
Ever since she was little, when she listened to Nana's stories
of the bogeyman down in the kitchen, she had feared the
dark, but now she did not dare turn on the lights or she
would frighten the tiny mummies during their erratic strolls.

Suddenly a hoarse, muffled sound broke the thick silence of the night, as if it was coming from the bottom of a
coffin, or so Blanca thought. She was beginning to fall
victim to a morbid fascination with things from beyond the
grave. She stopped in her tracks, her heart in her mouth, but
a second moan pulled her to her senses, giving her the
strength to continue toward Jean de Satigny's laboratory
door. She tried to open it, but it was locked. She pressed her
face to the door. It was then that she clearly heard the
moans, suffocated cries, and laughter, and no longer doubted
that something was going on with the mummies. She returned to her room relieved to know that her nerves were
not failing her but that something atrocious was going on in
her husband's secret den.

The next day Blanca waited for Jean de Satigny to finish
his meticulous toilette, eat his usual parsimonious breakfast,
read his newspaper cover to cover, and finally leave on his
morning walk, letting nothing in her placid, expectant mother's countenance betray her fierce determination. When Jean

went out, she called the high-heeled Indian and for the first
time gave him an order.

"Go to the city and buy me some candied papaya," she
told him brusquely.

The Indian set off at the slow trot typical of his race,
and she remained in the house with the other servants,
whom she feared far less than that strange individual with
the courtly inclinations. Since she estimated that she had a
couple of hours before he returned, she decided not to be too
hasty, and to proceed calmly. She was determined to clear up
the mystery of the furtive mummies. Convinced that in
daylight the mummies would be in no mood for clowning,
she went to the darkroom hoping that the door would be
open, but it was locked, as always. She tried all the keys on
her ring but none of them worked. Then she took the
biggest knife from the kitchen, slipped it into the doorjamb,
and forced it until the dried-out wood splintered and came
out in fragments. Thus she managed to pry the lock loose
from the frame and open the door. The damage to the door
was impossible to hide, and she realized that when her
husband saw it she would have to give some rational explanation, but she consoled herself with the argument that as
mistress of the house she had a right to know what was
going on beneath her roof. Despite her common sense,
which had withstood more than twenty years' worth of the
three-legged table and her mother's prognostications, she
was trembling as she crossed the threshold of the darkroom.

She groped for the light switch and flicked it on. She
found herself in a spacious room with black walls and thick
black curtains on the windows, through which not even a
feeble ray of sunlight filtered. The floor was covered with
dark, thick rugs. Everywhere were the bulbs, lamps, and
screens she had first seen Jean use at old Pedro García's
funeral, when he had been so enamored of photographing
the living and the dead that he made everyone uneasy and
the peasants ended up kicking his photographic plates to the
ground. She looked around in bewilderment: she was standing in the middle of the strangest scene. She continued
forward, sidestepping open trunks that held plumed garments from every period, curled wigs, and ostentatious hats.
She stopped before a golden trapeze, suspended from the

ceiling, on which hung a disjointed life-size puppet. In a corner she saw a stuffed llama; on the tables were bottles filled with amber-colored liquids, and on the floor the skins of exotic animals. But what most surprised her were the photographs. She stood open-mouthed before them. The walls of Jean de Satigny's studio were covered with distressing erotic scenes that revealed her husband's hidden character.

Blanca was slow to react, and it was a while before she realized what she saw, because she had no experience in such matters. Pleasure, to her, was the final, precious stage of the long road she had traveled with Pedro Tercero, on which she had moved unhurried and in good spirits, framed by the forests, the wheatfields, the river, and the immense sky, in the silence of the countryside. She had never felt the uncertainties of adolescence. While her classmates secretly read forbidden romances about passionate suitors and virgins aching to be so no longer, she sat in the shade of the plum trees in the convent courtyard, closed her eyes, and summoned with complete precision the magnificent vision of Pedro Tercero García holding her in his arms, stroking and kissing her, and eliciting from her the same profound harmony he drew from his guitar. Her instincts were satisfied as soon as they were awakened, and she had never imagined that passion could take other forms. These chaotic, tormented scenes were a thousand times more disconcerting than the scandalous mummies she had expected to find.

She recognized the faces of the household servants. There was the entire Incan court, as naked as God had put them on this earth, or barely clad in theatrical costumes. She saw the fathomless abyss between the thighs of the cook, the stuffed llama riding atop the lame servant girl, and the silent servant who waited on her at table, naked as a newborn babe, hairless and short-legged, with his expressionless stone face and his disproportionate, erect penis.

For an interminable second, Blanca was suspended in her own uncertainty; then she was overcome with horror. She managed to think clearly. She understood what Jean de Satigny had meant on their wedding night when he explained that he did not feel inclined to married life. She also glimpsed the sinister power of the Indian and the subtle mockery of the servants, and felt herself a prisoner in the anteroom of hell. Just then the child moved inside her and she jumped as if an alarm had just been sounded.

"My daughter! I have to get out of here!" she cried, hugging her womb. She ran out of the darkroom, crossed the entire house in a flash, and reached the street, where the leaden heat and the ruthless midday sun brought her back to reality. She understood that she would not get very far on foot with her nine-month belly. She returned to her bedroom, took all the money she could find, prepared a bundle containing some of the clothing from the splendid wardrobe she had knit, and left for the station.

Seated on the hard wooden bench near the tracks, with her bundle in her lap and her eyes full of fright, Blanca waited hours for the train, praying that the count, on returning home and discovering the damage to his laboratory door, would not come looking for her and force her to return to the evil kingdom of the Incas. She prayed for the train to be on time for once in its life so that she might arrive at her parents' before the creature that was crushing her insides and kicking at her ribs announced its arrival in the world. She prayed for the strength to endure this two-day journey. And she prayed that her desire to live would be stronger than this terrible sense of desolation that was beginning to paralyze her. She gritted her teeth and waited.

NINE

器

Little Alba

Alba was born feet first, which is a sign of good luck. Her Grandmother Clara searched her back and found the tiny star-shaped mark that distinguishes those born to true happiness. "There's no need to worry about this little girl. She will be lucky and she will be happy. She will also have a good complexion, because that is inherited, and at my age I have no wrinkles and I've never had a pimple," Clara declared two days after the birth. This is why they made no effort to prepare the child for life, since the stars had already conspired to endow her with so many gifts. Her sign was Leo. Her grandmother studied her astrological chart and recorded her destiny in white ink in an album with pages of black paper, in which she also pasted the child's first greenish locks of hair, the fingernails she clipped soon after her birth, and various portraits that allow one to see her as she was then: an extraordinarily tiny creature, almost bald, creased and pale, with no other sign of human intelligence than her sparkling black eyes, which bore an expression of ancient wisdom even when she was in the cradle. They were identical to those of her real father. Her mother wanted to call her Clara, but her grandmother did not believe in repeating names, because it created confusion in her notebooks that bore witness to life. They searched for a name in a thesaurus, where they found hers, the last in a chain of luminous words. Years later, Alba tormented herself with the thought that when she had a daughter there would be no other word with the same meaning to use as a name, but Blanca gave her the idea of using foreign languages, which offer a wide choice.

Alba was almost born in a narrow-gauged train, at three o'clock in the afternoon in the middle of the desert. That would have been fatal to her astrological chart. Fortunately, she managed to restrain herself within her mother for a few more hours and to enter the world in her grandparents' house, on the day, the hour, and in the place most propitious for her horoscope. Her mother arrived at the big house on the corner without advance notice. She was completely disheveled, covered with dust, bleary-eyed, and doubled over from the pain of the contractions with which Alba was pushing her way out. She knocked at the door in desperation, and when it opened, she rushed through, all the way to the sewing room, where Clara was putting the finishing touches on the last exquisite dress for her future granddaughter. There Blanca collapsed after her long journey, without explaining a thing, for her belly erupted in a long, liquid sigh and she felt as if all the water in the world were running out between her legs in a violent flush. At the sound of Clara's screams the servants came running, and so did Jaime, who was always in the house during that time, keeping watch on Amanda. They moved Blanca into Clara's room, and while they were laying her on the bed and pulling off her clothes, the minuscule human form of Alba began to appear. Her Uncle Jaime, who had assisted several births at the clinic, helped her into the world, grasping her firmly by the buttocks with his right hand while the fingers of his left groped in the darkness for the child's neck to remove the umbilical cord, which was strangling her. Meanwhile, drawn by the noise, Amanda ran in and pressed with all her weight on Blanca's belly while Clara, leaning over her daughter's suffering face, held a tea strainer covered with an ether-soaked rag to her nose. Alba was born quickly. Jaime removed the cord from around her neck, held her upside down and dangled her in the air, and with two resounding slaps introduced her into the suffering of life and the mechanics of breathing. But Amanda, who had read about the customs of African tribes and preached a return to nature, seized the newborn from his hands and gently placed her on the warm belly of her mother, where she found some consolation for the sadness of being born. Naked and embracing, mother and daughter lay resting while the others cleaned up the afterbirth and bustled about with the new sheets and the first batch of diapers. In the excitement of these first moments no one noticed the half-open door of the wardrobe, where little Miguel had observed the entire scene, paralyzed with fear, engraving in his mind forever the vision of a huge balloon of veins crowned with an enormous navel, from which that bruised creature emerged, wrapped in a hideous blue membrane.

Alba's name was entered in the Civil Registry and in the books of the parish with her father's French surname, but she never used it because her mother's was much easier to spell. Her grandfather, Esteban Trueba, did not approve of this bad habit. As he said every time he was given the opportunity, he had gone to a lot of trouble to be sure the child would have a known father and respectable name and would not have to use her mother's as if she were a child of shame and sin. Nor did he allow anyone to doubt the legitimate paternity of the count. Against all logic, he continued to hope that sooner or later the quiet, awkward little girl who glided through his house would display the Frenchman's elegant manners and refined charms. Clara made no mention of the matter either until much later, when she saw the little girl playing among the ruined statues in the garden and realized that she did not resemble anyone in the family, much less Jean de Satigny.

"I wonder where she got those old man's eyes?" she asked.

"They're her father's eyes," Blanca replied absent-mindedly.

"Pedro Tercero García, I suppose."

"Uh-huh."

It was the only time anyone ever mentioned Alba's origin within the family, because, as Clara noted, the issue was irrelevant since Jean de Satigny had disappeared from their life. They never heard a word about him, and no one bothered to investigate his whereabouts, not even to legalize Blanca's status, for she lacked the freedom of an unmarried woman and had all the limitations of a married one even though she had no husband. Alba never saw a picture of the count, for her mother did not leave a corner of the house untouched until she had destroyed them all, even those that showed them arm in arm on their wedding day. She had decided to forget the man she had married and act as if he had never existed. She never spoke of him again, nor did she offer any explanation for her flight from the conjugal abode. Clara, who had spent nine years without speaking, knew the advantages of silence and asked her daughter nothing, joining in her efforts to erase all memory of Jean de Satigny. Alba was told that her father was a distinguished and intelligent aristocrat who had unfortunately succumbed to fever in the northern desert. This was one of the few lies she had to put up with as a child; in everything else she was in direct contact with the prosaic truths of life. Her Uncle Jaime had taken it upon himself to destroy the myths that children come from under cabbage plants or are brought by stork from Paris, and her Uncle Nicolás had demolished those of the Three Kings, good fairies, and bogeymen. Alba had nightmares in which she saw her father's death. She dreamt of a young, handsome man dressed all in white, with patent-leather shoes and a straw hat, walking across the desert bathed in sunlight. In her dream the walker slackened his pace, hesitated, went slower and slower, stumbled and fell, picked himself up and stumbled again, burning with the heat, fever, and thirst. He pulled himself along the hot sand on his knees for a time, but in the end he lay stretched out in the vastness of those pale dunes as birds of prey circled over his inert body. She dreamt about him so many times that years later it came as a surprise when she was called to the central morgue to identify the body of the man she thought must be her father. By that time Alba was a bold young woman, much accustomed to adversity, so she went alone. She was met by a white-aproned technician, who led her down the long corridors of the ancient building to a large, cold room whose walls were painted gray. The man in the white apron opened the door of an immense refrigerator and withdrew a tray on which lay an old, swollen, bluish corpse. Alba examined it carefully, finding no resemblance to the image of her dreams. The man appeared to be an ordinary citizen, perhaps a post-office employee. She stared at his hands: they were

not those of a refined, intelligent aristocrat, but of a man
who has nothing interesting to say. But his identification
papers gave irrefutable proof that the sad, blue corpse was
Jean de Satigny, who had not died of fever in the golden
dunes of a child's nightmare, but of a simple stroke as he
crossed the street in his old age. But this all happened much
later. When Clara was alive and Alba was still a child, the
big house on the corner was a cloistered world in which she
grew up protected even from her own nightmares.

Alba was not yet two weeks old when Amanda left the
big house on the corner. Amanda had recovered her strength
and had no trouble reading the desire in Jaime's heart. She
took her little brother by the hand and left exactly as she had
arrived, without making noise or promises. The family lost
sight of her and the only one who could have gone to look
for her chose not to because he did not wish to hurt his
brother. After she left, Jaime drowned his sorrows in study
and work. He resumed his old habits, living like a hermit and
rarely appearing at the house. He never mentioned the young
woman's name and had nothing more to do with his brother.

The presence of his granddaughter sweetened Esteban
Trueba's character. The change was imperceptible, but Clara
noticed it. Slight symptoms gave him away: the sparkle in
his eyes when he saw the little girl, the expensive presents
he bought her, the anguish he felt if he heard her cry. Still, it
was not enough to bring him closer to Blanca. His relationship with his daughter had never been good, and after her
unfortunate marriage it had deteriorated to the point where
only the obligatory politeness Clara imposed allowed them
to live under the same roof.

In those days almost all the rooms in the Trueba house
were filled. The table was always set for the family, the
guests, and one extra place for anyone who might arrive
unannounced. The main door was left permanently open to
allow guests and visitors to come and go. While Senator
Trueba attempted to alter his country's destiny, his wife
sailed masterfully through the agitated seas of social life and
the other, more surprising ones of her spiritual voyage. Age
and experience had sharpened Clara's ability to divine the
occult and to move objects from afar. An exalted state of mind
could easily put her into a trance in which she would move

around the room while sitting in a chair, as if there were a hidden motor underneath the cushions. It was also during that time that a starving young artist, who had been given lodging in the house out of pity, paid for his stay by painting the only extant portrait of Clara. Much later, the impoverished artist was recognized as a master and today the painting hangs in a London museum, like so many works of art that left the country when people had to sell their furnishings to feed the victims of persecution. The canvas shows a middle-aged woman dressed in white, with silvery hair and the sweet gaze of a trapeze artist, resting in a rocking chair that hangs suspended just above the floor, floating amidst flowered curtains, a vase flying upside down, and a fat black cat that observes the scene like an important gentleman. Influence of Chagall, according to the catalogue, but that is not true. The picture captures precisely the reality the painter witnessed in Clara's house. That was the period when divine good humor and the hidden forces of human nature acted with impunity to provoke a state of emergency and upheaval in the laws of physics and logic. Clara's communication with wandering souls and extraterrestrials was conducted through telepathy, dreams, and the pendulum she used for that purpose, dangling it in the air above an alphabet she had arranged in proper order on the table. The pendulum's autonomous movement pointed to the letters, forming messages in Spanish and Esperanto, which proved that these, and not English, were the only languages of interest to beings from other dimensions, as Clara wrote in letters to the ambassadors of the English-speaking powers. They never answered her, and neither did the various ministers of education whom she wrote in order to explain her theory that instead of teaching English and French, which were languages for sailors, peddlers, and money lenders, the schools should insist that all the children in the country study Esperanto.

Alba's childhood was a mixture of vegetarian diets, Japanese martial arts, Tibetan dance, yogic breathing, relaxation and concentration with Professor Hausser, and many other interesting techniques, not to mention the contribution to her education made by her two uncles and the three enchanting

Mora sisters. Her Grandmother Clara managed to keep that immense covered wagon of a house rolling with its population of eccentrics, even though she had no domestic talent and disdained the basic operations of arithmetic to the point of forgetting how to add. The daily organization of the household and the keeping of accounts therefore fell to Blanca, who divided her time between the job of chief steward of that miniature kingdom and her work at her ceramic studio in the back of the courtyard, the ultimate refuge for her sorrows, where she gave classes for both mongoloids and young ladies and created incredible crèches full of monsters, which, against all logic, sold like hotcakes.

From a tender age it had been Alba's responsibility to put fresh flowers in the vases. She would open the windows to let in streams of air and light, but the flowers never lasted until nightfall because Esteban Trueba's thundering voice and slashing cane were even powerful enough to frighten nature. At the sound of his footsteps, household pets scattered and plants withered. Blanca was raising a Brazilian rubber tree, a shy, squalid little bush whose one attraction was its price: it was sold by the leaf. Whenever Trueba was heard arriving, whoever was closest ran to hide the rubber tree out on the terrace, because as soon as the old man entered the room, the plant lowered its leaves and began to exude a whitish fluid, like tears of milk, from its stem. Alba did not go to school; her grandmother held that anyone as favored by the stars as she was needed only to know how to read and write, and she could learn that at home. Clara was in such a hurry to make her literate that at the age of five the little girl was already reading the newspaper over breakfast and discussing the news with her grandfather. At six she had discovered the magic books in the enchanted trunks of her legendary Great-Uncle Marcos and had fully entered the world-without-return of the imagination. Nor did anyone worry about her health; they did not believe in the benefits of vitamins and thought that vaccinations were for chickens; besides, her grandmother studied the lines of her hand and said that she was made of iron and was assured of a long life. The only frivolous attention they lavished on her was to comb her hair with bay rum to mitigate the dark-green hue it had when she was born; this despite the fact that Senator

Trueba thought it should be left that way, since she was the only one who had inherited something from Rosa the Beautiful, even if, unfortunately, it was only the maritime color of her hair. To please him, Alba gave up the bay rum as an adolescent and rinsed her hair with parsley water, which allowed the green to reappear in its full leafiness. The rest of her was tiny and innocuous as opposed to the other women in her family, who were, almost without exception, splendid.

In the rare moments of leisure Blanca had to think about herself and her daughter, she regretted that her child was so silent and solitary, and that she had no playmates her own age. But Alba did not feel the least bit lonely. In fact there were times when she would have been delighted to escape her grandmother's clairvoyance, her mother's intuition, and the clamor of all the eccentric people who were constantly appearing, disappearing, and reappearing in the big house on the corner. It also worried Blanca that her daughter did not play with dolls, but Clara took her granddaughter's side, arguing that those tiny porcelain corpses with eyes that opened and shut and perverse, pouting mouths were repulsive. She herself constructed shapeless beings made of leftover scraps from the wool she used to knit for the poor. These creatures had no human traits, which made it much easier to cradle them, rock them, bathe them, and then throw them in the garbage. But the child's favorite plaything was the basement. Because of the rats, Esteban Trueba had ordered the door bolted shut, but Alba would slip down through a skylight and land noiselessly in that paradise of long-forgotten objects. The place was always dark and protected from the ravages of time, like a sealed pyramid. There were piles of cast-off furniture, tools of mysterious utility, broken machinery, and pieces of Covadonga, the prehistoric automobile that her uncles had taken apart and rebuilt into a racing car and that had ended its days as a heap of scrap iron. Alba used these things to build houses in the corners. There were trunks and suitcases filled with old clothes, which she used to stage her solitary plays, and a sad, dark, moth-eaten rug with the head of a dog, which when laid out on the floor resembled a wretched animal that had been split open. It was the last, ignominious vestige of faithful Barrabás.

One Christmas Eve, Clara gave her granddaughter a

fabulous present that occasionally superseded the fascination of the basement: a box filled with jars of paint, brushes, a small ladder, and permission to use the biggest wall in her bedroom whenever she wanted.

"This will give her an outlet for her feelings," Clara said, watching Alba balanced on the ladder, painting a train full of animals just below the ceiling.

With the passage of time, Alba filled not only one but all her bedroom walls with an immense fresco. In the midst of a Venusian flora and an impossible fauna of invented animals much like those Rosa had embroidered on her table-cloth and Blanca baked in her kiln, she painted all the wishes, memories, sorrows, and joys of her childhood.

Her two uncles were very close to her. Jaime was her favorite. He was a large, hairy man who shaved twice a day and still looked as if he had a four-day-old beard. He had black, evil-looking eyebrows that he combed upward to make his niece believe that he was in league with the devil, and hair stiff as a broom, which he slicked down to no avail and which was always damp. He came and went with his books under his arm and a plumber's bag in his hand. He had told Alba that he worked as a jewelry thief and that the dreadful bag contained his picklocks and brass knuckles. The child pretended to be frightened, but she knew her uncle was a doctor and that the bag contained the tools of his profession. Together they had invented certain imaginary games to entertain themselves on rainy afternoons.

"Bring on the elephant!" Uncle Jaime would command.

Alba would go out and return pulling an imaginary pachyderm on an invisible rope. They could spend a good half hour giving him the herbs elephants like to eat, bathing his skin with mud to protect it from the harsh effects of bad weather, and polishing his ivory tusks while they heatedly discussed the advantages and disadvantages of living in the jungle.

"This child is going to wind up stark raving mad!" Senator Trueba would say whenever he saw little Alba sitting on the balcony reading the medical treatises her Uncle Jaime lent her.

She was the only person in the house who had the key to her uncle's tunnel of books, along with his permission to take them out and read them. Blanca argued that her reading should be monitored because there were certain things that were inappropriate for her age, but her Uncle Jaime felt that people never read what did not interest them and that if it interested them that meant they were sufficiently mature to read it. He had the same theory about bathing and eating. He said that if the child did not want to take a bath, it was because she did not need to, and that she should be fed whatever she wanted whenever she was hungry, because the body knows its needs better than anyone. On this point, however, Blanca was inflexible, forcing her daughter to observe a strict schedule and the usual rules of hygiene. The upshot was that in addition to her normal baths and meals, Alba sucked the candies her uncle brought her and hosed herself down whenever she was hot, neither of these two activities having the slightest effect on her healthy constitution. Alba would have liked her Uncle Jaime to marry her mother, because it was safer to have him as a father than an uncle, but it was explained to her that this sort of incestuous union produces mongoloid offspring. As a result, she imagined that the pupils at her mother's Thursday workshops were her uncles' children.

Nicolás was also close to the little girl's heart, but there was something ephemeral and volatile about him. He was always in a hurry, always just passing through, as if he were jumping from one idea to another, and this made Alba uneasy. She was five years old when her Uncle Nicolás returned from India. Tired of invoking God through the three-legged table and a cloud of hashish, he had decided to seek Him in a region less harsh than his native land. He spent two months harassing Clara, following her around the house and whispering in her ear while she was asleep, until he finally convinced her to sell a diamond ring to pay his way to the land of Mahatma Gandhi. This time Esteban Trueba did not attempt to hold him back, because he thought a trip through that distant nation of starving people and nomadic cows would do his son a lot of good.

"If you don't die of a snakebite or some foreign plague, I hope you return a man, because I'm fed up with all your eccentricities," his father told him when he said goodbye to him on the pier.

Nicolás spent a year as a beggar, following the path of the yogis, across the Himalayas, through Katmandu, along the Ganges, and on to Benares, all on foot. By the end of this pilgrimage he was convinced that God exists, and had learned to pierce his cheeks and chest with hatpins and to live practically without eating. The family saw him coming toward the house one ordinary morning with an infant's diaper covering his private parts, his skin clinging to his bones, and that lost gaze so often observed in those who eat only vegetables. He was escorted by two incredulous policemen who were ready to arrest him unless he could prove that he really was the son of Senator Trueba, and by a knot of children who were running along behind him throwing garbage at him and laughing. Clara was the only one who had no difficulty recognizing him. His father reassured the policemen and ordered Nicolás to take a bath and put on some normal clothes if he wanted stay in the house, but Nicolás stared at him without seeing and did not reply. He had become a vegetarian. He did not eat meat, milk, or eggs. His diet was the same as a rabbit's, and his anxious face gradually came to resemble the face of that animal. He chewed each mouthful of his sparse nourishment fifty times. Meals became an endless ritual, during which Alba fell asleep on her empty plate and the servants dozed in the kitchen over their trays, while Nicolás solemnly chewed his food. Esteban Trueba stopped going to the house and took his meals at the club. Nicolás insisted he could walk barefoot on a bed of coals, but each time he announced a demonstration, Clara had an asthma attack and he was forced to stop. He spoke in Asiatic parables that could not always be understood. His only interests were of a spiritual nature. The materialism of domestic life and the excessive ministrations of his mother and his sister, who insisted on feeding and dressing him, irritated him, as did Alba's fascinated pursuit. She followed him around the house like a puppy, begging him to show her how to stand on her head and stick pins through her skin. He remained naked even after winter set in. He could go three minutes without breathing and was ready to demonstrate this accomplishment whenever anybody asked, which was quite often. Jaime said it was a shame that air was free, because according to his calculations Nicolás breathed only half of what a normal person did, although this did not appear to affect him in the least. He spent the winter locked in his room eating carrots, without complaining about the cold, and filling page after page with his minute handwriting in black ink. With the first signs of spring, he announced that his book was completed. He had one thousand five hundred pages and managed to convince his father and brother Jaime to pay for it, against whatever profits its sale might bring. After being corrected and printed, the one thousand five hundred pages reduced themselves to six hundred, yielding a voluminous treatise on the ninety-nine names of God and formulas for attaining nirvana through respiratory exercise. The book was not the success he had hoped for, and boxes filled with copies wound up in the basement, where Alba used them as bricks to build her trenches, until the day years later when they were used to fuel an infamous bonfire.

As soon as the book was off the presses, Nicolás cradled it lovingly in his arms, recovered his hyena smile, put on decent clothes, and announced that the time had come to bring The Truth to those of his generation who remained shrouded in darkness. Esteban Trueba reminded him that he was not welcome to use the house as an academy and warned him that he would not tolerate his putting pagan ideas into Alba's head, much less teaching her his fakir's tricks. Nicolás went off to preach at the cafeteria in the university, where he acquired an impressive number of followers for his classes in spiritual and respiratory exercise. He spent his free time riding his motorcycle and teaching his niece how to conquer pain and other weaknesses of the flesh. His method consisted of identifying whatever made her frightened. The child, who had a certain inclination for the macabre, would concentrate according to her uncle's instructions until she was able to visualize her mother's death as if it were really happening. She saw her chalk-white and cold, her beautiful purple eyes shut, lying in her coffin. She heard the weeping of the family. She saw the silent procession of friends file in, leave their calling cards on a tray, and walk out with bowed heads. She smelled the flowers and heard the neighing of the plumed horses of the funeral carriage. She felt how her feet hurt in her new mourning shoes. She imagined her loneliness, her abandonment, her orphanhood. Her uncle helped her think of all these things without crying, and taught her to relax and not resist the pain so that it would pass through her without stopping. Other times, Alba would squeeze a finger in the door and learn to withstand the burning pain without complaint. If she managed to get through an entire week without crying, overcoming all the tests Nicolás imposed, she won a prize, which almost always consisted of a motorcycle ride at breakneck speed—an unforgettable experience. Once they wound up in the middle of a herd of cows that were going toward the stable, along a road on the edge of the city where Nicolás had taken his niece as her reward. She would always remember the heavy animals, their slowness, their filthy tails hitting her in the face, the smell of dung, the horns grazing her, and the terrible sensation of emptiness in her stomach, of fantastic vertigo, of incredible excitement, a mixture of passionate curiosity and terror that she only felt again in a few fleeting moments of her life.

Esteban Trueba, who had always found it difficult to express his emotions and had had no access to tenderness ever since his relationship with Clara had deteriorated, transferred all his finest sentiments to Alba. The child meant more to him than his own children ever had. Every morning, still in her pajamas, she went to her grandfather's room. She entered without knocking and climbed into his bed. He would pretend to wake up with a start, even though he was actually expecting her, and growled that she should not disturb him and that she should go back to her room and let him sleep. Alba tickled him until, apparently defeated, he permitted her to look for the chocolate he always had hidden for her. Alba knew all his hiding places and her grandfather always used them in the exact same order, but so as not to disappoint him she spent a long time looking, and when she found it she shrieked with joy. Esteban never knew that his granddaughter hated chocolate and that she ate it only out of love for him. Those morning games satisfied the senator's need for human contact. The rest of the day he was busy with the Congress, the club, playing golf, his business, and his political meetings. Twice a year he went to Tres Marías with his granddaughter for two or three weeks. They both returned looking tanned, happier, and fatter. There they distilled a homemade brandy that was used as a drink, to light the stove, to disinfect wounds, and to kill cockroaches; they pompously called it "vodka." At the end of his life, when his ninety years had turned him into a twisted, fragile tree, Esteban Trueba would recall those moments with his granddaughter as the happiest of his whole existence. Alba too remembered the complicity of those trips to the country holding on to her grandfather's hand, the jaunts behind him in the saddle of his horse, the sunsets in the vast pastures, the long nights beside the living-room fireplace telling ghost stories and drawing pictures.

Senator Trueba's relationship with the rest of his family only worsened with time. Once a week, on Saturday, they all dined around the great oak table that had always been in the family and had first belonged to the del Valles; it was the most ancient of antiques, and had been used for laying out the dead, for Spanish dances, and for other unexpected needs. Alba was seated between her grandmother and mother, with a cushion on her chair so that her nose would reach her plate. The child watched the adults in fascination. There was her radiant grandmother, her teeth in place for the occasion, sending messages to her husband through her children or the servants; Jaime flaunting his bad manners by burping after each course and picking his teeth with his little finger to annoy his father; Nicolás with his eyes half closed chewing every bite fifty times; and Blanca chattering about anything she could think of just to create the illusion of a normal meal. Trueba remained relatively silent until his bad temper betrayed him and he began to argue with Jaime about the poor, the elections, the Socialists, and basic principles, or to insult Nicolás for his attempts to launch a balloon and practice acupuncture on Alba, or to punish Blanca with his harsh replies, his indifference, and his useless warnings that she had already ruined her life and that she would never inherit so much as a peso from him. The only one he did not confront was Clara, but, of course, he barely spoke to her. At times Alba caught her grandfather staring at Clara until he turned white and sweet, and looked like an old man they had never seen before. But this happened only rarely; typically, husband and wife ignored each other. Sometimes Senator Trueba lost his temper and screamed so much that he turned red and they had to throw a jugful of cold water in his face so that the fit would pass and his breathing would return to normal.

This was the period when Blanca's beauty was at its peak. She had a Moorish, languid, and abundant air about her, which induced repose and trust. She was tall and well endowed, of a rather helpless and tearful temperament that roused men's ancestral instinct for protection. Her father had no sympathy for her. He never forgave her love for Pedro Tercero García and made sure she did not forget that she was living off his pity. Trueba could not understand how his daughter had so many admirers, for she had none of the disarming gaiety and joviality he liked in women; besides, he felt that no normal man could want to marry a woman of ill health and uncertain civil status who already had a daughter. But Blanca did not seem the least surprised that men were interested in her. She was conscious of her beauty. Nevertheless, when she was with the gentlemen who called on her, she assumed a contradictory attitude, encouraging them with a batting of her Arabian eyes, but keeping them at a prudent distance. As soon as she saw that their intentions were serious, she broke off the relationship with a ferocious refusal. Some of them, those in a better economic position, attempted to win her heart by bribing her daughter. They showered Alba with expensive gifts and dolls with special mechanisms that enabled them to walk, cry, eat, and carry out other typically human feats, stuffed her with cream puffs and took her to the zoo, where the child wept with pity for the poor captive animals, especially the seal, who stirred dreadful omens in her soul. These visits to the zoo holding on to the hand of some conceited spendthrift suitor gave her a lifelong horror of enclosures, walls, cages, and isolation. Of all the contenders, the one who made the greatest progress toward winning Blanca's hand was the King of the Pressure Cookers. Despite his immense fortune and his peaceful, introspective character, Esteban Trueba detested him because he was circumcised and had a Sephardic nose and kinky hair. With his mocking, hostile attitude, Trueba managed to frighten off this man who had survived a concentration camp, overcome poverty and exile, and triumphed in the ruthless world of commerce. While their romance lasted, the King of the Pressure Cookers would come to call for Blanca and take her out to eat in the most exclusive restaurants; he drove a tiny car with only two seats, tractor tires, and the noise of a turbine under the hood, a unique model in its class, which provoked a rush of curiosity among the neighbors and derogatory remarks from the Trueba family. Ignoring her father's displeasure and the neighbors' nosy interest, Blanca would climb up into the vehicle with the majesty of a prime minister, dressed in her one and only black tailored suit and the white silk blouse she wore on all special occasions. Alba would kiss her goodbye and stand in the doorway, her mother's subtle jasmine perfume clinging to her nostrils and a knot of anxiety lying in her heart. Only her Uncle Nicolás's training helped her withstand her mother's outings without tears, because she feared that any day one of the suitors would convince her mother to marry him and Blanca would leave her all alone without a mother. She had decided a long time ago that she did not need a father, much less a stepfather, but that if she lost her mother she would plunge her head into a pail of water until she drowned, just as the cook did with the little kittens the cat gave birth to every four months or so.

Alba got over her fear that her mother would abandon her when she finally met Pedro Tercero. Her intuition told her that as long as that man existed, no one could win Blanca's love. It was a summer Sunday. Blanca set Alba's hair in corkscrew curls with a hot iron that singed her ears. She dressed her in white gloves and black patent-leather shoes and a straw hat with artificial cherries. Her Grandmother Clara laughed aloud when she caught sight of her, but her mother consoled her with two drops of her perfume on her neck.

"You're going to meet someone famous," Blanca said mysteriously as they left the house.

She took the child to the Japanese Gardens, where she bought her caramel on a stick and a bag of popcorn. They sat down on a bench in the shade, holding hands, surrounded by pigeons that were pecking at the corn.

She saw him approaching before her mother pointed him out to her. He was wearing a mechanic's overalls and

Franciscan sandals without socks, and he had a huge black beard that reached halfway down his chest. His hair was messy, but he had a magnificent smile, which immediately ranked him in the category of human beings who deserved to be painted into the gigantic fresco in her bedroom.

The man and the little girl looked at each other, recognizing themselves in the other's eyes.

"This is Pedro Tercero, the singer. You've heard him on the radio," her mother said.

Alba held out her hand and he squeezed it with his left one. Then she noticed that he was missing several fingers on his right hand, but he explained that he could play the guitar anyway, because there is always a way to do what you want to do. The three of them strolled together through the Japanese Gardens. In midafternoon they took one of the last electric streetcars that still existed in the city and went to have fried fish at a stall in the market. At dusk he escorted them as far as their street. When they said goodbye, Blanca and Pedro Tercero kissed each other on the mouth. It was the first time Alba had seen that in her life, because no one around her was in love.

From that day on, Blanca began going out alone every weekend. She said she was going to visit some distant cousins. Esteban Trueba got furious with her and threatened to expel her from his house, but Blanca was unyielding. She left her daughter with Clara and took the bus, carrying a clown's valise covered with flowers.

"I promise you I'm not getting married and that I'll be back tomorrow night," she would say to Alba when she said goodbye.

Alba liked to sit with the cook at siesta time, listening to popular singing on the radio, especially the songs of the man she had met in the Japanese Gardens. One day Senator Trueba entered the pantry and when he heard the voice on the radio he attacked the machine, smashing it with his cane until it was a pile of twisted wires and loose knobs, before the frightened eyes of his granddaughter, who could not understand her grandfather's sudden fit. The next day, Clara bought another radio so Alba could listen to Pedro Tercero whenever she felt like it, and old Trueba pretended not to notice.

That was still the era of the King of the Pressure Cookers. Pedro Tercero found out about his existence and had an attack of jealousy that was unwarranted if one compares the influence he had on Blanca with the timid siege of the Jewish merchant. As he had so many other times, he begged Blanca to leave the Trueba house, her father's ferocious guardianship, and the loneliness of her workshop filled with mongoloids and leisured ladies, and to go with him once and for all to live out the wild love they had been hiding ever since their childhood. But Blanca could not make up her mind. She knew that if she went with Pedro Tercero she would be banished from her social circle and from the position she had always had, and she also realized that she would never be accepted by Pedro Tercero's friends or be able to adjust to the modest life of a working-class quarter. Years later, when Alba was old enough to analyze this aspect of her mother's life, she concluded that she had not gone with Pedro Tercero simply because she did not love him enough, for there was nothing in the Trueba house that he could not have given her. Blanca was a very poor woman. She had money only when Clara gave her some or when she sold one of her crèches. She earned a wretched income, almost every cent of which she spent on doctors because work and necessity had not diminished her capacity for suffering imaginary illnesses; on the contrary, it seemed to be expanding year by year. She managed not to ask her father for anything, so as not to give him the least opportunity to humiliate her. From time to time, Clara and Jaime bought her clothes or gave her something for her basic needs, but usually she could not afford to buy a pair of stockings. Her poverty contrasted with the embroidered dresses and custom-made shoes in which Senator Trueba dressed his granddaughter Alba. Her life was hard. She rose at six every morning, winter and summer. Then, dressed in a rubber apron and wooden clogs, she lit her kiln, prepared her worktables, and pounded the clay for her classes, her arms up to her elbows in the coarse, cold mud. This was why she always had broken nails and cracked skin and why, with time, her fingers grew deformed. At that time of the day she felt inspired, and since there was no one to interrupt her, she could start her day by making extraordinary animals for her crèches. Afterward she had to see to the house, the servants, and the shopping until her classes began. Her pupils were daughters of the best families who had nothing to do and had taken up the fashion of ceramics, which was more elegant than knitting for the poor, as their grandmothers had done.

The idea of giving classes for mongoloids had come about by chance. One day an old friend of Clara's came to Senator Trueba's house with her grandson, a fat, soft teenager with the round face of a docile moon and an expression of unchanging tenderness in his tiny Oriental eyes. He was fifteen, but Alba realized he was like a baby. Clara asked her granddaughter to take the boy out to play in the garden and make sure he did not soil his clothes, drown in the fountain, eat dirt, or play with his fly. Alba quickly tired of watching him, and when she saw it was impossible to communicate with him in any coherent language, she took him to the ceramic studio, where Blanca, to keep him amused, tied an apron around him to protect him from stains and water and placed a ball of clay in his hands. The boy played with it for more than three hours, shaping a number of crude figures that he took to show his grandmother. This lady, who had practically forgotten he was with her, was utterly delighted; thus the idea was born that ceramics was good for mongoloids. Blanca ended up giving classes to a group of children who came to her studio every Thursday afternoon. They were delivered by truck and escorted by two nuns in starched white coifs, who sat in the garden drinking chocolate with Clara and discussing the virtues of cross-stitching and the hierarchy of sin, while Blanca and her daughter taught the children how to fashion worms, balls, squashed dogs, and misshapen vases. At the end of the year the nuns organized an exhibition and a party, and the dreadful works of art were sold for charity. Blanca and Alba had quickly understood that the children worked much better when they felt loved, and that the only way to communicate with them was through affection. They learned to hug them, kiss them, and fondle them until they wound up genuinely loving them. Alba waited all week for the truck with the retarded children to come, and she jumped with glee when they ran to hug her. But those Thursdays wore them out. Alba fell asleep exhausted, the sweet Asiatic faces of the children spinning in her mind, and Blanca invariably had a migraine. After the nuns left, their herd of mongoloids in hand and their white wings aflutter, Blanca hugged her daughter passionately, covered her face with kisses, and told her they should thank God that she was normal. For this reason, Alba grew up thinking that normality was a gift from heaven. She discussed it with her grandmother.

"In almost every family there's a fool or a crazy person," Clara assured her while she concentrated on her knitting—in all those years she had not learned to knit without looking. "You can't always see them, because they're kept out of sight as if they were something to be ashamed of. They're locked up in the back room so visitors won't see them. But actually there's nothing to be ashamed of. They're God's creatures too."

"But there's no one like that in our family, Grandmother," Alba replied.

"No. Here the madness was divided up equally, and there was nothing left over for us to have our own lunatic."

This was how her conversations with Clara went, and why, for Alba, the most important person in the house and the strongest presence in her life was her grandmother. She was the motor that drove the magic universe that was the rear section of the big house on the corner, where Alba spent her first seven years in complete freedom. She grew accustomed to her grandmother's eccentricities. She was not surprised, for example, to see her moving around the room in a trance, seated in an armchair with her legs tucked under her, pulled by an invisible force. She followed her on her pilgrimages to hospitals and almshouses, where Clara tried to track down her needy flock; she even learned, using four-ply wool and enormous needles, to knit the sweaters her Uncle Jaime gave away after he had worn them once, just so she could see her grandmother's toothless smile while she squinted at the stitches. Clara frequently used her to send messages to Esteban, which earned her the nickname "carrier pigeon." The little girl also took part in the Friday sessions, during which the three-legged table jumped in broad daylight without the aid of any special tricks, known form of energy, or outside leverage, as well as the literary soirées where she mingled with the acclaimed masters and a varying group of timid unknown artists whom Clara encouraged. In those days a large number of guests ate and drank in the big house on the corner. Almost all the most important people in the country took turns living there, or at least attending the spiritualist meetings, the cultural discussions, and the social gatherings. Among them was the Poet—years later considered the greatest of the century and translated into all the known languages on earth—on whose knees Alba often sat, little suspecting that one day she would walk behind his casket, with a bunch of bloody carnations in her hand, between two rows of machine guns.

Clara was still young, but to her granddaughter she looked very old because of her missing teeth. She had no wrinkles, and when her mouth was closed she gave the impression of extreme youth because of the innocent look on her face. She wore tunics of raw linen that looked like the robes crazy people wear, and in the winter she wore long woolen socks and fingerless gloves. She laughed at things that were not the least bit funny; on the other hand, she was incapable of understanding any joke, always laughing at the wrong time, and she could become very sad if she saw someone else behaving in a ridiculous fashion. Sometimes she had asthma attacks and would summon her granddaughter with a tiny silver bell she always carried on her person. Alba would come running to embrace her with consoling whispers, since they both knew from long experience that the only cure for asthma is the prolonged embrace of a loved one. She had laughing hazel eyes, shiny hair flecked with white and pulled into an untidy bun from which rebellious wisps escaped, and fine white hands with almond-shaped nails and long ringless fingers, which were useless except when it came to gestures of affection, arranging her divining cards, or putting in her denture before meals. Alba spent the day trailing after her, snuggling into her skirts and begging her to tell one of her stories or move the vases with the power of her mind. She found in her grandmother a sure refuge when she was haunted by nightmares or when her Uncle Nicolás's training became unbearable. Clara taught her how to take care of birds and speak to each of them in its own language, as well as how to read the premonitions in nature and knit chain-stitch scarves for the poor.

Alba knew that her grandmother was the soul of the big house on the corner. Everybody else learned it later, when Clara died and the house lost its flowers, its nomadic friends, and its playful spirits and entered into an era of decline.

Alba was six years old the first time she saw Esteban García, but she never forgot him. She had probably seen him before at Tres Marías, on one of her summer journeys with her grandfather. Old Trueba liked to take her out to see the property and—with a sweeping gesture that took in everything in sight, from the meadows to the volcano to the little brick houses—tell her that she must learn to love this land because one day it would be hers.

"My children are all fools. If they inherited Tres Marías, in less than a year it would be a ruin again, just as in my father's day," he told his granddaughter.

"All this is yours, Grandfather?"

"Every bit of it. From the Pan-American highway to those mountaintops over there. You see them?"

"Why, Grandfather?"

"What do you mean *why*? Because I'm the owner!"

"But why are you the owner?"

"Because it belonged to my family."

"Why?"

"Because they bought it from the Indians."

"And what about the tenants who've always lived here? Why aren't they the owners too?"

"Your Uncle Jaime is putting Bolshevik ideas into your head!" Senator Trueba would roar, sputtering with rage. "Do you know what would happen here without a *patrón*?"

"No."

"The place would go to hell! There would be no one to give orders, sell the crops, take responsibility for things—you understand? No one to take care of people, either. If anyone got sick or died or left a widow with a lot of kids, they'd all starve to death. Everyone would have a little piece of land that wouldn't produce enough for them to eat. They need someone to do their thinking for them, someone around to make decisions, someone to help them. I've been the best

patrón around, Alba. I may have a bad temper, but I'm fair. My
tenants live better than a lot of people in the city. They lack
for nothing, and even when there's a drought, or a flood, or
an earthquake, I see to it that no one suffers here. And that's
exactly what you'll have to do when you're old enough.
That's why I bring you to Tres Marías—so that you'll learn
to know each stone and each animal and, above all, each
person, by their first and last name. Do you understand?"

But in fact she had very little contact with the peasants
and was far from knowing each of them by name. This was
why she failed to recognize the swarthy, awkward, slow-
moving young man with the cruel eyes of a rodent who
knocked one afternoon at the door of the big house on the
corner. He was wearing a dark suit that was much too tight
for him. The cloth was worn to a shiny film on his knees,
elbows, and behind. He said he wanted to speak to Senator
Trueba and introduced himself as the son of one of the
tenants from Tres Marías. Despite the fact that in normal
times people of his condition entered through the service
entrance and waited in the pantry, he was shown to the
library, because that day there was a banquet in the house
that was to be attended by the whole directorate of the
Conservative Party. The kitchen had been invaded by an
army of cooks and their helpers whom Trueba had borrowed
from the club, and there was such confusion and pressure
that a visitor would have got in the way. It was a winter
afternoon, and the library was dark and silent, lit only by the
fire that was dancing in the chimney. It smelled of furniture
polish and leather.

"Wait here, but don't touch anything. The senator will
be in shortly," the maid said brusquely, leaving him alone.

The young man ran his eyes over the room, without
daring to make the slightest movement, simmering with
resentment at the thought that all this might have belonged
to him if only he had been legitimate; his Grandmother
Pancha García had explained it to him many times before she
died of chicken fever and left him a true orphan in that
crowd of brothers and cousins where he was nobody. Only
his grandmother had paid him any attention, and she never
let him forget that he was different from the others because
the *patrón's* blood ran in his veins. He felt suffocated as he

looked around the library. The walls were covered with shelves of polished mahogany except on either side of the fireplace, where there were two glass cases filled with marble and hard stones from the Orient. The room was two stories high, the only whim of the architect that Esteban Trueba had consented to. A balcony, to which one ascended via a spiral staircase made of wrought iron, took the place of the second story of shelves. This was where the finest paintings in the house were kept, for Esteban Trueba had made this his refuge, his office, his sanctuary, and he liked to have his most cherished objects close beside him. The shelves were filled from floor to ceiling with books and objets d'art. There was a heavy Spanish-style desk, huge black leather armchairs with their backs to the window, four Persian carpets on the oak parquet, and several reading lamps with parchment shades, strategically placed so that no matter where one sat there would always be good light for reading. This was where the senator preferred to hold his meetings, weave his intrigues, forge his deals, and, in his lonely hours, closet himself to release his rage, his frustrated desire, or his sorrow. But none of this was known to the peasant standing on the carpet, unsure of where to put his hands and perspiring heavily. That majestic, heavy, crushing library was exactly like the image he had of the *patrón*. He shuddered with hate and fear. He had never been in such a place, and until this moment he had thought that the most luxurious spot imaginable was the movie house in San Lucas, where the schoolteacher had once taken the whole class to see a Tarzan movie. It had not been easy for him to arrive at this decision, to convince his family, and to make the long trip to the capital alone and without a centavo to speak with the *patrón*. He could not wait till summer to tell him what was lodged in his chest. Suddenly he felt he was being watched. He turned around and found himself face to face with a little girl with braids and embroidered socks who was staring at him from the doorway.

"What's your name?" she asked.

"Esteban García," he replied.

"Mine is Alba Trueba. Will you remember my name?"

"I will."

They stared at each other a long time, until she began

to trust him and came forward. She explained that he would have to wait, because her grandfather had still not returned from Congress, and she told him that there was a mob of people in the kitchen on account of the party, and promised him that later on she would bring him some sweets. Esteban García felt more comfortable. He sat down in one of the black leather armchairs and little by little drew the child toward him and sat her on his knees. Alba smelled of bay rum, a sweet, fresh scent that mingled with the natural smell of sweaty little girl. The boy put his nose against her neck and inhaled that unknown perfume of cleanliness and well-being; without knowing why, his eyes filled with tears. He felt that he hated this little girl almost as much as he did old Trueba. She embodied everything he would never have, never be. He wanted to hurt her, destroy her, but he also wanted to continue smelling her, listening to her baby's voice, and having her soft skin within reach of his hand. He stroked her knees, just above the border of her embroidered socks. They were warm and had little dimples. Alba continued chattering about the cook who had stuck walnuts up the chickens' tails for the evening meal. He closed his eyes. He was shaking. With one hand he encircled the child's neck. He felt the tickle of her braids against his wrist and squeezed ever so gently, aware that she was so tiny he could strangle her with very little effort. He wanted to do it, feel her writhing and kicking at his knees, squirming as she fought for air. He wanted to hear her moan and die in his arms. He wanted to pull off her clothes. He felt violently aroused. With his other hand he ventured beneath her well-starched dress, running his fingers up her child's legs until he found the lace of her batiste petticoats and her woolen drawers with their elastic bands. He was panting. In a corner of his brain he had just enough sanity left to realize that he was poised on the edge of a bottomless pit. The child had stopped talking and was very still, staring up at him with her huge black eyes. Esteban García took her hand and placed it on his stiffened sex.

"Do you know what this is?" he asked hoarsely.

"Your penis," she replied, for she had seen it in the illustrations of her Uncle Jaime's medical books and on her

Uncle Nicolás whenever he walked around naked doing his Oriental exercises.

He jumped. He stood up suddenly and she fell to the carpet. He was surprised and frightened. His hands were shaking, his knees had become weak, and his ears were burning. Just then he heard Senator Trueba's footsteps in the hallway and seconds later, before he could catch his breath, the old man walked into the library.

"Why is it so dark in here?" he roared in his earthquake of a voice.

Trueba turned on the lights and seemed not to recognize the young man who was staring wild-eyed at him. He stretched his arms out to his granddaughter and she ran to him for cover for a moment, like a whipped puppy, but she quickly pried herself free and ran out, shutting the door behind her.

"Who are you, man?" he spat at the one who was also his grandchild.

"Esteban García. Don't you remember me, *patrón?*" the other managed to stammer.

Then Trueba recognized the crafty little boy who had betrayed Pedro Tercero years before and who had retrieved his amputated fingers. He understood that it would not be easy to send him away without giving him a hearing, despite the fact that as a rule matters concerning his tenants were supposed to be resolved by the foreman at Tres Marías.

"What do you want?" he asked.

Esteban García hesitated for a moment. He could not find the words he had so carefully prepared for months before daring to knock at the door of the *patrón's* house.

"Hurry up, I don't have much time," Trueba said.

Stuttering, García managed to make his plea: he had completed high school in San Lucas and wanted a recommendation to the police academy and a government subsidy to pay for his studies.

"Why don't you stay in the country like your father and grandfather?" the *patrón* asked him.

"Forgive me, *señor,* but I want to be a policeman," pleaded Esteban García.

Trueba remembered that he still owed him the reward for betraying Pedro Tercero García, and he decided that this was a good occasion to repay the debt and in the process acquire a useful friend in the police. You never know, he thought; I may need him someday. He sat down at his heavy desk, took out a piece of paper bearing the Senate letterhead, composed the recommendation in the usual terms, and handed it to the young man who stood waiting before him.

"Here, son. I'm glad you've chosen that profession. If you want to go around armed, you might as well be a policeman. That way you have impunity. I'm going to phone General Hurtado, a friend of mine, to make sure they give you the scholarship. If you need anything, just let me know."

"Thank you very much, *patrón.*"

"Don't mention it, son. I like to help my people out."

He said goodbye to him with a friendly pat on the shoulder.

"Why did they call you Esteban?" he asked him in the doorway.

"Because of you, sir," the young man answered, blushing.

Trueba did not give the matter a second thought. Tenants often used their *patrón*'s name for their children. It was a sign of respect.

Clara died on Alba's seventh birthday. The first omen of her death was perceptible only to her. She began to make secret preparations to depart. With great discretion she divided up her clothing among the servants and the followers she always had, keeping only what she absolutely needed. She put her papers in order, and salvaged her notebooks that bore witness to life from the hidden corners of the house. She tied them up with colored ribbons, arranging them according to events and not in chronological order, for the one thing she had forgotten to record was the dates, and in her final haste she decided that she could not waste time looking them up. When she was searching for the notebooks, the jewels began to appear in shoe boxes, in stocking wrappers, and on the bottom shelves of wardrobes, where she had kept them ever since the days when her husband gave them to her hoping to win her love. She placed them in an old woolen sock, fastened it with a safety pin, and handed them to Blanca.

"Put this away, darling. Someday they may be good for something besides masquerades," she said.

Blanca discussed the matter with Jaime and he began to keep an eye on his mother. He noticed that she was leading an apparently normal life but that she barely ate, sustaining herself with milk and a few spoonfuls of honey. Nor did she sleep very much. She spent the night writing or wandering through the house. She seemed to be detaching herself from the world, growing ever lighter, more transparent, more winged.

"One of these days she's going to fly away," Jaime said, worried.

Suddenly she began to suffocate. She felt the gallop of a wild horse in her chest and the anxiety of a rider rushing headlong into the wind. She said it was her asthma, but Alba noticed that she no longer rang the little silver bell so she would come and cure her with prolonged hugs. One morning she saw her grandmother opening the bird cages with inexplicable joy.

Clara wrote small cards to each of her loved ones, of whom there were many, and secretly placed them in a box beneath her bed. The next morning she did not get up, and when the maid brought in the breakfast tray she refused to have her open the curtains. She had begun to take leave even of the light, to enter slowly into darkness.

When he heard about this, Jaime went to see her. He insisted on examining her. He found nothing abnormal in her appearance, but he knew beyond a shadow of a doubt that she was going to die. He left her room with a broad, hypocritical smile, and once he was out of his mother's field of vision he had to lean against a wall, because his legs were giving out. He told no one in the house. He called a specialist from the school of medicine, who appeared that very day in the Trueba home. After seeing Clara, he confirmed Jaime's diagnosis. They assembled the whole family in the drawing room and without much ado announced that she would not live more than two or three weeks and that the only thing to be done was to sit with her, so that she would die happy.

"I think she's decided to die, and science has no cure for that," said Jaime.

Esteban Trueba grabbed his son by the collar and was on the verge of choking him. He pushed the specialist out the door and smashed all the lamps and china in the room.

Finally he fell to his knees, moaning like a newborn baby. Just at that moment, Alba entered the room and saw her grandfather reduced to her own height. She went up to him and stared him in the eyes, and when she saw his tears she threw her arms around him. It was the old man's weeping that told her what the matter was. She was the only one in the family who did not lose her serenity, thanks to her training in surmounting pain and the fact that her grandmother had often explained to her the circumstances and rituals of death.

"Just as when we come into the world, when we die we are afraid of the unknown. But the fear is something from within us that has nothing to do with reality. Dying is like being born: just a change," Clara had said.

She added that if she could easily communicate with those from the Hereafter, she was absolutely convinced that afterward she would be able to do the same with those of the Here-and-Now. Thus, instead of whimpering when the time came, she hoped Alba would be calm, because in her case death would not be a separation, but a way of being more united. Alba understood perfectly.

Soon afterward Clara seemed to enter a gentle sleep. Only the visible effort to take air into her lungs showed that she was alive. Still, asphyxiation did not seem to cause her undue anxiety now that she was not fighting for her life. Her granddaughter remained at her side the entire time. They had to improvise a bed for Alba on the floor because she refused to leave the room, and when they tried to take her out she had her first tantrum. She insisted that her grandmother was aware of everything and that she needed her. And this was true. Shortly before the end, Clara regained consciousness and was able to speak calmly. The first thing she noticed was Alba's hand in hers.

"I'm going to die, aren't I, darling?" she asked.

"Yes, Grandmother, but it doesn't matter, because I'm here with you," the child replied.

"That's good. Take out the box of cards that's under the bed and hand them out, because I won't have time to say goodbye to everyone."

Clara closed her eyes, breathed a contented sigh, and left for the other world without looking back. Gathered around her were all her family: Jaime and Blanca emaciated from the sleepless nights, Nicolás murmuring Sanskrit prayers, Esteban with his mouth and fists clenched tightly, infinitely furious and desolate, and little Alba, the only one who remained serene. There were also the servants, the Mora sisters, a couple of wretchedly poor artists who had survived in the house over the past few months, and a priest who had arrived at the summons of the cook, but he had nothing to do because Trueba forbade him to disturb the dying woman with last-minute confessions or sprinklings of holy water.

Jaime leaned over the body looking for some imperceptible heartbeat, but there was none.

"Mama's gone," he said, sobbing.

TEN

The Epoch of Decline

I can't talk about it. But I'll try to write it. It's been twenty years and for a long time my grief was unabating. I thought I would never get over it but now that I'm almost ninety I understand what she meant when she promised us she'd always keep in touch. Before, I used to walk around as if I were lost, looking for her everywhere. Every night when I got into bed, I used to imagine she was lying there beside me, the way she did when she had all her teeth and still loved me. I would turn out the light and close my eyes, and in the silence of my bedroom I tried to summon up her image. I called her when I was awake, and they say I did so in my sleep as well.

The night she died I locked myself in the room with her. After all those years without speaking, we spent her final hours lying side by side in the sailboat of the gentle blue silk sea, as she liked to call her bed, and I took the opportunity to tell her everything I couldn't say before, everything I'd been holding in since that terrible night when I beat her. I took off her nightgown and examined her meticulously for any trace of illness that might have justified her death; when I found none, I realized that she had simply fulfilled her mission in this life and that she had escaped to another dimension where her spirit, finally free of its material burden, would be more at home. There was no deformity or anything terrible about her death. I examined her at length, because it had been years since I'd had a chance to look at her the way I wanted to, and in that time my wife had changed, as we all do with the passage of time. She looked as beautiful as ever. She had lost weight and at first I thought she might have grown, because she looked taller, but then I realized it was just an optical illusion, the effect of my own shrinking. Before, I had always felt like a giant next to her, but when I lay down next to her on the bed I saw that we were almost the same size. Her mane of rebellious curls, which had charmed me so when we were married, was muted by a few white strands that lit her sleeping face. She was very pale, with shadows around her eyes. I noticed for the first time tiny, delicate wrinkles at the corners of her lips and on her forehead. She looked like a child. She was cold, but she was the same sweet woman as ever. I spoke to her gently, caressed her, and slept awhile when weariness overcame my grief. The irremediable fact of her death did nothing to alter our reunion. We were finally reconciled.

At daybreak I began to fix her up so she would look good when the others came in. I dressed her in the white tunic she kept in her wardrobe. I was surprised to see how little clothing she had; I'd always thought of her as an elegant woman. I found some woolen socks and put them on her so her feet wouldn't be cold, because she was always easily chilled. Then I brushed her hair, intending to put it up in the bun she always wore, but when I pulled the bristles through her hair the curls floated up around her face and I decided she looked prettier that way. I looked for her jewels but couldn't find them anywhere, so I took off the gold ring I had worn since the day we were engaged and slipped it on her finger to replace the one she removed when she cut me out of her life. I arranged the pillows, straightened the bed, put a few drops of cologne on her neck, and opened the window to let the morning in. When everything was ready, I opened the door and let my children and granddaughter say goodbye to her. They saw Clara smiling, clean, and beautiful, just as she always had been. I had shrunk four inches; my shoes were swimming on me, and my hair had gone completely white, but I wasn't crying anymore.

"You can bury her now," I said. "And while you're at it," I added, "you might as well bury my mother-in-law's head. It's been gathering dust down in the basement since

God knows when." I left the room, dragging my feet to keep my shoes from falling off.

This was how my granddaughter learned that the contents of the pigskin hatbox she used for celebrating black masses and decorating her playhouse in the basement was the head of her Great-Grandmother Nívea, which had remained unburied for years—first to avoid scandal, and later because in the turmoil of this house we simply forgot about it. We buried it in the strictest privacy, so as not to set people talking. After the employees of the funeral home had finished placing Clara in her coffin and turning the drawing room into a proper funeral chapel by hanging it with black and setting up white candles and an improvised altar on the grand piano, Jaime and Nicolás laid their grandmother's head—by then nothing more than a yellow toy with an expression of sheer terror—in the coffin beside her favorite daughter.

Clara's funeral was an event. Even I could not explain where all those people appeared from to mourn my wife. I hadn't realized she knew everyone. Interminable lines of people streamed by to shake my hand, cars blocked all the cemetery gates, and a hodgepodge of delegations—poor people, students, labor unionists, nuns, mongoloid children, bohemians, and spiritualists—came to pay her their respects. Almost all the tenants from Tres Marías made the trip by bus or train, some for the first time in their lives, to say goodbye to her. In the crowd I caught a glimpse of Pedro Segundo García, whom I hadn't seen in many years. I went to greet him, but he ignored my wave. His head bowed, he walked up to Clara's grave and threw a spray of half-withered wild flowers on it that looked as if they had been stolen from some garden. He was weeping.

Alba went to the funeral. Holding on to my hand, she watched the coffin being lowered into the earth in the provisional spot we had obtained. She listened to speeches extolling virtues her grandmother never had, and when she returned to the house she ran to lock herself in the basement, where she waited for Clara's spirit to communicate with her, just as Clara had promised. I found her there, smiling in her sleep, stretched out on the moth-eaten remnants of old Barrabás.

That night I couldn't sleep. The two loves of my life,

Rosa of the green hair and Clara the clairvoyant, the two sisters I adored, merged into one. At dawn I decided that if I hadn't been able to have them while I was alive, at least they would accompany me in death. I took a few sheets of paper from my desk and sat down to design the most fitting, most luxurious mausoleum in the world. It would be of salmon-colored Italian marble, with statues made of the same material showing Rosa and Clara with angel wings, because they were, and always would be, angels. One day I will lie between them there.

I wanted to die as soon as possible, because life without my wife had lost all meaning for me. I didn't know that I still had a lot to do in this world. Fortunately, Clara has returned, or perhaps she never left. I sometimes think that old age has affected my mind and that you can't just ignore the fact that I buried her twenty years ago. I suspect I'm seeing things, like a crazy old man. But those doubts melt away when I see her pass me in the halls or hear her laughing on the terrace. I know she's with me. I know she's forgiven my violent behavior and that she's closer to me now than she ever was before. She's still alive, and she's with me: Clara, the clearest.

Clara's death completely transformed life in the big house on the corner. Gone with her were the spirits and the guests, as well as that luminous gaiety that had always been present because she did not believe that the world was a vale of tears but rather a joke that God had played and that it was idiotic to take it seriously if He himself never had. Alba noticed the decline from the very first days. She saw it advancing slowly but inexorably. She noticed it before anybody else in the flowers wilting in their vases, saturating the air with a sickening odor that lingered while they dried up, lost their leaves, and fell apart, leaving only the musty stalks, which no one bothered to clean up until much later. Alba stopped cutting flowers to decorate the house. Then the plants died, because no one remembered to water them or talk to them as Clara had done. The cats crept away, disappearing just as they had arrived or been born in the cracks and crevices of the roof. Esteban Trueba dressed all in black and in a single night passed from his healthy middle years to a shrunken, stuttering old age, which, however, did nothing to curb his anger. He wore strict mourning attire for the rest of his life, even long after it had gone out of fashion and no one used it except the poor, who wore a black band around their sleeves. Under his shirt and close to his chest he wore a tiny suède bag that hung from a fine gold chain; in it were his wife's false teeth, which he treated as a token of good luck and expiation. Everybody in the family sensed that without Clara all reason for staying together had been lost: they had almost nothing to say to each other. Trueba realized that the only thing keeping him at home was the presence of his grand-daughter.

Over the course of the next few years the house changed into a ruin. No one tended the garden, either to water it or to weed it, until it was swallowed up by oblivion, birds, and wild grasses. The blind statues and the singing fountains filled with dry leaves, bird droppings, and moss. The broken, dirty arbors served as a refuge for wild animals and a garbage dump for the neighbors. The whole garden became a thick underbrush, like an abandoned town, through which one could scarcely walk without slashing a path with a machete. The topiaries that had once been pruned with aspirations toward the baroque finished in a hopeless, tortured state, besieged by snails and disease. Inside the house, the curtains slowly came unmoored from their rings and hung like the petticoats of an old woman, dusty and faded. Pieces of furniture, trampled on by Alba, who used them to build her houses and trenches, turned into corpses with exposed springs, and the huge tapestry in the drawing room lost the dauntless beauty of its bucolic Versailles setting to become the dart board of Nicolás and his niece. The kitchen was covered with soot and grease and full of empty cans and piles of newspaper; no longer did it produce platters of roast pork and aromatic dishes as it had before. The inhabitants of the house resigned themselves to eating chick-peas and rice pudding almost every day, for no one had the courage to face the procession of wart-faced, ill-tempered, and despotic cooks who succeeded each other in that kingdom of abused and blackened saucepans. The earthquakes, the door slammings, and Esteban Trueba's cane had opened cracks in the walls and splintered the doors, and the venetian blinds had slipped from their hinges. No one took the initiative to repair them. The taps began to leak, the pipes to sweat, the roof tiles to crack, and green stains to spread across the walls. Only Clara's blue silk-covered room remained intact. Within its walls were the blond wood furniture, two white cotton dresses, the empty canary cage, the basket with her unfinished knitting, her decks of magic cards, her three-legged table, and the stacks of notebooks in which she had recorded fifty years of life and which much later, in the solitude of the empty house and the silence of the dead and disappeared, I put in order and read, completely mesmerized, so I could construct this story.

Jaime and Nicolás lost what little interest they had in the family and showed no compassion for their father, who in his loneliness tried in vain to build a friendship with them that would fill the void left by a lifetime of bad relationships. They lived in the house because they had nowhere more suitable to eat and sleep, but they came and went like indifferent shadows, never stopping to notice the destruction. Jaime practiced his profession with the vocation of a true apostle. With the same tenacity his father had brought to the task of lifting Tres Marías out of ruin and making his fortune, he spent his strength working in the clinic and treating the poor without charge in his spare time.

"You're a hopeless loser, son," Trueba would say, sighing. "You have no sense of reality. You've never taken stock of how the world really is. You put your faith in utopian values that don't even exist."

"Helping one's neighbor is a value that exists."

"No. Charity, like Socialism, is an invention of the weak to exploit the strong and bring them to their knees."

"I don't believe in your theory of the weak and the strong," Jaime replied.

"That's the way it is in nature. We live in a jungle."

"Yes, because the people who make up the rules think like you! But it won't always be that way."

"Oh, yes, it will. Because we always win. We know how to move around in the world and how to use power. Listen to me, son. Pull yourself together and open your own clinic. I'll help you. But cut out your Socialist nonsense!" Esteban Trueba thundered, with no results.

After Amanda disappeared from his life, Nicolás seemed to find his emotional equilibrium. His experience in India had left him with a taste for spiritual endeavors. He abandoned the fantastic commercial escapades that had bedeviled his imagination in the early days of his youth, as well as his desire to possess every woman who passed in front of him, and turned his attention to his lifelong wish to find God on less traveled paths. He turned the same charm he had used to gather pupils for his Spanish dance class to collecting a growing number of disciples. Most of them were young people fed up with the good life, wanderers like him in search of a philosophy that would allow them to exist without participating in earthly strife. They formed a group that was prepared to receive the millennial knowledge Nicolás had acquired in the East. For a while they met in the back rooms of the abandoned part of the house, where Alba handed out walnuts and served them herbal teas while they meditated in a cross-legged position. When Esteban Trueba realized that behind his back these Contemporaries and Eponyms were breathing through their navels and taking off their clothes on the slightest pretext, he lost his patience and kicked them all out of his house, threatening them with his cane and shouting that he would call the police. Then Nicolás understood that there was no way he could continue teaching The Truth without money. He began to charge a modest fee for his knowledge, which enabled him to rent a house where he set up his academy of converts. Owing to legal constraints and the need for an official-sounding name, he called it the Institute for Union with Nothingness, or the I.U.N. But his father was not disposed to leave him in peace; Nicolás's followers began to appear in the newspaper with shaved heads, indecent loincloths, and beatific expressions, bringing public ridicule to the name of Trueba. As soon as they found out that the I.U.N. prophet was the son of Senator Trueba, the opposition blew the story out of proportion to make fun of him, using the son's spiritual quest as a political weapon against the father. Trueba resisted stoically until the day he found his granddaughter Alba with her head shaved like a billiard ball, endlessly repeating the sacred word *Om*. He had one of the worst tantrums of his life. He paid a surprise visit to his son's institute with two hired thugs, who broke what little furniture there was to pieces and were about to do the same to the peaceful worshippers when the old man, realizing that once again he had gone too far, ordered them to halt their destruction and wait for him outside. Alone with his son, he managed to control the furious tremor in his voice and to snarl at him that he was sick and tired of his clowning.

"I don't want to set eyes on you again until my granddaughter's hair has grown back!" he shouted before walking out with a final slam of the door.

Nicolás did not react until the next day. He began by throwing out the rubble his father's men had left and cleaning up his premises, breathing rhythmically to empty his insides of any trace of anger and to purify his spirit. Then, with his loinclothed followers bearing placards demanding religious freedom and respect for their civil rights, he marched them to the gates of Congress, where his disciples took out wooden flutes, bells, and some tiny makeshift gongs and made such a din that they stopped traffic. Once enough people had crowded around, Nicolás proceeded to remove all his clothes and, naked as a baby, lie down in the middle of the street with his arms stretched out, making a cross. There ensued such a commotion of screeching brakes, horns, screams, and whistles that alarm spread within the halls of Congress. In the Senate, discussion was suspended on the right of landowners to fence off neighboring paths with barbed wire, and the members of Congress appeared on the balcony to enjoy the spectacle of the son of Senator Trueba singing Asiatic psalms stark naked. Esteban Trueba ran down the broad stairs of Congress and hurled himself onto the street prepared to kill his son, but he was unable to get through the gates because he felt his heart explode with fury in his chest and a red veil clouded his sight. He fell to the ground.

Nicolás was removed in a police van and the senator in a Red Cross ambulance. Trueba's swoon lasted for three weeks and almost dispatched him to another world. When he was able to leave his bed, he grabbed Nicolás by the collar, pushed him onto an airplane, and shipped him overseas with instructions not to return for the rest of his life. However, he gave him enough money to settle down and live for a long time, because, as Jaime explained, that was one way to make sure Nicolás would not get involved in further acts of madness that could cast aspersions on his father abroad.

Over the course of the next few years Esteban Trueba kept abreast of the black sheep of the family through Blanca's sporadic correspondence with him. Thus he learned that in North America Nicolás had established another academy for uniting himself with nothingness, and that he had been so successful that he had acquired the wealth he had not been able to with his balloon or his sandwiches. He wound up lounging with his disciples in his very own rose-colored porcelain swimming pool and enjoying the full respect of the citizenry, having combined, without intending to, his quest for God with his luck in the world of business. Naturally, Esteban Trueba never believed a word of it.

The Senator waited for his granddaughter's hair to grow a little so no one would think she had ringworm; then he went to enroll her himself in a British school for young ladies, because he still believed that was the finest education, despite the contradictory results he had obtained with his two sons. Blanca went along with his decision, for she accepted that a good conjunction of planets in her daughter's astral chart would not provide Alba with everything she needed to get ahead in life. In this school Alba learned to eat boiled vegetables and burnt rice, to withstand the freezing courtyard, sing hymns, and give up worldly vanities except those in the realm of sports. She was taught to read the Bible, play tennis, and use a typewriter, which was the only useful thing she was left with after all those years in a foreign language. For Alba, who until then had never heard of sin or proper manners for young ladies, who was completely ignorant of the boundary between the human and the divine, the possible and the impossible, and who was used to seeing one of her uncles performing karate leaps completely naked in the hallways and the other buried under a mountain of books, not to mention her grandfather smashing telephones and the flowerpots to pieces with his cane, her mother sneaking out with her clownlike valise, and her grandmother moving the three-legged table and playing Chopin without opening the piano, the school routine was simply unbearable. She found the classes boring, and during recess she would sit in the farthest corner of the courtyard so no one could see her, trembling with the hope that someone would invite her to play and simultaneously praying that no one would notice her. Her mother had warned her not to try to explain to her classmates what she had learned about human nature in her Uncle Jaime's medical texts, and not to tell the teachers about the advantages of Esperanto over English. Despite these precautions, from the very first day, the headmistress had no trouble discerning the eccentricities of her new pupil. She observed her for a couple of weeks, and when she was certain of the diagnosis she summoned Blanca Trueba to her office and explained as politely as she could that the child was simply not cut out for a British education, and suggested that she try placing her in a school run by Spanish nuns, who might be better at controlling her wild imagination and correcting her appalling manners. But Senator Trueba was not going to let any Miss Saint John walk all over him, and he brought all his influence to bear to prevent her from expelling his granddaughter. He wanted her, at all costs, to learn English. He was convinced of the superiority of English over Spanish, which in his view was a second-rate language, appropriate for domestic matters and magic, for unbridled passions and useless undertakings, but thoroughly inadequate for the world of science and technology in which he hoped to see Alba triumph. He had finally come to accept—beaten into it by the tide of new ideas—that not all women were complete idiots, and he believed that Alba, who was too plain to attract a well-to-do husband, could enter one of the professions and make her living like a man. On this point Blanca supported her father, because she had felt in her own life the consequences of facing the world with an inadequate education.

"I don't want you to be poor like me or have to depend on a man for support," she told her daughter every time she saw her crying because she did not want to go to school.

They did not withdraw her from the school and she was forced to endure it for ten solid years.

For Alba, her mother was the only stable person in the drifting ship that was the big house on the corner after Clara's death. Blanca fought the destruction and decline with the ferocity of a lioness, but it was clear it was a losing proposition. She alone attempted to give the house the appearance of a home. Senator Trueba continued to live there, but he stopped inviting his friends and political cronies. He shut the drawing rooms and used only the library and his bedroom. He was deaf and blind to the needs of his house. He was very busy with his politics and his business, traveling constantly, financing new political campaigns, buying land and tractors, raising race horses, and speculating on the price of gold, sugar, and paper. He did not notice that the walls of his house were eager for a coat of paint, that the furniture was falling apart, and that the kitchen had turned into a pigsty. Nor did he see his granddaughter's worn sweaters or his daughter's antiquated clothing or her hands that had been ruined by household chores and clay. He did not behave this way out of avarice; it was simply that his family no longer interested him. At times he shook himself out of his indifference and showed up with some extraordinary, outsized present for his granddaughter, which only sharpened the contrast between the invisible wealth of his bank accounts and the austerity of the house. He gave Blanca varying amounts of money to maintain the dark, drafty, rambling, almost empty house, but she never had enough to cover all her expenses. She was continually borrowing from Jaime, and no matter how often she took a tuck in the budget here and a pleat there, by the end of the month she always had a stack of unpaid bills that kept piling up until she decided to take herself to the district of the Jewish diamond merchants to sell one of her gems, which had been bought a quarter of a century earlier in those very shops and which Clara had bequeathed to her tied up in the woolen sock.

Inside the house Blanca wore an apron and cloth sandals, which made her indistinguishable from the few remaining servants. When she went out, she wore her same black suit that had been ironed and reironed, with her same white silk blouse. After her grandfather had become a widower and stopped showing so much interest in her, Alba wore the hand-me-downs of some distant cousins who were either taller or shorter, which meant that in general the coats fit her like military greatcoats and the dresses were too short and tight. Jaime would have liked to do something for them, but his conscience told him it was better to spend his extra money buying food for the hungry than luxuries for his sister and his niece.

After her grandmother's death, Alba began to suffer nightmares from which she awoke screaming and feverish. She dreamt that everybody in the family was dying and that she was left to wander in the big house alone, with no other company than the faint, threadbare ghosts that wandered up and down the corridors. Jaime suggested that they move her into Blanca's room, which would soothe her nerves. From the moment she began to share her mother's room, she looked forward to bedtime with secret impatience. Curled up under the sheets, she watched her mother complete her nightly ritual and climb into bed. Blanca cleaned her face with Harem Cream, a pinkish grease that smelled of roses and was supposed to perform miracles on women's skin. She also brushed her long chestnut hair—now sprinkled with a few white hairs that were invisible to all but her—a hundred times. Blanca was prone to colds and slept winter and summer in woolen shifts she knit herself in her spare time. Whenever it rained, she put on a pair of gloves to relieve the arctic cold that had seeped into her bones from the damp clay she used, which all Jaime's injections and Nicolás's Chinese acupuncture were powerless to cure. Alba watched her come and go about the room, her novitiate's nightgown floating out from her body and her hair freed from its bun, wrapped in the gentle fragrance of her clean clothes and Harem Cream and lost in an incoherent monologue into which she poured complaints about the price of vegetables, the litany of her various aches and pains, her exhaustion from trying to run the house by herself, and her poetic fantasies of Pedro Tercero García, whom she would imagine among the clouds of sunset or in the golden wheatfields of Tres Marías. When she had finished her ritual, Blanca climbed into bed and turned out the light. Reaching across the narrow space between them, she took her daughter's hand and began to tell her stories from the magic books of the enchanted trunks of her Great-Uncle Marcos, which her poor memory had transformed into new tales. This was how Alba learned about a prince who slept a hundred years, damsels who fought dragons single-handed, and a wolf lost in a forest who was disemboweled by a little girl for no reason whatsoever. When Alba asked to hear these bizarre stories again, Blanca could not repeat them, for she had forgotten them. This led the little girl to write the stories down. She also began to record the things that struck her as important, just as her Grandmother Clara had before her.

Work on the mausoleum began soon after Clara's death, but it took almost two years to complete because I kept adding costly new details: tombstones with Gothic lettering in gold, a glass cupola to let the sunlight in, and an ingenious apparatus copied from the Roman fountains that allows a small interior garden, which I planted with roses and camellias, the favorite flowers of the two sisters who had won my heart, to be watered in perpetuity. The statues were a problem. I rejected several drawings because I didn't want a pair of moronic angels but faithful portraits of Rosa and Clara, with their faces, their hands, and their real shape. A Uruguayan sculptor finally did what I had in mind, and the statues turned out exactly as I wanted. When the project was complete, I came up against an unexpected obstacle: I was unable to transfer Rosa to the new tomb because the del Valle family objected. I tried to convince them, using every argument I could think of along with gifts and pressure, even bringing my political power to bear, but it was all in vain. My brothers-in-law were unyielding. I think they must have heard about Nívea's head and were angry with me for having kept it in the basement all that time. In light of their obstinancy, I called Jaime in and told him to get ready to accompany me to the cemetery to steal Rosa's body. He didn't look surprised.

"If they won't give her to us, we'll have to take her by force," I told him.

As is customary in this sort of affair, we went at night and bribed the guard, just as I had done years earlier when I wanted to stay with Rosa her first night there. We carried our tools down the cypress-lined path, found the del Valle family tomb, and embarked on the lugubrious task of opening it. We cautiously removed the heavy stone that safeguarded Rosa's eternal rest and slid the white coffin from its niche. The coffin was much heavier than we had expected, and we had to ask the guard to help. It was uncomfortable to work in that narrow, poorly lit space, getting in each other's way with our tools. When we were finished, we replaced the stone over the niche so that no one would suspect the grave was empty. We were bathed in sweat. Jaime had had the foresight to bring a canteen filled with brandy and we each took a swig to keep our spirits up. Even though neither of us was superstitious, that necropolis of crosses, cupolas, and tombstones had us pretty nervous. I sat down at the entrance to the tomb to catch my breath and realized there was precious little youth left in me if moving a coffin was enough to knock my heart off beat and make me see bright dots in the dark. I closed my eyes and thought of Rosa: her perfect face, her milky skin, her mermaid hair, her honeyed eyes that caused such havoc, her hands clasping the mother-of-pearl rosary, her nuptial flower crown. I sighed as I recalled the image of that beautiful virgin who had slipped through my hands and lain there waiting all those years for me to come and take her to the place where she belonged.

"Let's open it up, son. I want to see Rosa," I told Jaime.

He didn't try to talk me out of it, because he recognized the tone that creeps into my voice when I've made an irrevocable decision. We angled the lantern just so, and he loosened the bronze screws that had grown dark with time. We lifted the top, which was as heavy as a piece of lead, and in the white light of the carbide lantern I saw Rosa the Beautiful, with her orange-blossom crown, her green hair, and her unruffled beauty, just as I had seen her many years before, lying in her white coffin on my in-laws' dining room table. I stared at her in fascination, unsurprised that time had left her intact, because she was exactly as I'd seen her in my dreams. I leaned over and, through the glass covering her face, placed a kiss on the lips of my immortal beloved. At just that moment a breeze crept through the cypresses, slipped through a crack in the coffin, which until that instant had remained hermetically sealed, and in a flash the unchanged bride dissolved like a spell, disintegrating into a fine gray powder. When I raised my head and opened my eyes, the cold kiss still on my lips, Rosa the Beautiful was gone. In her place was a skull with empty sockets, a few strips of marble-colored skin clinging to its cheekbones, and a lock or two of moldy hair at its nape.

Jaime and the guard quickly slapped the coffin lid back on, placed Rosa in a wheelbarrow, and took her to the place that had been readied for her next to Clara in the salmon-colored mausoleum. I sat down on a grave in the middle of the cypresses and looked up at the moon.

Férula was right, I thought; I've been left all alone and my body and my soul are shriveling up. All that's left for me is to die like a dog.

Senator Trueba fought off his political enemies, who were making daily gains in the quest for power. While other leaders of the Conservative Party grew fat and old and spent their time in hair-splitting discussions, he devoted himself to work and study, crossing the country from north to south in a nonstop personal campaign, ignoring both his age and the muffled cry of his bones. He was re-elected senator in every parliamentary election. But he was not interested in power, wealth, or prestige. His one obsession was to destroy what he called "the Marxist cancer," which was slowly gaining ground among the people.

"You look under any stone and a Communist jumps out!" he said.

No one believed him. Not even the Communists. They made fun of his tantrums, his outdated cane, and his apocalyptic predictions, and said he looked like a crow in his mourning. When he brandished his statistics and the results of the last elections in front of them, his own party members suspected they were just the senile rantings of an old man.

"The day we can't get our hands on the ballot boxes before the vote is counted we're done for," Trueba argued.

"The Marxists haven't won by popular vote anywhere in the world," his confreres replied. "At the very least it takes a revolution, and that kind of thing doesn't happen in this country."

"Until it happens!" Trueba answered furiously.

"Relax, *hombre*. We're not going to let that happen," they consoled him. "Marxism doesn't stand a chance in Latin America. Don't you know it doesn't allow for the magical side of things? It's an atheistic, practical, functional doctrine. There's no way it can succeed here!"

Not even Colonel Hurtado, who saw traitors everywhere he looked, considered the Communists a danger. On more than one occasion he explained to Trueba that the Communist Party was composed of four bums without any statistical importance who followed Moscow's instructions with a piety worthy of a better cause.

"Moscow's on the other side of the globe, Esteban," Colonel Hurtado told him. "They have no grasp of the condition of this country. If you don't believe me, just look at them: they're more lost than Little Red Riding Hood. A while ago they published a manifesto calling on the peasants, sailors, and Indians to unite in the first national soviet, which from any point of view is a joke. How are the peasants supposed to know what a soviet is? The sailors are mostly at sea, and when they're not they're more interested in brothels than they are in politics. And the Indians! We've only got two hundred left. I doubt any more than that survived the massacres of the last century, but if they want to make a soviet on the reservations, that's their problem!" The colonel laughed.

"Yes, but it's not just Communists. There are Socialists, radicals, and lots of other splinter groups. They're all pretty much the same," Trueba replied.

To Senator Trueba, all political parties except his own were potentially Marxist, and he could not distinguish one ideology from another. Since he did not hesitate to explain his position in public every time he had the chance, for everyone but his own co-religionists he soon became a caricature of the picturesque, reactionary oligarch. The Conservative Party had to hold him back to keep him from saying things that could ruin their reputation. He was a furious crusader, ready to do battle in forums, press conferences, and universities; wherever no one else was brave enough to stand up, there he would be, unshakable in his dark suit, with his lion's mane of hair and his silver cane. He was the butt of cartoonists, thanks to whose constant mockery he became a popular figure and delivered a landslide vote for the conservatives in every election. He was fanatical, violent, and antiquated, but he represented better than anybody else the values of family, tradition, private property, law and order. Everyone recognized him on the street. People made up jokes and anecdotes about him that were the talk of the town. It was said that when he had his heart attack the day his son took off his clothes before the gates of Congress, the President of the Republic called him to his office to offer him the post of Ambassador to Switzerland, a job appropriate to his age that would allow him to recover his health. They said that Senator Trueba replied by slamming his fist down on the presidential desk, knocking down the flag and the bust of the Founding Father.

"I'm not going anywhere, Your Excellency!" he roared. "The minute I look away, the Marxists will pull that chair right out from under you!"

He was astute enough to be the first to call the left "the enemy of democracy," never suspecting that years later that would be the slogan of the dictatorship. He spent almost all his time and a good part of his fortune on the political front. He noticed that, despite the fact that he was constantly hatching new schemes, his finances seemed to have been dwindling since Clara's death; still, this caused him no undue alarm because he supposed that it was part of the natural order of things that she had breathed good luck into his life and that she could hardly continue to help him after her death. Besides, according to his calculations, he had enough to continue living like a rich man for the time that remained to him in this world. He felt old, and had decided that none of his three children deserved to inherit anything from him, and that he would secure his granddaughter's happiness by leaving her Tres Marías, even though the countryside was not as prosperous as before. Thanks to the new highways and cars, what had once been an expedition was now a mere six-hour drive from the capital; but he was always busy now and never had the time to make the trip. Every once in a while he spoke to his foreman on the telephone to go over the accounts, but these calls left him in a bad mood for several days afterward. His foreman was a man defeated by his own pessimistic views, and his news was mostly a series of misfortunes: the strawberries froze, the chickens caught the pip, the grapes rotted. Thus the countryside, which had been the source of his wealth, became a burden, and Senator

Trueba frequently had to withdraw money from his other businesses to prop up that insatiable land, which seemed to want to return to the days of oblivion, before he rescued it from misery.

"I have to go straighten things out. They need the *patrón*'s eye on them," he murmured.

"Things are getting stormy in the countryside, *patrón*," his foreman often warned him. "The peasants are up in arms. Every day there are new demands. It seems as if they want to be *patrones* themselves. The best thing you can do is sell the property."

But Trueba would not hear of selling. "Land is all you have left when everything else falls apart," he would repeat, almost exactly as he had at the age of twenty-five when his mother and sister were putting pressure on him for the same reason. But with the weight of age and politics, Tres Marías, like many other things that had once seemed essential, had ceased to interest him. Its only value was symbolic.

The foreman was right: those were stormy years. And that was precisely what Pedro Tercero García was proclaiming in his velvet voice, which, thanks to the miracle of radio, now reached the most remote corners of the country. In his mid-thirties, he still looked like a coarse peasant, although it had become more a matter of style since success and his knowledge of the world had softened his roughness and refined his ideas. He wore a woodsman's beard and the flowing hair of a prophet, which he trimmed himself, by memory, with a razor that had been his father's, anticipating by several years the style that was to become all the rage among protest singers. He wore canvas pants, homemade sandals, and a raw wool poncho in the winter. That was his battle dress, and it was how he appeared on the stage and on the covers of his records. Disillusioned with political organizations, he had distilled his thoughts down to three or four basic ideas, on which he built his whole philosophy. He was an anarchist. From the chickens and the foxes he had gone on to sing of life, friendship, love, and also revolution. His music was very popular, and only someone as stubborn as Esteban Trueba could ignore his existence. The old man had refused to allow radios in his house, both to prevent his granddaughter from listening to the soap operas and serials in which mothers lose their children and only recover them years later, and to spare himself the ill effects on his digestion of hearing the subversive songs of his enemy. He did, however, keep a modern radio in his bedroom, but he listened only to the news. He never suspected that Pedro Tercero García was his own son Jaime's best friend, or that he met with Blanca every time she left the house with her clownish suitcase, mumbling excuses. Nor did he know that on certain sunny Sundays Pedro Tercero took Alba hiking, and that as they sat looking out over the city, eating bread and cheese, before tumbling down the slopes, bursting with laughter like two happy puppies, he told her about the poor, the oppressed, the desperate, and other matters that Trueba did not want his granddaughter to know about.

Pedro Tercero watched Alba grow. He tried to be close to her but he never came to think of her as his daughter, because on that point Blanca was inflexible. She said that Alba had withstood many shocking things and that it was a miracle she had turned out to be a relatively normal child; the last thing she needed was any additional confusion about the circumstances of her birth. It was better for her to believe the official version. Besides, she did not want the child discussing this with her grandfather, which would certainly lead to disaster. In any case, the child's free spirit and rebellious nature were gratifying to Pedro Tercero.

"If she's not my daughter, she deserves to be," he would say proudly.

During all those years, Pedro Tercero never got used to the life of a bachelor, despite his success with women, especially the magnificent adolescents whom the laments of his guitar inflamed with love. Some of them forced their way into his life, and he thrived on the freshness of those love affairs. He tried to make these young girls happy for a short while, but from the very first moment of illusion he began to say goodbye, until he finally, delicately, left them. Frequently, when he was in bed with one of them and she was sighing in her sleep beside him, he would close his eyes and think of Blanca, with her ample, ripe body, her warm, generous breasts, the fine wrinkles at her mouth, and the shadows underneath her Arab eyes, and he would feel a cry pressing in his heart. He tried to stay with other women. He discovered many roads and many bodies trying to distance himself from her, but at the moment of greatest intimacy, the exact point of loneliness and the foreknowledge of death, Blanca was always the only one. The next morning, the whole slow process of withdrawing from his new love would begin. As soon as he was free again, he returned to Blanca, thinner, guiltier, and with deeper rings under his eyes, a new song on his guitar, and a wealth of never-ending caresses for her.

But Blanca was used to living by herself. When all was said and done, she had found peace in her household chores, her ceramics studio, and her crèches of made-up animals in which the only figures that corresponded to the laws of reality were the Holy Family lost in a crowd of monsters. The only man in her life was Pedro Tercero, for she was born to have one love. The strength of this immutable desire saved her from the mediocrity and sadness of her fate. She was faithful to him even in those moments when he lost himself in a sea of straight-haired, long-boned nymphs, and never loved him any the less for his digressions. At first she thought she would die every time he moved away from her, but she soon realized that his absences were only as long as a sigh and that he invariably returned more in love and sweeter than ever. Blanca preferred those furtive hotel rendezvous with her lover to the routine of everyday life, the weariness of marriage and the shared poverty at the end of every month, the bad taste in the mouth on waking up, the tedium of Sundays, and the complaints of old age. She was an incurable romantic. Every once in a while she was tempted to take her clown's suitcase and whatever was left of the jewels from the sock and go off with her daughter to live with him, but she always lost her nerve. Perhaps she feared the grandiose love that had stood so many tests would not be able to withstand the most dreadful test of all: living together. Alba was growing rapidly, and Blanca understood that she would not be able to rely much longer on the excuse that she had to watch over her daughter in order to postpone her lover's needs, but she still preferred to put off the decision to some other time. Actually, much as she feared routine, she was horrified by Pedro Tercero's way of living, and by his modest little house—in a working-class neighborhood among hundreds of others as poorly built—of boards and corrugated metal, with packed earth floors and a single light bulb hanging from the ceiling. For her, Pedro moved out of his neighborhood into a downtown apartment, thereby, without intending to do so, ascending to the middle class to which he had never aspired. But even this was not enough for Blanca, who found the apartment sordid, dark, and narrow and the building crowded. She said she could not let Alba grow up there, playing with other children in the street and on the steps, and attending public school. Thus Blanca's youth went by and she entered middle age, resigned to the fact that her only moments of pleasure would come when she dressed up in her best clothes, her perfume, and her whorish underwear, which captivated Pedro Tercero and which she hid, red with shame, in the bottom of her wardrobe, imagining the explanations she would have to give if anyone discovered them. This woman who was so down to earth and practical in all other aspects of life sublimated her childhood passion and lived it tragically. She fed it with fantasies, idealized it, savagely defended it, stripped it of its prosaic truth, and turned it into the kind of love one found in novels.

As for Alba, she learned not to mention Pedro Tercero García's name because she understood the effect it caused in the family. She guessed that something terrible had taken place between her grandfather and the man with the missing fingers who kissed her mother on the mouth, but everyone, even Pedro Tercero himself, gave evasive answers to her questions. Sometimes, in the intimacy of their bedroom, Blanca told her anecdotes about him and taught her his songs, warning her not to hum them in the house. But she never told her that he was her father, and she even seemed to have forgotten it herself. She recalled the past as a series of violent acts, abandonments, and sorrows, and she was not certain things had been the way she remembered. The episode of the mummies, the photographs, and the hairless Indian in Louis XV shoes that had prompted her flight from her husband's house had grown hazy with time. She had told and retold the story of the count's death of fever in the desert so often that she had come to believe it. Years later, the day her daughter came to tell her that the body of Jean de Satigny was lying in the icebox at the morgue, she was not relieved, for she had felt like a widow for years. Nor did she attempt to justify her lie. She took her old black tailored suit from the wardrobe, arranged the hairpins in her bun, and went with Alba to bury the Frenchman in the main cemetery, in a municipal grave, which was where the poor ended up, because Senator Trueba refused to make room for him in the salmon-colored mausoleum. Mother and daughter walked alone behind the black coffin they arranged to buy with Jaime's help. They felt a little ridiculous in the oppressive summer heat, with a bouquet of wilting flowers in their hands and not a single tear for the solitary body they were laying to rest.

"I see my father didn't have a single friend," Alba observed.

Even on that occasion Blanca did not tell her daughter the truth.

After I had settled Rosa and Clara in my mausoleum, I felt better because I knew that sooner or later the three of us would be reunited there, along with our other loved ones, like my mother, Nana, and even Férula, who I hope has forgiven me. I never imagined I was going to live as long as I have and that they'd have to wait so long for me.

Clara's bedroom was kept locked. I didn't want anybody going in there. I wanted everything to stay exactly where it was, so I'd be able to find her spirit whenever I wanted to. I began to suffer from insomnia, the old people's disease. Unable to sleep, I shuffled up and down the halls all night in my slippers that were too big for me, wrapped in the old ecclesiastical bathrobe I had kept for sentimental reasons, and railing against my fate like an old man at the end of his days. But with the first rays of sunlight I regained my desire to live. At breakfast, I appeared in my starched shirt and mourning suit, shaved and calm. I read the newspaper with my granddaughter, verified that my affairs were up to date, handled my correspondence, and went out for the rest of the day. I stopped eating in the house, even on the weekends, because without Clara's catalyzing presence there was no reason why I should put up with my children's bickering.

My only two friends tried to rid me of the grief in my

soul. They had lunch with me, played golf with me, challenged me to games of dominoes. We talked about business, politics, and, at times, about the family. One afternoon when they saw I was a little livelier than usual, they invited me to the Christopher Columbus, hoping that a pleasing woman would help me recover my good humor. None of the three of us was of an age for such adventures, but we had a couple of drinks and set off.

Though I had been in the Christopher Columbus years before, I had practically forgotten it. In recent times the hotel had acquired a certain prestige among tourists, and people traveled from the provinces to the capital just to see it and go back and tell their friends about it. When we arrived at the old house, which on the outside looked the same as it had for years, we were received by a doorman who led us in to the main room, where I remembered having been before in the days of the French madam—or, better put, the madam with the French accent. A young girl dressed like a schoolgirl offered us a glass of wine on the house. One of my friends tried to put his arm around her waist, but she warned him that she was only a servant and that he would have to wait for the professionals. Moments later a curtain opened and we saw a vision out of one of the ancient Arabian courts: a huge Negro so black that he looked blue, dressed in baggy carrot-colored silk trousers, a vest, a purple lamé turban, and Turkish slippers, with oiled muscles and a gold ring in his nose. When he smiled, we saw that all his teeth were made of lead. He introduced himself as Mustafá and handed us a photo album so we could choose our merchandise. For the first time in ages I laughed spontaneously; I found the idea of a catalogue of prostitutes very amusing. We flipped through the pictures, looking at women who were fat, thin, long-haired, short-haired, dressed as nymphs, amazons, nuns, and courtesans, but I was unable to decide because they all looked like trampled banquet flowers. The last three pages of the album were devoted to boys in Greek tunics, crowned with laurel, playing among false Hellenic ruins, with chubby bottoms and heavy eyelashes—repulsive. I have to admit I had never seen a fag close up except Carmelo, the one who dressed like a Japanese girl at the Red Lantern, so I was taken aback when one of my friends, a family man and a broker on the stock exchange, chose one of those fat-assed boys in the pictures. The boy appeared as if by magic from behind the curtains and led my friend off by the hand, giggling and wiggling his hips like a woman. My other friend chose a fat odalisque, with whom I doubt he was able to achieve any great feats, owing to his advanced age and fragile frame, but they, too, went out together, swallowed up by the curtain.

"I see the señor's having a hard time deciding," Mustafá remarked cordially. "Allow me to offer you the best in the house. I'm going to introduce you to Aphrodite."

And Aphrodite appeared in the room, with her hair piled three stories high, barely covered by a few layers of tulle and dripping with artificial grapes from her shoulders to her knees. It was Tránsito Soto, who had acquired a definite mythological look, despite the tasteless grapes and circus gauze.

"I'm glad to see you, *patrón,*" she greeted me.

She led me through the curtain into a small interior courtyard, the heart of that labyrinthine structure. The Christopher Columbus was built out of three old houses, strategically connected by a series of back courtyards, corridors, and specially constructed bridges. Tránsito Soto conducted me to a room that was nondescript but clean; its only sign of extravagance was a series of frescoes that were poor copies of the ones at Pompeii, which some mediocre painter had reproduced on the walls, and a large, slightly rusty antique bathtub with running water. I whistled in admiration.

"We've made a few changes in the décor," she said.

Tránsito took off her grapes and gauze and was once again the woman I remembered, only more appetizing and less vulnerable, but with the same ambitious look in her eyes that had captivated me when I first met her. She told me about the cooperative of prostitutes and homosexuals, which had had fantastic success. Together they had lifted the Christopher Columbus out of the ruin in which the phony French madam had left it, and had worked to transform it into a social event and historic monument whose reputation was passed by word of mouth from sailor to sailor on the farthest seas. The costumes had been the greatest success of all, because they awakened the customers' erotic fantasies, as did

the catalogue of whores, which they had managed to reproduce and distribute throughout certain provinces, arousing in
the men a desire one day to visit the famous brothel.

"It's boring to walk around in these rags and grapes,
patrón, but the men like it. When they leave, they tell others
and that brings us new customers. We're doing very well.
It's a good business, and no one here feels exploited. We're
all partners. This is the only whorehouse in the country with
its own authentic Negro. You might have seen others, but
they're all painted. But you can rub Mustafá with sandpaper
and he'll still be black. And this place is clean. You can drink
the water from the toilet bowl if you want to, because we
pour lye where you'd least expect it and we're all supervised
by the Board of Health. No venereal diseases here."

Tránsito removed her last veil, and her magnificent
nakedness so overwhelmed me that I immediately felt deathly
tired. My heart was weighed with sadness and my penis was
as flaccid as a withered, aimless flower between my legs.

"Ah, Tránsito," I said. "I think I'm too old for this."

But Tránsito Soto began to undulate the serpent around
her navel, hypnotizing me with the gentle curve of her belly
while she lulled me with that hoarse bird voice of hers, telling
me about the benefits of the cooperative and the advantages
of the catalogue. Despite everything, I had to laugh, and
gradually my own laughter began to affect me like a balm. I
tried to trace the serpent's path with my finger, but it slipped
away from me, zigzagging. I was astonished that this woman
who was no longer in her first or second youth should have
such firm skin and muscles that were capable of making that
reptile move as if it were alive. I bent down to kiss the tattoo
and was pleased to discover that she wasn't wearing perfume. The warm, safe scent of her belly entered my nostrils
and completely invaded me, awakening in my blood a fire I
had thought long since extinguished. Without ceasing to
speak, Tránsito opened her legs, casually separating the soft
columns of her thighs as if she were simply adjusting her
posture. I began to cover her with my lips, inhaling, pressing, and licking, until I forgot all about my grief and the
weight of the years, and my desire returned with the force of
other times, and without stopping my kisses and caresses I
pulled my clothes off in desperation, happy to discover my

masculinity intact and firm while I plunged into the warm, compassionate animal that was offering itself to me, rocked by the little hoarse bird, wrapped in the arms of the goddess, and shaken by the force of those hips until I lost all consciousness of things and exploded with pleasure.

Afterward we soaked together in the bathtub until my soul returned to my body and I felt practically cured. For a second I toyed with the fantasy that Tránsito was the woman I had always needed and that with her by my side I could return to the days when I was able to lift a sturdy peasant woman in the air, pull her up onto my horse's haunches, and carry her off into the bushes against her will.

"Clara . . ." I murmured without thinking, and I felt a tear roll down my cheek and then another and another until it became a downpour of grief, a torrent of sobs, a suffocation of nostalgia and sorrow that Tránsito Soto had no trouble understanding, for she had long experience with the heartaches of men. She let me weep out all the misery and loneliness of recent years and helped me out of the tub with a mother's care. She dried me off, massaged me until I was as soft as moistened bread, and pulled the covers over me when I closed my eyes in the bed. She kissed me on the forehead and tiptoed out of the room.

"I wonder who Clara is," I heard her murmur as she left.

ELEVEN

器

The Awakening

Around the age of eighteen, Alba left childhood behind for good. At the exact moment when she felt like a woman, she locked herself in her old room, which still held the mural she had started so many years before. Next she rummaged through her paint jars until she found a little red and a little white that were still fresh. Then she carefully mixed them together and painted a large pink heart in the last empty space on the wall. She was in love. Afterward she threw her paints and brushes into the trash and sat down to contemplate her drawings, which is to say, the history of her joys and sorrows. She decided that the balance had been happy and with a sigh said goodbye to the first stage of her life.

She finished school that year and decided to study philosophy for pleasure and music to annoy her grandfather, who believed that the arts were a waste of time and who constantly preached the virtues of the liberal or scientific professions. He also warned her against love and marriage, with the same insolence with which he insisted that Jaime should find a decent girl and settle down because he was turning into a hopeless bachelor. He said it was good for men to have a wife, but that women like Alba could only lose by marrying. Her grandfather's sermons went out the window when Alba set eyes on Miguel one unforgettable rainy afternoon in the cafeteria of the university.

Miguel was a pale student, with feverish eyes, faded trousers, and miner's boots, in his final year of law school.

He was a leftist leader, and he was afire with the most uncontrollable passion: justice. However, that did not prevent him from being aware that Alba was watching him. He looked up and their eyes met. They stared at each other, dazzled, and from that moment on they sought out every possible occasion to meet on the leafy promenades of the nearby park, where they walked with their arms full of books or dragging Alba's heavy cello in its case. On their initial encounter, she noticed that he wore a tiny insignia on his sleeve: a raised fist. She decided not to tell him that she was Esteban Trueba's granddaughter. For the first time in her life she used the surname that was on all her identification cards: Satigny. She quickly realized it would be best not to tell the rest of her fellow students either. On the other hand, she could boast that she was friends with Pedro Tercero García, who was very popular among the students, and with the Poet, on whose knees she had sat as a little girl and who was now known in every language and whose poetry was on the lips of all the students and scrawled in graffiti on the walls.

Miguel talked about revolution. He said that the violence of the system needed to be answered with the violence of revolution. But Alba was not interested in politics; she wanted only to talk about love. She was sick and tired of her grandfather's speeches, of listening to his arguments with her Uncle Jaime, and of endless electoral campaigns. The only political activity she had ever engaged in was the time she had gone with other students to throw stones for no apparent reason at the United States Embassy, for which she had been suspended from school for a week and which had nearly given her grandfather another heart attack. But at the university politics was unavoidable. Like all the young people who entered that year, she discovered the appeal of nightlong gatherings in cafés, talking about the necessary changes in the world and infecting each other with the passion of ideas. She would return home late at night, her mouth bitter and her clothes reeking of stale tobacco, her head burning with heroism, convinced that when the time came she would give her life for a noble cause. Out of love for Miguel, and not for any ideological conviction, Alba sat in at the university along with the students who had seized a building in support of a strike by workers. There were days of encampments, excited discussion, insults hurled at the police until the students lost their voices. They built barricades with sandbags and paving stones that they pried loose from the main courtyard. They sealed the doors and windows, intending to turn the building into a fortress, but the result was a dungeon that was harder for the students to leave than it was for the police to enter. It was the first time Alba had spent a night away from home. She was rocked to sleep in Miguel's arms between piles of newspapers and empty beer bottles, surrounded by the warm closeness of her comrades, all young, sweaty, red-eyed from smoke and lack of sleep, slightly hungry, and entirely fearless, because it was all more like a game than a war. They spent the first day so busy building barricades, mobilizing their innocent defenses, painting placards, and talking on the phone that they had no time to worry when the police cut off their water and electricity.

From the very first, Miguel became the soul of the occupation, seconded by professor Sebastián Gómez, who, despite his crippled legs, stayed with them to the end. That night they sang to keep their spirits up, and when they grew tired of harangues, discussions, and songs, they settled into little groups to get through the night as best they could. The last to rest was Miguel, who seemed to be the only one who knew what to do. He took charge of distributing water, transferring into receptacles even the water already in the toilet tanks, and he improvised a kitchen that, to everyone's amazement, produced instant coffee, cookies, and some cans of beer. The next day the stench of the waterless toilets was overpowering, but Miguel organized a cleanup and ordered that the toilets not be used: everyone should relieve themselves in the courtyard, in a hole that had been dug alongside the stone statues of the founder of the university. Miguel divided the group into squads and kept them busy all day with such efficiency that his authority went unnoticed. Decisions seemed to arise spontaneously from the groups.

"You'd think we were going to be in here for months!" Alba exclaimed, delighted at the prospect of being under siege.

The armored cars of the police stationed themselves out

on the street, surrounding the ancient building. A tense wait began, which would last for several days.

"Students all over the country, unions, and professional schools are going to join us. The government may fall," Sebastián Gómez commented.

"I doubt it," replied Miguel. "But the main thing is to establish the protest and not leave the building until they sign the workers' list of demands."

It began to drizzle and darkness came early in the lightless building. They lit a few improvised lamps made of tin cans filled with gasoline and a smoky wick. Alba thought the telephone had been cut, but when she tried to use it it still worked. Miguel explained that the police had reason to listen to their calls and he warned them how to conduct their conversations. In any case, Alba called home to let them know she would be staying with her comrades until victory or death, which sounded false the minute she said it. Her grandfather grabbed the phone from Blanca's hand. In a tone of voice she knew all too well, he told her that she had an hour to be home with a reasonable explanation for having stayed out all night. She replied that she could not leave, and that even if she could she would not think of doing so.

"You have no business being there with all those Communists!" Esteban Trueba roared. But he immediately softened his voice and begged her to leave before the police came in, because he was in a position to know that the government was not going to let them stay indefinitely. "If you don't come out voluntarily, they're going to send the mobile unit in and drive you out with clubs," the senator concluded.

Alba peeked through a chink in the window that was covered with planks of wood and bags of earth and saw the tanks lined up across the street and a double row of men in combat gear, with helmets, clubs, and gas masks. She realized that her grandfather was not exaggerating. Everybody else had seen them too, and some of the students were shaking. Someone said there was a new kind of bomb worse than tear gas, that provoked diarrhea attacks terrible enough to discourage the bravest, because of the stench and the ridicule they caused. To Alba the idea seemed terrifying. She had to make an effort not to cry. She felt stitches in her stomach and supposed they were from fear. Miguel put his arms around her, but that did not console her. They were both exhausted and were beginning to feel the effects of the sleepless night in their bones and in their soul.

"I don't think they'd dare break in here," Sebastián Gómez said. "The government's already got enough problems to deal with. It's not going to interfere with us."

"It wouldn't be the first time they've attacked students," someone said.

"Public opinion wouldn't stand for it," Gómez replied. "This is a democracy. It's not a dictatorship and it never will be."

"We always think things like that only happen elsewhere," said Miguel, "until they happen to us too."

The remainder of the afternoon passed without incident and by nightfall everyone was more relaxed despite the prolonged hunger and discomfort. The tanks remained in place. The young people played checkers and games of cards in the hallways, slept on the floor, and made defensive weapons with sticks and stones. Fatigue was visible on every face. The cramps in Alba's stomach were growing stronger, and she thought that if nothing was resolved by the morning she would have no other choice but to use the hole in the courtyard. It was still raining outide, and the routine of the city continued undisturbed. No one seemed to care about another student strike, and people walked past the tanks without stopping to read the placards hanging from the university façade. The neighbors quickly became accustomed to the presence of armed police, and when the rain stopped children ran out to play with a ball under the streetlights in the empty parking lot that separated the building from the police detachments. At moments Alba felt as if she were on a sailboat becalmed at sea, locked in an eternal, silent wait, peering out at the horizon for hours. With the passage of time and the increasing lack of comfort, the high-spirited camaraderie of the first day had turned to irritation and constant bickering. Miguel inspected the building and confiscated all the food supplies in the cafeteria.

"When this is gone, we'll pay the concessionaire for it. He's a worker like anybody else," he said.

It was cold now. The one who never complained, not

even of thirst, was Sebastián Gómez, who seemed as indefatigable as Miguel, even though he was twice his age and looked tubercular. He was the only professor who had stayed with the students when they seized the building. It was said that his crippled legs were the result of a burst of machine-gun fire in Bolivia. He was the ideologue who made his students burn with the flame that in most of them extinguished itself as soon as they graduated and joined the world they had once hoped to change. A small, spare man with an aquiline nose and sparse hair, he was lit by an inner fire that gave no respite. It was he who had christened Alba "the countess," because the first day of classes her grandfather had had the bad idea of sending her to school with his chauffeur and Professor Gómez had seen her arrive. By sheer chance his nickname had hit home; Gómez could not have known that in the improbable event that she should choose to do so, she could unearth the noble title of Jean de Satigny, which was one of the few authentic features of the French count who had given her his name. Alba did not resent his mocking nickname for her; in fact, on more than one occasion she had fantasized about seducing the stalwart professor. But Sebastián Gómez had seen a lot of girls like Alba and recognized the mixture of curiosity and compassion aroused by the sight of the crutches that supported his poor lifeless legs.

The next day went by without the mobile unit moving its tanks or the government giving in to the workers' demands. Alba began to wonder what the hell she was doing there; the pain in her abdomen was becoming unbearable and the need to take a bath with running water was beginning to obsess her. Each time she looked out at the street and saw the police, her mouth filled with saliva. By that point she had realized that her Uncle Nicolás's training was not nearly as effective in a moment of action as it was in the fiction of imagined suffering. Two hours later Alba felt a warm viscous liquid between her legs and saw that her slacks were stained with red. She was swept with panic. For the past few days the fear that this might happen had tormented her almost as much as hunger. The stain on her pants was like a flag, but she made no attempt to hide it. She curled up in a corner, feeling utterly lost. When she was little, her grandmother had taught her that everything associated with human functions is natural, and she could speak of menstruation as of poetry, but later on, at school, she learned that all bodily secretions except tears are indecent. Miguel noticed her shame and anguish. He went to the improvised infirmary to get a package of cotton and found some handkerchiefs, but it was soon clear that they were insufficient. By evening Alba was crying in humiliation and pain, terrified by the pincers in her guts and by this stream of blood that was so unlike her usual flow. She thought something must be bursting inside her. Ana Díaz, a student who, like Miguel, wore the insignia of the raised fist, observed that only rich women suffer from such pains; proletarian women do not complain even when they give birth. But when she saw that Alba's pants were a pool of blood and she was as pale as death, she went to speak to Sebastián Gómez, who said he had no idea how to resolve the problem.

"That's what happens when you let women get involved in men's affairs!" he roared.

"No! It's what happens when you let the bourgeoisie into the affairs of the people!" the young woman answered him indignantly.

Sebastián Gómez went over to the corner where Miguel had settled Alba, gliding up to her with difficulty because of his crutches.

"You have to go home, Countess," he said. "You're not contributing anything here. On the contrary, you're in the way."

Alba felt a wave of relief. She was too frightened, and this was an honorable way to leave that would allow her to return home without seeming like a coward. She argued a little with Sebastián Gómez to save face, but she almost immediately accepted the proposal that Miguel should go out with a white flag to parley with the police. Everybody watched him from the observation posts while he crossed the empty parking lot. The police had formed into narrow lines and ordered him through their loudspeaker to stop, lay his flag on the ground, and proceed with his hands behind his neck.

"This is like a war!" Gómez observed.

Soon afterward Miguel returned and helped Alba to her

feet. The same young woman who had previously criticized
Alba for complaining took her by the arm and the three of
them left the building, stepping around the barricades and
sandbags, illuminated by the powerful searchlights of the
police. Alba could barely walk. She felt ashamed and her
head was spinning. A police patrol came out to meet them
halfway, and Alba found herself a few inches from a green
uniform, with a pistol aimed directly at her nose. She raised
her eyes and looked into a dark face with the eyes of a
rodent. She recognized him right away: Esteban García.

"I see it's Senator Trueba's granddaughter!" García exclaimed ironically.

This was how Miguel learned that Alba had not been
entirely truthful. He felt betrayed. He deposited her into the
hands of the other man, turned on his heel, and left, dragging the white banner on the ground, without even looking
back to say goodbye, accompanied by Ana Díaz, who was as
surprised and furious as he was.

"What's the matter with you?" García asked, pointing
at Alba's pants. "It looks like an abortion."

Alba straightened her head and stared him straight in
the eye. "That is none of your business. Take me home!"
she ordered, copying the authoritarian tone her grandfather
employed with everyone he considered beneath his social
station.

García hesitated. It had been a long time since he had
heard orders from the mouth of a civilian, and for a moment
he was tempted to take her to the stockade and leave her
there to rot in a cell, bathed in her own blood, until she got
down on her knees and begged him, but his profession had
taught him that there were men more powerful than he and
that he could not afford the luxury of acting with impunity.
Besides, the memory of Alba in her starched dresses, drinking lemonade on the terrace of Tres Marías while he shuffled
around barefoot and sniffling in the chicken yard, and the
fear he still had of Senator Trueba were more powerful than
his desire to humiliate her. He could not bear the way she
stared at him and he lowered his head imperceptibly. He
turned around, barked out a brief instruction, and two policemen led Alba by the arms to a van. This was how she
reached her house. When Blanca saw her, her first reaction

was that the grandfather's predictions had been true and that the police had attacked the students with their clubs. She began to scream and did not stop until Jaime had examined Alba and assured her that she had not been injured and there was nothing wrong with her that a couple of injections and some rest would not cure.

Alba spent two days in bed, during which the student strike was peacefully terminated. The Minister of Education was relieved of his post and transferred to the Ministry of Agriculture.

"If he could be the Minister of Education without finishing school, there's no reason why he can't be the Minister of Agriculture without ever having seen a cow," Senator Trueba remarked.

While she was in bed, Alba had time to think back to when she had met Esteban García. Poring over her childhood memories, she remembered a dark-skinned boy, the library, the fireplace ablaze with enormous pine logs whose perfume filled the room, evening or night, and herself sitting on his knees. But that vision came and went quickly in her mind and she began to wonder whether she had dreamt it. The first definite image she had of him was later. She knew the exact date because it was her fourteenth birthday, and her mother had recorded it in the black album her grandmother had started when she was born. She had curled her hair in honor of the occasion and was out on the terrace in her coat, waiting for her Uncle Jaime to take her out to buy her present. It was very cold, but she liked the garden in wintertime. She blew on her hands and pulled up her coat collar to protect her ears. From where she was standing she could see the window of the library, where her grandfather was speaking with a man. The glass was clouded, but she recognized the uniform of a policeman and wondered what her grandfather could be doing with one of them in his library. The man had his back to the window and was sitting stiffly on the edge of a chair with a straight back and the pathetic air of a leaden soldier. Alba watched them for a while, until she guessed that her uncle must be about to arrive, and then she walked through the garden to a half-ruined gazebo. She rubbed her hands together to keep warm, brushed away the wet leaves that had fallen on the stone bench, and sat down to wait. Soon afterward, Esteban García encountered her there when he left the house and crossed the garden on his way toward the front gate. He stopped abruptly when he saw her. He looked all around him, hesitated for a moment, and then approached her.

"Do you remember me?" García asked.

"No ..." She spoke doubtfully.

"I'm Esteban García. We met at Tres Marías."

Alba smiled mechanically. He stirred up bad memories. There was something in his eyes that made her uneasy, but she could not say why. García swept the leaves away with his hands and sat down beside her in the gazebo, so near that their legs were touching.

"This garden looks like a jungle," he said, breathing very close to her.

He took off his police cap and she saw that his hair was short and stiff, groomed with hair tonic. Suddenly, García's hand was on her shoulder. The familiarity of his gesture disconcerted the girl, who was paralyzed for a second but quickly drew back, trying to struggle free. The policeman's hand squeezed her shoulder, and his fingers dug through the thick cloth of her coat. Alba felt her heart pound like a machine, and her cheeks turned red.

"You've grown, Alba. You almost look like a woman now," the man whispered in her ear.

"I'm fourteen. Today's my birthday," she said hesitantly.

"Then I have a present for you," Esteban García said, his mouth twisting into a smile.

Alba tried to turn her face away, but he held it firmly in both hands, forcing her to look at him. It was her first kiss. She felt a warm, brutal sensation as his rough, badly shaven skin scraped her face. She smelled his scent of stale tobacco and onion, and his violence. García's tongue tried to pry open her lips while his hand pressed against her jaw until he forced it open. She imagined that tongue as a warm, slimy mollusk, and she was overcome by a wave of nausea, but she kept her eyes open. She saw the hard cloth of his uniform and felt the ferocious hands wrap themselves around her neck; then without interrupting the kiss, the fingers began to tighten. Alba thought she was choking, and pushed him with such force that she managed to get away from him. García got up off the bench, smiling ironically. He had red splotches on his cheeks and was breathing rapidly.

"Did you like my present?" He laughed.

Alba watched him disappear across the garden with enormous strides, then sat down and wept. She felt dirty and humiliated. Afterward she ran into the house and washed her mouth with soap and brushed her teeth, as if that could remove the stain in her memory. When her Uncle Jaime came to find her, she clung to his neck, buried her face in his shirt, and told him that she did not want a present, she had decided to become a nun. Jaime gave one of his deep laughs that rose up from his stomach and that, since he was a taciturn man, she rarely heard.

"I swear I'm going to become a nun!" Alba sobbed.

"You'd have to be born all over again," Jaime replied. "Besides, you'd have to do it over my dead body."

Alba did not see Esteban García again until he was standing next to her in the university parking lot, but she could never forget him. She told no one of that repulsive kiss or of the dreams that she had afterward, in which García appeared as a green beast that tried to strangle her with his paws and asphyxiate her by shoving a slimy tentacle down her throat.

Remembering all that, Alba discovered that the nightmare had been crouched inside her all those years and that García was still the beast waiting for her in the shadows, ready to jump on top of her at any turn of life. She could not know it was a premonition.

Miguel's disappointment and rage at Alba's being the granddaughter of Senator Trueba vanished the second time he saw her wandering like a lost soul down the corridors near the cafeteria where they had met. He decided that it was unfair to blame the granddaughter for the ideas of the grandfather, and they resumed their stroll with their arms around each other. Soon their kisses were not enough and they began to meet in the rented room where Miguel lived. It was a mediocre boardinghouse for penniless students, presided over by a middle-aged couple with a calling for espionage. They watched with undisguised hostility when Alba went upstairs holding Miguel's hand, and it was a torture for her to overcome her timidity and face the criticism of those stares that ruined the joy of her meetings with Miguel. She would have preferred to avoid seeing them, but she rejected the idea of taking a hotel room together for the same reasons she did not want to be seen in Miguel's boardinghouse.

"You're the worst bourgeois I know!" Miguel would say, laughing.

Once in a while, he managed to borrow a motorcycle and they escaped for a few hours, traveling at reckless speed, crouched low on the machine, with frozen ears and anxious hearts. They liked to go to deserted beaches in the winter, where they walked on the wet sand, leaving their tracks to be lapped away by the waves, frightening the sea gulls and gulping great mouthfuls of salt air. In the summer they preferred the thickest forests, where they could frolic as they wished as soon as they got away from hikers and boy scouts. Alba soon discovered that the safest place of all was her own house, because in the labyrinth of the rear rooms, where no one ever went, they could make love undisturbed.

"If the servants hear noise, they'll think the ghosts are back," Alba said, and she told him of the glorious past of visiting spirits and flying tables in the big house on the corner.

The first time she led him through the back door of the garden, making a path in the jungle and stepping around the statues that were covered with moss and bird droppings, the young man did a double take when he saw the house. "I've been here before," he murmured, but he could not recall when, because that nightmare jungle and dilapidated mansion bore only meager resemblance to the luminous image he had treasured in his mind ever since his childhood.

One by one the lovers tried out all the abandoned rooms, and finally chose an improvised nest in the depths of the basement. It had been years since Alba had been there, and she had almost forgotten that it existed, but the minute she opened the door and inhaled its unmistakable odor, she felt again the old magical attraction. They used her Uncle Nicolás's books, the dishes, the boxes, the furniture, and the drapes of bygone days to arrange their astonishing nuptial chamber. In the center they created a bed by piling together several mattresses, which they covered with pieces of moth-

eaten velvet. From the trunks they took innumerable treasures. They made their sheets out of old topaz-colored damask
curtains. They unstitched the sumptuous dress of Chantilly
lace that Clara had worn the day Barrabás died, and made a
time-colored mosquito net, which also protected them from
the spiders that fell down unexpectedly from embroidering
on the ceiling. They lighted their way with candles and
ignored the rodents, the cold, and that fog from the other
world. They walked around stark naked in the eternal twi-
light of the basement, defying the humidity and drafts. They
drank white wine from crystal goblets that Alba took from
the dining room, and made a detailed inventory of each
other's bodies and the multiple possibilities of pleasure. They
played like children. It was difficult for her to recognize in
this sweet infatuated young man, who could laugh and romp
in an endless bacchanal, the eager revolutionary so committed to the idea of justice that he took secret courses in the
use of firearms and revolutionary strategy. Alba invented
irresistible techniques of seduction, and Miguel created new
and marvelous ways of making love to her. They were
blinded by the strength of their passion, which was like an
insatiable thirst. In their ambitious effort to possess each
other totally, there were not hours or words enough to tell
each other their most intimate thoughts and deepest memories. Alba stopped practicing the cello, except to play it
naked on the topaz bed, and she attended classes at the
university with a hallucinated look in her eyes. Miguel put
off his thesis and his political meetings, because he and Alba
wanted to be together every hour of the day. They used the
least distraction on the part of the inhabitants of the house to
sneak down to the basement. Alba learned to lie and dissim-
ulate. On the pretext that she had to study late at night, she
left the room she had shared with her mother ever since her
grandmother died and set up a room on the first floor, facing
the garden, so she could let Miguel in through the window
and lead him on tiptoe through the sleeping house to their
enchanted lair. But they did not meet only at night. Love's
impatience was sometimes so unbearable that Miguel ran the
risk of daytime visits, slinking through the bushes like a thief
until he reached the basement door, where Alba waited for
him, her heart in her mouth. They embraced with the des-

peration of a parting and slipped down to their refuge suffocating with complicity.

For the first time in her life, Alba wanted to be beautiful. She regretted that the splendid women in her family had not bequeathed their attributes to her, that the only one who had, Rosa the Beautiful, had given her only the algae tones in her hair, which seemed more like a hairdresser's mistake than anything else. Miguel understood the source of her anxiety. He led her by the hand to the huge Venetian mirror that adorned one wall of their secret room, shook the dust from the cracked glass, and lit all the candles they had and arranged them around her. She stared at herself in the thousand pieces of the mirror. In the candlelight her skin was the unreal color of wax statues. Miguel began to caress her and she saw her face transformed in the kaleidoscope of the mirror, and she finally believed that she was the most beautiful woman in the universe because she was able to see herself with Miguel's eyes.

That seemingly interminable orgy lasted more than a year. Finally, Miguel finished his thesis, graduated, and began to look for work. When the pressing need of unsatisfied love had passed, they regained their composure and were able to return to normal. Alba made an effort to take an interest in her studies again, and he turned once more to his political activities, because events were taking place at breakneck pace and the country was torn apart by a series of ideological disputes. Miguel rented a small apartment near the place where he worked, and this was where they made love; in the year they had spent frisking naked in the basement they had both contracted chronic bronchitis, which dampened somewhat the attraction of their subterranean paradise. Alba helped decorate the new apartment, hanging curtains and political posters everywhere she could and even suggesting that she might move in with him, but on this point Miguel was unyielding.

"Bad times are coming, my love," he explained. "I can't have you with me, because when it becomes necessary I'm going to join the guerrillas."

"I'll follow you wherever you go," she promised.

"You can't do that for love. You do it out of political

conviction, and that's something you don't have," Miguel replied. "We can't afford the luxury of accepting amateurs."

His words seemed cruel to Alba, but it was several years before she was able to understand their full meaning.

Senator Trueba was already old enough to retire, but the thought had not even crossed his mind. He read the daily papers and muttered under his breath. Things had changed a good deal in the preceding years, and he felt overtaken by events that he had not expected to live long enough to have to confront. He had been born before the city had electric lights and had lived to see a man walking on the moon, but none of the upheavals of his long existence had prepared him for the revolution that was brewing in his country, right under his eyes, and that had everyone in a state of agitation.

The only person who did not speak about what was happening was Jaime. To avoid arguing with his father, he acquired the habit of silence and soon discovered it was far more comfortable. The only time he abandoned his Trappist laconism was when Alba went to visit him in his tunnel of books. His niece always arrived in her nightgown, her hair wet from the shower, and sat at the foot of his bed to tell him happy stories, because, as she put it, he was a magnet for other people's problems and irreversible disasters, and someone had to keep him posted about spring and love. But her good intentions clashed with her need to talk with her uncle about the things that preoccupied her. They never agreed. They shared the same books, but when it came time to analyze what they had read, their opinions were different. Jaime made fun of her political ideas and bearded friends, and scolded her for having fallen in love with a café terrorist. He was the only one in the family who knew about Miguel.

"Tell that spoiled brat to come and spend a day in the hospital with me. We'll see if he still wants to waste his time on pamphlets and speeches," he said to Alba.

"He's a lawyer, Uncle, not a doctor," she replied.

"I don't care. We need whatever we can get. Even plumbers would be a help."

Jaime was convinced that after so many years of struggle the Socialists were finally going to win. This he attributed to the fact that the people had become conscious of their needs and their own strength. Alba would repeat Miguel's words: that only through armed struggle could the bourgeoisie be toppled. Jaime was horrified by any form of extremism and held that guerrilla warfare is only justified by tyranny, where the only solution is to shoot it out, but that it would be an aberration in a country where change can be obtained by popular vote.

"Don't be so naïve, Uncle. You know that's never happened," Alba answered. "They'll never let your Socialists win!"

She tried to explain Miguel's point of view: that it was not possible to keep waiting for the slow passage of history, the laborious process of educating and organizing the people, because the world was moving ahead by leaps and bounds and they were being left behind; and that radical change is never brought about willingly and without violence. History confirmed this. The argument went on and on, and they became locked in a confused rhetorical exchange that left them exhausted, each accusing the other of being more stubborn than a mule. But in the end they kissed each other good night and both were left with the feeling that the other was an extraordinary human being.

One night at dinner, Jaime announced that the Socialists were going to win, but since he had been saying that for twenty years, no one believed him.

"If your mother were alive, she'd say that those who always win are going to win again," Senator Trueba replied disdainfully.

But Jaime knew what he was talking about. He had heard it from the Candidate. They had been friends for years, and Jaime often went to play chess with him at night. He was the same Socialist who had had his eye on the Presidency for the past eighteen years. Jaime had first seen him behind his father's back, when the Candidate rode the trains of victory in a cloud of smoke during the electoral campaigns of his youth. In those days, the Candidate was a robust young man with the angular face of a hunting dog, who shouted impassioned speeches over the hissing and heckling of the landowners, and the silent fury of the peasants. It was the era when the Sánchez brothers had hanged the Socialist leader at the crossroads and when Esteban

Trueba had whipped Pedro Tercero García in front of his father for spreading Father José Dulce María's strange interpretations of the Bible among the tenants. Jaime's friendship with the Candidate was born by chance one Sunday night when he was summoned from the hospital to make an emergency house call. He arrived at the appropriate address in an ambulance, rang the doorbell, and was ushered in by the Candidate himself. Jaime had no trouble recognizing him, because he had seen his picture many times and he had not changed much since the time he had seen him on the train.

"Come in, Doctor. We were expecting you," the Candidate said.

He led him to the maid's room, where his daughters were attempting to help a woman who appeared to be choking. Her pop-eyed face was purple, and her monstrously swollen tongue was hanging from her mouth.

"She was eating fish," one of the daughters explained.

"Bring the oxygen that's in the ambulance," Jaime said, preparing a syringe.

He remained with the Candidate, sitting beside him next to the bed until the woman began to breathe normally and was able to get her tongue back in her mouth. They discussed Socialism and chess, and it was the beginning of a strong friendship. Jaime introduced himself with his mother's surname, which was the one he always used, never imagining that the next day the party's security service would inform the Candidate that he was the son of Senator Trueba, his worst political enemy. The Candidate, however, never mentioned this, and right up to the final hour, when they shook each other's hand for the last time in the din of fire and bullets, Jaime wondered if he would ever have the courage to tell him the truth.

His long experience of defeat and his knowledge of the people allowed the Candidate to realize before anyone else that this time he was going to win. He told Jaime this, cautioning him not to let anybody know, so that the right would go into the elections sure of victory, as arrogant and divided as ever. Jaime replied that even if they told everyone, no one would believe it—not even the Socialists themselves—and as proof he told his father.

Jaime continued working fourteen hours a day, includ-

ing Sundays, and took no part in the political process. He
was frightened by the violent turn the struggle had taken,
polarizing everyone into two extremes and leaving the center
to a flighty, indecisive group that was waiting to see who
the winner might be so they could vote for him. He refused
to be provoked by his father, who seized every opportunity
to warn him of the handiwork of international Communism
and the chaos that would sweep the country in the improbable event of a victory of the left. The only time Jaime lost his
patience was one morning when he awoke to find the city
plastered with angry posters that portrayed a full-bellied,
lonely woman vainly attempting to wrest her son from the
arms of a Communist soldier who was dragging him off to
Moscow. It was part of the terror campaign organized by
Senator Trueba and his co-religionists, with the help of
foreign experts who had been especially imported to that
end. This was too much for Jaime. He decided that he could
no longer live beneath the same roof as his father. He closed
the door to his tunnel, packed his clothes, and went to sleep
at the hospital.

The pace of events escalated during the final months of
the campaign. Portraits of the candidates were on every wall;
pamphlets were dropped from airplanes and carpeted the
streets with printed refuse that fell from the sky like snow.
Radios howled the various party slogans and preposterous
wagers were made by party members on both sides. At night
gangs of young people took to the streets to attack their
ideological rivals. Enormous demonstrations were organized
to measure the popularity of each party, and each time the
city was jammed with the same numbers of people. Alba was
euphoric, but Miguel explained that the election was a joke
and that whoever won, it would make no difference because
you would just be changing the needle on the same old
syringe, and that you cannot make a revolution at the ballot
box but only with the people's blood. The idea of a peaceful,
democratic revolution with complete freedom of expression
was a contradiction in terms.

"That poor boy is crazy!" Jaime exclaimed when Alba
told him what Miguel had said. "We're going to win and
he'll have to swallow his words."

Up until that moment, Jaime had always managed to

avoid Miguel. He did not wish to know him, for he was tormented by a secret unconfessable jealousy. He had helped bring Alba into the world and had sat her on his knee a thousand times; had taught her to read, paid for her schooling, and celebrated all her birthdays. Feeling like a father, he could not shake off his uneasiness on seeing her become a woman. He had noticed her change in recent years, and had deceived himself with false arguments, even though his long experience in taking care of other human beings had taught him that only the knowledge of love could bring such splendor to a woman's looks. He had seen Alba mature practically overnight, leaving behind the vague shape of adolescence to assume the body of a satisfied and gentle woman. With absurd intensity he hoped against hope that his niece's infatuation would prove to be a passing fancy, because deep down he could not accept that she should need another man more than she needed him. Still, he could not continue to ignore Miguel. It was during this time that Alba told him Miguel's sister was ill.

"I want you to speak to Miguel. He'll tell you about his sister. Would you do that for me?" Alba pleaded.

When Jaime met Miguel in a neighborhood café, all his suspicion was swept away be a wave of sympathy, because the man across the table from him nervously stirring his coffee was not the petulant extremist bully he had expected, but a tremulous, sensitive young man who was fighting off tears as he described the symptoms of his sister's illness.

"Take me to see her," Jaime said.

Miguel and Alba led him to the bohemian quarter. In the center of town, only yards away from the modern buildings made of steel and glass, streets of painters, ceramists, and sculptors had sprung up on the side of a steep hill. There they had built their burrows, dividing ancient houses into tiny studios. The craftmen's workshops had glass roofs to let the sky in, while the painters survived in dark hovels that were a paradise of misery and grandeur. Confident children played in the narrow streets, beautiful women in long tunics carried babies on their backs or anchored on their hips, and bearded, sleepy, indifferent men watched the stream of life pass by from chairs they had set up on street corners or in doorways. Miguel, Alba, and her brother stopped before a French-style house that looked like a cream cake, with cherubs carved along the friezes. They ascended a narrow staircase that had been built as an emergency exit in case of fire but that the numerous subdivisions of the house had transformed into the only means of entrance. As they climbed, the staircase turned on itself and wrapped them in the penetrating smell of garlic, marijuana, and turpentine. Miguel stopped on the top floor before an orange door. He took out a key, turned it in the lock, and they went in. Jaime and Alba felt as if they had stepped into an aviary. The room was round, and capped by an absurd Byzantine cupola surrounded with windows, through which one could see all the rooftops of the city and feel close to the clouds. Doves had nested on the windowsill, adding their excrement and feathers to the spattered panes. Seated on a chair before the only table in the room was a woman in a ragged robe adorned with an embroidered dragon on its front. It took Jaime a few seconds to recognize her.

"Amanda . . . Amanda . . ." he whispered.

He had not seen her in more than twenty years, when the love they both felt for Nicolás was stronger than the love between them. In that time the dark, athletic young man with the damp slicked-down hair, who used to walk back and forth reading aloud from his medical textbooks, had become a man slightly curved from the habit of bending over his patients' beds. Though he now had gray hair, a serious face, and wire-rimmed glasses, he was basically the same person as before. But to have recognized Amanda, he must have loved her a great deal. She looked older than she could possibly have been, and she was very thin, just skin and bones, with a wan, yellow complexion and neglected, nicotine-stained hands. Her eyes were red and bloated, without luster, and her pupils were dilated, which gave her a frightened, helpless look. She saw neither Jaime nor Alba, looking only at Miguel. She tried to get up, but she stumbled and swayed. Her brother jumped to catch her, holding her against his chest.

"Did you two know each other?" Miguel asked in surprise.

"Yes, a long time ago," Jaime replied.

He felt it would be useless to discuss the past and that

Alba and Miguel were too young to understand the sense of irreparable loss he was feeling at that moment. With a single brushstroke the image of the gypsy girl he had treasured all those years had been erased, the only love in his solitary fate. He helped Miguel lay the woman on the sofa she used as a bed and put a pillow under her head. Amanda held her robe with both hands, weakly trying to protect herself and mumbling incoherently. She was shaken by a series of convulsions and panted like a tired dog. Alba watched in horror. Only when Amanda was lying still, with her eyes closed, did she recognize the woman who smiled in the little photograph Miguel always carried in his wallet. Jaime spoke to her in a voice unfamiliar to Alba and gradually managed to calm her. He caressed her with the tender, fatherly touch he sometimes used with animals, until the woman finally relaxed and allowed him to roll up the sleeves of her old Chinese robe, revealing her skeletal arms. Alba saw that they were covered with thousands of tiny scars, bruises, and holes, some of which were infected and full of pus. Then he uncovered her legs: her thighs were also tortured. Jaime looked at her sadly, comprehending in that moment the abandon, the years of poverty, the frustrated loves, and the terrible road this woman had traveled before reaching the point of desperation where they now found her. He remembered her as she had been in her youth, when she had dazzled him with the flutter of her hair, the rattle of her trinkets, her bell-like laughter, and her eagerness to embrace outlandish ideas and pursue her dreams. He cursed himself for having let her go and for all the time they both had lost.

"She's got to be hospitalized. Only a detoxification program can save her now," he said. "She's going to go through hell."

TWELVE

The Conspiracy

Just as the Candidate had predicted, the Socialists, in alliance with the other parties of the left, won the Presidential election. The balloting proceeded without incident on a shining September morning. Those who had always won, accustomed to being in power since time immemorial even though their strength had greatly waned in recent years, spent the weeks before the elections preparing for their triumph. Liquor stores sold out their stock, marketplaces sold their last fresh fish, and bakeries worked double shifts to meet the demand for cakes and pastries. In the High District there was no alarm at the first partial returns from the provinces, which favored the left, because everyone knew that it was the votes from the capital that would be decisive. Senator Trueba followed the returns from his party headquarters, perfectly relaxed and good-humored, laughing disdainfully when any of his men showed signs of nervousness at the unmistakable advance of the opposition candidate. In anticipation of victory, he had broken his strict mourning and placed a red rose in the buttonhole of his lapel. When he was interviewed on television, the entire country heard him say, "We who have always won will win again," and then he invited everyone to join him in a toast to "the defenders of democracy."

In the big house on the corner, Blanca, Alba, and the servants were sitting in front of the television, sipping tea and eating toast. They were intently following the election returns, jotting down the results as they were announced, when they saw Trueba on the screen, looking older and more stubborn than ever.

"He's going to have a fit," Alba said. "Because this time the other side is going to win."

Soon it was evident to everyone that only a miracle would alter the results, which were growing clearer throughout the day. In the white, blue, and yellow houses of the High District, venetian blinds were lowered, doors were bolted, and the flags and portraits of their candidate, which people had already hung from balconies, were hurriedly pulled inside. Meanwhile, in the shantytowns and working-class neighborhoods whole families—parents, children, and grandparents—took to the streets in their Sunday best, gaily making their way toward the center of the city. They carried portable radios to follow the latest returns. In the High District, a few students, afire with idealism, made faces at their relatives huddled before the television screen with grim expressions and went out to join the procession. Marching in orderly columns, their clenched fists raised, workers began to arrive from the industrial belt on the outskirts of the city, singing campaign songs. They converged in the center of the city, shouting in a single voice that the people united would never be defeated. They took out white handkerchiefs and waited. At midnight it was announced that the left had won. In the twinkling of an eye, the scattered groups filled out, swelled, and lengthened, and the streets filled with euphoric people jumping up and down and shouting and hugging each other and laughing. They lit torches, and the jumble of voices and dancing in the streets became a disciplined, jubilant procession that advanced toward the well-tended avenues of the bourgeoisie, creating the unaccustomed spectacle of ordinary citizens—factory workers in their heavy work shoes, women with babies in their arms, students in shirt-sleeves—calmly marching through the private, expensive neighborhood where they had rarely ventured before, and in which they were complete foreigners. The noise of their songs, the sound of their footsteps, and the glow of their torches penetrated the shuttered, silent houses where those who believed their own prophecies of terror trembled in fear, expecting at any moment to be cut to pieces by the masses or, if they were lucky, to be stripped of their possessions and packed off to Siberia. But no roaring crowd forced their doors or trampled their flowerbeds. People surged forward without so much as touching the luxury cars that lined the streets—pouring into and out of squares and parks they had never entered in their lives and stopping to marvel at the shopwindows, which sparkled as if it were Christmas and in which were displayed objects they did not even know how to use—and continued peacefully on their way. When the columns passed in front of her house, Alba ran out and joined them, singing at the top of her voice. The people marched all night, beside themselves with joy. Inside the mansions of the rich, the bottles of champagne remained unopened, lobsters languished on their silver trays, and pastries swarmed with flies.

At daybreak, in the crowd that was finally beginning to disperse, Alba glimpsed the unmistakable figure of Miguel shouting and waving a flag. She pushed her way toward him, calling his name in vain, because he could not hear her in the confusion. When she was standing in front of him and he finally saw her, he passed the flag to the person next to him and threw his arms around her, lifting her off the ground. They were both exhausted, and while they kissed, they wept with joy.

"I told you we'd win, Miguel!" Alba said, laughing.

"We've won, but now we'll have to defend our victory," he replied.

The next day, the same people who had spent the night in frightened vigil in their houses poured out onto the streets like a crazed avalanche to storm the banks, demanding their money. Anyone who had anything of value decided to keep it under the mattress or send it overseas. Within twenty-four hours, property values had been halved and every available flight out of the country was booked in the hysteria to escape before the Russians came and strung barbed wire along the borders. The people who had marched in triumph went to watch the bourgeoisie standing in line and fighting to get through the doors of the banks, and roared with laughter. In a few hours the country had split into two irreconcilable groups, a division that began to spread within every family in the land.

Senator Trueba spent the night in his party headquarters, forcibly restrained by his followers, who were convinced that if he went outside the crowd would recognize him and immediately hang him from the first lamppost they could find. Trueba was more surprised than angry. He could not believe what was happening, even though he had been singing the same old song for years about how the country was crawling with Marxists. But he was not depressed; far from it. In his old fighter's heart fluttered a sense of elation he had not felt for years.

"It's one thing to win an election and quite another to be President," he remarked mysteriously to his teary co-religionists.

The idea of eliminating the new President, however, was not yet on anybody's mind, for his enemies were sure they would put an end to him through the same legal channels that had carried him to triumph. That was what Esteban Trueba was thinking. The next day, when it was clear that there was no need to fear the festive crowds, he left his refuge and headed to a country house on the outskirts of the city, where a secret lunch was held. There he met with other politicians, a group of military men, and gringos sent by their intelligence service to map a strategy for bringing down the new government: economic destabilization, as they called their sabotage.

It was an enormous colonial-style house surrounded by a flagstone patio. When Senator Trueba arrived, there were already several cars parked in front of it. He was received effusively, because he was one of the undisputed leaders of the right and because, having prepared for what might happen, he had made the necessary contacts months in advance. After the meal—cold fish with avocado sauce, roast suckling pig in brandy, and chocolate mousse—they dismissed the waiters and bolted the doors to the dining room. There they sketched out the main lines of their strategy. When they were finished, they stood and made a toast to the fatherland. Everyone, except the foreigners, was willing to risk half his personal fortune in the endeavor, but only old Trueba was also willing to give his life.

"We won't give him any peace, not even for a minute. He'll have to resign," he concluded firmly.

"And if that doesn't work, Senator, we have this," said General Hurtado, placing his service pistol on the table.

"We're not interested in a military coup, General," the head of Embassy intelligence replied in studied Spanish. "We want Marxism to be a colossal failure and for it to fall alone, so we can erase it from the people's minds throughout the continent. You understand? We're going to solve this problem with money. We can still buy a few members of Congress so they won't confirm him as President. It's in your Constitution: he didn't get an absolute majority, and Congress has to make the final choice."

"Get that idea out of your head, mister!" Trueba exclaimed. "You're not going to bribe anyone around here! The Congress and the armed forces are above corruption. It would be better if we used the money to buy the mass media. That would give us a way to manipulate public opinion, which is the only thing that really counts."

"You're out of your mind! The first thing the Marxists are going to do is destroy freedom of the press!" several voices said.

"Believe me, gentlemen," Senator Trueba replied. "I know this country. They'll never do away with freedom of the press. Besides, it's in their platform: they've sworn to respect democratic rights. We'll catch them in their own trap."

Senator Trueba was right. They were unable to bribe the members of Congress, and on the date stipulated by law the left calmly came to power. And on that date the right began to stockpile hatred.

After the election everyone's life changed: those who thought they would be able to continue as before soon realized that was an illusion. For Pedro Tercero García the change was brutal. He had managed to avoid the snares of a routine, living as free and poor as a wandering minstrel, having never worn leather shoes, a tie, or a wristwatch, and indulging himself in the luxuries of affection, candor, shabbiness, and the siesta, for he was not accountable to anyone. It had become increasingly difficult for him to find the requisite anxiety and sorrow for new songs, because in the course of time he had found great inner peace. The rebelliousness that had inspired him in his youth had given way to the gentleness of a man satisfied with himself. He was as austere as a Franciscan. He had no ambition for either money or power. The only blot on his peace of mind was Blanca. He had lost interest in having dead-end love affairs with adolescent girls and now believed that Blanca was the only woman he was meant to love. He tallied up all the years he had loved her clandestinely and could not recall a moment of his life when she had not been present—at least in his thoughts. After the election, his equilibrium was destroyed by the urgency of working with the government. There was no way he could refuse because, as it was explained to him, the parties of the left had a shortage of skilled men for the many positions to be filled.

"But I'm just a peasant. I have no training," he argued, trying to excuse himself.

"It doesn't matter, *compañero*. You're popular. Even if you put your foot in it, people will forgive you," they replied.

So it was that he found himself sitting behind a desk for the first time in his life, with a personal secretary at his disposal and a grandiose portrait of the Founding Father at some valiant battle hanging behind him. Pedro Tercero García stared out the barred window of his luxurious office and could see only a small square of gray sky. His job was not a sinecure. He worked from seven in the morning until late at night, and by the time he left work he was so tired that he was incapable of striking a single chord on his guitar, much less making love to Blanca with his accustomed passion. When they were able to arrange a meeting, surmounting all of Blanca's usual obstacles in addition to the new ones imposed by Pedro's job, they would find themselves more full of anguish than desire. They made love wearily, interrupted by the telephone and harried by time, of which there was never enough. Blanca stopped wearing her risqué lingerie, because she decided that it was an unnecessary provocation that made her look ridiculous. In the end they met only so that they could sleep in each other's arms like a pair of grandparents, and to hold friendly conversations about their daily problems and the serious matters that were shaking the country to its core. One day Pedro Tercero realized he had gone a whole month without making love and that, what was even worse to him, neither of them had really wanted to. This shocked him. He knew there was no reason for him to be impotent at his age, and was forced to attribute it to the kind of life he was leading and the bachelor ways he had developed. He imagined that if he could lead a normal life with Blanca, one in which she would be waiting for him every evening in a peaceful home, everything would be different. He announced he would marry her once and for all, because he was fed up with furtive love and too old to continue living like this. Blanca gave him the same answer she had given him so many time before.

"I have to think it over, my love," she said.

She was sitting naked on Pedro Tercero's narrow bed. He studied her dispassionately and saw that time was beginning to ravage her beauty: she was fatter and sadder, with hands deformed now by rheumatism, and the magnificent breasts that years earlier had kept him awake at night were slowly but surely approaching the broad lap of a matron firmly settled in her years. Still, he found her just as beautiful as he had when he was young, when they had made love in the reeds along the banks of the river at Tres Marías, and it was precisely this thought that made him regret that his exhaustion was stronger than his passion.

"You've been thinking it over for almost half a century," he said. "That's long enough. It's now or never."

Blanca was not surprised, for it was not the first time he had given her an ultimatum. Each time he broke off with one of his young mistresses and returned to her side, he demanded that she marry him, in a desperate attempt to hang on to her love and find forgiveness. When he agreed to move out of the working-class neighborhood where he had been happy for years and to resettle in the middle-class apartment, he had said the same thing.

"Either you marry me now or we never see each other again."

Blanca did not realize that this time Pedro Tercero's mind was made up.

They separated angrily. She got dressed, quickly gathering her clothes, which were strewn across the floor, and wrapped her hair into a bun that she moored to her head with a handful of hairpins she retrieved from the bed. Pedro Tercero lit a cigarette and did not take his eyes off her while she dressed. Blanca finished putting on her shoes and waved goodbye to him from the doorway. She was sure that he would call her the next day for one of his spectacular reconciliations. Pedro Tercero turned his face to the wall. A bitter grin had transformed his mouth into a single line. It would be two years before they met again.

In the days that followed, Blanca waited for him to get in touch with her, according to their timeworn pattern. He had never failed her, not even when she had married and they had spent a year apart. Even then it was he who had come looking for her. But after three days with no word from him she began to be alarmed. She tossed and turned in her bed, tormented by an unrelenting case of insomnia. She doubled her dose of tranquilizers, took refuge once again in her migraines and neuralgias, and, in an attempt to stay busy and not think, she stupefied herself by cooking hundreds of crèche monsters in her kiln for Christmas. Still, she was unable to suppress her impatience. Finally she called the Ministry. A female voice replied that Compañero García was in a meeting and could not be interrupted. The next day Blanca called again. She continued to call all the rest of that week, until she realized she would never get through to him that way. She forced herself to swallow the enormous pride she had inherited from her father, put on her best dress and striptease garter belt, and set out to visit him at his apartment. Her key did not fit the lock and she was obliged to ring the bell. The door was opened by a mustached giant with the eyes of a schoolgirl.

"Compañero García isn't here," he said, without asking her in.

It was then she understood that she had lost him. She had a fleeting vision of her future, seeing herself in a vast desert where she was wasting away, devoting herself to tasks that used up her time, without the only man she had ever loved and far from the arms she had slept in since the long-gone days of her early childhood. She sat down on the stairs and burst into tears. The man with the mustache quietly shut the door.

She told no one what had happened. Alba asked her

about Pedro Tercero and she answered evasively, saying that he was extremely busy with his new job in the government. She continued giving her classes for young ladies of leisure and mongoloid children, and even began to teach ceramics in the shantytowns, where the women had organized to learn new trades; and, for the first time, she took an active role in the political and social life of the country. Organization was necessary, because the "road to Socialism" quickly became a battlefield. While the people were celebrating their victory, letting their hair and beards grow, addressing each other as *"compañero,"* rescuing forgotten folklore and native crafts, and exercising their new power in lengthy meetings of workers where everyone spoke at once and never agreed on anything, the right was carrying out a series of strategic actions designed to tear the economy to shreds and discredit the government. They controlled the influential mass media and possessed nearly limitless financial resources, as well as the support of the gringos, who had allocated secret funds for the program of sabotage. Within a few months the results could be seen. For the first time in their lives, people had enough money to cover their basic needs and to buy a few things they had always wanted, but now they were unable to do so because the stores were nearly empty. Shortages of goods, which was soon to be a collective nightmare, had begun. Women woke at dawn to stand in endless lines where they could purchase an emaciated chicken, half a dozen diapers, or a roll of toilet paper. Shoe polish, needles, and coffee became luxury items to be gift-wrapped and given as presents for birthdays and other special occasions. The anxiety of scarcity had arrived: the country was swept with rumors about products supposedly going to disappear, and people bought anything they could, without thinking, as a precaution. They stood in line without even knowing what was being sold, just so they would not lose a chance to buy something, even if they did not need it. A new occupation was born: professional line standers, who held other people's places for a reasonable sum. There were also peddlers of sweets who took advantage of the lines to hawk their goods, and people who rented blankets for the long nighttime lines. The black-market flourished. The police tried to restrain it, but it was like a plague that seeped in everywhere, and no matter how much they checked the trucks and stopped people carrying suspicious packages, they could not prevent it. Children made transactions in schoolyards. In the hysteria to get things, there were all sorts of confusions: people who had never smoked wound up paying an exorbitant sum for a pack of cigarettes, and those without children found themselves fighting over cans of baby formula. Spare parts for kitchens, for industrial machinery, and for cars disappeared from the market. Gasoline was rationed, and the lines of automobiles could last two days and a night, constricting the city like a gigantic motionless boa tanning itself in the sun. There was not enough time to stand in so many lines, and since office workers had to get around the city on foot or by bicycle, the streets filled with panting cyclists that looked like a frenzy of Dutchmen. This was the state of things when the teamsters declared their strike; by the second week, it was clear that this was not a union matter but a political one, and that the men had no intention of returning to work. The Army wanted to take control because the produce was rotting in the fields and there was nothing for housewives to buy in the markets, but the drivers had dismantled their engines and it was impossible to move the thousands of trucks that were strewn along the highways like so many fossilized remains. The President appeared on television asking the people to be patient. He warned the country that the teamsters were in the pay of the imperialists and that they would stay out on strike indefinitely; people would be wise, he said, to plant their own vegetables in their yards and on their terraces, at least until another solution was found. Meanwhile, the people, who were accustomed to poverty and most of whom had never eaten chicken except at Christmas and on Independence Day, did not give up the euphoria of the first days of victory. They organized themselves as if for war, determined not to let the economic sabotage spoil what they had won. They continued celebrating in a festive spirit and singing that the people united would never be defeated—even though each time they sang, it sounded more out of tune because divisiveness and hatred were inexorably growing.

Like everyone else, Senator Trueba also found his life changed. His enthusiasm for the struggle he had undertaken restored his former vigor and relieved some of the pain in his aching bones. He worked as he had in his heyday. He made numerous conspiratorial trips abroad and traveled the country tirelessly from north to south on planes, cars, and trains, on none of which were there now such things as first-class tickets. He endured the extravagant dinners with which his hosts received him in each city, town, and village he visited by pretending to have the appetite of a prisoner, despite the fact that his aging digestive tract was no longer up to such acrobatics. He lived in meetings. At first his long democratic experience impeded his ability to set traps for the new government, but he soon gave up the idea of obstructing it by legal means and came to accept the fact that the only way to unseat it was by using illegal ones. He was the first to declare in public that only a military coup could halt the advance of Marxism because people who had anxiously waited fifty years to be in power would not relinquish it because there was a chicken shortage.

"Stop acting like a bunch of faggots and take out your guns!" he shouted when there was talk of sabotage.

He made no secret of his ideas. He broadcast them to the four winds. Still dissatisfied, he went to the military school from time to time to throw corn at the cadets, shouting through the fence that they were all a bunch of chickens. He was forced to hire a pair of bodyguards to protect him from his own excesses. However, he often forgot that he had engaged them, and when he felt them spying on him he would have a tantrum, insulting them and threatening them with his cane until he was practically choking, his heart was beating so hard. He was convinced that if anyone tried to assassinate him, these two stocky morons would be powerless to prevent it, but he trusted that their presence would at least scare off spontaneous detractors. He also tried to place his granddaughter under surveillance, for he thought that since she moved in a circle of Communists, at any moment someone might mistreat her because of her relationship with him. But Alba would not hear of it. "A hired bully is the same as a confession of guilt. I have nothing to be afraid of," she said. He did not dare insist; he was tired of fighting with the members of his family, and, besides, his granddaughter was the only person in the world with whom he could express tenderness and who was able to make him laugh.

Meanwhile, Blanca had organized a network for obtaining provisions through the black-market and her contacts in the working-class neighborhood where she went to teach ceramics to the women. She had to work and worry for every bar of soap or bag of sugar she could find. Eventually she developed a cunning she had not suspected in herself, managing to store all kinds of things in the empty rooms of the house, including some things that were downright useless, like the two barrels of soy sauce she bought from a Chinese immigrant. She sealed the windows, put padlocks on the doors, and wore the keys around her waist, not removing them even when she took a bath, because she distrusted everyone, including Jaime and her daughter, and not without reason. "You look like a jailer, Mama," Alba would say, alarmed at this mania for insuring the future by embittering the present. Alba felt that if there was no meat they should eat potatoes, and that if there were no shoes they should wear sandals; but Blanca, horrified at her daughter's simplicity, held to the theory that, whatever happened, one should not lower one's standard of living, which she used to justify the time she spent in her smuggler's ploys. Actually, they had never lived so well since Clara's death, because for the first time since that date there was someone in the house to see to domestic order and take charge of what went into the pots. Crates of food were delivered regularly from Tres Marías, and Blanca promptly hid them. The first time, almost everything rotted, and the stench issued forth from the locked rooms, spreading through the house and seeping out into the neighborhood. Jaime suggested to his sister that she either donate, trade, or sell any perishable items, but Blanca refused to share her treasures. Alba understood then that her mother, who up till then had seemed like the only sane person in the family, also had a streak of madness. Alba made a hole in the wall, through which she removed part of what Blanca stored. She learned to do it so carefully, stealing cupfuls of sugar, rice, and flour, breaking off pieces of cheese, and spilling open the sacks of dried fruit to make it look like the work of mice, that it took Blanca more than four months to suspect her. At that point she made a written inventory of everything in her pantry and began to put a cross next to the things she removed for household use, convinced that the new system would bring the thief to light. But Alba took advantage of any carelessness on her mother's part to make new crosses on the list; in the end Blanca was so confused she did not know if she had erred in her accounting, if they were eating three times more than she had calculated, or if it was true that there were still ghosts in that accursed mansion.

The product of Alba's thefts wound up in the hands of Miguel, who distributed it in poor neighborhoods and in factories, along with his revolutionary pamphlets calling on the people to join in an armed struggle to bring down the oligarchy. But no one paid any attention to him. They were convinced that since they had come to power through legal means, no one could take it away from them, at least not until the next Presidential election.

"They're fools! They don't realize that the right is arming itself!" Miguel said to Alba.

Alba believed him. She had seen enormous wooden crates unloaded in the courtyard of her house in the middle of the night and their contents silently stored, under Trueba's orders, in another of the unused back rooms of the house. Like her mother, her grandfather put a padlock on the door, and kept the key around his neck in the same suède pouch where he carried Clara's teeth. Alba told this to her Uncle Jaime, who, having made peace with his father, had moved back into the house. "I'm almost certain that they're weapons," she confided. Jaime, who at that time was preoccupied and more or less continued to be until the day they killed him, could not believe it, but his niece was so insistent that he agreed to ask his father at the dinner table. The old man's answer removed any doubts.

"In my house I do as I see fit and store as many boxes as I feel like! Don't stick your nose into my affairs!" Senator Trueba thundered, slamming his fist on the table so that the glassware jumped, and stopping the discussion in its tracks.

That night Alba went to see her uncle in his tunnel of books and proposed that they apply the same system to his father's weapons as she had to her mother's provisions. And so they did. They spent the rest of the night boring a hole in

the wall of the room adjacent to the arsenal, which they hid
with a large wardrobe on one side and on the other with the
forbidden boxes themselves. This entrance enabled them,
armed with a hammer and a pair of pliers, to gain access to
the room Trueba had shut. Alba, who already had experience
in this line of work, suggested that they start with the boxes
on the bottom. They found a military cache that left them
openmouthed, for they had never seen such perfect instruments
of death. In the days that followed, they stole everything
they could, leaving the empty boxes under the other ones
after filling them with stones so they would go unnoticed if
anybody tried to lift them. Between them they pulled out
pistols, submachine guns, rifles, and hand grenades, which
they hid in Jaime's room until Alba could take them in her
cello case to a safer place. Senator Trueba saw his granddaughter walk by pulling the heavy case, never suspecting
that the bullets he had worked so hard to bring across the
border and into his house were rolling about in the velvet
lining. Alba wanted to hand the confiscated weapons over to
Miguel, but her Uncle Jaime convinced her that Miguel was
no less a terrorist than her grandfather and that it would be
better to get rid of them in such a way that they would not
harm anyone. They discussed various alternatives, from throwing them in the river to burning them on a pyre, but finally
decided that the most practical solution would be to bury
them in plastic bags in a safe, secret location, in case they
were ever needed for a nobler cause. Senator Trueba was
surprised to see his son and granddaughter planning an
outing to the mountains, for neither Jaime nor Alba had
participated in any sport since they left the English school
and had never shown the slightest inclination for the discomforts of hiking in the Andes. One Saturday morning they
drove off in a borrowed jeep, supplied with a tent, a basket
of food, and a mysterious suitcase that they had to carry
between them because it was as heavy as a corpse. In it were
the weapons they had stolen from the old man. They took
off enthusiastically in the direction of the mountains, driving
as far as they could and then continuing on foot until they
found a tranquil spot in the midst of that wind- and cold-
swept vegetation. There they dropped their gear and clum-
sily pitched their tent, dug holes, and buried the plastic bags,

carefully indicating each spot with a little pile of stones. They spent the rest of the weekend trout-fishing in the nearby river and roasting their catch on a fire of brambles, exploring the hills like children, and talking about the past. At night they drank hot wine with cinnamon and sugar and, huddled in their shawls, raised a toast to the face old Trueba would make when he discovered that he had been robbed, laughing until the tears rolled down their cheeks.

"If you weren't my uncle, I'd marry you," Alba joked.

"What about Miguel?"

"He'd be my lover."

Jaime did not think that was amusing, and the remainder of the trip he was withdrawn. That night they climbed into their sleeping bags, put out the paraffin lantern, and lay in silence. Alba fell asleep almost immediately, but Jaime, his eyes open in the darkness, saw the sun come up. He liked to say that Alba was a daughter to him, but that night he caught himself thinking that he wished he was neither her uncle nor her father but Miguel. He thought about Amanda and regretted that she no longer moved him, and when he searched his memory for the last embers of their excessive passion he could not find them. He had become a recluse. At first, he had been very close to Amanda because he had taken charge of her treatment and had seen her nearly every day. She had been in agony for several weeks, until she was able to live without drugs. She also gave up cigarettes and alcohol and began to lead a healthy, orderly existence; she put on weight, cut her hair, made up her large eyes again, and went back to wearing her tinkling necklaces and bracelets in a pathetic attempt to remove the tarnished image of herself. She was in love. She went from depression to a state of permanent euphoria. Jaime was the focus of her obsession. As proof of her love, she offered him the enormous effort she had made to free herself from her numerous addictions. Jaime scarcely encouraged her, but he lacked the fortitude to reject her, because he felt that the illusion of love might help in her recovery although he knew that for the two of them it was too late. All he did was try to maintain a certain distance, on the pretext of being a hopeless bachelor when it came to matters of the heart. He was satisfied with his furtive encounters with an occasional willing nurse from the clinic or his sad visits to brothels, which were enough to meet his most pressing needs in the rare free moments his work afforded him. Despite himself, however, he was involved in a relationship with Amanda that he had desperately wished for in his youth but that no longer touched him deeply and he felt incapable of sustaining. He was inspired only with compassion, but this was one of the strongest emotions he was capable of feeling. In a lifetime of living with misery and pain, his soul had not hardened; if anything it was increasingly vulnerable to pity. The day Amanda threw her arms around his neck and told him that she loved him, he hugged her back mechanically and kissed her with a feigned passion so that she would not notice he did not desire her. He now found himself trapped in a demanding relationship at an age when he no longer saw himself capable of tumultuous love. I'm no good at these things anymore, he would think after those exhausting sessions with Amanda, who, in order to charm him, resorted to the most extreme expressions of her love, leaving both of them undone.

His relationship with Amanda and Alba's insistence often brought him in contact with Miguel. There was no way to avoid meeting him on certain occasions. Jaime did his best to seem indifferent, but in the end Miguel captivated him. He had matured, and was no longer an excitable youth, but his politics had not changed in the least; he still believed that it would be impossible to defeat the right without a violent revolution. Jaime did not agree, but he was fond of Miguel and admired his courage. Nevertheless, he could not help thinking of him as one of those fatal men possessed by a dangerous idealism and an intransigent purity that color everything they touch with disaster, especially the women who have the misfortune to fall in love with them. He also disliked his ideological position; he was convinced that left-wing extremists like Miguel were doing more to harm the President than those on the right. None of this, however, prevented him from feeling well disposed toward him or recognizing the strength of his convictions, his natural gaiety, his capacity for tenderness, and the generosity that made him willing to give his life for ideals that Jaime shared but lacked the courage to take to their ultimate conclusion.

That night Jaime slept fitfully and uneasily, uncomfortable in his sleeping bag as he listened to his niece breathing close beside him. When he awoke, she was already up and about and was heating coffee for breakfast. A chill wind was blowing and the sun lit the mountain peaks with golden reflections. Alba threw her arms around her uncle and gave him a kiss, but he kept his hands in his pockets and did not return the gesture. He was perturbed.

Tres Marías was one of the last haciendas in the South to be expropriated under the agrarian reform. The same peasants who had been born there and had farmed the land for generations formed a cooperative and took title to the property, because it had been three years and five months since they had last seen their *patrón* and they had long since forgotten his hurricane-like temper. The foreman, terrified by the turn of events and the fiery tone of the meetings the tenants held in the schoolhouse, gathered up his belongings and disappeared without a word to anyone, not even Senator Trueba, for he did not wish to face his anger and he felt he had done his duty by warning him many times in the past. With his departure Tres Marías was left adrift for quite a while. There was no one to give orders and no one to obey them; the peasants, for the first time in their lives, were savoring the taste of freedom and the experience of being their own *patrón*. They divided up the pastureland and each grew whatever he wanted, until the government sent an agronomist who gave them seed on credit and brought them up to date on the demands of the market, the difficulties of transporting produce, and the advantages of fertilizers and disinfectants. But the peasants paid him little attention, since he seemed like a city slicker and it was easy to see that he had never had a plow in his hand; still, they celebrated his arrival by opening the sacred wine cellar of their former *patrón,* sacking his aged wines, and slaughtering his breeding bulls in order to eat their testicles with onion and basil. After the agronomist had left, they also ate the imported cows and all the brood hens. Esteban Trueba discovered that he had lost his land when they notified him that they were going to pay him for it with government bonds that had a thirty-year maturation and at the same price he had listed on his tax statement. He lost control. He went to his arsenal, picked up a machine gun he did not know how to use, and—without telling anyone, not even his bodyguards—ordered his chauffeur to drive him straight to Tres Marías. He traveled for many hours, blind with rage and without any clear plan in mind.

When they arrived, the chauffeur had to slam on the brakes because a thick wooden beam had been thrown across the gate to the hacienda as a roadblock. One of the tenants was standing guard, armed with a pike and an unloaded shotgun. Trueba got out of the car. When he saw the *patrón,* the poor man frantically rang the schoolhouse bell, which had been hung nearby in case they needed to sound an alarm, and quickly threw himself to the ground. A hail of bullets sailed past his head and embedded themselves in the neighboring trees. Trueba did not stop to see if he was dead. With unusual dexterity for a man his age, he headed down the path to the hacienda without looking to either side, so that the blow to the back of his head took him by surprise and he fell flat on his face in the dust before he even realized what had happened. The next thing he knew he was in the dining room of the main house lying face up on the table, his hands tied and a pillow under his head. A woman was pressing moist compresses to his forehead, and gathered around him were almost all his tenants, staring at him with intense curiosity.

"How do you feel, *compañero?*" someone asked.

"Sons of bitches! I'm nobody's *compañero!*" the old man roared, trying to sit up.

He struggled and shouted so much that they loosened his bonds and helped him to his feet, but when he attempted to leave he saw that the windows had been bricked in from outside and that the door was locked. They tried to explain to him that things had changed and that he was no longer the *patrón,* but he refused to listen. He was foaming at the mouth and his heart was about to burst. Cursing like a madman, he threatened them with such punishment and vengeance that they could only respond with laughter. Finally they grew bored and left him alone, locked in the dining room. Esteban Trueba collapsed into a chair, thoroughly drained from the exertion. Hours later he was informed that he was now a hostage and that they wanted to film him for television. Alerted by his chauffeur, his two bodyguards and a number of excited young members of the Conservative Party had made the trip to Tres Marías armed with sticks, brass knuckles, and chains, but when they arrived to rescue him they found a double guard posted at the gate, training the barrel of Senator Trueba's own machine gun on them.

"No one's taking our hostage *compañero* anywhere," one of the peasants said, and in order to emphasize the words they sent the would-be rescuers packing with a short volley fired into the air.

A television truck arrived to film the incident, and the tenants, who had never seen anything like it, let the truck through the gate and posed for the cameras with their broadest smiles, standing around their prisoner. That night, people all around the country saw on their television screens the leader of the opposition tied to a table and foaming at the mouth with rage, bellowing such vile curse words that the tape had to be censored. The President saw it too and the matter did not amuse him, for he realized it could be the detonator that would set off the powder keg on which his government was delicately perched. He called out the national guard to rescue the senator. When they reached the ranch, the peasants, emboldened by the support they had received from the press, refused to let them in, demanding a court order. The provincial judge, seeing that he could get himself in a fix and might wind up on national television excoriated by the leftist press, promptly went on a fishing trip. The guardsmen were forced to wait outside the gate of Tres Marías until they received an order from the capital.

Blanca and Alba found out, along with everybody else, when they saw it on the news. Blanca waited until the following morning without making any comment, but when she heard that the guardsmen had failed to rescue her father, she decided that the moment had come for her to see Pedro Tercero García again.

"Take off those filthy slacks and put on a decent dress," she ordered Alba.

They appeared at the Ministry without an appointment. A male secretary tried to make them stay in the waiting room, but Blanca pushed him away and proceeded with a firm step, dragging her daughter after her. She opened the door without knocking and burst into Pedro Tercero's office. She had not seen him for two years, and she almost turned and left, thinking she had entered the wrong office, because in that short time the man of her life had grown thin and old. He looked very tired and sad, and even though his hair was still black and shiny it was thin and short. He had trimmed his beautiful beard and was dressed in a bureaucrat's gray suit and a faded tie of the same color. Only by the look in his old black eyes did Blanca recognize him.

"Jesus! How you've changed," she exclaimed.

To Pedro Tercero, however, Blanca seemed more beautiful than he remembered, as if absence had rejuvenated her. In those two years he had had time to regret his decision and to learn that without Blanca he had lost his taste for the young girls who had previously attracted him. And when he spent twelve hours a day sitting at a desk, far from his guitar and the inspiration of the people, he had few opportunities to feel happy. The more time passed, the more he missed Blanca's calm, restful love. But the minute he saw her step across the threshold with her determined air, accompanied by Alba, he understood that she had not come to see him for sentimental reasons; he guessed that her visit was prompted by the scandal of Senator Trueba.

"I've come to ask you to accompany us," Blanca said without prefacing her remarks. "Your daughter and I are going to Tres Marías to rescue the old man."

That was how Alba learned that her father was Pedro Tercero García.

"All right. Let's stop at my house to pick up my guitar," he replied, already rising from his chair.

They left the Ministry in a black car resembling a hearse with official license plates. Blanca and Alba waited in the street while he ran up to his apartment. When he returned, he had recovered some of his old charm. He had changed out of his gray suit into his overalls and poncho of past years; he was wearing sandals and had slung his guitar over his shoulder. Blanca smiled at him for the first time, and he bent down and kissed her quickly on the mouth. The first sixty miles of the trip were spent in silence, until Alba managed to get over her surprise and ask in a quavering voice why they had not told her sooner that Pedro Tercero was her father, and spared her endless nightmares about a count dressed in white who had died of fever in the desert.

"Better a dead father than an absent one," Blanca enigmatically replied, and she never mentioned it again.

They arrived at Tres Marías at dusk. In front of the gate they met a large crowd gathered in amiable conversation around a bonfire on which a pig was roasting. It was the guardsmen, the journalists, and the peasants, who were finishing off the last of the senator's bottles. A few dogs and several children were playing in the glow of the flames, waiting for the shiny pink suckling pig to be served. The members of the press recognized Pedro Tercero García immediately because they had interviewed him many times, the guardsmen recognized his unmistakable face as that of the popular singer, and the peasants knew him because they had seen him born on this land. They welcomed him home with great affection.

"What brings you here, *compañero*?" someone asked.

"I've come to see the old man," Pedro Tercero said, smiling.

"You can go through, *compañero*, but alone. Doña Blanca and the señorita Alba will join us in a glass of wine."

The two women sat by the fire with the others, and the sweet smell of charred meat reminded them that they had not eaten since that morning. Blanca knew all the tenants and had taught many of them to read in the little schoolhouse of Tres Marías, so they began to talk about the bygone days when the Sánchez brothers imposed their law on the region, when old Pedro García had ended the plague of ants, and when the President had been an eternal candidate, standing in the station to harangue them from the train of his defeat.

"And to think that one day he would be our President!" someone said.

"And that one day the *patrón* would have less say at Tres Marías than us!" another said, laughing.

They led Pedro Tercero García directly into the kitchen. The oldest tenants were standing by the door, guarding the entrance to the dining room where their former *patrón* was being held prisoner. Though they had not seen Pedro Tercero in years, everyone remembered him. They sat down at the table to have a glass of wine and recall the distant past, the days when Pedro Tercero was not a legend in the peasants' memory but a rebellious boy in love with the daughter of his *patrón*. After that, Pedro Tercero picked up his guitar, rested it on his knee, shut his eyes, and sang with his velvety voice the song about the foxes and the hens. All the old people joined in the refrain.

"I'm going to take the *patrón* with me, friends," he said slowly during a pause in the singing.

"That's out of the question, son," someone replied.

"Tomorrow the national guard's going to show up here with a court order and carry him out like a hero," Pedro Tercero said. "It will be better if I take him with me now, with his tail between his legs."

They argued for a long while, and finally they led him into the dining room and left him alone with the hostage. It was the first time the two men had been face to face since the fateful day when Trueba had made him pay for his daughter's virginity with an axe. Pedro Tercero remembered him as an angry giant with a snakeskin whip and a silver cane, at whose step the tenants trembled and whose thunderous voice and feudal arrogance made all of nature quake. He was surprised to find the resentment he had stored up over all these years melt away in the presence of this bent and shrunken old man who was staring up at him in fright. Senator Trueba had exhausted his rage, and the night he had spent tied to a chair had left him with a pain in all his bones and the fatigue of a thousand years in his back. At first he had difficulty in recognizing Pedro, but when he saw that he was missing three of the fingers on his right hand, he understood that this was the end of the nightmare in which he was immersed. They stared at each other in silence for several seconds, each thinking that the other was the very incarnation of everything most hateful in the world, but unable to find the old fire of hatred in their hearts.

"I've come to get you out of here," Pedro Tercero said.

"Why?" the old man asked.

"Because Blanca asked me to," Pedro Tercero replied.

"Go to hell," Trueba said without conviction.

"Fine. That's where we're going. You're coming with me."

Pedro Tercero proceeded to untie his bonds, which had been wrapped around his wrists to keep him from pounding on the door. Trueba averted his glance to keep from looking at Pedro Tercero's mutilated hand.

"Get me out of here without their seeing me. I don't want the journalists to make fun of me," Senator Trueba said.

"I'm taking you out the same way you came in, through the gate," Pedro Tercero said, and he started walking.

Trueba followed him with his head bowed. His eyes were red, and, for the first time he could remember, he felt defeated. They crossed the kitchen and still the old man did not look up. They went through the house and followed the path that led from the main building to the outside gate, accompanied by a group of unruly children who skipped along beside them and an entourage of silent peasants who followed behind. Blanca and Alba were sitting with the journalists and guardsmen, eating roast pig with their fingers and drinking mouthfuls of red wine straight from a bottle that was being passed from hand to hand. When she saw her grandfather, Alba was troubled; she had not seen him so dejected since the day Clara died. Swallowing what was in her mouth, she ran to greet him. They hugged each other tightly and she whispered something in his ear, which apparently made Senator Trueba regain his dignity, for he raised his head and smiled with his old pride into the lights of the cameras. The journalists filmed him climbing into a black car with official plates, and people wondered for weeks what all the foolishness had been about, until other, far more serious events eclipsed all memory of the incident.

That night the President, who had acquired the habit of outwitting his insomnia by playing chess with Jaime, discussed the matter between two games, while his astute eyes, hidden behind thick lenses in dark frames, scrutinized his friend's face for the least hint of discomfort, but Jaime continued to place his pieces on the board without saying a word.

"Old Trueba's got his balls in the right place," the President said. "He really should be on our side."

"Your move, Señor President," Jaime replied, pointing to the board.

In the following months, the situation deteriorated greatly, like a country at war. Spirits ran high, especially among the women of the opposition, who paraded in the streets pounding their empty pans in protest against the shortages in the stores. Half the population hoped to overthrow the government and the other half defended it, and no one had time to worry about work. One night Alba was astonished to find the streets in the center of the city dark and almost deserted. Garbage had not been collected all that week, and stray dogs were scavenging among mountains of waste. Telephone poles were covered with posters faded by the winter rains, and every available inch of space was filled with the slogans of the two opposing sides. Half the street lamps had been smashed, and there were no lights on in any of the buildings; the only illumination came from a few sad bonfires fed by newspaper and wooden planks, around which the small groups that stood guard in front of the ministries, the banks, and the offices were warming themselves, taking turns to make sure the gangs of the extreme right that roamed the streets at night did not jump them in the dark. Alba saw a van pull up before one of the public buildings. A group of young men in white helmets piled out, armed with buckets of paint and brushes, and proceeded to cover the walls with light-colored paint. Then they drew huge multicolored doves, butterflies, and bloody flowers, with hand-lettered verses by the Poet and appeals for the people to unite. These were the youth brigades, who thought they could save the revolution with patriotic murals and inflammatory doves. Alba went up to them and pointed to the mural on the other side of the street. It was stained with red paint and contained a single word printed in enormous letters: Djakarta.

"What does that mean, *compañero?*" she asked one of them.

"I don't know," he replied.

And none of them knew why the opposition had painted that Asiatic word on the walls; they had never heard about the piles of corpses in the streets of that distant city. Alba climbed on her bicycle and pedaled home. After the gasoline rationing and the public transport strike, she had unearthed this childhood toy from the basement as her only means of getting around. She was thinking of Miguel, and a dark foreboding gripped her throat.

It had been ages since she had gone to class, and time hung heavy on her hands. The professors had declared an indefinite strike and the students had taken over all the buildings. Bored with practicing the cello at home, she used the time when she was not sleeping with Miguel, strolling with Miguel, or talking with Miguel to work at the hospital in the Misericordia District, where she helped her Uncle Jaime and a few other doctors who continued to practice there despite an order from the school of medicine to stop work so as to sabotage the government. It was a Herculean task. The hallways were piled with patients who had to wait for days, like a moaning herd, to be examined. The orderlies no longer brought supplies. Jaime would fall asleep with his scalpel in his hand, so busy that he often forgot to eat. He had lost weight and looked haggard. He was working eighteen-hour shifts, and when he could finally lie down on his cot, he was often unable to sleep. His mind raced at the thought of all the patients who were waiting for him, the lack of anesthesia, syringes, and cotton, and the realization that even if he could be multiplied by a thousand it would still not be enough, because it was like trying to stop a train with your bare hands. Amanda also worked in the clinic as a volunteer, both to be close to Jaime and to keep busy. In the exhausting days spent taking care of unknown patients, she regained the light that had illuminated her from within when she was young, and for a time she had the illusion of being happy. She wore a blue smock and rubber shoes, but when she was around him Jaime was convinced he heard the tinkle of the glass beads she used to wear. He was glad to have her there and he wished he loved her. The President appeared on television almost every night to denounce the ruthless war being waged by the opposition. He was very tired, and at times his voice would crack. People said that he was drunk, and that he spent his nights in orgies with mulattas flown in from the tropics to warm his bones. He announced that the striking teamsters were receiving fifty dollars a day from abroad to keep the country at a standstill. People responded that he was being sent coconut ice cream and Soviet arms via diplomatic pouch. He said that his enemies were conspiring with the generals to launch a coup d'état because they would rather see democracy dead than be governed by him. They accused him of telling paranoid lies and of stealing paintings from the National Museum to hang in his mistress's bedroom. He warned that the right was armed and determined to sell the country to imperialism, and they replied that his pantry was stocked with breasts of fowl while the masses had to stand in line to buy the neck and wings of the same bird.

The day Luisa Mora rang the bell of the big house on the corner, Senator Trueba was in his study doing his accounts. She was the last remaining Mora sister. Reduced to the size of a wandering but completely lucid angel, she was in full possession of her indomitable spiritual energy. Trueba had not seen her since Clara's death, but he recognized her by her voice, which still sounded like an enchanted flute, and by her perfume of wild violets, which, although somewhat tempered by time, was still noticeable even at a distance. As she entered the room, she brought with her the winged presence of Clara, floating in the room before the loving eyes of her husband, who had not seen her in several days.

"I've come to bring you some bad news, Esteban," Luisa Mora said after she had settled into the armchair.

"Ah, dear Luisa! I've had enough of that," he said, sighing.

Luisa told him what she had discovered in the stars. She had to explain the scientific method she had used in order to overcome the senator's pragmatic resistance. She told him she had spent the past ten months studying the astrological charts of each important person in the government and the opposition, including Trueba himself. When she compared the charts, they showed that at this exact historic moment there would be a terrible sequence of events, bringing blood, pain, and death.

"I don't have the slightest doubt about it, Esteban," she concluded. "Terrible times lie ahead. There will be so many dead they will be impossible to count. You will be on the side of the winners, but victory will only bring you suffering and loneliness."

Esteban Trueba felt uneasy in the presence of this unusual soothsayer, who had disturbed the peace of his library and upset his liver with her astrological rantings, but because of Clara, who was watching him out of the corner of her eye from across the room, he did not have the strength to send her away.

"But I didn't come here to upset you with news that's beyond your control, Esteban. I came to speak with Alba, because I have a message for her from her grandmother."

The senator sent for Alba. The girl had not seen Luisa Mora since she was seven, but she remembered her perfectly. She embraced her gently so as not to crush the fragile marble bones, and anxiously inhaled a mouthful of her unmistakable perfume.

"I came to tell you to be careful, child," Luisa Mora said after she had dried her tears. "Death is at your heels. Your Grandmother Clara is doing all she can to protect you in the Hereafter, but she sent me to tell you that your spiritual protectors are powerless when it comes to major cataclysms. She says it would be wise for you to take a trip, that you should cross the ocean. You'll be safe there."

At this point in the conversation Esteban Trueba lost his patience. He was convinced he was dealing with a crazed old woman. Ten months and eleven days later he would recall Luisa Mora's prophetic words, when they took Alba away in the middle of the night, while the curfew was in force.

✼

THIRTEEN

The Terror

The day of the coup the sun was shining, a rare event in the timid spring that was just dawning. Jaime had worked practically all night and by seven in the morning his body had had only two hours of sleep. He was awakened by the ring of the telephone. It was a secretary, her voice slightly agitated, who scared his drowsiness away. She was calling from the Presidential Palace to inform him that he should present himself there as soon as possible; no, the President was not ill; no, she was not sure what was happening, she had simply been instructed to call all the President's doctors. Jaime dressed like a sleepwalker and got into his car, grateful that his profession entitled him to a weekly ration of gasoline; otherwise he would have had to go by bicycle. He arrived at the palace at eight o'clock and was surprised to see the great square completely empty and a large detachment of soldiers stationed at the gates to the seat of the government. They were in full battle dress, with helmets and guns. Jaime parked his car in the deserted square without noticing the soldiers who were motioning him not to stop. He got out of the car and was immediately surrounded.

"What's this, *compañeros?* Have we gone to war with China?" Jaime smiled.

"Keep going. You can't stop here. Traffic is prohibited," an officer ordered.

"I'm sorry, but I received a call from the President's

office," Jaime said, showing them his identification card. "I'm a doctor."

They escorted him to the heavy wooden doors of the Presidential Palace, where a group of guardsmen were standing watch. They let him through. Inside the building, the commotion resembled that of a shipwreck. Employees were running up and down the stairs like seasick rats and the President's private guard were pushing furniture against the windows and distributing pistols to those who were closest to him. The President came out to greet him. He was wearing a combat helmet, which looked incongruous with his fine sports clothes and Italian shoes. Then Jaime understood that something momentous was taking place.

"The Navy has revolted, Doctor," the President explained tersely. "It's time to fight."

Jaime picked up a telephone and called Alba, told her not to leave the house, and asked her to warn Amanda. He never spoke with her again. In the next hour a few ministers and political leaders arrived, and telephone negotiations with the insurgents were begun in order to gauge the magnitude of the insurrection and to find a peaceful settlement. But by nine-thirty in the morning all the armed units in the country were under the command of officers sympathetic to the coup. In barracks across the country, purges had begun of all those remaining loyal to the Constitution. The commander of the national guard ordered his men at the palace to leave because the police had just joined the coup.

"You can go, *compañeros,* but leave your guns behind," the President said.

The guardsmen were confused and ashamed, but the commander's order was final. Not one of them dared to accept the challenge in the gaze of the Chief of State. They left their arms in the courtyard and began to file out with lowered heads.

One of them turned when he reached the door. "I'm staying with you, *Compañero* President," he said.

By midmorning it was clear that dialogue would not resolve the situation and almost everyone began to leave. Only close friends and the private guard remained behind. The President had to order his daughters to leave; they had to be removed forcibly, and they could be heard from the street calling his name. Some thirty people were left in the building, holding out in the drawing rooms on the second floor. Among them was Jaime, feeling as if he were in the middle of a nightmare. He sat down on a red velvet chair with a gun in his hand, staring at it blankly; he did not know how to use it. It seemed to him that time was moving very slowly. His watch showed that only three hours of this bad dream had passed. He heard the voice of the President speaking to the nation on the radio. It was his farewell.

"I speak to all those who will be persecuted to tell you that I am not going to resign: I will repay the people's loyalty with my life. I will always be with you. I have faith in our nation and its destiny. Other men will prevail, and soon the great avenues will be open again, where free men will walk, to build a better society. Long live the people! Long live the workers! These are my last words. I know my sacrifice will not have been in vain."

The sky began to cloud. Isolated gunshots were heard in the distance. At that moment, the President was speaking on the phone with the head of the uprising, who was offering him a military plane to leave the country with his family. But he was not the kind of man to become an exile in some distant place where he would spend the rest of his life vegetating with other deposed leaders who had left their countries on a moment's notice.

"You were wrong about me, traitors. The people put me here and the only way I'll leave is dead," he replied serenely.

Then came the roar of the airplanes, and the bombing began. Jaime threw himself to the floor with everyone else, unable to believe what he was seeing; until the day before, he had been convinced that nothing like this would ever happen in his country and that even the military respected the law. Only the President was on his feet. He walked to the window carrying a bazooka and fired it at the tanks below. Jaime inched his way to him and grabbed him by the calves to make him get down, but the President replied with a curse and remained erect. Fifteen minutes later the whole building was in flames, and it was impossible to breathe because of the bombs and the smoke. Jaime crawled among the broken furniture and bits of plaster that were falling around him like a deadly rain, attempting to help the wounded, but he could only offer words of comfort and close the eyes of the dead. In a sudden pause in the shooting, the President gathered the survivors and told them to leave because he did not want any martyrs or needless sacrifice; everyone had a family, and important tasks lay ahead. "I'm going to call a truce so you can leave," he added. But no one moved. Though a few of them were trembling, all were in apparent possession of their dignity. The bombing was brief, but it left the palace in ruins. By two o'clock in the afternoon the fire had consumed the old drawing rooms that had been used since colonial times, and only a handful of men were left around the President. Soldiers entered the building and took what was left of the first floor. Above the din was heard the hysterical voice of an officer ordering them to surrender and come down single file with their hands on their heads. The President shook each of them by the hand. "I'll go last," he said. They never again saw him alive.

Jaime went downstairs with the others. Soldiers had been stationed on each step of the broad stone staircase; they seemed to have lost their senses. They kicked and beat those coming down the stairs with the butts of their guns, as if possessed by a new hatred that had just been invented and had bloomed in them in the space of a few hours. A few of them fired their guns over the heads of those who had surrendered. Jaime received a blow to his stomach that made him double up in pain, and when he was able to stand his eyes were full of tears and his pants moist with excrement. The soldiers continued to beat them all the way into the street, where they were ordered to lie face down on the ground. There they were trampled on and insulted until there were no more Spanish curse words left; then someone motioned to one of the tanks. The prisoners heard it approach, shaking the pavement with its weight like an invincible pachyderm.

"Make way, we're going to run the tank over these bastards!" a colonel shouted.

Jaime looked up from the ground and thought he recognized the man; he reminded him of a boy he used to play with at Tres Marías when he was a child. The tank snorted past, four inches from their heads, amidst the hard laughter of the soldiers and the howl of the fire engines. In the distance they could hear the sound of war planes. A long while later they divided the prisoners into groups, according to their guilt. Jaime was taken to the Ministry of Defense, which had been transformed into a barracks. They made him walk in a squatting position, as if he were in a trench, and led him into an enormous room filled with naked men who had been tied up in lines of ten, their hands bound behind their backs, so badly beaten that some could hardly stand. Rivulets of blood were running down onto the marble floor. Jaime was led into the boiler room, where other men were lined up against the wall beneath the watchful eye of a pale soldier who kept his machine gun trained on them. There he stood motionless for a long time, managing to stay erect as if he were sleepwalking, still not understanding what was happening and tormented by the screams coming through the walls. He noticed that the soldier was watching him. Suddenly the man lowered his gun and came up to him.

"Sit down and rest, Doctor. But if I tell you to, stand up immediately," he said softly, handing him a lighted cigarette. "You operated on my mother and saved her life."

Jaime did not smoke, but he savored that cigarette, inhaling as slowly as he could. His watch was destroyed, but his hunger and thirst led him to believe that it was night. He was so tired and uncomfortable in his stained trousers that he did not even wonder what was going to happen to him. His head was beginning to nod when the soldier came over to him again.

"Get up, Doctor," he whispered. "They're coming for you now. Good luck!"

A moment later two men walked in, handcuffed him, and led him before an officer who was in charge of interrogating the prisoners. Jaime had seen him on occasion in the company of the President.

"We know you have nothing to do with this, Doctor," he said. "We just want you to appear on television and say that the President was drunk and he committed suicide. After that you can go home."

"Do it yourself. Don't count on me, you bastards," Jaime said.

They held him down by the arms. The first blow was to his stomach. After that they picked him up and smashed him down on a table. He felt them remove his clothes. Much later, they carried him unconscious from the Ministry of Defense. It had begun to rain, and the freshness of the water and the air revived him. He awoke as they were loading him onto an Army bus and sat him down in the last seat. He saw the night through the window and when the vehicle began to move he could see the empty streets and flag-decked buildings. He understood that the enemy had won and he probably thought about Miguel. The bus pulled into the courtyard of a military regiment. They took him off the bus. There were other prisoners in the same condition. They tied their hands and feet with barbed wire and threw them on their faces in the stalls. There Jaime and the others spent two days without food or water, rotting in their own excrement, blood, and fear, until they were all driven by truck to an area near the airport. In an empty lot they were shot on the ground, because they could no longer stand, and then their bodies were dynamited. The shock of the explosion and the stench of the remains floated in the air for a long time.

In the big house on the corner, Senator Trueba opened a bottle of French champagne to celebrate the overthrow of the regime that he had fought against so ferociously, never suspecting that at that very moment his son Jaime's testicles were being burned with an imported cigarette. The old man hung a flag over the entrance of his house and did not go outside to dance because he was lame and because there was a curfew, but not because he did not want to, as he jubilantly announced to his daughter and granddaughter. Meanwhile, hanging on to the telephone, Alba was attempting to get word on those she was most worried about: Miguel, Pedro Tercero, her Uncle Jaime, Amanda, Sebastián Gómez, and so many others.

"Now they're going to pay for everything!" Senator Trueba exclaimed, raising his glass.

Alba snatched it from his hand and hurled it against the wall, shattering it to bits. Blanca, who had never had the courage to oppose her father, did not attempt to hide her smile.

"We're not going to celebrate the death of the President or anybody else!" Alba said.

In the pristine houses of the High District, bottles that had waited for three years were opened and the new order was toasted. All that night helicopters flew over the working-class neighborhoods, humming like flies from another world.

Very late, almost at dawn, the phone rang. Alba, who had not gone to bed, ran to answer it. She was relieved to hear Miguel.

"The time has come, my love. Don't look for me or wait for me. I love you," he said.

"Miguel! I want to go with you!" Alba cried.

"Don't mention me to anybody, Alba. Don't see any of our friends. Destroy all your address books, your papers, anything that has to do with me. I'll always love you. Remember that, my love," Miguel said, and he hung up.

The curfew lasted for two days, which to Alba seemed an eternity. On the radio they played martial music, and on television they showed only landscapes from around the country and cartoons. Several times a day the four generals of the junta appeared on the screen, seated between the coat of arms and the flag, to announce various edicts: they were the new heroes of the nation. Despite the order to shoot anyone who ventured outside, Senator Trueba crossed the street to attend a celebration in his neighbor's house. The hubbub of the party did not concern the soldiers patrolling the streets because it was a neighborhood where they expected no opposition. Blanca announced that she had the worst migraine of her life and locked herself in her room. During the night, Alba heard her rummaging in the kitchen and concluded that her mother's hunger must have overcome her headache. Alba spent two days walking around the house in circles in a state of sheer despair, going through the books in Jaime's tunnel and on her own shelves and destroying anything that might be compromising. It was like a sacrilege. She was sure that when her uncle returned he would be furious with her and lose all trust in her. She also destroyed the address books with her friends' phone numbers, her most treasured love letters and even her photographs of Miguel. Indifferent and bored, the maids entertained themselves throughout the curfew by making empanadas;

all, that is, except the cook, who wept nonstop and anxiously awaited the moment when she would be able to go out and join her husband, with whom she had been unable to communicate.

When the curfew was lifted for a few hours to enable people to go out and buy food, Blanca was amazed to see the stores filled with the products that during the preceding three years had been so scarce and that now appeared in the shopwindows as if by magic. She saw piles of butchered chickens and was able to buy as many as she wanted even though they cost three times as much as usual, since free pricing had been decreed. She noticed many people staring curiously at the chickens as if they had never seen them before, but few were buying, because they could not afford them. Three days later the smell of rotting meat infected every shop in the city.

Soldiers nervously patrolled the streets, cheered by many people who had wished for the government's defeat. Some of them, emboldened by the violence of the past few days, stopped all men with long hair or beards, unequivocal signs of a rebel spirit, and all women dressed in slacks, which they cut to ribbons because they felt responsible for imposing order, morality, and decency. The new authorities announced that they had nothing to do with actions of this sort and had never given orders to cut beards or slacks, and that it was probably the work of Communists disguised as soldiers attempting to cast aspersions on the armed forces and make the citizenry hate them. Neither beards nor slacks were forbidden, they said, although of course they preferred men to shave and wear their hair short, and women to wear dresses.

Word spread that the President had died, and no one believed the official version that he had committed suicide.

I waited until things had stabilized a little. Three days after the Military Pronunciamiento, I drove to the Ministry of Defense in my Congressional car, surprised that no one had come to invite me to participate in the new government. Everyone knows I was the Marxists' chief enemy, the first to oppose Communist dictatorship and to dare say in public that only the military could prevent the country from falling into the clutches of the left. I was also the one who made almost all the contacts with the high command of the military, who was the intermediary with the gringos, and who used my own name and money to buy arms. In other words, I had more at stake than anyone. At my age I was not interested in political power. But I was one of the few people around who could advise them, because I'd held many posts over the years and I knew better than anyone what this country needed. What could a bunch of temporary colonels do without loyal, honest, experienced advisers! Just make a mess of things. Or be deceived by those sharp characters who know how to turn this kind of situation into personal profit, something that's already happening. No one knew then that things were going to turn out the way they have. We thought military intervention was a necessary step for the return to a healthy democracy. That's why I thought it was so important to cooperate with the authorities.

When I arrived at the Ministry of Defense, I was surprised to see that the building had become a pigsty. Orderlies were swabbing the floors with mops, some of the walls were riddled with bullet holes, and crouched soldiers were running around as if they were in the middle of a battlefield or expected the enemy to drop from the roof. I had to wait nearly three hours to see an officer. At first I thought that in all that chaos they simply hadn't recognized me and that was why they were treating me with so little respect, but then I realized what was going on. The officer received me with his boots up on the desk, chewing a greasy sandwich, badly shaven, with his jacket unbuttoned. He didn't give me a chance to ask about my son Jaime or to congratulate him for the valiant actions of the soldiers who had saved the nation; instead he asked for the keys to my car, on the ground that Congress had been shut down and that all Congressional perquisites had therefore been suspended. I was amazed. It was clear then that they didn't have the slightest intention of reopening the doors of Congress, as we all expected. He asked me—no, he ordered me—to show up at the cathedral at eleven the next morning to attend the Te Deum with which the nation would express its gratitude to God for the victory over Communism.

"Is it true the President committed suicide?" I asked.

"He's gone," he answered me.

"Gone? Where to?"

"He's gone to Hell!" he said, laughing.

I walked out onto the street feeling extremely disconcerted, leaning on my chauffeur's arm. We had no way to get home; there were neither taxis nor buses, and I'm too old to walk. Fortunately we saw a jeep full of policemen and they recognized me. I'm easy to spot, as my granddaughter Alba says, because I have the unmistakable appearance of an angry old crow and I always wear my mourning clothes and carry my silver cane.

"Get in, Senator," a lieutenant said.

They helped us up into the jeep. The men looked tired and I could tell they hadn't slept. They told me they had been patrolling the city for the past three days, staying awake on coffee and pills.

"Did you meet any resistance in the shantytowns or slums?" I asked.

"Very little. People are calm," the lieutenant said. "I hope things get back to normal quickly, Senator. We don't like this. It's a dirty business."

"Don't say that. If you people hadn't acted, the Communists would have staged a coup themselves, and right this minute all of us here plus another fifty thousand people would be dead. I suppose you knew they had a plan for imposing their dictatorship?"

"That's what they told us. But where I live they've arrested a lot of people. My neighbors look at me with fear. The same thing happens to the rest of my men. But you have to follow orders. The nation comes first, right?"

"That's the way it is. I'm also sorry about what's going on, Lieutenant. But there was no other way. The regime was rotten. What would have happened to this country if you people hadn't taken up your arms?"

But deep down I wasn't so sure. I had a feeling things weren't turning out the way we had planned and that the situation was slipping away from me, but at the time I kept my doubts to myself, reasoning that three days are very few to put a country back together and that probably the vulgar officer who received me at the Ministry of Defense represented an insignificant minority within the armed forces. The majority were like the scrupulous lieutenant who had driven me home. I supposed that in no time at all order would be restored and that once the tension of the first few days had ebbed I would get in touch with someone better placed within the military hierarchy. I regretted not having spoken to General Hurtado. I held off out of respect and also, I must admit, out of pride, because he should have sought me out and not vice versa.

I didn't learn of my son Jaime's death until two weeks later, after our euphoria over the triumph had waned when we saw people going around counting the dead and those who had disappeared. One Sunday a soldier silently appeared at the house and went into the kitchen to tell Blanca everything he had seen in the Ministry of Defense and what he knew about the dynamited bodies.

"Dr. del Valle saved my mother's life," the soldier said, looking at the floor, his helmet in his hand. "That's why I came to tell you how they killed him."

Blanca called me in so I could hear what the soldier had to say, but I refused to believe it. I said he must have been confused, that it couldn't have been Jaime but someone else he had seen in the boiler room, because Jaime had no reason to be in the Presidential Palace the day of the Military Pronunciamiento. I was sure my son had managed to escape abroad by crossing some border pass or had taken refuge in some embassy, on the assumption that he was being looked for. Besides, his name had not appeared on any of the lists of people sought by the authorities, so I deduced that Jaime had nothing to fear.

A long time would have to pass—several months, in fact—before I understood that the soldier had told the truth. In my deluded solitude, I sat waiting for my son in the armchair of my library, my eyes glued to the doorsill, calling to him with my mind, as I used to call for Clara. I called him so many times that I finally saw him, but when he came he was covered with dried blood and rags, dragging streamers of barbed wire across the waxed parquet floors. That was how I learned that he had died exactly as the soldier reported. Only then did I begin to speak of tyranny. My granddaughter Alba, however, saw the true nature of the dictator long before I did. She picked him out from among all the generals and military men. She recognized him right away, because she had inherited Clara's intuition. He's a crude, simple-looking man of few words, like a peasant. He seemed very modest, and few could have guessed that one day they would see him wrapped in an emperor's cape with his arms raised to hush the crowds that had been trucked in to acclaim him, his august mustache trembling with vanity as he inaugurated the monument to the Four Swords, from whose heights an eternal torch would illuminate the nation's destiny—except that, owing to an error by the foreign technicians, no flame would ever rise there, only a thick cloud of kitchen smoke that floated in the sky like a perennial storm from some other climate.

I began to think I had been wrong to do as I had and that perhaps after all this was not the best way to overthrow Marxism. I felt more and more alone, for no one needed me anymore. I no longer had my sons, and Clara, with her habits of silence and distraction, seemed like a far-off ghost. Even Alba grew daily more remote. I hardly ever saw her in the house. She went by me like a gust of wind in her horrible long cotton skirts, with her incredible green hair like Rosa's, busy in all sorts of mysterious chores that she carried out with the complicity of her mother. I'm sure that behind my back the two of them were weaving every kind of intrigue. My granddaughter was in a state, just like Clara in the days of the typhus epidemic, when she took everybody else's suffering onto her own back.

Alba did not have long to mourn her Uncle Jaime's death. The needs of others were so pressing that she was forced to put her grief aside for later. She did not see Miguel again until two months after the coup, and she began to fear that he too was dead. Still, she did not look for him; he had given her strict instructions in that regard and besides, she had heard that his name was on the lists of those who had been ordered to appear before the new authorities. That gave her hope. As long as they're looking for him, he's still alive, she concluded. She tortured herself with the idea that they might capture him alive, and invoked the spirit of her grandmother to ask her to prevent that from happening. "I'd rather see him dead a thousand times over, Grandmother," she begged.

She knew what was taking place in the country, which was why she walked around with knots in her stomach, why her hands shook, and why, whenever she heard that someone had been taken prisoner, she broke out in a rash from head to foot, like someone with the plague. But there was no one with whom she could speak about these things, not even her grandfather, because people preferred not to know.

After that terrible Tuesday, Alba had to rearrange her feelings in order to continue living; to accept the idea that she would never again see those she loved the most, her Uncle Jaime, Miguel, and many others. She blamed her grandfather for what had taken place, but then, seeing him hunched in his armchair calling out to Clara and his son in an interminable murmur, her love for the old man returned and she ran to embrace him, running her hands through his white hair and comforting him. She felt that everything was made of glass, as fragile as a sigh, and that the machine-gun fire and bombs of that unforgettable Tuesday had destroyed most of what she knew, and that all the rest had been smashed to pieces and spattered with blood. As days, weeks, and months went by, what had at first appeared to be spared also began to show signs of destruction. She noticed that friends and relatives were avoiding her. Some crossed the street so as not to say hello to her, or turned away when she drew near. She imagined the word had spread that she was helping the victims of the persecution.

And it was true. From the very first days, the most pressing need was to secure asylum for those in danger of death. At first it almost seemed like fun, because it kept her from thinking of Miguel, but Alba soon realized it was no game. Everywhere there were posters reminding citizens that it was their duty to inform on Marxists and turn in the fugitives or else they would be marked as traitors and brought to justice. Alba miraculously rescued Jaime's car, which had survived the bombing and had been sitting for a week where he had parked it. She painted two large sunflowers on the doors with the brightest yellow she could find, to distinguish it from other cars and make her new job easier. She had to memorize the location of all the embassies, the shifts of the guardsmen who stood watch in front of them, the height of their walls and width of their doors. Word that someone

needed asylum would reach her unexpectedly, often through
a stranger who approached her on the street and who she
imagined had been sent by Miguel. She would drive to the
appointed place in broad daylight and when she saw someone motioning to her, recognizing the yellow flowers on her
car, she stopped for a minute to let the man jump in. They
never spoke on the way, because she preferred not to know
his name. There were times when she had to spend the
whole day with him, or even hide him for a night or two
before finding the right moment to slip him into one of the
more accessible embassies, climbing a wall behind the guards'
backs. This system turned out to be more reliable than
working out complicated arrangements with the nervous
ambassadors of the foreign democracies. She would never
hear another word about the person she had helped, but she
retained forever their trembling gratitude and once it was
over she breathed a sigh of relief that at least this time
someone had been saved. Occasionally she had to do the
same thing with women who feared being separated from
their children, and no matter how much Alba promised them
that she would bring their children to them afterward through
the front door, knowing as she did that not even the most
timid ambassador would turn her down, the mothers refused
to leave their children behind, and even the children had to
be thrown over the walls or slipped through the iron gates.
Soon all the embassies were ringed with barbed wire and
machine guns and it was impossible to continue taking them
by storm; but then there were other needs to keep her busy.

It was Amanda who first put her in touch with the
priests. The two friends would get together to whisper about
Miguel, whom neither of them had seen, and to remember
Jaime with dry-eyed yearning; there was no official proof
that he had died and their desire to see him again was
stronger than the soldier's tale. Amanda had resumed her
compulsive smoking; her hands shook and her gaze wandered. At times her pupils were dilated and she moved
slowly, but she continued working in the hospital. She told
Alba that she frequently took care of patients who were faint
with hunger.

"The families of prisoners, disappeared people, and the
dead have nothing to eat. The unemployed don't either.

Barely a plate of corn mush every other day. The children are so undernourished that they fall asleep in school."

She added that the glass of milk and the crackers that schoolchildren used to receive each day had been discontinued, and that mothers were quieting their children's hunger with cups of tea.

"The only ones trying to help are the priests," Amanda said. "People don't want to know the truth. The Church has organized soup kitchens to feed children under seven a hot meal six times a week. Of course that's not enough. For every child who eats a plate of lentils or potatoes once a day, there are five outside looking in because there's not enough to go around."

Alba realized that they had returned to the old days when her Grandmother Clara went to the Misericordia District to replace justice with charity. Except that now charity was frowned upon. She noticed that whenever she went to the houses of her friends to ask for a package of rice or a tin of powdered milk no one dared to turn her down the first time, but afterward they avoided her. At first Blanca helped her. Alba had no trouble obtaining the key to her mother's pantry, arguing that there was no need to hoard ordinary flour and poor men's beans when you could buy Baltic crab and Swiss chocolate. This enabled her to stock the priests' kitchens for a time, which, however, seemed all too brief to her. One day she took her mother to one of the soup kitchens. When Blanca saw the long unpolished wooden table where two rows of children were awaiting their portions with pleading eyes, she began to cry and wound up spending two days with a splitting headache. She would have gone on crying if her daughter hadn't forced her to get dressed, forget about herself, and look for help, even if it meant she had to steal from her father's household budget. Senator Trueba would not discuss the subject; like everyone else in his class, he denied the existence of hunger just as vehemently as he denied that of the prisoners and the torture; this meant that Alba could not rely on him, and later, when she could no longer rely on her mother either, she was forced to take more drastic measures. The farthest her grandfather went was to his club. He never went downtown, much less to the outskirts of the city or the shantytowns. It was no effort for him to believe that the misery his granddaughter reported was a Marxist fabrication.

"Communist priests!" he shouted. "That's the last thing I need to hear!"

But when children and women began to appear outside people's houses at every hour of the day and night begging for something to eat, Trueba—instead of ordering the gates to be shut and lowering the blinds so he wouldn't have to see them, like everyone else—raised Blanca's monthly stipend and said there should always be hot food on hand to give away.

"This is just a temporary situation," he assured them. "As soon as the military can straighten out the chaos that the Marxists left the country in, this kind of problem will be resolved."

The newspapers said that the beggars in the streets, a sight that had not been seen in years, had been sent by international Communism to discredit the military junta and undermine the return to order and progress. Cement walls were erected to hide the most unsightly shantytowns from the eyes of tourists and others who preferred not to see them. In a single night, as if by magic, beautifully pruned gardens and flowerbeds appeared on the avenues; they had been planted by the unemployed, to create the illusion of a peaceful spring. White paint was used to erase the murals of doves and to remove all political posters from sight. Any attempt to write political messages in public was punished with a burst of machine-gun fire on the spot. The clean, orderly, silent streets were reopened to commerce. Soon the beggar children disappeared, and Alba noticed that the stray dogs and piles of garbage were gone too. The black-market came to an end at the very moment when the Presidential Palace was bombed, because speculators were threatened with martial law and execution by firing squad. Items whose very name was unheard of began to be sold in stores, along with things that only the rich had previously been able to buy as contraband. The city had never looked more beautiful. The upper middle class had never been so happy: they could buy as much whisky as they wanted, and automobiles on credit.

In the patriotic euphoria of the first few days, women brought their jewels to the barracks to help finance the national reconstruction. They even handed over their wedding rings, which were replaced with copper bands that bore the national seal. Blanca had to hide the woolen stocking that contained the jewels Clara had left her, to prevent Senator Trueba from handing them over to the authorities. They saw the birth of a proud new class. Illustrious ladies dressed in foreign clothes, as exotic and shimmering as fireflies, paraded themselves in the fashionable entertainment centers on the arm of the proud new economists. A caste of military men arose to fill key posts. Families who had previously considered it a disgrace to count a member of the military among their number were now pitted against each other in the struggle to see who could get their sons into the war academies and were offering their daughters to soldiers. The country filled with men in uniform, with war machines, flags, hymns, and parades, because the military understood the need for the people to have their own rituals and symbols. Senator Trueba, who despised these things on principle, realized what his friends at the club had meant when they had assured him that Marxism did not stand a chance in Latin America because it did not allow for the magical side of things. "Bread, circuses, and something to worship are all they need," the senator concluded, regretting in his conscience that there should be a lack of bread.

A campaign was orchestrated to erase from the face of the earth the good name of the former President, in the hope that the masses would stop mourning him. His house was opened and the public was invited to visit what they called "the dictator's palace." People could look into his closets and marvel at the quantity and quality of his suède jackets, go through his drawers, and rummage in his pantry to see the Cuban rum and bag of sugar he had put away. The most crudely touched-up photographs were circulated, depicting him dressed as Bacchus with a garland of grapes around his head, cavorting with opulent matrons and athletes of his own sex in a perpetual orgy. No one, not even Senator Trueba, believed they were authentic. "This is too much, this time they've gone too far," he muttered when he saw them.

With a stroke of the pen the military changed world history, erasing every incident, ideology, and historical figure of which the regime disapproved. They adjusted the maps because there was no reason why the North should be placed on top, so far away from their beloved fatherland, when it could be placed on the bottom, where it would appear in a more favorable light; and while they were at it they painted vast areas of Prussian-blue territorial waters that stretched all the way to Africa and Asia, and appropriated distant countries in the geography books, leaping borders with impunity until the neighboring countries lost their patience, sought help from the United Nations, and threatened to send in tanks and planes. Censorship, which at first covered only the mass media, was soon extended to textbooks, song lyrics, movie scripts, and even private conversation. There were words prohibited by military decree, such as the word *"compañero,"* and others that could not be mentioned even though no edict had swept them from the lexicon, such as "freedom," "justice" and "trade union." Alba wondered where so many Fascists had come from overnight, because in the country's long democratic history they had not been particularly noticeable, except for a few who got carried away during World War II and thought it amusing to parade in black shirts with their arms raised in salute—to the laughter and hissing of bystanders—and had never won any important role in the life of the country. Nor did she understand the attitude of the armed forces, most of whom came from the middle and working class and had traditionally been closer to the left than to the far right. She did not understand the state of civil war, nor did she realize that war is the soldiers' work of art, the culmination of all their training, the gold medal of their profession. Soldiers are not made to shine in times of peace. The coup gave them a chance to put into practice what they had learned in their barracks: blind obedience, the use of arms, and other skills that soldiers can master once they silence the scruples of their hearts.

Alba abandoned her studies; the school of philosophy, like many others that open the gateway of the mind, was closed. Nor did she continue with her music, because her cello seemed frivolous to her under the circumstances. Many professors were fired, arrested, or simply disappeared, in accordance with a blacklist in the hands of the political police. Sebastián Gómez was killed in the first raid, betrayed by his own students. The university was filled with spies.

The upper middle class and the economic right, who had favored the coup, were euphoric. At first they were a little shocked when they saw the consequences of their action; they had never lived in a dictatorship and did not know what it was like. They thought the loss of democratic freedoms would be temporary and that it was possible to go without individual or collective rights for a while so long as the regime respected the tenets of free enterprise. Nor did they put much stock in international condemnation, which lumped them in the same category as the other tyrannies of the region, because it seemed a small price to pay for the defeat of Marxism. When foreign investment capital began to flow into the country, they naturally attributed it to the stability of the new regime, ignoring the fact that for every peso that entered the country, two were lost to interest. When almost all the national industries were gradually shut down and businesses were beginning to go bankrupt, defeated by the massive importation of consumer goods, they said that Brazilian stoves, Taiwanese cloth, and Japanese motorcycles were superior to anything that had ever been manufactured in the country. Only when the concessions of the mines were returned to the North American companies after three years of nationalization did a few voices suggest that this amounted to giving the country away wrapped in cellophane. But when the lands that the agrarian reform had parceled out were returned to their former owners, they were reassured: things were returning to the good old days. They realized that only a dictatorship could act with the necessary force and without accounting to the people to guarantee their privileges, so they stopped talking about politics and accepted the idea that they held economic power, but the military was going to rule. The right's only task was to advise the military in the elaboration of new edicts and new laws. Within days they had eliminated labor unions. The union leaders were either in jail or dead, political parties had been indefinitely recessed, and all student-worker organizations, and even professional associations, had been dismantled. Gatherings of any size were forbidden. The only place people could congregate was in church, so religion quickly became fashionable, and priests and nuns were forced to postpone their spiritual tasks in order to minister to the earthly needs of their lost flocks. The government and the business community began to view them as potential enemies, and some dreamt of resolving the problem by assassinating the cardinal when it was clear that the Pope in Rome had no intention of removing him from his post and sending him to an asylum for insane priests.

A large part of the middle class rejoiced at the military coup, because to them it signaled a return to law and order, to the beauty of tradition, skirts for women and short hair for men, but they soon began to suffer from the impact of high prices and the lack of jobs. Their salaries were not sufficient to buy food. There was someone to mourn for in every family, and the middle class could no longer say, as they had in the beginning, that if he was imprisoned, dead, or exiled it was because he deserved it. Nor could they go on denying the use of torture.

While luxury stores, miraculous finance companies, exotic restaurants, and import business were flourishing, the unemployed lined up outside factory gates waiting for a chance to work at the minimum wage. The labor force was reduced to slavery, and for the first time in many decades management was able to fire people at will without granting any severance pay and to have them thrown in jail for the slightest protest.

During the first months, Senator Trueba shared the opportunism of his class. He was convinced that a period of dictatorship was necessary to bring the country back into the fold it never should have left. He was one of the first landowners to regain his land. Tres Marías was returned to him in ruins but intact down to the last square yard. He had waited more than two years for this moment, nursing his anger. Without giving it a second thought he left for the countryside with half a dozen hired thugs to avenge himself to his heart's content against the peasants who had dared to defy him and rob him of his property. They arrived on a fine Sunday morning shortly before Christmas, entering the hacienda with all the clamor of a pirate crew. His men spread out, rounding people up with curses, blows, and kicks. Then they gathered humans and animals in the courtyard, poured gasoline on the little brick houses that had once been Trueba's pride and joy, and set fire to them and everything inside them. They shot the animals to death. They burned the fields, the chicken coops, the bicycles, and even the cradles of newborn babies, in a noontime witches' Sabbath that nearly made Trueba die of joy. He dismissed all the tenants, warning them that if he ever caught them prowling around his property they would suffer the same fate as their animals. He watched them depart poorer than ever in a long, sad procession, with their children, their old people, and the few dogs that had survived the shooting, and some chickens saved from the inferno, dragging their feet along the dusty road that led away from the land where they had lived for generations. At the gate to Tres Marías there was a group of wretched people waiting with anxious eyes. They were peasants who had also been expelled from their hacienda, arriving as humbly as their ancestors of the preceding century to beg the *patrón* to give them work in the coming harvest.

That night Esteban Trueba lay down in the iron bed that had belonged to his parents, in the old main house where he had not slept in years. He was tired. The smell of the fire, and the animals that had had to be burned so that their rotting corpses would not infect the air, clung to his nostrils. The remains of the little houses were still burning; everywhere around him was death and destruction. But he knew that he could restore the land again, just as he had once before, because the pastures were intact and so was his strength. Despite the pleasure of his revenge, he was unable to sleep. He felt like a father who has punished his children too severely. All that night he kept recalling the faces of the peasants, whom he had seen come into this world on his property, as they moved off along the highway. He cursed his bad temper. Nor was he able to sleep well the rest of that week, and when he finally did he dreamt of Rosa. He decided not to tell anyone what he had done, and promised himself that Tres Marias would again become the model farm it had once been. He let it be known that he was willing to have his tenants back—under certain conditions, of course—but none of them returned. They had scattered through the countryside, across the mountains and along the coast. Some had walked all the way to the mines, others to the islands of the South, all of them seeking their families' daily bread wherever they could find it. Disgusted with himself, the *patrón* returned to the city, feeling older than ever. His soul weighed heavy.

The Poet was dying in his house by the sea. He had been ailing, and the recent events had exhausted his desire to go on living. Soldiers broke into his house, ransacked his snail collection, his shells, his butterflies, his bottles, the ship figureheads he had rescued from so many seas, his books, his paintings, and his unfinished poems, looking for subversive weapons and hidden Communists, until his old poet's heart began to falter. They took him to the capital, where he died four days later. The last words of this man who had sung to life were: "They're going to shoot them! They're going to shoot them!" Not one of his friends could be with him at the hour of his death; they were all outlaws, fugitives, exiles, or dead. His blue house on the hill lay half in ruins, its floor burnt and its windows broken. No one knew if it was the work of the military, as the neighbors said, or of the neighbors, as the military said. A wake was held by those few who were brave enough to attend, along with journalists from all over the world who came to cover his funeral. Senator Trueba was his ideological enemy, but he had often had him in his house and knew his poetry by heart. He appeared at the wake dressed in rigorous black, with his granddaughter Alba. Both stood watch beside the simple wooden coffin and accompanied it to the cemetery on that unfortunate morning. Alba was holding a bouquet of the first carnations of the season, as red as blood. The small cortege walked on foot, slowly, all the way to the cemetery, between two rows of soldiers who had cordoned off the streets.

People went in silence. Suddenly, someone hoarsely called out the Poet's name and in a single voice everyone replied, "Here! Now and forever!" It was as if they had opened a valve and all the pain, fear, and anger of those days had issued from their chests and rolled onto the street, rising in a terrible shout to the thick black clouds above. Another shouted, "*Compañero* President!" and everyone answered in a single wail, the way men grieve: "Here! Now and forever!" The Poet's funeral had turned into the symbolic burial of freedom.

The cameramen of Swedish television were filming close by Alba and her grandfather, to send back to Nobel's frozen land the terrifying image of machine guns posted on both sides of the street, people's faces, the flower-covered coffin, as well as the silent group of women clustered in the doorway of the morgue, two blocks from the cemetery, reading the names on the lists of dead. Voices mingled in a single chant and the air filled with forbidden slogans as, face to face with the guns that were shaking in the soldiers' hands, they shouted that the people united would never be defeated. The cortège passed in front of a construction site and the workers dropped their tools, removed their helmets, and, with bowed heads, formed a single line. A man with a shirt frayed at the cuffs, without a jacket and wearing broken shoes, marched along reciting the Poet's most revolutionary poems, his grief streaming down his face. Senator Trueba gazed at him in astonishment.

"It's a shame he was a Communist!" the senator told his granddaughter. "Such a fine poet, and such confused ideas! If he had died before the coup, I suppose he would have received a national tribute."

"He knew how to die, just as he knew how to live, Grandfather," Alba replied.

She was convinced that he had died at the proper time, because no tribute could have been any greater than this modest procession of a handful of men and women who lowered him into a borrowed grave, shouting his verses of freedom and justice for the last time. Two days later a notice from the military junta appeared in the papers, decreeing national mourning for the Poet and authorizing those who wanted to do so to fly the flag at half-mast in front of their houses. The permission was valid from the moment of his death until the day the notice appeared.

In the same way that she could not sit down to mourn her Uncle Jaime, Alba could not lose her head thinking of Miguel or grieving for the Poet. She was absorbed in the task of tracking down the disappeared, comforting the victims of torture who returned with their backs flayed and their eyes unfocused, and searching for food for the priests' soup kitchens. Still, in the silence of the night, when the city lost its stage-set normality and operetta peace, she was besieged by the agonizing thoughts she had repressed during the day. At that time of night, the only traffic consisted of trucks filled with bodies and detainees, and police cars that roamed the streets like lost wolves howling in the darkness of the curfew. Alba shook in her bed. She saw the ghosts of all those unknown dead, heard the great house pant with the labored breath of an old woman. Her hearing sharpened and she felt the dreadful noises in her bones: a distant screeching of brakes, the slam of a door, gunfire, the crush of boots, a muffled scream. Then the long silence would return, lasting until dawn, when the city reawakened and the sun seemed to erase the terrors of the night. She was not the only one in the house who lay awake at night. She often came upon her grandfather in his nightshirt and slippers, older and sadder than during the day, heating up a cup of bouillon and muttering the curses of a buccaneer because his bones and his soul were killing him. Her mother also rummaged in the kitchen or walked like some midnight apparition through the empty rooms.

Thus the months went by, and it became clear to everyone, even Senator Trueba, that the military had seized power to keep it for themselves and not to hand the country over to the politicians of the right who had made the coup possible. The military were a breed apart, brothers who spoke a different dialect from the civilians and with whom any attempt at dialogue would be a conversation of the deaf, because the slightest dissent was considered treason in their rigid honor code. Trueba realized that they had messianic plans that did not include the politicians. One day he was discussing the situation with Blanca and Alba. He expressed his regret that the Army's action, whose purpose had been to eliminate the threat of a Marxist dictatorship, had condemned the country to a dictatorship far more severe, one that, to all evidence, was fated to last a century. For the first time in his life, Senator Trueba admitted he had made a mistake. Sunk in his armchair like an old man at the end of his days, they saw him shed silent tears. He was not crying because he had lost power. He was crying for his country.

Then Blanca knelt beside him and took his hand. She confessed that Pedro Tercero was living like a hermit in one of the abandoned rooms Clara had had built in the time of the spirits. The day after the coup, the lists of people who were supposed to present themselves to the authorities had been published and the name of Pedro Tercero García was among them. There were some who, convinced that in their country nothing like this could ever happen, had gone on their own to surrender to the Ministry of Defense and had paid for it with their lives. But Pedro Tercero had had a premonition of the ferocity of the new regime long before anyone else, perhaps because during those three years he had come to know the armed forces and no longer believed that they were any different from those elsewhere in the world. That same night, while the curfew was in force, he had crawled to the big house on the corner and knocked at Blanca's window. When she looked out, her eyes blurred from her migraine, she did not recognize him because he had shaved his beard and was wearing spectacles.

"They've killed the President," Pedro Tercero said.

She hid him in one of the empty rooms. She set up an emergency refuge, never thinking that she would have to keep him hidden for several months while the soldiers combed the country looking for him.

Blanca assumed that it would occur to no one to think that Pedro Tercero García was in Senator Trueba's house at the very moment when the senator was attending the Te Deum in the cathedral. It was the happiest period in Blanca's life.

But for Pedro Tercero the hours passed as slowly as if he were in jail. He spent his day shut within four walls behind a locked door, so that no one would happen to walk in to clean his room, and with the blinds lowered and the curtains drawn. Daylight could not come in, but he was able to recognize it by the tenuous change in the cracks of the blinds. At night he opened the window as wide as he could to air out the room—where he had to keep a covered pail in which to relieve himself—and to inhale great mouthfuls of the air of freedom. He spent his time reading Jaime's books, which Blanca brought him on the sly, and listening to the street sounds and to the whisper of the radio, which he kept at the lowest volume. Blanca managed to bring him a guitar and stuffed some rags beneath the strings so no one would hear him composing muted songs of widows, orphans, prisoners, and the disappeared. He tried to work out a schedule to organize his day. He did calisthenics, read, studied English, took a siesta, wrote music, and did some more calisthenics, but even with all this he had endless amounts of spare time until he finally heard the key turn in the lock and saw Blanca coming through the door with newspapers, food, and clean water for him to wash with. They made love desperately, inventing forbidden formulas that fear and passion transformed into wild journeys to the stars. Blanca had already resigned herself to chastity, middle age, and her various aches and pains, but the shock of love had brought her a new youth. The sheen of her skin, the rhythm of her gait, and the cadence of her voice all became more pronounced. She smiled inwardly and walked around like a woman asleep. She had never been more beautiful. Even her father noticed, attributing it to the peace of abundance. "Ever since Blanca stopped having to stand in line, she looks like a new woman," Senator Trueba remarked. Alba also noticed it. She watched her mother. Her strange somnambulism seemed suspicious to her, as did her new mania for taking food to her room. On more than one occasion, she set out to spy on her during the night, but she was overcome by the fatigue of her own many acts of consolation, and when she had insomnia she was afraid to venture into the empty rooms that were full of whispering ghosts.

Pedro Tercero grew thin and lost the good humor and sweetness that had characterized him up till then. He was bored. He cursed his voluntary imprisonment, and raged impatiently for news of his friends. Only Blanca's presence could pacify him. When she entered the room, he hurled himself upon her like a madman to calm the terrors of the day and the tedium of his weeks. He began to be obsessed by the idea that he was a coward and a traitor for not having shared the fate of so many others, and felt that it would be more honorable to surrender and meet his fate. Blanca tried to dissuade him with the best of arguments, but he seemed not to hear her. She tried to hold him back with the force of her newfound love, fed him with her hands, bathed him by rubbing him with a damp cloth and dusting him with powder like an infant, cut his hair and fingernails, and even shaved him. Finally she had no choice but to put tranquilizers in his food and sleeping pills in his water, which stunned him into a profound, tormented sleep, from which he would awake with a dry mouth and a sadder heart. After a few months Blanca realized that she could not hold him prisoner indefinitely and gave up her plans to reduce his spirit in order to make him her permanent lover. She understood that he was being eaten up alive because for him freedom was even more important than love, and that there were no magic pills that would make him change his mind.

"Help me, Father!" Blanca begged Senator Trueba. "I have to get him out of the country."

The old man was paralyzed with bewilderment, recognizing how worn out he was, when he tried to summon up his fury and his hatred and was unable to find them. He thought of the peasant who had shared his daughter's love for half a century and was unable to find a single reason for detesting him, not even his poncho, his Socialist beard, his tenacity, or his damned fox-chasing hens.

"Hell!" he exclaimed. "We'll have to get him asylum, because if they find him here we'll all be screwed" was all he could think to say.

Blanca threw her arms around his neck and covered him with kisses, weeping like a child. It was the first spontaneous hug she had given her father since her most remote childhood.

"I can get him into an embassy," Alba said. "But we have to wait for the right moment and he'll have to leap over a wall."

"That won't be necessary, my dear," Senator Trueba replied. "I still have some influential friends in this country."

Forty-eight hours later the door to Pedro Tercero García's room swung open. This time, instead of Blanca, Senator Trueba was standing in the doorway. The fugitive thought his final hour had arrived and, in a strange way, he was happy.

"I've come to get you out of here," Trueba said.

"Why?" Pedro Tercero asked.

"Because Blanca asked me to," the other answered.

"Go to hell," Pedro Tercero said.

"Fine, that's where we're going. You're coming with me."

The two of them smiled simultaneously. The silver limousine of a Nordic ambassador was waiting in the courtyard. Pedro Tercero was put in the trunk of the car, curled up like a package, and covered with market baskets full of fruit and vegetables. Blanca, Alba, Senator Trueba, and their friend the ambassador rode inside the car. The chauffeur drove them to the residence of the Papal Nuncio, passing in front of a police barricade without anyone attempting to stop them. There was a double guard stationed at the nunciature gate, but when they recognized Senator Trueba and saw the diplomatic plates on the car, they let them in with a salute. Behind the gate, safely within the seat of the Vatican, they let Pedro Tercero out from under a mountain of lettuce leaves and bruised tomatoes. They led him to the office of the Nuncio, who was waiting for him dressed in his bishop's cassock and holding a new safe-conduct pass that would allow him to go abroad with Blanca, who had decided to live out in exile the love she had postponed since her childhood. The Nuncio welcomed them. He was an admirer of Pedro Tercero García and had all his records.

While the priest and the Nordic ambassador discussed the international situation, the family said goodbye. Blanca and Alba wept disconsolately. They had never been separated before. Esteban Trueba gave his daughter a long hug. He did not cry, but his mouth was clamped shut and he shook from the effort of holding back his sobs.

"I haven't been a good father to you, my dear," he said. "Do you think you'll ever be able to forgive me and forget the past?"

"I love you so much, Papa!" Blanca wept, throwing her arms around his neck, clasping him to her ardently, and covering his face with kisses.

After that the old man turned to Pedro Tercero and looked him in the eye. He stretched out his hand, but he did not know how to shake Pedro's hand because it was missing several fingers. Instead, he opened his arms and the two men said goodbye in a tight knot, free at last of the hatred and rancor that had poisoned their lives for so many years.

"I'll take good care of your daughter and I will try to make her happy," Pedro Tercero García said, his voice breaking.

"I have no doubt of that. Go in peace, my children," the old man murmured.

He knew he would never see them again.

Senator Trueba was left alone in the house with his granddaughter and a few remaining servants. At least that was what he thought. But Alba had decided to adopt her mother's plan and was using the abandoned wing of the house to hide people for a night or two until she found a safer place or a way to get them out of the country. She helped those who lived in shadow, fleeing by day and mingling with the bustle of the city, but who had to be hidden by nightfall, always in a different place. The most dangerous time was during the curfew, when fugitives could not be out on the street and the police could hunt them down at will. Alba thought her grandfather's house was the last place they would search. Slowly but surely she transformed the empty rooms into a labyrinth of secret nooks where she hid those she took under her wing, sometimes whole families. Senator Trueba used only the library, the bathroom, and his bedroom. There he lived surrounded by his mahogany furniture, his Victorian glass cabinets, and his Persian carpets. Even for a man so little given to intuition as he was, the dark mansion was disquieting: it seemed to hold a hidden monster. Trueba could not understand the reason for his uneasiness, because he knew that the strange noises the servants said they heard were made by Clara as she wandered through the house in the company of her spirit friends. He had often come upon his wife gliding through the sitting rooms, in her white tunic, with her young girl's laugh. He pretended not to see her, not moving and even holding his breath so as not to frighten her. If he closed his eyes and pretended to be asleep, he could feel her fingers gently stroking his forehead, her fresh breath touching him like a breeze, her hair brushing against his hand. He had no reason to suspect anything irregular, and yet he tried not to venture into the enchanted realm that belonged to his wife. The farthest he went was the neutral zone of the kitchen. His old cook had left because her husband had been accidentally shot, and her only son, who as doing his military service in a village in the South, had been hanged from a post with his guts wrapped around his neck, the people's revenge for his having carried out the orders of his superiors. The poor woman had lost her mind and soon afterward Trueba lost his patience, fed up with finding in his food the hairs she had torn from her head in her unending grief. For a while, Alba experimented with the pots, using a cookbook, but despite her good intentions Trueba wound up dining almost every night at his club, so he could have at least one decent meal a day. That gave Alba greater freedom for her traffic in fugitives and greater safety for bringing people in, and taking them out of the house before curfew, without her grandfather suspecting.

One day Miguel appeared. She was entering the house in the broad light of the siesta hour when he came walking toward her. He had been waiting for her hidden in the thick weeds of the garden. He had dyed his hair pale yellow and was wearing a blue checked suit. He looked like an ordinary bank employee, but Alba recognized him immediately and was unable to stifle the shout of joy that rose up from within her. They embraced in the garden, in view of the passersby and anyone who cared to look, until they came to their senses and understood how dangerous it was. Alba led him inside the house, to her bedroom. They fell onto the bed in a knot of arms and legs, each calling the other by the secret names they had used in the days of the basement. They made love impatiently until they felt that the very life was flowing out of them and their souls were bursting. Then they were forced to lie quiet, listening to the pounding of their hearts, in order to calm down a little. Looking at him for the first time, Alba saw that she had been cavorting with what looked like a total stranger, who not only had the hair of a Viking but also lacked the beard of Miguel and his small round schoolmaster's spectacles, and seemed much thinner. "You look horrible!" she whispered in his ear. Miguel had become one of the guerrilla leaders, fulfilling the destiny he had been moving toward ever since he was a teenager. Many men and women had been interrogated to find out his whereabouts, a fact which weighed on Alba's spirit like a millstone, but for him it was simply another part of the horror of war, and he was prepared to suffer the same fate when the moment came to cover up for others. Meanwhile, he fought clandestinely, faithful to his theory that the violence of the rich must be met by the violence of the people. Alba, who had imagined a thousand times over that he was a prisoner or that he had been put to death in the most dreadful manner, wept with joy as she savored his scent, his texture, his voice, his warmth, the brush of his hands—callused from handling weapons and the habit of crawling on all fours—praying, cursing, and kissing him at the same time that she hated him for all the accumulated suffering and wished she could die there on the spot so she would never have to feel his absence again.

"You were right, Miguel," Alba said, burying her face in his shoulder. "Everything happened exactly as you said."

Then she told him of the weapons she had stolen from her grandfather and hidden with her Uncle Jaime, and she offered to take him to look for them. She would also have liked to give him those she had been unable to steal, which had remained in the house, but a few days after the coup the civilian population had been ordered to surrender anything that could pass for arms, from scout knives to children's penknives. People had left their little bundles wrapped in newspaper at the doors of the churches, because they were afraid to take them to the barracks, but Senator Trueba, who had real weapons in his possession, was not the least bit worried; his had been stockpiled for killing Communists, as everybody knew. He called up his friend General Hurtado, who sent a truck to pick them up. Trueba led the soldiers to his personal arsenal, and, mute with surprise, was amazed to find that half the boxes were filled with stones and straw, but he realized that if he admitted to the loss he would be compromising a member of his own family or getting himself into a jam. He began to make apologies, which no one paid any attention to, since the soldiers could hardly know how many weapons he had purchased. He suspected Blanca and Pedro Tercero García, but his granddaughter's flushed cheeks also made him wonder. After the soldiers had removed the boxes, handing him a signed receipt, he took Alba by the shoulders and shook her as he never had before, to make her confess that she had something to do with the missing machine guns and rifles.

"Don't ask me questions you don't want to know the answer to," Alba replied, looking him in the eye. They never spoke of the matter again.

"Your grandfather is a bastard, Alba," Miguel told her. "Someday someone will kill him and give him what he deserves."

"He'll die in bed. He's very old now," Alba said.

"He who lives by the sword must die by the sword. Maybe I'll kill him myself one of these days."

"God forbid, Miguel, because then I'd have to do the same to you," Alba answered fervently.

Miguel explained to her that they would not be able to see each other for a long while, perhaps never again. He tried to make her understand the danger of being the woman of a guerrilla, even if she was protected by her grandfather's name, but she wept so and hugged him with such anxiety that he was forced to promise her that they would find a way to meet from time to time, even at the risk of their lives. Miguel also agreed to go with her and dig up the guns and ammunition buried in the mountains, because that was what he most needed in his reckless fight.

"I hope they haven't rusted in the ground," Alba murmured. "And that I'll be able to remember exactly where we hid them, because it was more than a year ago."

Two weeks later, Alba organized an outing for the children from the soup kitchen. They used a truck they were lent by the parish priests. She carried baskets of food, a bag of oranges, balls, and a guitar. None of the children paid attention when she stopped along the way to pick up a blond man. Alba drove the heavy van with its load of children along the same mountain route she had followed with her Uncle Jaime. She was stopped by two patrols and had to open all the food baskets, but the children's contagious gaiety and the innocent contents of the baskets sent all suspicion flying. They arrived calmly at the place where the arms were buried. The children played hide-and-seek. Miguel organized a football match. Then he sat them in a circle and told them stories, and afterward they all sang until they were hoarse. Later he sketched a map of the site to enable him to return with his comrades under cover of darkness. It was a happy day in the country, during which they were able to forget for a few hours the tension of the state of war and enjoy the warm mountain sun, listening to the children's shouts as they raced among the rocks, their stomachs full for the first time in months.

"I'm scared, Miguel," Alba said. "Aren't we ever going to be able to lead a normal life? Why don't we go abroad? Why don't we escape now, while we still can?"

Miguel pointed to the children, and Alba understood what he meant.

"Then let me go with you!" she begged, as she had so many times before.

"Right now we can't take someone who hasn't been trained. Much less a girl in love." Miguel smiled. "It's more important for you to continue what you're doing. These poor kids need all the help they can get until things get better."

"At least tell me how to find you!"

"If the police ever get hold of you, it's better if you don't know anything," Miguel replied.

She shuddered.

During the following months, Alba began to sell the furniture in the house. At first she dared to take only what was in the abandoned rooms and the basement, but when she had sold everything there she took the antique chairs from the drawing room, one by one, the baroque room dividers, the colonial chests, the engraved screens, and even the dining-room linens. Trueba noticed, but said nothing. He supposed that his granddaughter was giving the money to a forbidden cause, just as he imagined she had done with the weapons she had stolen, but he preferred not to know about it in order to retain his precarious stability in a world that was crumbling beneath his feet. He realized that all he really cared about was losing his granddaughter, because she was his last link to life. This was why he also said nothing when she took the paintings from the walls and the antique carpets to sell them to the nouveaux riches. He felt very old and tired, and did not have the strength to fight. His ideas were not as clear as they had been and the line between what was good and what was bad had blurred. During the night, when he was overcome by sleep, he had nightmares of small brick houses in flames. He thought that if his only heir was going to squander his fortune, he would do nothing to stop her, because he was going to be in his grave soon and all he would take with him was his shroud. Alba tried to speak to him, to explain what she was doing, but the old man refused to hear the story of the starving children who received a dish of charity with the profit from his Aubusson tapestry, or the unemployed who were able to last another week thanks to his jade Chinese dragon. All this, he continued to maintain, was a monstrous Communist lie; but in the remote event that it was true, it would still not be Alba's responsibility to shoulder the burden, but the government's or, as a last resort, the Church's. Nevertheless, the day he came home and did not see Clara's portrait hanging in the entry, he decided that matters had gone too far and confronted his granddaughter.

"Where the devil is the portrait of your grandmother?" he lowered.

"I sold it to the British consul. He told me he would put it in a museum in London."

"I forbid you to take another thing out of this house! Starting tomorrow, you'll have your own bank account, for pin money," he said.

Esteban Trueba soon saw that Alba was the most expensive woman of his life, and that a whole harem would have cost him less than that green-haired granddaughter. He never reproached her, for his good luck had returned and the more he spent the more he had. After political activity had been forbidden, he had more time for his business matters, and he calculated that, against all his predictions, he was going to die a very rich man. He placed his money in the new investment houses that promised to multiply money overnight. He discovered that being rich was terribly annoying because it was so easy to make money and so difficult to find an incentive for spending it. Not even his granddaughter's prodigious talent for extravagance was able to make a dent in his purse. He enthusiastically embarked on the reconstruction and improvement of Tres Marías, but after that he lost all interest in any other endeavor because he noticed that, thanks to the new economic system, there was no need to work hard and produce, inasmuch as money makes money and his bank accounts grew fatter every day without the slightest effort on his part. Thus, tallying up his accounts, he took a step he had never thought he would take in his life: once a month he sent a check to Pedro Tercero García, who was living with Blanca in exile in Canada, where they both felt completely fulfilled in the peace of satisfied love. Pedro Tercero composed revolutionary songs for workers, students, and, above all, the upper middle class, which had made his music, successfully translated into French and English, their own despite the fact that chickens and foxes are underdeveloped creatures that lack the zoological splendor of the eagles and wolves of that frozen country of the North. Meanwhile, placid and happy, Blanca was in splendid health for the first time in her life. She set up an enormous kiln in her house to fire her crèches of monsters, which sold extremely well as examples of indigenous folk art, just as Jean de Satigny had predicted twenty-five years earlier, when he had wanted to export them. The combination of this business, her father's checks, and assistance from the Canadian government gave them more than enough to live on. Just to be on the safe side, however, Blanca hid the woolen sock with Clara's jewels in the most secret place she could find. She hoped that she would never have to sell them, and that one day they would shine for Alba.

Esteban Trueba never knew that the political police had his house under surveillance until the night they came for Alba.

They were both asleep, and by sheer chance there was no one hidden in the labyrinth of empty rooms in the back of the house. The slam of rifle butts against the door shook the old man from his sleep with a clear foreboding of misfortune. But Alba had already been awakened by the sound of brakes, the loud footsteps, and the hushed orders, and had begun to dress herself, because she had no doubt that her time had come.

Throughout these months, the senator had learned that not even his own record as a supporter of the coup was any guarantee against terror. But he had never imagined that he would see a dozen plainclothesmen break into his house under cover of curfew, armed to the teeth, to drag him from his bed and push him into the sitting room, without even allowing him to put on his slippers or throw a shawl over his shoulders. He saw them kick open Alba's bedroom door and storm in with machine guns in their hands, and he saw his granddaughter waiting for them; she was already dressed, and though her face was pale, she looked serene. He saw them push her out and take her at gunpoint to the drawing room, where they ordered her to stand beside him and not move. She obeyed without saying a word, oblivious to her grandfather's anger and the violence of the men who were ransacking the house, kicking down doors, rifling wardrobes, knocking over furniture, ripping open mattresses, emptying dresser drawers, kicking the walls, and shouting orders in their search for hidden guerrillas, contraband weapons, and any other evidence they could find. They pulled the maids from their beds and locked them in a room where an armed man stood guard. They ransacked the bookshelves in the study, sending the senator's bibelots and works of art crashing to the floor. The books from Jaime's den were piled in the courtyard, doused with gasoline, and set on fire in an infamous pyre that was fed with the magic books from the enchanted trunks of Great-Uncle Marcos, the remaining copies of Nicolás's esoteric treatise, the leather-bound set of the complete works of Marx, and even Trueba's opera scores, producing a scandalous bonfire that filled the neighborhood with smoke and that, in normal times, would have brought fire trucks from every direction.

"Hand over all your notebooks, your address books, your checkbooks, and all your personal documents!" shouted the man who seemed to be in charge.

"I'm Senator Trueba! For God's sake, don't you recognize me?" the grandfather shrieked in desperation. "You can't do this to me! This is an outrage! I'm a friend of General Hurtado's!"

"Shut up, you old shit! You don't open your mouth until I tell you to!" the man replied brutally.

They forced him to surrender the contents of his desk, and put everything that interested them into paper bags. While one group finished checking the house, another continued throwing books out the window. Four smiling, mocking, threatening men remained in the drawing room. They put their feet up on the furniture, drank the senator's Scotch straight from the bottle, and broke his classical records one by one. Alba calculated that at least two hours had passed. She was shaking, but not from cold—from fear. She had supposed this moment would come one day, but she had always had the irrational hope that somehow her grandfather's influence would protect her. At the sight of him sitting fearfully on the sofa, tiny and wretched as a sick old man, she understood that she could expect no help.

"Sign here!" the man in charge ordered Trueba, shoving a piece of paper in his face. "It's a declaration that we entered with a court order, showed you our identification cards, and that everything proceeded properly, with all due respect and proper manners, and that you have no complaints. Sign it!"

"I'll never sign this!" the old man shouted furiously.

The man spun around and slapped Alba in the face, a blow that knocked her to the floor. Senator Trueba was paralyzed with terror and surprise. He realized that his hour of truth was finally upon him, after living almost ninety years as his own boss.

"Did you know that your granddaughter is the whore of a guerrilla?" the man asked.

Dejected, Senator Trueba signed the paper. Then he painfully made his way to his granddaughter and put his arms around her, caressing her hair with unaccustomed tenderness.

"Don't worry, my dear. Everything will turn out fine. They can't do anything to you. This is all a terrible mistake," he murmured. "Be calm."

But the man shoved them apart and shouted to the others that it was time to go. Two of the men took Alba out, practically lifting her off the floor. The last thing she saw was the pathetic figure of her grandfather, pale as wax, trembling in his nightshirt and shoeless, promising her from the doorway that the next day he would get her out, that he would go to speak with General Hurtado, that he would take his lawyers to find her wherever they took her, that he would bring her home.

They lifted her into a van alongside the man who had hit her and another who was whistling at the wheel. Before they put adhesive tape over her eyelids, she looked back one last time at the empty, silent street, surprised that despite the uproar and burning books not a single neighbor had stuck his head out to see what was going on. She supposed that, just as she had done so many times herself, they were peering through the chinks of their venetian blinds and the space between their curtains, or else they had put pillows over their heads so they would not have to know what was going on. The van started to move. Blind for the first time in her life, she lost all sense of time and space. She felt a large, wet hand on her leg, kneading, pinching, climbing, and exploring, and then a heavy breath on her face whispering, "I'm going to warm you up, whore, you'll see," and other voices and laughter, while the van turned and turned in what seemed to her an endless ride. She did not know where they were taking her until she heard the rush of water and felt the wheels of the van cross planks of wood. Then she knew her destiny. She invoked the spirits of the days of the three-legged table and her grandmother's restless sugar bowl, and all the spirits capable of bending the course of events, but they appeared to have abandoned her, for the van continued on its way. She felt it brake, heard the heavy doors of a gate squeak open and shut behind them after they drove through. It was then that Alba entered the nightmare that her grandmother had apparently not seen on her astrological chart when she was born, and that Luisa Mora had seen in a fleeting premonition. The men helped her down. She had not taken two steps before she felt the first blow strike her ribs and she fell on her knees, the breath knocked out of her. Two men lifted her by the armpits and dragged her a long way. She felt the earth beneath her feet and then the harsh surface of a cement floor. They stopped.

"This is Senator Trueba's granddaughter, Colonel," she heard one say.

"So I see," another man replied.

Alba immediately recognized the voice of Esteban García. At that moment she understood that he had been waiting for her ever since the distant day when he had sat her on his knees, when she was just a child.

FOURTEEN

The Hour of Truth

Alba was curled up in the darkness. They had ripped the tape from her eyes and replaced it with a tight bandage. She was afraid. As she recalled her Uncle Nicolás's training, and his warning about the danger of being afraid of fear, she concentrated on trying to control the shaking of her body and shutting her ears to the terrifying sounds that reached her side. She tried to visualize her happiest moments with Miguel, groping for a means to outwit time and find the strength for what she knew lay ahead. She told herself that she had to endure a few hours without her nerves betraying her, until her grandfather was able to set in motion the heavy machinery of his power and influence to get her out of there. She searched her memory for a trip to the coast with Miguel, in autumn, long before the hurricane of events had turned the world upside down, when things were still called by familiar names and words had a single meaning; when people, freedom, and *compañero* were just that—people, freedom, and *compañero*—and had not yet become passwords. She tried to relive that moment—the damp red earth and the intense scent of the pine and eucalyptus forests in which a carpet of dry leaves lay steeping after the long hot summer and where the coppery sunlight filtered down through the treetops. She tried to recall the cold, the silence, and that precious feeling of owning the world, of being twenty years old and having her whole life ahead of her, of making love slowly and calmly, drunk with the scent of the forest and their love, without a past, without suspecting the future, with just the incredible richness of that present moment in which they stared at each other, smelled each other, kissed each other, and explored each other's bodies, wrapped in the whisper of the wind among the trees and the sound of the nearby waves breaking against the rocks at the foot of the cliff, exploding in a crash of pungent surf, and the two of them embracing underneath a single poncho like Siamese twins, laughing and swearing that this would last forever, that they were the only ones in the whole world who had discovered love.

Alba heard the screams, the long moans, and the radio playing full blast. The woods, Miguel, and love were lost in the deep well of her terror and she resigned herself to facing her fate without subterfuge.

She calculated that a whole night and the better part of the following day had passed when the door was finally opened and two men took her from her cell. With insults and threats they led her in to Colonel García, whom she could recognize blindfolded by his habitual cruelty, even before he opened his mouth. She felt his hands take her face, his thick fingers touch her ears and neck.

"Now you're going to tell me where your lover is," he told her. "That will save us both a lot of unpleasantness."

Alba breathed a sigh of relief. That meant they had not arrested Miguel!

"I want to go to the bathroom," Alba said in the strongest voice she could summon up.

"I see you're not planning to cooperate, Alba. That's too bad." García sighed. "The boys will have to do their job. I can't stand in their way."

There was a brief silence and she made a superhuman effort to remember the pine forest and Miguel's love, but her ideas got tangled up and she no longer knew if she was dreaming or where this stench of sweat, excrement, blood, and urine was coming from, or the radio announcer describing some Finnish goals that had nothing to do with her in the middle of other, nearer, more clearly audible shouts. A brutal slap knocked her to the floor. Violent hands lifted her to her feet. Ferocious fingers fastened themselves to her breasts, crushing her nipples. She was completely overcome by fear. Strange voices pressed in on her. She heard Miguel's name but did not know what they were asking her, and kept repeating a monumental *no* while they beat her, manhandled her, pulled off her blouse, and she could no longer think, could only say *no, no,* and *no* and calculate how much longer she could resist before her strength gave out, not knowing this was only the beginning, until she felt herself begin to faint and the men left her alone, lying on the floor, for what seemed to her a very short time.

She soon heard García's voice again and guessed it was his hands that were helping her to her feet, leading her toward a chair, straightening her clothes, and buttoning her blouse.

"My God!" he said. "Look what they've done to you! I warned you, Alba. Try to relax now, I'm going to give you a cup of coffee."

Alba began to cry. The warm liquid brought her back to life, but she could not taste it because when she swallowed it was mixed with blood. García held the cup, guiding it carefully toward her lips like a nurse.

"Do you want a cigarette?"

"I want to go to the bathroom," she said, pronouncing each syllable with difficulty with her swollen lips.

"Of course, Alba. They'll take you to the bathroom and then you can get some rest. I'm your friend. I understand your situation perfectly. You're in love, and that's why you want to protect him. I know you don't have anything to do with the guerrillas. But the boys don't believe me when I tell them. They won't be satisfied until you tell them where Miguel is. Actually they've already got him surrounded. They know exactly where he is. They'll catch him, but they want to be sure that you have nothing to do with the guerrillas. You understand? If you protect him and refuse to talk, they'll continue to suspect you. Tell them what they want to know and then I'll personally escort you home. You'll tell them, right?"

"I want to go to the bathroom," Alba repeated.

"I see you're just as stubborn as your grandfather. All right. You can go to the bathroom. I'm going to give you a chance to think things over," García said.

They took her to a toilet and she was forcd to ignore

the man who stood beside her, holding on to her arm. After that they returned her to her cell. In the tiny, solitary cube where she was being held, she tried to clarify her thoughts, but she was tortured by the pain of her beating, her thirst, the bandage pressing on her temples, the drone of the radio, the terror of approaching footsteps and her relief when they moved away, the shouts and the orders. She curled up like a fetus on the floor and surrendered to her pain. She remained in that position for hours, perhaps days. A man came twice to take her to the bathroom. He led her to a fetid lavatory where she was unable to wash because there was no water. He allowed her a minute, placing her on the toilet seat next to another person as silent and sluggish as herself. She could not tell if it was a woman or a man. At first she wept, wishing her Uncle Nicolás had given her a special course in how to withstand humiliation, which she found worse than pain, but she finally resigned herself to her own filth and stopped thinking about her unbearable need to wash. They gave her boiled corn, a small piece of chicken, and a bit of ice cream, which she identified by their taste, smell, and temperature, and which she wolfed down with her hands, astonished to be given such luxurious food, unexpected in a place like that. Afterward she learned that the food for the prisoners in that torture center was supplied by the new headquarters of the government, which was in an improvised building, since the old Presidential Palace was a pile of rubble.

She tried to count the days since she was first arrested, but her loneliness, the darkness, and her fear distorted her sense of time and space. She thought she saw caves filled with monsters. She imagined that she had been drugged and that was why her limbs were so weak and sluggish and why her ideas had grown so jumbled. She decided not to eat or drink anything, but hunger and thirst were stronger than her determination. She wondered why her grandfather still had not come to rescue her. In her rare moments of lucidity she understood that this was not a nightmare and that she was not there by mistake. She decided to forget everything she knew, even Miguel's name.

The third time they took her in to Esteban García, Alba was more prepared, because through the walls of her cell she could hear what was going on in the next room, where they were interrogating other prisoners, and she had no illusions. She did not even try to evoke the woods where she had shared the joy of love.

"Well, Alba, I've given you time to think things over. Now the two of us are going to talk and you're going to tell me where Miguel is and we're going to get this over with quickly," García said.

"I want to go to the bathroom," Alba answered.

"I see you're making fun of me, Alba," he said. "I'm sorry, but we don't have any time to waste."

Alba made no response.

"Take off your clothes!" García ordered in another voice.

She did not obey. They stripped her violently, pulling off her slacks despite her kicking. The memory of her adolescence and García's kiss in the garden gave her the strength of hatred. She struggled against him, until they got tired of beating her and gave her a short break, which she used to invoke the understanding spirits of her grandmother, so that they would help her die. But no one answered her call for help. Two hands lifted her up, and four laid her on a cold, hard metal cot with springs that hurt her back, and bound her wrists and ankles with leather thongs.

"For the last time, Alba. Where is Miguel?" García asked.

She shook her head in silence. They had tied her head down with another thong.

"When you're ready to talk, raise a finger," he said.

Alba heard another voice.

"I'll work the machine," it said.

Then she felt the atrocious pain that coursed through her body, filling it completely, and that she would never forget as long as she lived. She sank into darkness.

"Bastards! I told you to be careful with her!" she heard Esteban García say from far away. She felt them opening her eyelids, but all she saw was a misty brightness. Then she felt a prick in her arm and sank back into unconsciousness.

A century later Alba awoke wet and naked. She did not know if she was bathed with sweat, or water, or urine. She could not move, recalled nothing, and had no idea where she was or what had caused the intense pain that had reduced her to a heap of raw meat. She felt the thirst of the Sahara and called out for water.

"Wait, *companēra*," someone said beside her. "Wait until morning. If you drink water, you'll get convulsions, and you could die."

She opened her eyes. They were no longer bandaged. A vaguely familiar face was leaning over her, and hands were wrapping her in a blanket.

"Do you remember me? I'm Ana Díaz. We went to the university together. Don't you recognize me?"

Alba shook her head, closed her eyes, and surrendered to the sweet illusion of death. But she awakened a few hours later, and when she moved she realized that she ached to the last fiber of her body.

"You'll feel better soon," said a woman who was stroking her face and pushing away the locks of damp hair that hid her eyes. "Don't move, and try to relax. I'll be here next to you. You need to rest."

"What happened?" Alba whispered.

"They really roughed you up, *companēra*," the other woman said sadly.

"Who are you?" Alba asked.

"Ana Díaz. I've been here for a week. They also got my *companero*, Andrés, but he's still alive. I see him once a day, when they take them to the bathroom."

"Ana Díaz?" Alba murmured.

"That's right. We weren't so close back then, but it's never too late to start. The truth is, you're the last person I expected to meet here, Countess," the woman said gently. "Don't talk now. Try to sleep. That way the time will go faster for you. Your memory will gradually come back. Don't worry. It's because of the electricity."

But Alba was unable to sleep, for the door of her cell opened and a man walked in.

"Put the bandage back on her!" he ordered Ana Díaz.

"Please . . . Can't you see how weak she is? Let her rest a little while. . . ."

"Do as I say!"

Ana bent over the cot and put the bandage over her eyes. Then she removed the blanket and tried to dress her, but the guard pulled her away, lifted the prisoner by her arms, and sat her up. Another man came in to help him, and between them they carried her out because she could not walk. Alba was sure that she was dying, if she was not already dead. She could tell they were walking down a hallway in which the sound of their footsteps echoed. She felt a hand on her face, lifting her head.

"You can give her water. Wash her and give her another shot. See if she can swallow some coffee and bring her back to me," García said.

"Do you want us to dress her?"

"No."

Alba was in García's hands a long time. After a few days, he realized she had recognized him, but he did not abandon his precaution of keeping her blindfolded, even when they were alone. Every day new prisoners arrived and others were led away. Alba heard the vehicles, the shouts, and the gate being closed. She tried to keep track of the number of prisoners, but it was almost impossible. Ana Díaz thought there were close to two hundred. García was very busy, but he never let a day go by without seeing Alba, alternating unbridled violence with the pretense that he was her good friend. At times he appeared to be genuinely moved, personally spooning soup into her mouth, but the day he plunged her head into a bucket full of excrement until she fainted from disgust, Alba understood that he was not trying to learn Miguel's true whereabouts but to avenge himself for injuries that had been inflicted on him from birth, and that nothing she could confess would have any effect on her fate as the private prisoner of Colonel García. This allowed her to venture slowly out of the private circle of her terror. Her fear began to ebb and she was able to feel compassion for the others, for those they hung by their arms, for the newcomers, for the man whose shackled legs were run over by a truck. They brought all the prisoners into the courtyard at dawn and forced them to watch, because this was also a personal matter between the colonel and his prisoner. It was the first time Alba had opened her eyes outside the darkness of her cell, and the gentle splendor of the morning and the frost shining on the stones, where puddles of rain had collected overnight, seemed unbearably radiant to her. They dragged the man, who offered no resistance, out into the courtyard. He could not stand, and they left him lying on the ground. The guards had covered their faces with handkerchiefs so no one would ever be able to identify them in the improbable event that circumstances changed. Alba closed her eyes when she heard the truck's engine, but she could not close her ears to the sound of his howl, which stayed in her memory forever.

Ana Díaz helped her to resist while they were together. She was an indomitable woman. She had withstood every form of cruelty. They had raped her in the presence of her lover and tortured them together, but she had not lost her capacity to smile or her hope. She did not give in even when they transferred her to a secret clinic of the political police because one of the beatings had caused her to lose the child she was carrying and she had begun to hemorrhage.

"It doesn't matter," she told Alba when she returned to her cell. "Someday I'll have another one."

That night Alba heard her cry for the first time, covering her face with her blanket to suffocate her grief. She went to her and put her arms around her, rocking her and wiping her tears. She told her all the tender things she could think of, but that night there was no comfort for Ana Díaz, so Alba simply rocked her in her arms, lulling her to sleep like a tiny baby and wishing she could take on her shoulders the terrible pain of Ana's soul. Dawn found them huddled together like two small animals. During the day, they anxiously awaited the moment when the long line of men went by on their way to the latrine. They were blindfolded, and to guide themselves each had his hand on the shoulder of the man ahead of him, watched over by armed guards. Among the prisoners was Andrés. From the tiny barred window of their cell the women could see them, so close that if they had been able to reach out they could have touched them. Each time they passed, Ana and Alba sang with the strength of their despair, and female voices rose from the other cells. Then the prisoners would stand up tall, straighten their backs, and turn their heads in the direction of the women's cells, and Andrés would smile. His shirt was torn and covered with dried blood.

One of the guards was moved by the women's hymns. One night he brought them three carnations in a can of water to put in their window. Another time he came to tell Ana Díaz that he needed a volunteer to wash one of the prisoners' clothes and clean out his cell. He led her to where Andrés was and left them alone together for a few minutes. When Ana Díaz returned, she was transfigured. Alba did not dare speak to her, so as not to break the spell of her happiness.

One day Colonel García was surprised to find himself caressing Alba like a lover and talking to her of his childhood in the country, when he would see her walking hand in hand with her grandfather, dressed in her starched pinafores and with the green halo of her hair, while he, barefoot in the mud, swore that one day he would make her pay for her arrogance and avenge himself for his cursed bastard fate. Rigid and absent, naked and trembling with disgust and cold, Alba neither heard nor felt him, but that crack in his eagerness to torture her sounded an alarm in the colonel's mind. He ordered Alba to be thrown in the doghouse, and furiously prepared to forget that she existed.

The doghouse was a small, sealed cell like a dark, frozen, airless tomb. There were six of them altogether, constructed in an empty water tank especially for punishment. They were used for relatively short stretches of time, because no one could withstand them very long, at most a few days, before beginning to ramble—to lose the sense of things, the meaning of words, and the anxiety of passing time—or simply, beginning to die. At first, huddled in her sepulcher, unable either to stand up or sit down despite her small size, Alba managed to stave off madness. Now that she was alone, she realized how much she needed Ana Díaz. She thought she heard an imperceptible tapping in the distance, as if someone were sending her coded messages from another cell, but she soon stopped paying attention to it because she realized that all attempts at communication were completely hopeless. She gave up, deciding to end this torture once and for all. She stopped eating, and only when her feebleness became too much for her did she take a sip of water. She tried not to breathe or move, and began eagerly to await her death. She stayed like this for a long time.

When she had nearly achieved her goal, her Grandmother Clara, whom she had invoked so many times to help her die, appeared with the novel idea that the point was not to die, since death came anyway, but to survive, which would be a miracle. With her white linen dress, her winter gloves, her sweet toothless smile, and the mischievous gleam in her hazel eyes, she looked exactly as she had when Alba was a child. Clara also brought the saving idea of writing in her mind, without paper or pencil, to keep her thoughts occupied and to escape from the doghouse and live. She suggested that she write a testimony that might one day call attention to the terrible secret she was living through, so that the world would know about this horror that was taking place parallel to the peaceful existence of those who did not want to know, who could afford the illusion of a normal life, and of those who could deny that they were on a raft adrift in a sea of sorrow, ignoring, despite all evidence, that only blocks away from their happy world there were others, these others who live or die on the dark side. "You have a lot to do, so stop feeling sorry for yourself, drink some water, and start writing," Clara told her granddaughter before disappearing the same way she had come.

Alba tried to obey her grandmother, but as soon as she began to take notes with her mind, the doghouse filled with all the characters of her story, who rushed in, shoved each other out of the way to wrap her in their anecdotes, their vices, and their virtues, trampled on her intention to compose a documentary, and threw her testimony to the floor, pressing, insisting, and egging her on. She took down their words at breakneck pace, despairing because while she was filling a page, the one before it was erased. This activity kept her fully occupied. At first, she constantly lost her train of thought and forgot new facts as fast as she remembered them. The slightest distraction or additional fear or pain caused her story to snarl like a ball of yarn. But she invented a code for recalling things in order, and then she was able to bury herself so deeply in her story that she stopped eating, scratching herself, smelling herself, and complaining, and overcame all her varied agonies.

Word went out that she was dying. The guards opened the hatch of the doghouse and lifted her effortlessly, because she was very light. They took her back to Colonel García, whose hatred had returned during these days, but she did not recognize him. She was beyond his power.

On the outside, the Hotel Christopher Columbus looked as ordinary as an elementary school, just as I remembered. I had lost count of the years that had passed since I had last been there, and I tried to tell myself that the same Mustafá as before would come out to greet me, that blue Negro dressed like an Oriental apparition, with his double row of leaden teeth and the politeness of a vizier, the only authentic Negro in the country since all the others were painted, as Tránsito Soto had assured me. But that was not what happened. A porter led me to a tiny cubicle, showed me to a seat, and told me to wait. After a while, instead of the spectacular Mustafá, a lady appeared who had the unhappy, tidy air of a provincial aunt, dressed in a blue uniform with a starched white collar. She gave a start when she saw how old and helpless I was. She was holding a red rose.

"The gentleman is alone?"

"Of course I'm alone!" I shouted.

The woman handed me the rose and asked me which room I preferred.

"It makes no difference," I replied, surprised.

"We can offer you the Stable, the Temple, and the Thousand and One Nights. Which one do you want?"

"The Thousand and One Nights," I said, for no particular reason.

She led me down a long hallway that was lined with green lights and bright-red arrows. Leaning on my cane, dragging my feet along, I followed her with great difficulty. We arrived in a small courtyard with a miniature mosque that had been fitted with absurd arched windows made of painted glass.

"This is it. If you want something to drink, order it by phone," she said, pointing.

"I want to speak with Tránsito Soto. That's why I've come," I said.

"I'm sorry, but Madam doesn't see private individuals, only suppliers."

"I have to speak with her! Tell her that Senator Trueba is here. She knows who I am."

"I already told you, she won't see anyone," the woman replied, crossing her arms.

I picked up my cane and told her that if Tránsito Soto did not appear in person within ten minutes, I would break all the windows and everything else inside that Pandora's box. The woman in the uniform jumped back in fright. I opened the door of the mosque and found myself inside a cheap Alhambra. A short tiled staircase covered with false Persian carpets led to a hexagonal room with a cupola on the roof, where someone who had never been in an Arab harem had arrayed everything thought to have existed in one: damask cushions, glass incense burners, bells, and every conceivable trinket from a bazaar. Through the columns, which were infinitely multiplied by the clever placement of the mirrors, I saw a blue mosaic bathtub that was as big as the room and a pool large enough to bathe a cow in—or, more to the point, for two playful lovers to cavort in. It bore no resemblance to the Christopher Columbus I remembered. I lowered myself painfully onto the round bed, suddenly feeling very tired. My bones ached. I looked up, and the mirror on the ceiling returned my image: an old, shriveled body, the sad face of a biblical patriarch furrowed with bitter wrinkles, and what was left of a mane of white hair. "How time has passed!" I sighed.

Tránsito Soto entered without knocking.

"I'm glad to see you, *patrón*," she said, as she always greeted me.

She had become a slender, middle-aged woman with her hair in a bun, wearing a black woolen dress with two strands of simple pearls around her neck, majestic and serene; she looked more like a concert pianist than the owner of a brothel. It was hard for me to connect her to the woman I had known, who had a tattooed snake around her navel. I stood up to greet her, and found I was unable to be as informal as I'd been before.

"You're looking well, Tránsito," I said, figuring she must be past sixty-five.

"Life has been good to me, *patrón*. Do you remember

that when we met I told you one day I'd be rich?" She smiled.

"Well, I'm glad you have achieved that."

We sat down side by side on the round bed. Tránsito poured us each a glass of cognac and told me that the cooperative of whores and homosexuals had done stupendously well for ten years, but that times had changed and they had had to give it a new twist, because thanks to the modern ways—free love, the pill, and other innovations—no one needed prostitutes, except sailors and old men. "Good girls sleep with men for free, so you can just imagine the competition," she said. She explained that the cooperative had begun to go downhill and that the partners had had to look for higher-paying jobs and that even Mustafá had gone back to his country. Then she had realized that what was really needed was a hotel for rendezvous, a pleasant place where secret couples could make love and where a man would not be embarrassed to bring a girl for the first time. No women: those were furnished by the customer. She had decorated it herself, following the whims of her imagination and taking her customers' taste into account. Thus, thanks to her commercial vision, which had led her to create a different atmosphere in every available corner, the Hotel Christopher Columbus had become the paradise of lost souls and furtive lovers. Tránsito Soto had made French sitting rooms with quilted furniture, mangers with fresh hay and papier-mâché horses that observed the lovers with their immutable glass eyes, prehistoric caves with real stalactites, and telephones covered with the skins of pumas.

"Since you're not here to make love, *patrón*, let's go talk in my office," Tránsito Soto said. "That way we can leave this room to customers."

On the way she told me that after the coup the political police had raided the hotel a couple of times, but that each time they dragged the couples out of bed and lined them up at gunpoint in the main drawing room, they had found a general or two, so the police had quickly stopped annoying her. She had an excellent relationship with the new government, just as she had had with the preceding ones. She told me that the Christopher Columbus was a thriving business and that every year she renovated part of the decor, replacing the stranded hulls of Polynesian shipwrecks with severe monastic cloisters, and baroque garden swings with torture racks, depending on the latest fashion. Thanks to the gimmickry of the mirrors and lights, which could multiply space, transform the climate, create the illusion of infinity, and suspend time, she could bring all this into a residence of relatively normal size.

We arrived at her office, which was decorated like the cockpit of an airplane and from which she ran her incredible organization with the efficiency of a banker. She told me how many sheets had to be washed, how much toilet paper bought, how much liquor was consumed, how many quail eggs prepared daily—they're aphrodisiacs—how many employees she needed, and how much she paid for water, electricity, and the phone in order to keep that outsized aircraft carrier of forbidden love afloat.

"And now, *patrón*, tell me what I can do for you," Tránsito Soto finally said, settling into the reclining seat of an airplane pilot while she toyed with the pearls around her neck. "I suppose you've come because you want me to repay the favor that I've owed you for half a century, right?"

Then, having waited for her to ask me that, I opened the floodgates of my soul and told her everything; I didn't hold back anything and didn't stop for a second from beginning to end. I told her that Alba is my only granddaughter, that I'm practically all alone in the world, and that my body and my soul have shrunken away, just as Férula predicted with her curse; that all that awaits me now is to die like a dog, and that my green-haired granddaughter is all I have left, the only person I really care about; that unfortunately she turned out to be an idealist, a family disease, one of those people cut out to get involved in problems and make those closest to her suffer; that she took it into her head to help fugitives get asylum in the foreign embassies, something she did without thinking, I'm sure, without realizing that the country is at war, whether war against international Communism or its own people it's hard to tell, but war one way or the other, and these things are punishable by law, but Alba always has her head in the clouds and doesn't realize she's in danger, she doesn't do it to be mean, really, just the opposite, she does it because her heart knows no

limits, just like her grandmother, who still runs around
ministering to the poor behind my back in the abandoned
wing of the house, my clairvoyant Clara, and anyone who
tells Alba people are after him gets her to risk her life for
him, even if he's a total stranger, I've already told her, I
warned her time and again they could lay a trap for her and
one day it would turn out that the supposed Marxist was an
agent of the secret police, but she never listened to me, she's
never listened to me in her life, she's more stubborn than I
am, but even so, it's not a crime to help some poor devil get
asylum every once in a while, it's not so serious that they
should arrest her without taking into account that she's my
granddaughter, the granddaughter of a senator of the Republic, a distinguished member of the Conservative Party, they
can't do that to someone from my own family, in my own
house, because then what the hell is left for everybody else,
if people like us can be arrested then nobody is safe, that
more than twenty years in Congress aren't worth a damn
and all the acquaintances I have, I know everybody in this
country, at least everyone important, even General Hurtado,
who's my personal friend but in this case hasn't lifted a
finger to help me, not even the cardinal's been able to help
me locate my granddaughter, it's not possible she could just
disappear as if by magic, that they could take her away in
the night and that I should never hear a word of her again,
I've spent a whole month looking for her and I'm going
crazy, these are the things that make the junta look so bad
abroad and give the United Nations reason to screw around
with human rights, at first I didn't want to hear about the
dead, the tortured, and the disappeared, but now I can't keep
thinking they're just Communist lies, because even the gringos, who were the first to help the military and sent their
own pilots to bombard the Presidential Palace, are scandal-
ized by all the killing, it's not that I'm against repression, I
understand that in the beginning you have to be firm if you
want a return to order, but things have gotten out of hand,
they're going overboard now and no one can go along with
the story about internal security and how you have to eliminate your ideological enemies, they're finishing off everyone, no one can go along with that, not even me, and I was
the first to throw corn at the military cadets and to suggest

the coup, before the others took it into their heads, and I was the first to applaud them, I was present for the Te Deum in the cathedral, and precisely because I was I can't accept that this sort of thing should happen in my country, that people disappear, that my granddaughter is dragged from my house by force and I'm powerless to stop them, things like this never happened here and that's why I've come to see you, Tránsito, because fifty years ago when you were just a skinny little thing in the Red Lantern I never thought that one day I'd be coming to you on my knees to beg you to do me this favor, to help me find my granddaughter, I dare to ask you such a thing because I know you're on good terms with the new government, I've heard about you, Tránsito, I'm sure no one knows the top brass of the armed forces better than you do, I know you organize their parties for them and that you have access to places I could never penetrate and that's why I'm asking you to do something for my granddaughter before it's too late, I've gone weeks without sleeping, I've been to every office, every ministry, seen all my old friends, and no one's been able to do anything, they don't want to see me anymore, they make me wait outside for hours, please, Tránsito, ask me for anything you want, I'm still a wealthy man even though under the Communists things got a little tough for me, you probably heard, you must have seen it in the papers and on television, a real scandal, those ignorant peasants ate my breeding bulls and hitched my racing horses to the plow and in less than a year Tres Marías was in ruins, but now I've filled the place with tractors and I'm picking up the pieces, just as I did before, when I was young, I'm doing the same thing now that I'm an old man, but I'm not done for, while those poor souls who had the title to my property—my property—are dying of hunger like a bunch of miserable wretches, poor things, it wasn't their fault they were taken in by that damned agrarian reform, when it comes right down to it I've forgiven them and I'd like them to return to Tres Marías, I've even placed notices in the papers summoning them back, someday they'll return and I'll have no choice but to shake their hands, they're like children, but anyway that's not what I came to talk to you about, Tránsito, I don't want to waste your time, what counts is that I'm well placed and my affairs are sailing along, so I can give you anything you ask for, anything, so long as you find my granddaughter Alba before some madman sends me any more chopped-off fingers or starts to send me cut-off ears and winds up driving me stark raving mad or giving me a heart attack, forgive me for getting all worked up like this, my hands are shaking, I'm very nervous, I can't explain what happened, a package in the mail and in it only three human fingers, cleanly amputated, a macabre joke that brings back memories, but memories that have nothing to do with Alba, my granddaughter wasn't even born then, I'm sure I have a lot of enemies, all of us politicians have enemies, it's not surprising there should be some maniac out there who wants to torture me by sending me fingers through the mail just when I'm out of my mind about Alba's arrest, to put terrible ideas into my head, and if I weren't at the end of my rope and hadn't exhausted all my other possibilities I wouldn't bother you with this, please, Tránsito, in the name of our old friendship, have pity on me, I'm just a poor destroyed old man, have pity on me and look for my granddaughter Alba before they send her to me in the mail all cut up in little pieces, I sobbed.

Tránsito Soto has gotten where she has because, among other things, she knows how to pay her debts. I suppose she used her knowledge of the most secret side of the men in power to return the fifty pesos I once lent her. Two days later she called me on the phone.

"It's Tránsito Soto, *patrón.* I did what you asked me to."

Epilogue

My grandfather died last night. He did not die like a dog, as he feared he would, but peacefully, in my arms. In the end, he confused me with Clara, and at times with Rosa, but he died without pain or anguish, more lucid than ever and happy, conscious, and serene. Now he's laid out on the sailboat of the gentle sea, smiling and calm, while I write at the blond wood table that belonged to my grandmother. I've opened the blue silk curtains to let the morning in and cheer up the room. A new canary is singing in the antique cage hanging by the window, and from the center of the room the glass eyes of Barrabás stare up at me. My grandfather told me Clara fainted the day he put the skin of the animal down as a rug, thinking it would please her. We both laughed until we cried and decided to go down to the basement and look for the remains of poor old Barrabás, sovereign in his indefinable biological constitution, despite the passage of time and so much neglect, and to put him where my grandfather had laid him half a century earlier in homage to the woman he loved most in his life.

"Let's leave him here," he said. "This is where he always should have been."

I arrived at the house on a sparkling winter morning in a wagon drawn by a scrawny horse. With its double row of centenarian chestnut trees and its seignorial mansions, the street looked like an improbable setting for such a modest vehicle, but when it pulled up before my grandfather's house it fit in very well. The big house on the corner was sadder and older than I had remembered, and looked absurd, with its architectural eccentricities, its pretensions to French style, its façade covered with diseased ivy. The garden was a tangle of weeds and almost all the shutters were hanging from their hinges. As always, the gate was open. I rang the bell, and after a while I heard a pair of sandals approach, and a maid I had never seen before came to the door. She looked at me blankly as I inhaled the marvelous scent of wood and seclusion of the house where I was born. My eyes filled with tears. I ran to the library, sensing that my grandfather would be waiting for me where he always sat, and there he was, shrunken in his armchair. I was surprised to see how old he looked, how small and trembling. All that remained from before was his leonine white mane and his heavy silver cane. We threw our arms around each other and remained locked together for a long while, whispering Alba, Grandfather, Grandfather, Alba, and then we kissed each other and when he saw my hand he began to cry and curse and smash his cane against the furniture, the way he used to, and I laughed because he was not as old or as worn out as he had looked at first.

That same day my grandfather wanted us to leave the country. He was afraid for me. But I explained that I could not leave, because far away from my country I would be like those trees they chop down at Christmastime, those poor rootless pines that last a little while and then die.

"I'm no fool, Alba," he said, staring me straight in the eye. "The real reason you want to stay here is Miguel. Isn't that so?"

I was taken aback. I had never spoken to him of Miguel.

"Ever since I met him, I knew I would never get you out of here," he told me sadly.

"You met him? Is he alive, Grandfather?" I shook him, grabbing hold of his clothes.

"He was last week, my dear, the last time we saw each other," he said.

He told me that after they arrested me Miguel had appeared one night at the big house on the corner. He almost gave my grandfather a stroke, but in a few minutes he realized that the two of them had a common goal: to rescue me. Afterward Miguel often came to see him. He kept him company and they pooled their efforts to discover where I was being held. It was Miguel who had the idea of going to see Tránsito Soto. My grandfather would never have thought of it.

"Listen to me, señor. I know who has the power in this country. My people have infiltrated everywhere. If there's anyone who can help Alba now, it's Tránsito Soto," he assured him.

"If we can get her out of the hands of the police, she'll have to leave here, son. You two go together. I can get you safe-conduct passes out of the country and you'll never need money," my grandfather offered.

But Miguel looked at him as if he were an old lunatic and proceeded to explain to him that he had a mission to fulfill and could not flee.

"I had to resign myself to the idea that you would stay here in spite of everything," my grandfather said, embracing me. "Now tell me about it. I want to know it all, down to the last detail."

So I told him. I told him that after my hand became infected they had taken me to a secret clinic where they send the prisoners they don't want to die. There I was attended by a tall, fine-featured doctor who seemed to hate me as much as Colonel García and refused to give me any painkillers. He used each treatment to regale me with his personal theory about how to rid the country—and if possible, the world—of Communism. Aside from that, he left me in peace. For the first time in several weeks, I had clean sheets, enough to eat, and natural light. I was looked after by a male nurse named Rojas, a heavyset man with a round face, who always wore a dirty blue smock and was endowed with enormous kindness. He fed me, told me endless stories about distant football teams I had never heard of, and obtained painkillers with which he injected me on the sly until he managed to put a stop to my delirium. In this clinic, Rojas had already cared for an interminable procession of unlucky souls. He had been able to verify that most of them were neither killers nor traitors, and he was therefore well disposed toward the prisoners. It often happened that he had no sooner finished putting someone back together than the same prisoner was taken to be tortured again. "It's like shoveling sand into the sea," he used to say, sadly shaking his head. I found out that some of them asked him to help them die, and in at least one case I think he did. Rojas kept an exact tally of everyone who entered and left, and he could recite their names, dates of entry and departure, and their circumstances without hesitation. He swore to me that he had never heard of Miguel, and that gave me the courage to keep living, even though I sometimes fell into a black pit of depression and began to recite the refrain about how much I wanted to die. He was the one who told me about Amanda. They arrested her around the same time they arrested me. By the time they took her to Rojas, there was nothing he could do. She died without betraying her brother, fulfilling a promise she had made him many years before, the day she first took him to school. The only consolation is that she died much faster than they would have liked, because her body was so weak from drugs and from her infinite despair over Jaime's death. Rojas took care of me until my fever had subsided, my hand began to heal, and I returned to my senses; after that he had no more excuses to keep me there. But they did not send me back to Esteban García, as I had feared. I suppose it was then that the beneficent influence of the woman with the pearls went into effect, the one my grandfather and I went to see to thank her for saving my life. Four men came to get me in the night. Rojas woke me up, helped me dress, and wished me good luck. I gave him a grateful kiss.

"Goodbye, little one! Change your bandage, don't let it get wet, and if the fever comes back it means it's infected again," he told me from the doorway.

They led me into a narrow cell where I spent the rest of the night sitting in a chair. The next day they took me to a concentration camp for women. I will never forget the moment when they took my blindfold off and I found myself in the middle of a sun-filled, square courtyard, surrounded by women who were singing the Ode to Joy, just for me. My friend Ana Díaz was among them and ran to embrace me. They quickly laid me on a camp bed and explained the rules of the community and my responsibilities.

"Until you're better, you don't have to wash or sew, but you have to help with the children," they decided.

I had managed to resist the inferno with a certain integrity, but when I felt so much support, I broke down. The smallest expression of tenderness sent me into a crying fit. I spent the night with my eyes wide open, wrapped in the closeness of so many women, who took turns watching over me and never left me alone. They helped me when I began to suffer from bad memories or when I saw Colonel García coming to plunge me back into his world of terror, or when, with a sob, I imagined Miguel arrested.

"Don't think about Miguel," they told me, they insisted. "You mustn't think about your loved ones or about the world that lies beyond these walls. It's the only way to survive."

Ana Díaz obtained a notebook and gave it to me. "For you to write in, to see if you can get out whatever's worrying you inside, so you'll get better once and for all and join our singing and help us sew," she said.

I showed her my hand and shook my head, but she put the pencil in my left hand and told me to write with it. I began slowly. I tried to organize the story I had started in the doghouse. My companions helped me whenever my patience flagged and the pencil began to shake in my hand. There were times when I threw it all away, but I would quickly retrieve the notebook and lovingly smooth its pages, filled with regret, because I did not know when I could get another one. At other times I would wake up sad and filled with foreboding. I would turn my face to the wall and refuse to speak to anyone, but the women did not leave me alone. They shook me, made me work, made me tell stories to the children. They changed my bandage with great care and put the paper in front of me.

"If you want, I'll tell you my story so you can write it down," one said. Then they laughed and made jokes, arguing that everybody's story was the same and that it would be better to write love stories because everyone likes them. They also forced me to eat. They divided up the servings with the strictest sense of justice, each according to her need; they gave me a little more because they said I was just skin and bones and not even the most desperate man would ever look at me. I shuddered, but Ana Díaz reminded me that I was not the only woman who had been raped, and that, along with many other things, it was something I had to forget. The women spent the whole day singing at the top of their lungs. The guards would pound on the wall.

"Shut up, whores!"

"Make us if you can, bastards! Let's see if you dare!" And they sang even stronger but the guards did not come in, for they had learned that there is no way to avoid the unavoidable.

I tried to record the small events of the women's section of the jail: that they had arrested the President's sister, that they had taken our cigarettes away, that new prisoners had arrived, that Adriana had had another one of her attacks and had stood over her children threatening to kill them; how we had had to pull them away from her and I had sat with a child in each arm and told them magic stories from the enchanted trunks of my Great-Uncle Marcos until they fell asleep, and how in the meantime I thought about the fate of the children growing up in that place with a mother who had gone mad, cared for by other, unfamiliar mothers who had not lost their voice for lullabies, and I wondered, as I wrote, how Adriana's children would be able to return the songs and the gestures to the children and grandchildren of the women who were rocking them to sleep.

I was in the concentration camp only a few days. One Wednesday afternoon, the police came to get me. I had a moment of panic, thinking they were taking me back to Esteban García, but my companions told me that if the men were in uniform they were not part of the security police, and that reassured me a little. I left the women my woolen sweater, so they could unravel it and knit something warm for Adriana's children, along with the money I had had when I was arrested, which, with the military's scrupulous honesty for the unimportant, had been returned to me. I put my notebook in my slacks and hugged each of the women one by one. The last thing I heard when I left was the chorus of my friends singing to give me courage, just as they did with all the women when they arrived or left the camp. I wept as I walked. I had been happy there.

I told my grandfather that they had put me in a van and

driven me blindfolded, during curfew. I was shaking so hard that my teeth were chattering. One of the men who was with me in the back of the truck put a piece of candy in my hand and gave me a few comforting pats on the shoulder.

"Don't worry, señorita," he told me in a whisper. "Nothing's going to happen to you. We're going to release you, and in a few hours you'll be back with your family."

They left me in a dump near the Misericordia District. The same man who gave me the candy helped me down.

"Careful with the curfew," he whispered in my ear. "Don't move till sunrise."

I heard the engine and thought they were going to run me down and that my name would appear in the papers saying I had died in a traffic accident, but the vehicle drove away without touching me. I waited for a while, paralyzed with fear and cold, until I finally decided to pull off the blindfold and see where they had left me. I looked around. It was an empty lot full of garbage, with rats scampering among the refuse. There was a pale moon that allowed me to make out in the distance the outlines of a wretched slum, with houses made of cardboard, planks, and corrugated metal. I realized I must pay attention to what the guard had said and stay there until morning. I would have spent the night there, but suddenly a boy appeared, crouching in the shadows. He motioned to me. Since I had nothing to lose, I walked toward him, stumbling. When I reached him, I saw his small, anxious face. He threw a blanket over my shoulders, took me by the hand, and led me to the settlement without saying a word. We walked squatting, avoiding the street and the few lamps that were lit. A couple of dogs began to bark, but no heads appeared to see what was going on. We crossed a dirt courtyard, where pieces of clothing hung like pennants from a wire, and entered a dilapidated hut like all the others. Inside, a single bulb cast its somber light. I was moved by the extreme poverty: the only furniture was a pine table, two crude chairs, and a bed on which several children were sleeping. A short, dark woman came out to meet me. Her legs were crossed with veins and her eyes were sunk in a web of generous wrinkles that did not make her look old. She smiled, and I saw that some of her teeth were missing. She came up to me and straightened the blanket with a brusque, timid gesture that took the place of the hug she was afraid to give me.

"I'm going to give you a little cup of tea. I don't have any sugar, but something warm will do you good," she said.

She told me they had heard the van and knew what it meant to hear a vehicle in that out-of-the-way place during curfew. They had waited until they were sure it had gone away and then she had sent the boy out to see what had been left. They had expected to find a body.

"They sometimes leave us the bodies of people they've shot," she said. "To intimidate us."

We stayed up all night talking. She was one of those stoical, practical women of our country, the kind of woman who has a child with every man who passes through her life and, on top of that, takes in other people's abandoned children, her own poor relatives, and anybody else who needs a mother, a sister, or an aunt; the kind of woman who's the pillar of many other lives, who raises her children to grow up and leave her and lets her men leave too, without a word of reproach, because she has more pressing things to worry about. She looked like so many others I had met in the soup kitchens, in my Uncle Jaime's clinic, at the church office where they would go for information on their disappeared, and in the morgue where they would go to find their dead. I told her she had run an enormous risk rescuing me, and she smiled. It was then I understood that the days of Colonel García and all those like him are numbered, because they have not been able to destroy the spirit of these women.

The next morning, she took me to a close family friend who had a horse-drawn cart for hauling freight. She asked him to take me home, and that's how I arrived here. Along the way I could see the city in all its terrible contrasts: the huts surrounded by makeshift walls to create the illusion that they do not exist, the cramped, gray center, and the High District, with its English gardens, its parks, its glass sky-scrapers, and its fair-haired children riding bicycles. Even the dogs looked happy to me. Everything in order, everything clean, everything calm, and that solid peace of a conscience without memory. This neighborhood is like another country.

My grandfather listened sadly. A world he had thought was good had crumbled at his feet.

"Well, since it looks as if we're going to stay here and wait for Miguel, we're going to fix this place up a little," he said after a moment's silence.

And so we did. At first we spent the whole day in the library, worried that they could return for me and take me back to García, but then we decided that the worst thing is to be afraid of fear, as my Uncle Nicolás had said, and that we had to use the entire house and start to live a normal life. My grandfather engaged a special company to come in with polishing machines and clean the house; they washed the windows, painted, and disinfected the place from top to bottom until it was livable again. Half a dozen gardeners and a tractor got rid of the weeds. They brought in a lawn rolled up like a carpet, an ingenious invention of the gringos, and in less than a week we even had tall birches; water gushed from the singing fountains, and the Olympian statues once again stood tall and proud, free at last of so much bird droppings and neglect. We went together to buy birds for the cages that had been empty ever since my grandmother, sensing that she was about to die, had opened them and let the birds fly out. I put fresh flowers in the vases and platters of fruit on all the tables, as Clara had in the days of the spirits, and the air filled with their fragrance. Afterward my grandfather and I walked arm in arm through the house, stopping in each place to remember the past and salute the imperceptible ghosts of other eras, who, despite all the ups and downs, have remained in place.

It was my grandfather who had the idea that we should write this story.

"That way you'll be able to take your roots with you if you ever have to leave, my dear," he said.

We unearthed the old albums from the forgotten nooks and crannies of the house. Here, on my grandmother's table, is the stack of photographs: Rosa the Beautiful beside a faded swing; my mother, with Pedro Tercero García at the age of four, feeding corn to the chickens in the courtyard of Tres Marías; my grandfather when he was young and stood six feet tall, irrefutable proof that Férula's curse came true and that his body shrank in the same proportions as his soul; my uncles Jaime and Nicolás, one dark, somber, gigantic, and vulnerable, the other lean, graceful, volatile, and smiling;

also Nana and the del Valle great-grandparents before they were killed in the accident; everyone, in short, except the noble Jean de Satigny, of whom no scientific trace remains and whose very existence I have begun to doubt.

I began to write with the help of my grandfather, whose memory remained intact down to the last second of his ninety years. In his own hand he wrote a number of pages, and when he felt that he had written everything he had to say, he lay down on Clara's bed. I sat beside him to wait with him, and death was not long in coming, taking him by surprise as he lay sleeping peacefully. Perhaps he was dreaming that it was his wife who held his hand and kissed his forehead, because in his final days she did not leave him for a second, following him around the house, peering over his shoulder when he was reading in his library, lying down beside him and leaning her beautiful curly head against his shoulder when he got into bed. At first she was just a mysterious glow, but as my grandfather slowly lost the rage that had tormented him throughout his life, she appeared as she had been at her best, laughing with all her teeth and stirring up the other spirits as she sailed through the house. She also helped us write, and thanks to her presence Esteban Trueba was able to die happy, murmuring her name: Clara, clearest, clairvoyant.

When I was in the doghouse, I wrote in my mind that one day Colonel García would stand before me in defeat and that I would avenge myself on all those who need to be avenged. But now I have begun to question my own hatred. Within a few short weeks, ever since I returned to the house, it seems to have become diluted, to have lost its sharp edge. I am beginning to suspect that nothing that happens is fortuitous, that it all corresponds to a fate laid down before my birth, and that Esteban García is part of the design. He is a crude, twisted line, but no brushstroke is in vain. The day my grandfather tumbled his grandmother, Pancha García, among the rushes of the riverbank, he added another link to the chain of events that had to complete itself. Afterward the grandson of the woman who was raped repeats the gesture with the granddaughter of the rapist, and perhaps forty years from now my grandson will knock García's granddaughter down among the rushes, and so on down through the centuries in an unending tale of sorrow, blood, and love. When I was in the doghouse, I felt as if I were assembling a jigsaw puzzle in which each piece had a specific place. Before I put the puzzle together, it all seemed incomprehensible to me, but I was sure that if I ever managed to complete it, the separate parts would each have meaning and the whole would be harmonious. Each piece has a reason for being the way it is, even Colonel García. At times I feel as if I had lived all this before and that I have already written these very words, but I know it was not I: it was another woman, who kept her notebooks so that one day I could use them. I write, she wrote, that memory is fragile and the space of a single life is brief, passing so quickly that we never get a chance to see the relationship between events; we cannot gauge the consequences of our acts, and we believe in the fiction of past, present, and future, but it may also be true that everything happens simultaneously—as the three Mora sisters said, who could see the spirits of all eras mingled in space. That's why my Grandmother Clara wrote in her notebooks, in order to see things in their true dimension and to defy her own poor memory. And now I seek my hatred and cannot seem to find it. I feel its flame going out as I come to understand the existence of Colonel García and the others like him, as I understand my grandfather and piece things together from Clara's notebooks, my mother's letters, the ledgers of Tres Marías, and the many other documents spread before me on the table. It would be very difficult for me to avenge all those who should be avenged, because my revenge would be just another part of the same inexorable rite. I have to break that terrible chain. I want to think that my task is life and that my mission is not to prolong hatred but simply to fill these pages while I wait for Miguel, while I bury my grandfather, whose body lies beside me in this room, while I wait for better times to come, while I carry this child in my womb, the daughter of so many rapes or perhaps of Miguel, but above all, my own daughter.

My grandmother wrote in her notebooks that bore witness to life for fifty years. Smuggled out by certain friendly spirits, they miraculously escaped the infamous pyre in which so many other family papers perished. I have them here at my feet, bound with colored ribbons, divided according to events and not in chronological order, just as she arranged them before she left. Clara wrote them so they would help me now to reclaim the past and overcome terrors of my own. The first is an ordinary school copybook with twenty pages, written in a child's delicate calligraphy. It begins like this: *Barrabás came to us by sea . . .*

About the Author

ISABEL ALLENDE is Chilean and worked for many years as a journalist. *The House of the Spirits* was a bestseller in both Europe and the United States, written "to keep alive the memory" of her family and country. Niece of assassinated President Salvador Allende, she now lives in exile in Venezuela, and has recently completed her second novel.